Q–16

and the Lord of the
Unfinished Tower

A.A. Jankiewicz

To Doris,

I hope you enjoy!

Q-16 and the Lord of the Unfinished Tower

Works by A.A. Jankiewicz

<u>Q-16 Series</u>

Q-16 and the Eye to All Worlds
Q-16 and the Lord of the Unfinished Tower

<u>Short Stories</u>

'The Space Driver' in The Welcome: and other Sci Fi Stories by Tom Benson
'Skyris' in Brave New Girls Stories of Girls Who Science and Scheme edited by Paige Daniels & Mary Fan

*To my uncle Krzysiek, wherever you are,
I hope they have a Polish translation out.*

*To those who inspired me,
but are now gone from this world,
I hope I can pay it forward with these scribbles of mine.*

And to all those who know the meaning of these words,

*Jeszcze Polska nie zginęła,
Kiedy my żyjemy.
Co nam obca przemoc wzięła,
Szablą odbierzemy.*

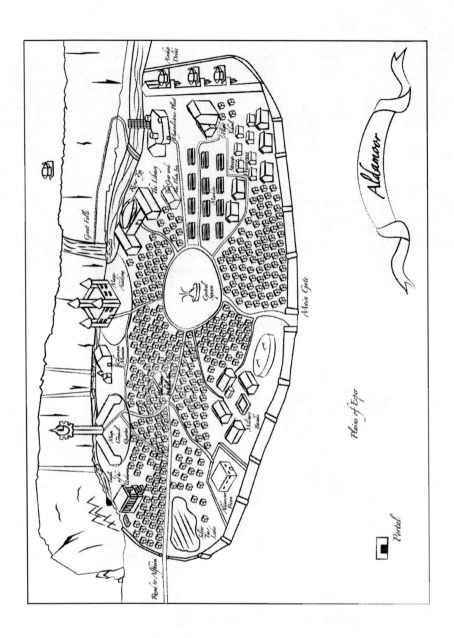

Allanor

5

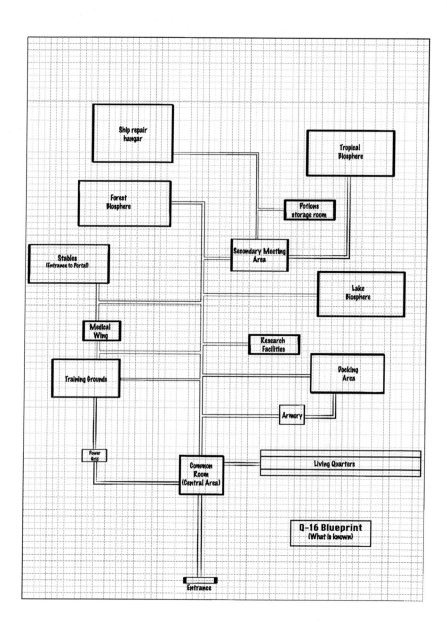

Ship repair hangar

Tropical Biosphere

Forest Biosphere

Potions storage room

Stables (Entrance to Portal)

Secondary Meeting Area

Lake Biosphere

Medical Wing

Research Facilities

Training Grounds

Docking Area

Armory

Power Grid

Common Room (Central Area)

Living Quarters

Q-16 Blueprint
(What is known)

Entrance

6

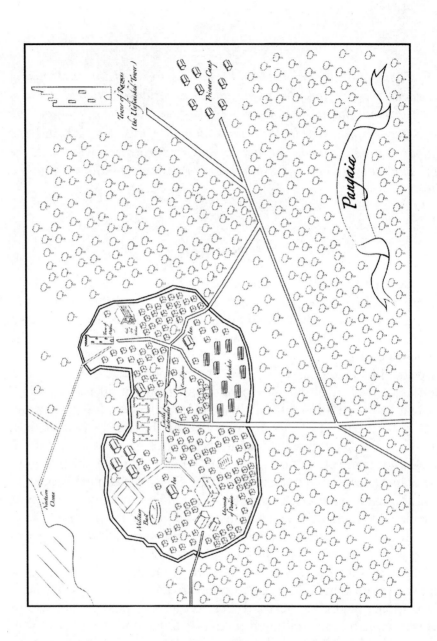

Change. The eternal cycle of life moving forward and never taking a second glance back. All living things experience it and it is one's decisions that shape the future of who they are to become. They are the lines between duty and love, pride and humility, false heroism and true valour. Though it comes no matter how one tries to postpone it, the ultimate outcome belongs to the heart of the one standing within the storm.

ഹര

Prologue

Dimmer, dimmer and dimmer. From out of the blinding light emerged tall blades of deep green grass that blew in the wind, their sound the only one to be heard for miles. Though they seemed to stretch for eternity in all directions, their confusing sways ended in the shadows of a great black structure beyond which the lights of a vast city could be made out as it got ready for slumber. The structure had lain untouched by all hands except that of nature itself for years but, tonight had been different. The homage it had craved for so long had finally been paid. Tiny, almost unnoticeable beside the behemoth, a broken star-shaped mask glinted in the dark of night, waiting for the ritual to be complete. As the last rays of the blinding light coming from the entrance ceased into nothingness, the clang of chain mail could be heard from deep within the corridor. The louder it became, the more it resembled a rhythmic sound not much different from a machine.

Amarok Mezorian's patience was well rewarded when a pearl-white armoured hand grabbed at the side of the wall, claw-like gauntlets raking across the rock. Pulling itself free of the dark and letting go of the stone, the armoured being strode forward a few steps. Its head thrown back and chest forward, it stood at over six feet tall with a tattered crimson cape trailing behind it. Fatigue, however, had its way and the warrior fell to the floor face first. The heavy helmet dropped away to reveal a cascade of golden blonde hair that fell past the shoulders of the armoured giant. Shaking off the shock, the man peered up with glistening blue eyes and a fortnight's growth of facial hair on pale skin.

8

Not bothering to look at his saviour, he questioned in a voice that seemed to make everything else around him stop. "Where...where am I?"

"Gaia, my lord." The masked being knelt before him.

Groggy, the man in armour stood up, straightening himself as before, and looked into the night that held all in the thralls of sleep. His surroundings made no sense to him. Where was his great city? All he saw was grass and in the distance what looked like the shapes of immense trees. Looking down at his mighty armoured hands, the warrior noted the amount of rust upon his gauntlets and curling his fist, he watched as they crumbled, plate that had once meant to withstand wars, no more fragile than paper. Then it all came crashing back, the betrayal, the anger, the pain. All he had left behind came back to him and the king that once was lost found his way again.

"How long have I been in this sleep, Amarok?" he spoke again, venom leaking through his teeth with each word.

"Well near over twelve thousand years, my lord," the masked man responded without hesitation.

Snarling upon hearing this, the lord turned around and looked upon the decimated stonework that hailed the starry sky above in a jagged smile. Further beyond the trees, he then noticed the tall city walls where his brother's tower had been. "We have much rebuilding to do."

Chapter 1

Over a year later...

The red filmy shapes from beyond her eyelids greeted Annetta Severio into the world, accompanied by the sound of her alarm clock buzzing incessantly. She growled unconsciously and covered herself up with her blanket. A moment of peace seemed to come over her as the buzzing faded from her mind and she was back in the plains surrounding the castle, racing on Firedancer along the grass.

An all too familiar female voice of authority, however, interrupted the daydream from progressing further. "Annetta! Wake up! You're going to be late for school!"

Bolting alert at the sound of her mother's voice, she threw away the sheets. "Okay! Okay! Okay! I'm awake!"

Sitting up on her bed, Annetta oriented herself with the surroundings in the room. Pushing back her messy copper bangs, she remembered she was indeed at home and not within one of the rooms in Q-16. Knowing this, she got up and stretched.

She began her everyday routine in the same way as it had been as far back as she could remember. Grabbing a fresh set of jeans, a t-shirt and undergarments, Annetta made her way into the bathroom and set everything on the counter. As she began readying herself, she looked into the mirror. Staring back at Annetta was a tough looking eighteen-year-old girl with blue eyes and reddish brown hair that went past her shoulders, with thick bangs.

Getting dressed, she made note of the three thin scars that remained since the battle with Mislantus a year ago, one on her arm, one on her torso and one on her back. They were a small price to pay in the long run. She was also struck again by the way her body had changed since she had first learned of her heritage and had begun her training. What once had been a small and wispy girl was now a young woman corded in muscle. It was not the kind of muscle that a girl got from cheerleading or dance either, graceful and slender. It was the kind one got from heavy labour and swinging a sword, the body of a fighter or, as many snickered at her, a man. It made Annetta feel unattractive some mornings. The older she got, it seemed, the more she noticed these things, especially when other girls whispered in the halls about it when she passed by. It being one of those days where she wanted to forget it, she pulled her black t-shirt down as quickly as she could and continued on with her routine. Going to put on her socks, she noticed the pair did not match, one being blue with black stripes while the other was blue with a solid black heel and toes. The girl sighed in frustration, as this was not the first time this had happened. Chucking the socks into the basket her mother kept with all of the mismatched pairs, she went to her drawer to grab another. Finally, brushing her hair, she headed down for breakfast.

Though it had been almost a year since the Severio family had moved into a detached two-story house in the suburbs, Annetta was still having trouble remembering some mornings that there were stairs. From time to time when asleep, her feet would slip on the thick carpet, resulting in rug burn on her legs. It being one of those mornings, she managed to do just that.

The decision for the move had come when the landlord of their previous building had become suspicious of the volume people going in and out all the time and had demanded a higher rate for the apartment, thinking more tenants had moved in with them, to which Annetta's father, Arieus Severio, simply said no and decided it was about time for them to finally own their own little patch of land where no one would question who came in or out at any given time.

Coming to the bottom of the stairs, still grumbling about her slip, Annetta made her way into the kitchen to see her mother Aurora pouring coffee into a travel mug, while her younger brother Xander munched away on cereal at the kitchen table.

"Morning." Annetta greeted everyone present before going over to the cupboard and pulling out some bread to place in the toaster oven.

"About time you woke up. You'll be late for school if you don't hurry up and I don't have time to drive you," her mother warned her as she finished up. "I need to head off now, so...Xander make sure your sister is ready for school."

"Yes, mom," the young boy answered between taking a spoonful of food.

"Shouldn't it be the other way around?" Annetta raised an eyebrow as her mother dashed out of the kitchen and into the hallway.

"Not when I last found you in the Lab instead of attending your chemistry test," her mother called from the hall as the door shut behind her. The sound of a car engine followed soon after, signalling her leave.

Annetta still found it odd how easily her parents had adapted to having Q-16 be part of their lives once more. The Lab, a nickname her grandfather had given the base, had been reused by her and her friends in order to keep it a secret when spoken about in public. She sighed, lowering her head into her folded arms across the back of a chair. Ever since the battle with Mislantus, her parents had been trying to be part of her life in the Lab more and more, leaving Annetta with no place to run to when hiding from her parents was needed. Though they did not venture down often, it felt like an invasion of privacy for Annetta, who was not used to having her immediate family in the Lab while she was training with Puc or any of the others.

A heavy hand landed on Annetta's shoulder, almost causing her whole body to bounce on impact. Looking up, she found herself staring into a familiar pair of smiling grey eyes, lined with a crescent moon scar and shaggy dirty blonde hair. They belonged to none other than Lincerious Heallaws, known more commonly to everyone as Link. He was a Gaian militiaman that had come to the Lab through a portal when Annetta and her friend Jason had first discovered the base beneath the sea. The girl looked up at him, stone faced from the previous encounter with her mother.

"Why so glum?" he asked, taking a seat beside Xander. "Hey, what's up?"

"Parents," Xander told him, looking at his sister.

"Parents," she echoed through her teeth as the timer on the toaster ended and she got up.

Link formed an 'oh' with his lips as he watched Annetta shuffle around the kitchen, preparing her breakfast.

"Xander, if you wanna walk to school with us you gotta hurry it up," Annetta told him as she pulled out a plate.

"I'm more ready than you are," he responded. "All I gotta do is grab my bag."

"Yeah, but you usually go and put on a game and disappear from the face of the Earth while doing it," she retorted. "I'm not gonna sound trumpets just so you can hear when we are leaving, dude."

"Ugh, fine…I'm gonna go sit in my room then and not play video games," he griped under his breath. Putting his plate in the dishwasher, he stalked off.

Annetta exhaled in annoyance. The older her brother seemed to get, the harder it was to be the cool big sister because he was developing an attitude. She watched him leave, then turned back to her toast.

Relaxing his shoulders against the back of the chair, Link decided to change the subject. "So, are you excited about graduating this year?"

Annetta took a bite of her toast and savouring the flavour of the crunchy bread, she swallowed before responding. "Meh. It's just another year dead and gone. Also, am I the only one who keeps losing socks?"

"Now that you mention it, I did find a mismatched pair a few weeks ago. Yeah, but you have prom, and then you need to think about universities and colleges and-"

"Link, it's only like, what, the end of October? My next priority is Halloween costumes," she rebutted before he could finish his train of thought.

"Oh, right. That thing where people dress up and kids go door to door for candy," Link summarized in his own words, then added, "I can solve that for you. Why don't you just wear your armour to school?"

"Yeah, right, like Puc would allow that," snorted Annetta as she wolfed down her the rest of her food.

"Sure he would. I mean, come on, it's the one time of the year he doesn't need to dress up when he's here." The Gaian youth grinned, only to have a dish towel thrown at his face.

"Hurry up or we're gonna be late," Annetta said, moving past Link to brush her teeth.

"Says the girl getting ready to the guy who is ready." He rolled his eyes and waited for her to finish.

&⊃⊂&

Backpack slung casually over one shoulder, Jason Kinsman leaned against the back fence of the school, waiting for his friends to show up. The slowly chilling autumn wind ruffled his dark brown hair, sending goosebumps down his neck, causing him to wrap his hooded sweatshirt tighter around him. He refused to wear a fall jacket just yet, enjoying the last bits of warm weather that were salvageable in the approaching negative numbers.

Beside him, Sarina, a girl of auburn hair, sat upon the ground, deeply engaged in reading a very old hardcover book, its dust jacket practically gone. The daughter of Mislantus had adapted well to her new life on Earth, never having looked back. Her choice to remain in

Q-16 had been without hesitation. Soon after that decision, what she had once known as anger, fear and enslavement had been replaced with freedom, friendship and a family.

The boy shifted from his position, dropping the bag. "I wonder if Annetta slept in again."

"She was down there pretty late," Sarina responded, never raising her gaze from the page. "I'm surprised her parents didn't end up dragging her out again."

"Yeah," Jason sighed. He'd been more fortunate with his lot after everything had settled down at the end of the Second Great War. His mother had firmly stuck to her promise of not taking part in the events of the other worlds anymore. He knew full well, however, that her words had come out of the pain it had brought her for many years prior to him ever seeing the behemoth doors many miles down under the ocean.

Before any further conversation could be exchanged, the call of the first morning bell roared through the yard of the school. From all edges of the field, young, eager students flocked to the entrances of the main building or lined up beside the portables that were their homerooms. Sarina closed her book and opening her bag, she placed it in gently in order not to ruin it any further. She then looked up at Jason, who seemed torn between the responsibility of school and the loyalty to his friend.

"J.K., she will understand, you need to get to class on time." Sarina touched Jason's arm, to which the youth snapped out of his psychological dilemma and nodded. Shouldering their bags, the couple began to walk off towards class, fingers entwined, as they prepared for the turbulence of another day.

෨෬

Picking up her late slip, Annetta walked as briskly as she could to class, a sweaty mess beneath the tattered large jean jacket. Her efforts to make it before the morning announcements were foiled when the national anthem began to play. Straightening her back, the girl stood at attention, listening to the all-too-familiar tune that she had grown up hearing each and every morning that she had come to school. Annetta's mind wandered during such times in a whirlwind of thought, unable to maintain focus.

Her latest favourite daydream had become reliving the many times she was given the leisure of free time down in the Lab. She would often go out riding on her horse Firedancer around Severio Castle. It was not that she did not enjoy the company of her friends, but there were times when she felt a great need to be alone. There was something satisfying about the long bumpy ride down the stony road to the castle and beyond it. There was a sense of freedom in the blue sky above and something magic about the great limestone hills that seemed to roll endlessly.

Before Annetta could immerse herself more, the anthem stopped and she was back. The muscles in her legs coiled and stretched as she started out back into a sprint, not caring if anyone would stop to tell her to slow down. Some distance behind, she heard the distinct shuffling of Link's sneakers on the ground as he darted after her, having gotten his slip. She did not take time to wait for him, and nearly missing her classroom door, she slid on the tiled floor to a halt.

Looking into the tiny window of the door, Annetta took note of a tall heavyset man with balding black hair and a bushy black beard that seemed to be so thick it looked like a second set of hair. He seemed to be walking around and handing out papers to the class while speaking in a deep baritone voice that carried outside the room, though muffled.

"Great, Martinson is giving a pop quiz," Annetta seethed through her teeth as the sound of Link's shoes caught up to her.

"Why are you standing there?" Link raised his head and looked into the glass.

The inaudible speaking stopped and the teacher cocked his head to the side, peering straight into the little window back at Link, who lowered his head as though someone was about to swing a battle axe at it. Seconds later, the door handle twisted and a female student opened the door with a curious look on her face.

"Miss Annetta Severio and her sidekick, Mr. Link Heallaws," Mr. Martinson's voice boomed, laced thick with sarcasm as he glared at the two late comers with his hazel eyes. "So grand you could both grace us with your presence. Would you care to participate in marking our quizzes from last week, or should I take a rain check?"

Link avoided eye contact, unable to utter a syllable. He did not particularly like the sardonic Biology teacher. He found it was best always to scuffle off to the side and try to be as unnoticed as possible for the rest of the class.

Annetta, on the other hand, was a different case altogether, having had practice in such situations with a certain mage from Aldamoor.

Looking down with a smirk, she glanced back up at the teacher standing in the midst of the class.

"Well, sir, you know, we did just save the world and have to change out of our masks and capes. It was a bit hard to get here by the last bell when we couldn't find a phone booth to change in, what with everyone using cellphones nowadays," Annetta jested, shrugging her shoulders, to which the classroom behind her snickered.

Communicated to in his own weapon, the corner of Mr. Martinson's mouth twitched as he glared at those in the class, silencing them. He then turned to Annetta, who had given Link enough time to get to his seat and be forgotten about.

"Very droll, Miss Severio, slip on my desk and in your seat," the teacher huffed as he turned back to his blackboard. "Now, everyone pull out a different coloured pen and write your name in the top left hand corner of the paper, so I can know who marked whom."

Her words to the teacher said, Annetta did as she was told. Flopping down at her desk, she noticed in her peripheral vision both Jason and Sarina writing on the papers before them intently. Behind, Link settled in his desk, pulling out what supplies were needed. All around her, her classmates settled into the mundane routine of class. Seeing the pen she'd had in her desk was gone she frowned. It had been the eighth one that week. Pulling out another pen from her bag without second thought, she accepted the paper given to her and began to scribble down her name.

Chapter 2

The first two periods of the day flew by. Before Annetta knew it, the bell rang for their lunchtime break and she found herself walking to her corner of the fence with her friends. The schoolyard was a far more peaceful place this year, with Richard Finn having transferred to another school and his companions having scattered to the wind. Annetta did not mind the lack of confrontation. It was a relaxing change for her final year of high school. Reaching their destination, the girl slid down against the fence and sat on the grass, pulling out her sandwich. Though the wind blew fiercely in her face, making it difficult to see at times, she did her best to ignore it and focused on those around her.

"I almost forgot how much work high school is," groaned Jason. "Two essays for the rest of the semester plus all the rough drafts and other research for Biology alone? I mean, where are we gonna find time for all of this?"

"Let me put it in plain speech, J.K. They don't care," Annetta responded, taking a bite of her sandwich. "I guess we just gotta tough it out. I mean, it's not going to get any easier you know."

"Yeah, yeah, but I gotta vent somewhere you know?" the boy sighed, flopping down on the grass beside Sarina, who already had her nose in a book. Jason raised an eyebrow at her. "Aren't you going to eat?"

"I finished eating while you guys were talking," she responded bluntly, turning the page.

Jason shrugged and peered over her shoulder to see the writing. "You're really into that thing, aren't you? What's it about anyways?"

Sarina closed the book. "Not something you would understand."

"Touchy today, isn't she? What did you do, J.K.?" Link mused, looking over at the other boy teasingly.

Jason opened his mouth to protest, but before he could say anything, the girl replied, "Oh, he didn't do anything. I was being serious when I said he would not understand. It's a book on herbs and how to recognize them in the wild, along with their various medicinal properties."

Before the conversation could continue, Annetta heard and felt a faint buzzing on her left wrist. Confused as to why the Communication and Time Synchronizer was going off in the middle of her school day, she rolled up her sleeve to see 05 flashing across the faceplate. She looked over at the others, who had stopped chatting amongst themselves and huddled close to the buzzing watch.

Pressing the button to answer, Annetta waited a moment before speaking to it, "01 here...uh...what's going on Puc? You know we're in school, right?"

"I am well aware of your whereabouts, 01, as I am also aware that you are not within your classroom's vicinity. Am I correct?" the cold voice of the elven mage came through the speaker. **"And what have I told you about using names when speaking over the C.T.S.?"**

"I know, but it just sounds funny, alright?" Annetta ran a hand through her hair in order to keep it from getting in her face.

"Regardless, it is for your own safety," he stated. **"Now, my reason for contacting you so abruptly is that I have just received an envoy from the Ogaien and your presence, along with Jason's, will be required for participation in the Riva Mortem."**

"The what now?" Jason raised an eyebrow.

"I will explain everything when you get down to the Lab promptly after your classes. It is considered a great honour to be admitted to such an event. I want no dallying or wandering off. We will meet in the common room and proceed from there, understood?"

"Sure thing." Jason nodded in response.

"Good, and that means no riding off into the middle of nowhere, 01. 05 out." The light faded on the screen, allowing the time to display it again before the girl could object to the invasion of her freedom.

"Riva Mortem. What is that supposed to be?" Annetta scrunched up her nose, the wind causing her hair to tickle her face.

Link glanced over at her. "Guess we will find out once we get there. No point in worrying about it now."

"Yeah, not like we could even decline the invitation or anything," Annetta muttered, leaning against the fence, getting frustrated with her hair and pushed it back once more. "I hate how, we still get treated like kids."

"You mean by Puc? It's his duty," Sarina stated. "He's just doing what he has done all along, since before we were all born."

Annetta glanced over at Sarina while she sat with the giant book still in her lap. Ever since Sarina had decided to stay with them, she had been helping Puc around the Lab due to his apprentice Darius Silver having left to pursue finishing his studies back in Aldamoor. "I keep forgetting you're his pet now."

"I'm not his pet!" Sarina protested. "I just understand where he's coming from. When I was on my father's ship, there were events I was expected to attend with him, like the unveiling of a new weapon or a combat tournament. We had people like Puc who informed us of these things and managed what time we had in order not to be tardy for them. He's just trying to make you look good. That's all."

"Well, I can still find it annoying." Annetta shrugged and sighed, closing her eyes. "Maybe tomorrow I can go riding with Firedancer after training."

Link pulled out an apple from his bag and bit into it, the juice running down his chin and hand, causing him to pull it away and let it drip onto the grass beside him. "You're always off with him. Just what do you do in Severio Castle, anyways? You must have ridden every trail possible with him. There's probably no grass left."

Annetta smiled shyly, looking down at her cyan sneakers. "It's not something I can explain, I just like going off on my own. It helps me relax."

"It gives her time to daydream without Puc around telling her not to," Jason chuckled, pulling out his soup thermos. "Careful, Anne, you don't wanna space out and hit a branch."

Link and Sarina joined in the laughter with Jason, and even after a moment, Annetta cracked a grin. She knew full well if she tried to dive further into the topic of discussion there would just be more friendly jabs, which would make Annetta feel bad for having said anything at all. It was best to let them think what they liked, she thought, for some things were far too complicated to explain.

Chapter 3

A pair of inhuman blue eyes scanned the ink scribbles made on frail parchment, illuminated by the glow of a candle. Although the power worked fine within the confines of Q-16, Puc Thanestorm still preferred to use fire as his source of light, finding it more predictable than that of a generator. He had spent many years before with his close companion Brakkus in such conditions. It almost seemed wrong to not continue doing so, even if it was just in memory of the slain Hurtz.

Turning the page, his concentration was interrupted when he heard the distinct sound of feet shuffling along a metallic surface, and young voices speaking energetically to one another. Pushing back his shoulder length black hair from his face, he noted the time on the grandfather clock in the corner of the room.

Extinguishing the candles with the tips of his finger, the elven mage of Aldamoor grabbed his ornate gnarled wooden staff, and with a whirl of his dark robes, he was on his way to meet his charges.

He arrived in the common room, a large area consisting of multiple couches and armchairs all pushed together in a large circle, to find not a single soul in sight.

"Typical," he muttered to himself, knowing it would take the four youth far longer to reach the area than it should due to their stress-free pace. He then sat down on one of the sofas, placing his staff beside himself and waited.

His patience had almost run out by the time Annetta, Jason, Link and Sarina finally arrived. He did his best to show no disdain. There really was no point to it, after all. They would just do it again to spite him.

"Hey Puc, sorry it took us so long, we had-" Annetta began to explain herself, only to be cut off by the mage's raised hand.

"Spare me the storytelling so that we may get down to business." The mage rose from his seat and produced a folded piece of parchment from the breast pocket of his robe. "An Ogaien messenger left this for you both today, requesting your participation in the Riva Mortem that is to be held two days from now."

Annetta accepted the paper from the mage and looked over the overly-pronounced cursive, only to realize she could not understand it at all, due to it being written in Ogaien and not English. They had learned after the fight with Mislantus that none of the worlds truly spoke the same language and that it was the passage through a portal that translated everything into one common tongue for them all to be able to hear one another. If one spoke English, one would hear English and if other spoke the Ogaien tongue or the language of the Minotaurs, they would hear those languages, as Puc had explained to them. The written language, however, did not get translated and that was where the mage had proven highly skilled. Ever since the end of the fight, all races that comprised the Four Forces kept in contact with them through envoys that would come to speak with Puc, letting him know of various events that went on within the worlds. The girl was grateful more than ever for having him around to help meet all the demands placed upon her and Jason's shoulders as the heirs of Orbeyus and Arcanthur, be it meetings with leaders or attending ceremonies, even if it became bothersome at times. Studying the scribbles a minute longer, she handed it back, positive that Puc had read it correctly.

"Okay, so what does that mean for us exactly? Sounds like a festival or something." Jason rubbed his chin, feeling the few hairs there under his thumb.

"It is in a manner of speaking, I suppose." Puc motioned for them to sit, as it would take some time to explain. "The Riva Mortem is part of a tournament, created to honour the Ogaien Goddess Tiamet as the one who bestows life and takes it. It consists of a series of games, the nature of which I think all of you know."

Sarina felt her body become queasy and shifted her feet in her shoes, as she did not like where this was going. "You mean of death."

Puc nodded his head in her direction and continued. "The Riva Mortem itself is a game in which teams of six players face off on fully spike-armoured Aiethon and compete to use a spear to throw a charred animal carcass over a post on a field that is over a hundred yards long. It is a brutal affair that more often than not ends in at least one death. The first team to get the carcass over the post is named the victor. The twist in the Riva Mortem is this: One of the teams is always comprised of prisoners, and if they win, they are allowed to walk free."

Link squirmed in his seat. "That sounds pretty barbaric. Should such a thing be allowed?"

"It is their way, and it is not our place to criticize it," Puc replied. "It is always easier for an outsider to belittle those of another race and to see them as primitive. Their folly lies in their unwillingness to accept the other as equal and just in their own way, even if they do not see the merit of it."

Jason looked over at Sarina, trying to get a read on her face, but after seeing no sympathy, he turned to Puc. "You have to agree. I mean, that does sound pretty extreme."

"Puc is right, though," Sarina interjected. "We shouldn't be criticizing how they do things. If I'm not correct, some of your ancient cultures practiced such things as well."

"Yeah, and there's a reason they aren't around anymore," Jason muttered back.

Puc folded his hands in his lap and waited for Jason and Sarina to stop bickering. He did not have the patience to deal with silencing the couple and had learned to allow them to sort things out between one another. His eyes turned to Annetta, whom for once did not have a word to say. The girl leaned against one of the sofa armrests with her hands in her pockets in deep contemplation, her brows knotted beneath the growth of shaggy bangs, her jaw strained.

"Does something trouble you, Annetta?" he spoke to her.

The girl snapped out of her trance and looked over at him. "Hmm? Oh, not really. Well, I was just wondering are there any other rules we need to be aware of. I mean, you did say people die in this sort of thing, and we're supposed to be going up against prisoners."

The mage's lips curled slightly upwards in a pseudo-smile. The girl had become quite critical and observant in the past year, something she had not possessed before. "The Aiethon's spiked armour will be a grave concern of yours. You will only have one free arm to maneuver the spear with."

Hearing what was being discussed, Link nudged Jason, who was still speaking with Sarina. The Gaian youth raised a finger to his lips and pointed in the direction of the mage, causing them to become silent and listen in on what he and Annetta were speaking about.

The girl felt the eyes of her friends fall to her, but did her best to ignore them and focus on the mage. "Are other weapons allowed on the field at all, even as a backup?"

"They are, but do not expect to use them, for as I said, you will be more preoccupied with trying to avoid the spikes than the fight. This is not a regular battle on horseback. It is a contest of skill and precise timing."

22

Annetta bit down on her upper lip, unsure if there was anything else she wanted to ask. She knew there was no point in asking for pointers for such an event, there was neither time to prepare nor anything the mage could do to help them. It would all come down to nerves.

Link took the opportunity to step in where she had left off. "Did the letter say if they only requested Annetta and Jason, or will I be able to participate? The teams should have six contestants and if one of the slots isn't taken, then I want to go as well."

"To my knowledge, they only requested Annetta and Jason to participate, but your point is valid, Lincerious. I will ask Natane," the mage replied.

"Ask about me as well," Sarina added.

"What?" Jason's eyes widened. "You can't go with us, this isn't a game. I'm not going to be able to protect you. No way!"

"Kinsman," Puc hissed, causing the boy to lower his head. "Mind your tongue."

Sarina felt her face heat up from the comment made by him, causing her body to shift back a pace. Her dark eyes glared at Jason in confusion and anger. "I think that it's my choice whether I want to go or not."

She felt the green eyes of the boy gaze back at her, the corner of his mouth twitching as if to say something. Not wanting to hear it, she left, walking past the others into the confines of the base.

Puc waited for her to leave before focusing upon Jason, who stood rooted to his spot, dumbfounded. The youth realized he was being watched and turned to the elf.

"There looks to be trouble in paradise, Kinsman." Puc stated and then inclined his head in the direction the girl left. "Best go after her."

Blood rising to his face, causing him to blush, Jason ran off without another word after Sarina.

Puc exhaled roughly and raised himself from the seat, grabbing his staff. He turned to Annetta and Link, who were still before him. "You know the drill. Sparring in the training grounds."

&⊃&

The sounds of his breathing and of his shoes squeaking across the metal floor were the only companions Jason had in his journey catching up to Sarina. Seeing the dark-haired figure on the horizon was the only thing to slow his pace to a jog. The feeling of blood rushing to his neck dissipating, he stopped beside her, huffing and bracing his knees so as to not fall over. The girl, however, did not stop walking.

Trying to go further, Jason felt his legs turn to jelly, forcing him to stay put. Cursing at his cardiovascular performance for being so low, he looked up in her direction. "Can you at least tell me what I did?"

"Oh, I think you know pretty well," she answered, still walking.

Growling, the boy straightened his posture, the tension in his muscles lessening. "You give me too much credit, you know?"

Crossing her arms across her chest, Sarina wrinkled her nose and closed her eyes, facing away from him. She had no intention of further interaction for the time being.

Uncertain if he should approach her or not, Jason ran a hand through his ruffled hair and scratched the back of his neck, watching the girl from across the hall, his girl. It had not been a secret after the end of the battle with Mislantus that the two of them had been drawn to one another. It had not taken long after that for the labels of girlfriend and boyfriend to be attached to them, especially with the constant teasing of Annetta at every step. Sighing, Jason took a few steps towards her slowly.

"Look, if it's about the barbarism comments, I'm sorry, I was just trying to get on Puc-"

"I think you know full well what upset me," the girl said, still not bothering to face him, her voice the consistency of a storm of needles.

"I'm sorry," he managed to choke out of himself. "I may have overreacted but I had good reason. Puc said people die, and I just don't want you to get hurt is all. I don't know what I'd do if something happened to you, much less what I would say to Matt once he got back from wherever he is now. He'd probably skewer me on the spot."

Sarina sighed, her arms still crossed tightly as she turned around to look at him, an earnest expression drawn across his face as he stared her down, the look of a lost boy. The contours of her own features softened as she came closer to him.

"Maybe I was the one that overreacted," she said, finally. "It's just that... my father would always try to use the same argument. Even though I know he never meant it."

Jason continued to look down at his scuffed-up running shoes. Taking his time to stick his hands in his pockets, he tried to come up with what he should say and what he should avoid saying.

"It hadn't crossed my mind," he spoke after having collected his thoughts, "Honest. I was so worried I hadn't even thought about what I was saying. All I know was that it felt right and that it made sense. I mean, I think you out of everyone should know I'm nothing like him."

The girl nodded her head in agreement, pulling at a loose strand of hair and twirling it around her finger. "I know. It's like I said, I overreacted. It still doesn't change my mind about going with you."

Jason threw his hands up in the air, slapping them against his sides for emphasis. "You've gotta be kidding me, right? What part me worrying for your safety and not wanting you to go did you miss?"

"None, I can simply take care of myself," she stated bluntly, and turned to walk back in the direction they had come from. "Now come on. I have a feeling Puc wants you to spar."

"Just hold on a moment." Jason veered over to her and placed his hands on her shoulders, looking her in the eye. "You haven't had half the training we've had with Annetta or Link and you intend on getting involved in this thing, this game we have to play against prisoners. I mean, no offence or anything, but Annetta is built like a tank, and-"

"You don't know half the things I'm capable of," she retorted with a smile, cutting him off, taking his hands off her, and resuming her walk.

Turning to watch her go, Jason attempted to shut his hanging mouth, the flame of his argument never given time to build any potential. Regaining his senses, the boy shook his head and followed.

80G3

Steel clashed on steel with rhythmic humming in the massive stone arena surrounded by tall glass windows. Columns of uninhabited seats watched as two figures moved quickly across the rocky surface, blinding reflective lights flashing from their weapons every so often. Annetta faced Link, their blades crossing one another in the dance of their swordsmanship. They were only ever interrupted by the eventual struggle and blocking of the tower shield the girl carried. They did not use their actual swords, not wanting to damage the edges of the weapons. Instead, they carried practice ones, dull-edged swords they had picked out from the armoury.

Puc watched from the side, leaning on his staff as he analyzed every move made by the two young warriors. They were so into the heat of their own battle that they did not notice Jason or Sarina enter to stand beside the mage.

"Who's winning?" Jason asked.

Puc continued to watch without making eye contact with the new arrivals, and simply said, "Neither of them, for the time being."

"Oh, good, at least Annetta will be broken in when I have to fight her." The boy stretched his arms and waved them around in large circles in order to get his blood flowing better.

The elf did not reply directly again, his eyes following Annetta and Link intently. "Did you sort it?"

"Sort what?" Jason raised an eyebrow.

"The contretemps you two were having?" he asked yet again.

The boy's attention was taken from the poor conversation when Annetta jumped away from a direct attack at her midsection, diving down into a crouching position and raising her shield to block an upper attack. The impact of the blow upon the shield caused her whole body to jump slightly, but the girl wasted no time waiting for recovery and drove her sword point forward, attempting to stab at her opponent, who stepped back just in time to not be gutted, but with no guard or option of fleeing. Link raised his arms in a yielding fashion, causing Jason to snap back to the conversation with Puc.

"Uh, yeah we solved them," he replied, looking over at Sarina.

The mage continued to keep his focus upon the two within the rink. "Good footwork, Lincerious, but you need some work on being able to detect unevenness in the flooring. You are too sure on an even floor, and I do not like it. Annetta, I do not want to see any more of those mid- thrusts, they are moribund in a battle scenario and will only work well in a rehearsed duel."

Puc then turned to Jason and Sarina. "Well, that is a pity, because you are both next in the arena."

"I'm sorry, what?" Jason raised his voice a pitch upon hearing the bold words of the elf. "I'm not fighting Sarina, no way. I've never fought against her, she's never been part of-"

The eyes of the elf zeroed in on the boy. "And when you stood against your foes on the field, did you question if you had fought them and if they had experience or not?"

Jason felt the logic behind what Puc was saying to be irrelevant to the current situation, but feeling the heat of the gaze boring into him, he replied anyways, "Well, no, but-"

"And if a doppelgänger stood here and in this moment in place of Sarina, would you question then? Trust me when I say this, boy, you may even learn a thing or two from her in the process."

Jason could not believe what he was being made to do and looked over at Sarina, who stood quietly beside him without saying a word. Annetta wiped the sweat from her brow and walked over to the practice weapons rack. She pulled out a sword and handed it to Sarina before she sat down in the seats behind them, exhaling deeply. Link also took a seat beside her without a second thought, huffing wearily from the effort of the brawl. Jason growled under his breath and pulled out a dulled mace that they had managed to find for him so he would not fall out of practice. His glance once more turned reluctantly to Sarina.

"I really don't want to do this," he muttered, his feet feeling like concrete as he dragged them across the floor.

Sarina did not respond and simply went into her fighting stance, her eyes locked on Jason.

Puc walked to the side of the arena beside Annetta and Link, clearing the path. Once in position, he announced, "You may begin."

The boy licked his lips nervously, reaffirming the tight grip on his weapon and began to move sideways in a clockwise direction. He had no desire to hit Sarina, and he was doing everything possible to postpone the fight. Every step he took seemed to feel like his shoes were filled with lead and twice as sensitive, feeling every light anomaly underfoot.

Unsure of what he was doing, Sarina followed his lead and walked in a circle as well, not letting her guard down.

Rolling his eyes, the mage interjected, "Unknown's bane, you are to be sparring, not dancing! Sarina, if he is unwilling, then you land the first blow."

As if on command, the blade crossed with the mace, sending Jason staggering a pace back from the shock. He had not expected such a well-placed hit from the girl, nor one so strong. Pushing her weapon back, he attacked with the mace, an overhead strike that was sure to knock the sword from Sarina's hand. His effort was thwarted when the girl nearly planted the sword in his belly upon seeing the opening. Jason's ability to teleport was the only thing that had saved him.

Annetta and Link watched the fight from the side. Though Link thought nothing of what was going on, Annetta had a very different feeling about it. Not only had she never seen Sarina spar with them before, she was doing it very well. Wrinkling her nose in confusion, she leaned over to the mage.

"Was there something we missed?" she asked him.

The stone faced elf turned ever slightly to make eye contact with her. "She was the daughter of Mislantus the Threat. If you thought just because she was locked up all her life she was never trained in weapons use, think again."

"You'd never think it," muttered the girl.

"You forget one key thing, Annetta. Sarina is not human, as much as she may look like it," Puc replied, looking back on the fight to see Jason taking blow after blow from the girl with very little retaliation. "Had enough, Kinsman?"

Jason staggered back once more. Taking another attack from Sarina, he was forced to one knee. He looked over at the mage, who stared back at him judgmentally. "Not just yet."

His attention turned away from Sarina, however, cost him valuable defence power and the mace quickly flew out of his hands, landing some distance away on the floor. The tip of Sarina's sword remained pointed at his throat, causing his face to heat up from surprise.

"Not just yet, indeed," Puc mused with a smirk on his face. "You can put those away. I can see you have clearly been blinded by love and there is no point in continuing this sordid torture."

Biting his tongue in order not to reply, Jason got up once Sarina had taken away the sword. He then marched over to where his mace lay and picking it up in a fluid motion, went to deposit it with a scowl on his face. His temper even prevented him from making any comment to the elf as he passed by him. He could not remember the last time he had so easily been bested in a fight. It seemed unthinkable to him. The only excuse he had for himself was that he had not seen it coming and even that was not enough to satisfy him.

Puc noted the behaviour and turned to the others. "I think we can call it a day for now. Check your mounts to make sure everything is in order for the trip, so that there is sufficient time to replace and repair what is needed. We will meet again tomorrow, and I will walk you through what you need to know."

Sarina nodded and went after an angry Jason, as did Link, who hoped to somehow comfort his friend. Annetta lingered while everyone left, remaining beside the mage. He regarded her actions with curiosity, knowing full well the young woman was always first out the door.

"What ails you?" he asked once they were alone.

"Uh, nothing, I just feel like we ought to know more about this Riva Mortem thing. I just want to do everything as best as I can," Annetta spoke, rubbing her arm where Link had smacked her with the flat of his sword.

Puc noticed her body language and turned to move to his quarters, motioning for her to come with him so that he could examine the damage done. "You will perform as you always have, and it will be well. You have nothing to worry about. I do not see why you are troubled so much."

"Okay, well, have you been on an Aiethon? Those things are huge, and I'm pretty sure they have a mind of their own," grumbled Annetta, "Secondly, you never really gave us lessons in handling a spear efficiently."

"Annetta, a spear is no different-"

The girl's ranting continued over the mage's words, her arms thrown up in frustration as they walked. "Yes, it totally is different! We're going into a battlefield with no knowledge of how to wield the weapons that are being given to us! You might as well give us all pitchforks and ask us to perform because it'll make no difference in what we're going to be doing out there."

Puc stopped in his tracks, closing his eyes and shaking his head with a sigh. The young Severio child had proven at times more difficult than he remembered her elders being. Opening his eyes again, he looked down at the stubborn looking girl with ruffled reddish-brown hair and an angry scowl.

"You are really that concerned about using a spear properly?" he concluded.

"Among other things," she stated, fixing the shoulder of her shirt, which had come out of place during the sparring. "I know the others won't ask, so I have to. I mean, like it or not, I'm still the heir of Orbeyus you know? There are things that are expected of me because of it."

Switching the staff from one hand to another, the mage continued to walk beside her, their voices accompanied by the sound of their feet upon the steel floors. The halls around them had remained unchanged since the initial arrival of Annetta and Jason, mostly due to the fact that many of the things within the base had remained untouched, their origins forgotten. Gathering his thoughts finally, Puc stopped and turned fully to Annetta.

"From the time I laid eyes on you over a year ago, I said to myself that you were far too young to be engaged in the things which were to come. It would be a lie if I said this was all going to be easy," he spoke, and started walking once more towards his quarters.

"Look, I know it won't be, alright?" Annetta huffed, not sure how to further beat her point home. "I'm just asking for advice is all, I guess."

The mage paused and slowly turned again. The face he looked upon seemed in a state of forlorn chaos, a spectre of someone who was drowning at sea and had nothing left to hold onto, except one plank that lay before them. If they did not reach for it, then it would mean their end. The severity of it all made the mage nearly cough up a laugh in the back of his throat. She may have looked an adult in the eyes of many, but beneath it all still reigned a child's heart.

"Believe me when I tell you this, you are more prepared than you know," Puc said, coming closer to the girl. "An Aiethon, you will find, is not much different than a horse, though it may look like it will strip the flesh off your bones with its teeth. A spear you will find not much different in use than a sword, for I do hope you know which end you will need to hold when the game begins."

Annetta gave a stiff laugh, and even the mage joined her in a small tight-lipped smile for a split second.

The elf continued, having diffused the tension. "Tell me, do you remember the battle in Aerim when we went to find Prince Snapneck in Yarmir's lair?"

"Our first real fight." She nodded.

"Yes. You also had no idea what to expect then. There was no preconception of how it was all to turn out, apart from your need to win. Try to think of the Riva Mortem in this spectrum as well."

The girl sighed, not satisfied with the answer. "It's easier said than done now after everything."

"Try either way," Puc stated, "and when I said you were far too young, I never meant you were incapable. They are two very different things."

The youth gave a stiff bob of her head, still not feeling fully comfortable with everything. Somehow in her own mind, she had pictured all her doubts washing away, whereas they had only been pushed to the back of her mind, still throbbing like a weak migraine. Her further contemplations on the issue were interrupted when a hand clamped down on her shoulder and she looked over to see Puc standing beside her.

"Trouble yourself no more with idle thoughts," he spoke to her. "Thinking of such events never did anyone good. They are best dealt with by being in the moment. Now come, that bruise will be a hard one to explain to your teachers if not taken care of."

He waited no more for her after the fact, the wooden staff echoing on the floor as he moved further away. Annetta watched the robes of the mage billow around him, seeming to become a dark mist on the horizon the further away he moved. Seeing his point, she went to rejoin him.

Chapter 4

Two days passed by quickly, and before either Annetta or Jason knew, everyone was assembled in the stables, preparing everything that was needed to make the journey to the Yasur Plains. Packs and saddles were hoisted onto uneasy steeds as every corner of the establishment seemed to beam with life. Annetta and Sarina checked the horses to make sure each animal had been groomed prior to saddling, while Link and Jason put on the blankets and saddles, securing them to the backs of the animals. Chatter flew through the air like clouds of arrows, despite how grizzly the event seemed and how much Puc had drilled them the day before on what needed to be done when handling a spear, at the insistence of Annetta, and participating in the event.

Puc entered after some time, once more donning the deep crimson robes he always wore when he rode to meet with the Ogaien. He carried a satchel slung across his shoulder, which, with the addition of his staff made him look more a traveller than a mage. His appearance also meant an instant death to the conversation which had been going prior to his arrival.

The mage of Aldamoor did not miss a beat and glanced around him. "How go the preparations? From the amount of buzzing I heard beyond the doors, I would say everything is complete."

Stupefied in their tracks, the four looked at one another. Despite the mage's assessment ringing true, no one spoke up. After a moment, Sarina took a step forward. "Everything has been prepared. We're just missing the Severio banner itself."

"The colours will be at the castle grounds. We will fasten them to Firedancer there," he responded briefly before looking to the rest. "If nothing else need be accounted for, we move out."

Climbing onto their horses and making sure once more that everything was secure, they headed out. Carefully one by one, they led their steeds onto the green pasture that surrounded the stables. Turning to an all-too-familiar dirt trail that lay neatly trampled out among the tall green blades, the companions moved towards the red and black wall that lay ahead of them, the portal leading to the Eye to All Worlds.

Seeing as no one moved in a hastened pace to lead, Puc urged his horse, a calm grey mare that had been nicknamed Ebony for the black markings on her legs, forward. "I do not see why you are all standing about like a bunch of gaping trolls. You know the drill by now."

Snapping out of her daze, Annetta shook her head as though she were trying to make whatever it was that had latched onto her leave. "Sorry, I think it's just beginning to hit us all, you know?"

"What is to be will be. There is no turning back now." Looking down at his horse, the mage made sure to tighten his grip on the reins before uttering the command, "Fly."

As soon as the words left his lips, Ebony darted forward and pierced the red and black watery wall before them, disappearing with her rider.

Annetta looked over at Link, Jason and Sarina, who glanced back at her with neutral expressions. Seeing their melancholy facades, the girl sucked some air into her lungs and exhaled heavily, allowing the last words of the mage to wash over her. "Look, Puc has a point. Whatever is gonna happen is gonna happen, and I think we're all forgetting one important and very key fact in all of this."

"And what would that be, warrior princess?" Jason raised an eyebrow.

Annetta did not reply to the comment, simply rolling her eyes in response. Nudging Firedancer closer, the girl leaned her saddle in towards him. "This isn't the first fight we're gonna be in. We've been training every day and from the sound of it, those Ogaien we are gonna face won't have. So, I say we turn those frowns upside down because they're just making us all upset. Is there a point to all of it? I don't really think so."

"Just when did you have time to pop some positivity pills?" Jason snorted.

Annetta ignored him again, not really in the mood to reply to his sarcasm. She then veered her horse around, and with a sharp command, bolted through the portal. Flinching slightly from the after effects of crossing the massive wall, the girl allowed her gaze to linger on the stone structure in the valley below, surrounded by mountains of limestone. There, in the midst of it all, stood Severio castle, hailing the new arrivals with its cerulean tower heads raised in salute from the white castle walls.

"Took you long enough." The voice of the mage interrupted her mesmerizing connection with the scenery. "Are Lincerious, Jason and Sarina planning on joining us anytime in this fine century?"

Messy hair gliding across her shoulders as she turned, the girl faced Puc and nodded. "Yeah, they're coming. We just all needed a moment."

"I understand this is the first task of its kind that you have had to undertake since the battle with Mislantus, but you are all getting worked up for no reason," he huffed, adjusting the grip on his staff. "I suppose this is why they say teenagers are a difficult breed."

Before the ranting could be continued, Link, Jason and Sarina appeared, stopping their horses beside Annetta and Puc's.

"Good of you to decide to join us. I was preparing to set up camp soon." Puc glared at them.

"Look, we had cold feet," Jason rebutted "Don't tell me you never did when getting ready to go do something like this."

The stern-faced elf did not so much as move a muscle as he continued to watch the boy. After having proved his point, he turned to Annetta. "You know where the standard is kept. Lincerious, I would request that you accompany her in order to make sure that it is secure. The last thing we want is to have it fall as we reach Natane. Meet us at the gate to the Yasur Plains. I will disperse the cloaking potions before we cross."

"What about us?" Jason asked, looking over at Sarina, who had already urged her horse to move forward after the mage.

Taking pity on him, Sarina stopped and turned around her saddle. "Isn't it obvious? We just go with him."

Jason bit his upper lip in embarrassment and nodded his head slowly as he nudged his horse to follow Sarina's, calling out to her. "You know, just because I'm psychic doesn't mean I can read minds. Puc of all people should know that!"

&)(&

Potions having been taken and everything accounted for, the companions headed through the carved archway into Salaorin, the home of the Ogaien. Though Annetta and her friends had been there multiple times since their first visit to the bizarre world made of flames, it always struck them by surprise. The red sky above seemed almost pleasant despite the angry hue it held, and all around the glowing orange grass seemed to cover the hooves of their mounts. Above these, the black sleek twisted trunks of trees greeted them on the distant horizon, decorated with bright fiery leaves that twinkled like an odd assortment of stars on a very small patch of sky. Before they could look around further, however, the sounds of hooves on dry hard ground came at them, and the forms of two riders could be seen fast approaching.

A cloud of dust and sparks materialized before them. Within its centre, the Ogaien riders brought their mounts to a standstill, their reptilian faces focused on them intently, frizzled black hair cascading down their backs from the hastened journey.

"Greetings, Anuli and Amayeta." Puc did not miss a beat in his response to the appearance of the warriors. "We have arrived as promised."

"And with good time to spare, I see," Anuli replied. "Come, the Great Mother awaits to welcome you so that you may prepare. There is much to be discussed in terms of strategy."

Urging their horses into a canter, everyone began to move in the direction of the settlement within the Yasur Plains.

"Strategy?" Annetta asked, pushing Firedancer to catch up with their escorts.

"On this day we fight alongside you, heir of Orbeyus," Amayeta explained. "Six have always been the champions of Tiamet and six the scourge of Pioren, our sacrifice."

The girl turned to Puc, wanting to understand why the mage would not be participating with them in the battle. His cloak fluttered lightly on the wind as Ebony followed the other horses without question. Feeling the weight of the girl's gaze, the elf returned it.

"Sarina rides in my place. Only six may ride per team," he explained. "Anuli and Amayeta have waited for the right to prove themselves in the Riva Mortem since they became aware of its importance in their society. I as an outsider have no right to take such an honour away from them."

"If it's such a great honour, then why are we taking the place of four other Ogaien who could be participating?" Jason butted in.

Puc looked at the boy and replied, "Because it was requested of the Great Mother herself that four warriors of Orbeyus's alliance were to ride as a way of proving themselves to Tiamet and thus cementing their worth in the eyes of the Dragon Goddess. You and Annetta are the leaders of the Four Forces. Sarina and Lincerious are two of your closest followers, so it is only natural that they go with you."

"It was seen in a vision," Anuli stated, "while the Great Mother prayed, and so it must be done."

Annetta nodded and continued on her way without another word, watching underfoot to make sure Firedancer was not stepping onto any uneven ground. Though she had come to terms with there being expectations from her as the heir, she still did not like it when those expectations were foretold or seen in visions. It made the anxiety all the greater, as though someone had, in place of a boulder, set a mountain on her shoulders to carry.

"Breathe," she muttered to herself, clutching the reins tighter. "Just because someone said something, it doesn't mean a thing."

ഇരുന

Though the journey seemed endless, Annetta and the others soon rode through the gates of the encampment found on the Yasur Plains. The companions were greeted amidst the chaotic preparations for the festival with a quick bow of the head from any who turned to see them pass by. It was not until they reached the main tent of the Great Mother that a proper welcome was bestowed upon them. Natane stood at the mouth of her hut, flanked by two female warriors on foot. Though fierce in its disposition until the last minute, the face of the Ogaien leader softened as soon as the horses came to a stop.

"Greetings to you all." Natane's green eyes sparkled, contrasting the crimson tinted atmosphere. "I hope your journey was free of obstacles."

"There were none, Great Mother," Puc answered, all too happy to be off his horse. "How go the preparations?"

Natane turned to her guards and with a wave of her hand, had them attending to the horses, taking the reins from the new arrivals. Their places at her side were quickly filled by Amayeta and Anuli. Her red and orange reptilian face then turned back to the mage and the others. "All goes well. Come, so that you may see the arena."

Annetta took a deep breath, put on her neutral face and followed Puc. The soft orange grass brushed about her feet as she went after him, her ears picking up the sounds of shouting, whetstones and Aiethon as they moved about the camp. Seeing no one close to her side, she turned around to see where Jason, Sarina and Link were. She saw Link a few steps behind her, while Jason and Sarina stayed further back, engaged in conversation. She stopped and waited for the Gaian to catch up with her.

"Did anyone ever tell you that you walk really slowly?" she said, teasingly.

"I wasn't aware it was a contest," the youth replied as he pushed his bangs back with his hand. "Otherwise I would have put more effort into it."

Annetta felt the corners of her mouth form into a closed-lip smile, only to be distracted by a laugh from Sarina and Jason as they caught up to them. Crossing her arms, she cleared her throat, "My, aren't you both chatty today. Care to share?"

"Sarina, she-" Jason choked on his laughter as Sarina smacked his arm. "Sorry, Anne, you had to have been there."

"My voice cracked," Sarina sighed. "Nothing unusual."

Annetta raised an eyebrow and formed an 'oh' shape with her mouth before nodding her head. She looked over at Link, who seemed not to understand what was so amusing about a change of pitch in vocal chords. Then again, neither did Annetta, the more she thought about it. Their silent exchange of thought was cut off by the sound of Natane's voice.

"We have arrived," the Great Mother announced.

Turning in the direction of the call, Annetta and her friends walked over to catch up to Puc and Natane. Passing by the last of the huts that made up the encampment, they came upon a large rectangular clearing from which the grass had been stripped clean. To either end were two poles and flat black stones were being set to separate them from the rest of the field by Ogaien. Elevated seats were also being erected from the far side, and sharpened spikes were being placed in the ground, surrounding the flattened area.

"A Riva Mortem of this magnitude has not been held in many years," Natane spoke, "And it shall be remembered for many after when the blood of the slain shall stain the ground."

Jason shifted uneasily in his shoes as he looked over at Sarina and then turned back to face the Great Mother. "Do people...I mean... is there a lot of death in a Riva Mortem?"

"Only as much as is required by the Goddess Tiamet at a given time. In some Riva Mortems past, there have been no recorded deaths at all."

"That's a bit of a relief," Jason sighed, relaxing.

"In some, however, none stood living by the end of the contest. Champions and scourge fell on each other's spears and the field lay littered in red." Natane concluded.

Jason's lips tightened after hearing the last part. Prying them open, he replied, "Well, hopefully, she's not feeling too angry today."

"Not up to us mortals," Natane chuckled. "I must leave for now. I am needed to see to other things."

Puc bowed upon hearing the Ogaien. "I will see to them being ready Great Mother. You have my word."

"I leave it in your hands, Thanestorm," she replied.

Annetta watched as Natane left with her two daughters. After she was sure they were far enough away, she sighed and slouched against the wall of the closest hut.

"Great, another fate thing," she muttered, crossing her arms repeatedly.

"It's like the Great Mother said, we can't do anything about it," Link spoke, looking over at the girl. "You said it yourself, too, we just gotta roll with it."

"Still bugs me, though," she grumbled back.

The mage smirked lightly as he walked towards them, having heard the conversation. "You know, I used to be of the same mind once, Annetta."

"And let me guess, thunder hit you and you became a believer," she replied with a smug look on her face, half-expecting to be right.

The elf's expression did not falter, adjusting the grip on his staff and he continued. "No, far from it, I simply heard a tale from one of my teachers when I was young which made me see things in a different light. It was the tale of two young mages who studied at the Academy together. They were without equal in their skill. It was even thought that in the future, they would compete for the title of First Mage. One day, however, a prophet who was in town foretold the doom of one of them. The youth on which the death sentence hung dedicated himself fiercely to his studies, spending all his waking moments in focus on preparations so that when death was to claim him, he could be ended standing on his own two feet. The youth who was told he would be spared, however, saw no point in honing his skill any longer, for once his peer was dead he would be the greatest in all the land. The day came, however, when the Fire Elves invaded the shores of Aldamoor, breaching its walls. Many died, and the fighting spread like wildfire into the Academy. Amongst those caught in the battle were the two students. Once the chaos had cleared, it was discovered that the student which had been foretold to live had been slain and the one that had been told he would die, lived. Do you know why this was?"

Link knotted his eyebrows. "It was a trick, and the prophecy was misinterpreted."

Puc raised his hand. "Wrong, but a good guess. The prophecy was correct, however, the fault lies in the one who put all his trust in words alone. It was once said by the Unknown himself, trees that are said to be barren can still flourish if given the chance. It is up to us to truly decide our fate. Prophecy is but words spoken. How we choose to react to them are our own decisions, and they are what mark our destinies."

Annetta felt the words partially bounce off of her. Looking down at her shoes with her arms crossed, she knew Puc was right. Actions and not words decided the fate of a person. She couldn't help the fact however that on another level, the idea of a vision being the reason for her participation in the upcoming event made her insides churn with unease. She exhaled deeply through her mouth, feeling the cool blast of air run all the way down to where her jeans met her sneakers and turned her gaze back to the mage.

"So…where do we go to suit up?"

Chapter 5

Crossing the field being prepared for the festivities, Annetta, Jason, Link and Sarina were led to a large tent by Amayeta while Puc left with Anuli to find Natane. The inside of the structure was dark and smelt strongly of hay, burlap and wood. It was not by any means meant to be a residence of any finery, but a simple place of waiting out until the appointed time.

"You have been told by Thanestorm," Amayeta began once everyone was inside, "what is expected on the field during the Riva Mortem, I would assume?"

Sarina was the first to answer. "Six players to each team wielding spears on armed Aiethon, and the goal is to fling a charred animal carcass across the posts."

"Correct." Amayeta nodded her head. "In order to help distinguish which team is which, the players also wear coloured hide tunics, shin and arm guards. Do not count on these to save your skin from the point of an Ogaien spear, however. They are meant for decoration and nothing more."

Jason frowned, crossing his arms. "Well, that sounds pretty grim."

"Grim it may be, Kinsman but this is our way and has been for many years," Amayeta replied with a slight sharpness to her voice. Picking up a large bag, she tossed it in the middle of where the four of them stood, "We ride today marked in crimson. Let no scourge know if we bleed and let all the world see their marks when they ride today in pale hides of white."

Annetta reached into the bag and produced a red garb. Touching the velvety underside of the rawhide, she could see why it would offer no defence against enemy spears. She then turned her gaze back to Amayeta's green reptile eyes.

"Will we be told when to proceed?" she asked.

"We will join you with Anuli in good time. For now, dress, prepare and pray to whichever gods you salute. Pray that they give you the strength and speed needed to seize victory. I go now to find my sister and will return in due time so that we may all retrieve our Aiethon."

"Just one more question." Jason interrupted Amayeta's exit. "If for some reason we use our psychic powers, would we get in trouble for it?"

Amayeta paused to think on the subject before answering. "There are none to my knowledge, though it would be wise to not use it too rashly I would say. Some Ogaien may oppose it."

Annetta and Jason nodded in reply. As soon as the Ogaien warrior left the tent, the tension seemed to lessen all around the youth. Sitting down on one of the benches with a thud, Annetta examined the red leather tunic in her hands more precisely, noting all the scratches and imperfections laid into it from years of use. She wondered how many Ogaien had worn it before her and how many had died in it.

Still standing where they were, Sarina and Link both reached into the bag and began pulling on arm guards, trying to find a pair that fit either of them. Jason watched them both, then noticed his friend sitting on her own. He walked in her direction.

"Come on, Anne, it won't be so bad," Jason said as he sat down beside her. "It's six on six and I remember us in worse odds than that. There's no magic and no psychic abilities on their team either in this, just us."

Annetta smiled weakly and began picking at one of the larger loose pieces of leather that had been sliced pretty badly. "I don't get how you can take this so lightly after everything we've been through."

"Because we've gotten better since then," Jason scoffed, throwing his hands up. "You said it yourself earlier that we need to make the best of it and just go with the flow. You were right, things have changed since our first fight, and we aren't completely useless. Back then we barely knew how to create psychic fire, much less how to use our abilities or to fight. I don't know about you, Anne, but I like to think our hard work with Puc will pay off."

"Maybe it will," the girl replied. "But I also don't think we have to tickle a sleeping dragon, so to speak."

"Anne, it's just a fight, it's no different than-"

"It is different." Annetta rose from her seat and stared him down. "We fought before for very different reasons. We fought to save people, to save our own lives. This is just a contest, a tournament. This is not a fight of our choosing and honestly, not a fight I want to be part of. I'm just doing it because we have to. It's what we're expected to do."

Link looked over at Annetta from the pile of uniforms, having already slipped on one of the red tunics. "What if you think of this as something you need to do in order to protect your friends from harm?"

"Doesn't change the reason we're here to begin with," Annetta huffed back, pulling her hair into a ponytail for the upcoming event with a hair tie she'd brought with her.

"No, maybe it doesn't, but I mean…together we can watch each other's backs," Link continued. "Even in all the battles we fought before, we didn't plan to be in them. We got thrown into them by other forces at work. This isn't that much different if you think about it."

Annetta felt herself clenching her teeth even harder, to the point she thought they would break under the pressure of her jaws. Collecting her thoughts, she loosened the muscles in her face and pulled on the red garb, allowing it to slide all the way down. It was far too big for her and she would need to shorten it somehow in order not to trip on it. Pulling up the ends, she began tying them together around her waist. After some work and a final tight tug, she managed to get the leather to sit just slightly below her hips.

"As I said before, I'm here to do my duty and nothing more. It doesn't mean I have to like it." She gave a final grunt and left the tent to get some fresh air.

⌘

Outside on the field, in the thralls of the afternoon sun, the last of the raised benches had been completed by the workers and a crowd began to swarm around its lower levels. Having arrived early with Natane, Puc looked out over the sights before him from one of the upper levels in a box-like pavilion that had been provided for Natane and her closest guests. Though he knew full well the proceedings, something still clenched inside of him with anxiety's iron grip. A blast from a wide black horn on the far side of the field heralded the flocks of Ogaien to begin assembling in their seats for the event in greater numbers.

"It will not be long now." Natane broke the silence. "It will take a little while for all to gather. We have three other camps here with us today, those of Mothers Nita, Ahota and Enola. They too took up spears during the Second Great War under my command and were all too eager to see the heir and her companions this day. On the third sounding, the riders will assemble on the grounds and on the fourth, it will begin."

Black hair sliding over his crimson robes, the mage twisted slightly to face the Great Mother, who had seated herself in one of the chairs provided in their box. Loosening the grip on his staff, he walked over to join her without a word and took his place.

Natane's serpentine eyes looked at the elf with curiosity. "How fare you these days, Thanestorm?"

"I am well, Great Mother," he responded reflexively. "There is no cause for me to be otherwise."

The Ogaien leader seemed unsatisfied with the shallow answer. Her tongue flickered in and out a few times as if analyzing the words spoken. "You may be honest with me. I have known you many years now and still, you treat me at a distance. Tell me, have I done something to offend thee? In Annetta's service, or perhaps in Orbeyus's?"

"You have never done anything of the sort, Great Mother," he replied once more and straightening his posture, he looked down at his hands. "Forgive me if I seem distant, but I have learned over the years that dwelling on emotion does not do anyone any good in the long run."

"And whose wise words are those?" Natane chuckled. "They are certainly not Ogaien. We may be cruel, harsh and indomitable at times but to those, we call kin and friend, our passion burns as deep as the flames of Tiamet herself."

"I know so for a fact." Puc looked out at the rapidly filling stadium around him. "The words are not of Ogaien origin, nor of any whom have ever walked in the service of the Severio clan. They come from a place far deeper and more primitive. They come from experience in loss."

"I feel I should have left you in the Visium far longer than you stayed," Natane sighed in defeat. "This is not about the Hurtz or Orbeyus, is it?"

A slight smile crossed the face of the elf. "No, those souls have been laid to rest. Caution's scars are etched into the flesh far deeper."

There was stillness among the two for a time, the sound of the crowds filling in for what would have normally been the sounds of wind against vegetation. Clearing his throat, the blue-eyed mage looked in the direction of the dragon-featured woman at his side. "I meant what I said about being well, however. All scars will heal eventually if given a chance to do so with a helping hand."

Natane's red and golden face stretched into a smile as the second blast was sounded and the assembled Ogaien cheered at the impending festivities. In the midst of the celebrating, three Ogaien warriors made their way to the box where Puc and Natane resided. Seeing the new arrivals, the mage rose to his feet on instinct. They looked virtually indistinguishable in their builds, were it not for one of them having a large scar running parallel on her face from temple to jaw, the second wearing her hair in a braid and the third having her hair shaved to either side with a short Mohawk.

Turning her head, the Great Mother greeted those who had appeared. "And as spoken, Mothers Nita, Ahota and Enola."

"Praised be the Great Mother, keeper of dreams," Enola, the one with the braid spoke as she knelt.

"May she know many more days in the service of the Goddess Tiamet," Nita, the one with the scar added.

"Into eternity," said the third, Ahota, bowing low.

"Rise, sisters. You honour me far too much," Natane answered and bid them to stand. "You all remember Thanestorm, I assume?"

"A face quite hard to forget," Ahota replied, getting up. "Pale flesh and blue eyes are not a common thing on Salaorin, no matter where you go."

Enola nodded her head and turned to Puc directly, "We are pleased to have you here, Thanestorm, and more so that the invitation to participate in the Riva Mortem was taken up by young Annetta and her companions."

"She did so with eagerness," Puc replied briefly, feeling flooded by the newcomers.

"We are surprised, however," Nita said, "that you do not ride with her today."

Puc turned his eyes to Nita, his face not betraying the slightest hint of insult. "I was to ride with her, however another, younger face wished to prove herself on this day, and who am I to deny the right? Let the young collect the glory they crave so in old age they may stand aside for those yet to come after them."

"Wise words." Ahota gave a grin in response. "We may make an Ogaien out of you yet."

"Come and sit," Natane interrupted, "The third blast will sound soon."

As everyone took their seats, Puc felt his lips stretch out into something resembling a small smile and turned to Ahota. "I am afraid water does not mix well with fire."

The overpowering sound of the third horn blast came just as promised and the crowds on the benches roared even louder, most rising from their seats, fervent to have the festivities begin. Puc, Natane and the other leaders of the Ogaien camps stirred upon hearing it. The noise soon died down, the trudging of Aiethon hoofs causing all to come to silence.

ꜱꝋꝶ

From both far sides of the stadium came two rows of three riders. Fanning out into a single line as they rode to the middle, they came to a halt but a few feet from their opponents, their Aiethon mounts uneasy from the quick halt in their course. Annetta and her companions were then forced to face their opponents for the first time.

The so-called scourge, dressed in white as they had been branded, did not look very different to her from that of other Ogaien warriors she had come in contact with. Four were female and two were male. The males both had their heads completely shaved, and could only be told apart by their varied physiques, one being slimmer than the other, and a large pink scar crisscrossing the chest of the bigger one. The women, of varied height, all had their hair cut ruggedly short in order to make them seem indistinguishable from one another. All their spears had a white piece of leather tied to the spear points, causing the weapons to look like white flags of surrender.

"Pale skins to show the colours of their blood as they fall, or the blood of the champions," Amayeta explained to Annetta. "Best hope it will only be their own."

"No kidding." she felt the Aiethon under her move a little uneasily and reined it in tighter.

Feeling something like the sensation of needles hit her, Annetta looked over to the opposing side to find the Ogaien female before her sizing her down with eyes such a pale shade of green they almost had a milky look to them. They were eyes that seared with venom. The girl knew the poison well, pure desire to win.

Far from them in her high booth, Natane rose. Grabbing her spear she walked to the edge of the platform for all to see. Slamming the butt of her weapon on the wood, a silence fell so deep that the only thing which could be heard was the distant billowing of leaves on the wind.

"My sisters and brothers in Tiamet's blood," the Great Mother called out to those gathered with her arms outstretched. "Today we come together in honour of the feast of our Goddesses battling with the thunder scourge Pioren. It was a dark time, a savage time, and it all was before our own time. For it was on this fated day that, with Tiamet's blood spilt upon the ground, the race of Ogaien was made. To remember and honour the blood spilt, I give you the champions and scourge of this day's Riva Mortem."

The gathered crowds exploded in a tidal wave of cheers. Below them, Annetta and the others waited in anticipation, not fully sure what to expect. A lone female rider in a black hide cloak appeared from the sidelines, with a spear in her right hand raised up to the sun. The girl, squinting her eyes, noticed the black mass which hung from the end of it, a charred mound which resembled badly burnt bread. It landed on the floor before them with a thud, a light layer of dust rising around it. Though it did not look it, Annetta knew that the object before them was the charred animal carcass. The stench of scorched flesh filled her nostrils.

A final, baritone blast sounded from the horn, and it began. Anuli leapt from the side at the black mass, piercing it with her spear. Before the dust settled, she was already off with Amayeta at her side, two of the scourge closing in on her, the rest in tow.

Shaking off the shock, Annetta turned to her companions quickly to see them intact. Certain they were safe, she veered her Aiethon around in the direction of the chase. The sound of thundering hooves and the roar of the crowd overpowered much of her concentration as she clung to the reins. From what she could make out, Anuli still had the lead. Her focus was breached when a sharp pain shot through her right leg like a hundred thorns. Snapping her neck to the side, she saw the milky eyed Ogaien had rammed her Aiethon's armour into her leg, causing the leather guard to shred from the impact. Digging her heels into the beast she rode, the girl managed to gain some distance from her opponent.

Not much farther behind, Link rode, watching every move Annetta made, making sure not to lose sight of her. His efforts were thwarted when a spear point nicked and missed his face, causing a trickle of blood to run down his already scarred cheek. He turned to see one of the male Ogaien with his arm bent back, ready to strike at him once more. The Gaian youth quickly brought his own spear to the forefront, clashing it with his opponent's.

Heading up the rear were Sarina and Jason, as well as two other riders from the opposing team. The spear arms of all four adversaries pumped furiously, delivering blow upon blow as their Aiethon charged ahead.

ຂງ໑

From above, Puc observed with Natane and the others. His fist was curled over his lips as he watched intently, calculating everything in his head. It had been good fortune that Anuli had jumped at the carcass when she did, giving her the leverage the team needed. All seemed to go smoothly thus far and if it played out, then it would be over soon.

"These outlanders ride well," Ahota mused, breaking the silence. "I had not expected them to look so natural in the saddle of an Aiethon."

"Hush, all is well now, but this is just the beginning of the match," Enola replied. "This Riva Mortem is far from over. Blood must be spilt this day."

"True. The question remains, whose?" Ahota's green serpentine eye's twinkled like large emeralds.

Puc glanced at the speakers, not moving a muscle in his body as he did so. He would not let them know he was even aware of their prattle. Looking down, he could see that Annetta and her friends holding their own on the field. The question remained, for how long could they do it? In retrospect, it felt there could have been more he could have done on his part. His mind meticulously picked out little things he could have told them that he had not been aware of before as being of any use. It drove him mad for not having done so. He knew, however, that any betrayal of his uncertainty in their victory now would serve as fodder to those around him.

ℬℭ

Having gained some space from her rival, Annetta focused on catching up to Anuli and Amayeta to make sure they were covered. The second Anuli had lunged on her Aiethon for the carcass, Annetta understood that she had been asked to play defence for them while the sisters raced forward to the goal post.

Her thoughts were again interrupted when a black shape darted past her face and collided with Anuli. A blood-curdling shriek erupted from the disturbed Aiethon upon which the Ogaien warrior sat. The girl did not immediately register what had happened and what the shape had been. Her eyes adjusting, Annetta could see the black spear protruding from Anuli's back. The Aiethon came to a slow canter, then a standstill. Finally, with her head lolling to the side, the Ogaien fell from the saddle.

Jason and Sarina both stopped in their tracks as the crowd roared with cheers for the bloodshed. The shock of the quick death made the hairs on their neck stand on end. Neither of them had expected such a thing.

Taking time to parade about, the pale-eyed Ogaien that had thrown the spear raised her hands up and rode to the body, retracted the weapon from it. The horn sounded in the distance, announcing a death on the field. She then speared the carcass and was off in the opposite direction, a smug look of triumph across her serpentine face.

"All who call me scourge, I am Gezana of the Yasur Plains, and the one who will water this land with the blood of your outland champions this day!" she shouted as she raced past the masses.

Blood boiling, Annetta gave a war cry and was off. No threat would hold her rage down, and tucking the spear under her arm like a lance, she charged.

"Annetta!" Link called watching her thunder past him atop the Aiethon. The look she had in her eyes worried him. There had only been a few instances he had seen her that angry and it generally meant there was no reasoning with her. He could quite literally feel her rage. The strange sixth sense had awakened in him after the death of Brakkus. He was able to sense the girl whenever she was in danger. What's more was that he could feel other emotions like joy, sadness and rage. He'd confronted Puc on the issue before, to which the mage simply had told him that Brakkus had been Orbeyus's sworn protector, and perhaps the oath he had spoken had somehow bound him to the girl. At first, the idea of being bound to someone like that had scared him, but the longer the gift remained with him, the more he grew accustomed to it, just as he was to the beastly form which dwelled inside.

Jason pulled up beside him. "Now what do we do?"

"Cover her, and make sure she doesn't get speared as well," the Gaian replied, getting ready to urge his Aiethon into a run after her.

Amayeta pulled up to the boys right after. If the Ogaien warrior woman was mourning for her sister, it was difficult to see on her hard dragon-featured face. Tongue flickering in and out, she turned to them. "One of you on the right, and the other on the left. I will flank directly from the rear. Do not let any get within shooting distance of her."

"Question for ya," Jason interjected. "Is this one of those instances using psychic abilities would be okay?"

"As I said, there are no rules against it but use your common sense," she replied and was off.

Jason exhaled. "That's what I wanted to hear."

Already farther ahead than the others, Annetta pushed her Aiethon with all ferocity, her eyes set on her target in unwavering ambition. Though she had seen many soldiers die during the battle against Mislantus, she had never expected something so cowardly to befall someone she had personally known. The event replayed in her mind over and over again as a helpless choking feeling grappled at her throat. No matter how much she examined it, there truly had been nothing the girl could have done, but it did not change the way she felt about it. Uncontrollable rage pulsed through her veins in rhythm with the hoof beats upon the field as she closed in on the victim of her rage.

Behind, Jason, Sarina, Link and Amayeta had fanned out their positions into an arc, doing their best to keep an eye out on Annetta as she charged ahead. They were soon flanked by the Ogaien on the opposing team, who did not hesitate to each pick a target of their own.

From her marked place, Sarina turned to her left to see one of the male Ogaien slowly inching closer to her, its Aitheon's head bobbing back and forth like an animated toy. Not losing focus, the girl faced forward, only to feel her Aiethon buck from behind. Turning around, the girl managed to duck from the oncoming spear, which lodged itself deeply in her Aiethon's hindquarters. Whining, the creature began to crumple, losing control of its back legs.

Jason's head whipped to the side, hearing the sound of a falling body. "Sarina!"

Cringing, the girl did her best to hold onto the animal as it slid down. Pulling back on the reins, she tried to get it to rise again, but the creature would not yield to her command. Feeling a shadow creep up behind her shoulders she turned to see the raised spear of the Ogaien pointed to her face. The stare was cut short when a black shape flew through the air and slammed into the Ogaien so hard it knocked him flat off his mount.

Jason arrived seconds after, looking down at Sarina. "You okay?"

"I'm fine." She shook her head. "I could have handled it, you know."

"Yeah, just like how you were handling getting your Aiethon back up," he replied as he extended a hand to her. "I don't know what the rules are for having you with me, but come on."

The crowds cheered behind them as Sarina gripped Jason's hand and hoisted herself into the back of his saddle, pulling Jason's spear free from the dead rider as they passed by it.

Further in front, Link and Amayeta rode side by side, fending off the enemy riders. The range between Link, Amayeta and Annetta slowly increased with the onslaught of spears being thrust in their direction. Managing to overpower one of the female riders, Amayeta let go of her reins entirely. Taking hold of the enemy's weapon, she drove it back with all her strength, causing the end of the weapon to pierce the Ogaien's flesh. Driving the spear home with one final thrust, Amayeta watched with satisfaction as her prey slid from the saddle in much the same fashion her sister did. She was unable to enjoy the kill, for a sharp pain sliced through her left shoulder. Dropping her spear from the shock, she faced the second male Ogaien, his visage parted in a reptilian snarl. Grabbing his spear with her right hand she braced herself for a struggle. Her anticipation was cut short when another spear erupted from her foe's chest, causing blood to splash on his light hides. The weapon retracted itself from the Ogaien, allowing him to fall from the saddle with animated grace. His image was replaced with that of Link holding a bloodied spear behind him.

"Never in my wildest visions had I imagined an otherworld male to come to my aid," the Ogaien spoke.

"You haven't met much otherworld males, we tend to do those sort of things," Link replied. His attention was averted from the conversation however when he heard the sound of an Aiethon shrieking up ahead of them. "Annetta."

The legs of the black Aiethon pumped at their maximum speed as Annetta remained almost flat in the saddle with the spear at her side, her teeth gritting in fury as the mount inched in closer and closer to her prey. Finally, unable to contain her anger, Annetta launched herself from where she sat with a cry, tackling Gezana, putting her spear around the Ogaien's neck and beginning to pull it back, tightening her grip.

Gurgling and gasping for air, Gezana dropped her spear with the carcass and began clawing at the girl's hands, trying to find a weak spot. Giving up hope, the Ogaien warrior curled her fist and sent her elbow to the girl's kidney, causing Annetta to lose her hold.

"Dishonourable little outlander wench," Gezana spat. "How dare you leave the saddle of your Aiethon!"

"Same as how you stabbed my friend in the back," Annetta groaned as she attempted to recover from the blow. Reasserting her grip, she pulled harder.

Grasping the spear, Gezana managed to aim her elbows back again and hit Annetta square in the gut, knocking the wind out of her. The Ogaien then seized the opportunity and slammed the back of her fist straight into Annetta's face. Howling, the girl let go completely and found herself drop sideways off the mount. Grabbing onto the spiked armour from the side, she managed to keep herself from falling off completely.

Seeing a clear advantage, Gezana began to kick at the girl, trying to pry her off like a piece of chewing gum from the bottom of a shoe.

Clenching her teeth tighter, Annetta clung to the uneven spikes that were fastened all over the beast's body, but each time that she tried to haul herself back up, she was forced down under the Ogaien's boot. The muscles in her arms and legs seemed to catch on fire the longer she held on. Amayeta had said they could use their abilities if need be but, she was determined to avoid doing so for as long as possible. She had learned from Puc was to respect the cultures of others. A final thrust from her opponent's leg knocked the last bit of strength from the girl, causing her fingers to finally surrender.

Annetta did not have a chance to contemplate her next move nor even her next thought when she felt a firm hand grab hold of her own. Looking up, she found herself staring into Link's grey eyes, his scarred face twisted from the effort of both holding her up and keeping a grip on his reins. Hoisting her up with an awkward motion, the youth turned his head slightly to her. "Are you alright?"

"I won't die if that's what you're asking," she replied, wrapping her arms around his torso so she would not fall. "Now what?"

"Jason and Sarina managed to take two of them out, Amayeta got another-" Link was cut off as he grabbed the girl and ducked beneath a spear flying in their direction. "They've gotten bolder."

"I think if you're fighting for your life, nothing can be considered too bold," the girl replied.

Amayeta pulled up seconds later and holding the reins of Annetta's Aiethon in her free hand, she gave it to the girl. "I believe you lost this."

"Do I lose brownie points?" she asked sheepishly and quickly got back onto it. The trio then took off again, staying in close proximity.

"No, but we may lose the games if this Gezana throws the carcass. You were too careless, Severio. It takes a team to win this, not a single warrior."

Annetta felt the same sensation she always did when she was being scolded, of her ears going flat against her skull like that of an animal. She had managed to cool off a little, but she was still angry at what had occurred.

Amayeta exhaled, clenching her spear tighter. "Anuli knew what could befall her in the arena, and there was no shame in her death. Now come, we waste time. Flank my back."

Amayeta urged her Aiethon harder then and went on ahead of Annetta and Link without further speech.

"Doesn't change the fact it was a cheap shot," the girl muttered and did as she was told.

Whipping her head to the side, Annetta managed to watch as an approaching challenger fell when Jason's spear found its mark, the Ogaien dropping from the saddle like a lifeless sack of grain. Tearing the weapon free, Jason along with Sarina joined up to Annetta and Link.

"You okay, Anne?" Jason asked.

"I've been better if that's what you are asking," she replied in a dry, focused tone.

Jason held back any further conversation from the girl. He could still feel the heat of her anger which seared from her tongue.

In the front, Amayeta had caught up to Gezana, both Ogaien's mounts racing furiously to the end, mouths frothing from exhaustion. Taking the butt of her spear, Amayeta thrust it into her opponent's face, causing Gezana to lose balance, along with her grip on the spear. Though she had hidden her emotions well enough before, the Ogaien warrior was not about to pass up a chance to let her sister's murderer get away easy. Gezana's pale eyes snapped back to attention at her foe as she recovered. Her spear gone from her hand, the scourge aimed a well-placed fist at Amayeta's face.

Growling, Amayeta retaliated once more with the back end of the spear, this time aiming for the ribs. One step ahead, Gezana grabbed the weapon and began pulling it in her own direction. Gritting her razor-like teeth, Amayeta did her best to hold her grip.

Behind them, Annetta raced alongside Link and Jason, with Sarina in the back of his saddle. Her eyes were glued to the Ogaien warrior before her, having taken very seriously the task which had been assigned. Her concentration was interrupted by an incoherent shout from the side and the feeling of an object colliding into her body with a sharp pain in her right shoulder. Everything came into focus a second later as she cried out, a dark shape, a spear point, protruding from her shoulder joint, her arm going numb from the throbbing. A strong arm then supported her from the side, not allowing her to fall. Biting back tears, Annetta turned to see Link huddling beside her on his mount, his arm outstretched awkwardly as he held her up.

In front, Amayeta had won her struggle and having grabbed the carcass with Gezana's spear still intact, she held it overhead and was making her way down the field to the opposite end to throw it. The crowds roared, waves of heads in the stands moving in a chaotic dance as the games concluded themselves moments later.

Chapter 6

What happened next, Annetta could barely remember. Her mind had been in a state of explosive agony as she was rushed back to the tent where they had waited for the games to begin. She remembered Puc rushing in with Natane and a space being cleared in the middle of the room. She had somehow been dismounted and placed on a bench. Then, she had been given a foul-tasting leather cloth to bite down on. Everything after became so blurry that there was no trace of it in her mind.

She awoke sometime later on a wooden cot, every muscle in her body limp with exhaustion. Despite this, she tried to get up to see where she was but found she lacked the strength to do so. Moving her head to the right, she noted the sling draped across her arm and the multiple bandages all along her shoulder.

Puc's voice came from the other side. "Your infraspinatus was completely punctured. I've managed to patch it up as best as I could but, I will need access to my supplies back at the Lab."

Groggily, Annetta turned to face the other way. The mage was sitting in a chair some distance from the bed, watching her. His red robes were stained in darker patches from blood.

The girl raised an eyebrow. "I got stabbed in my what now?"

Before Puc could explain, the flap of the tent opened. Sunlight poured in, and along with it, the figures of Jason, Link and Sarina. Their wounds, though minor compared to Annetta's, were also dressed, and each of them wore a relieved expression on their face.

"Anne! You're alive!" Jason squealed with glee as he attempted to go give her a hug, only to have the mage swing his staff in front of him and block the youth.

"I do not know the full extent of the damage," Puc said. "If the bone is fractured, you could cause more by applying pressure."

"Oh, right," Jason backed away. "So…do we put a fragile sticker on her, then?"

"Very funny," Annetta muttered through her teeth.

Puc gave a small huff and turned to the youth. "That will not be necessary, and now that I have you all here I need to ask, what in the infernal realms of hell happened out there?"

Annetta, Jason, Link and Sarina all looked at one another in turn, confused by the words the mage had uttered.

Jason turned back to him, "What do you mean?"

"I mean that for almost two years now you have been training to fight and on the field, it looked as though all your lessons fell on deaf ears. What happened?"

Annetta felt her face go a little pale, "Nerves happened, that's what. You think it's easy to remember everything we learned just spur of the moment, especially when someone just died in front of us. As for us not using our abilities much, Amayeta said to use our psychic abilities minimally. She also said to use our better judgment."

Puc kept his gaze fixed on the girl. "Clearly you still lack much of it. Did you take into account that an average Ogaien can throw twice as far as a human being?"

Confused, Annetta furrowed her brows, "But you've always emphasized that we shouldn't use our abilities when we participate in these things."

"Perhaps then you misinterpreted what I said," Puc said. "All of the events you have previously participated in never involved the possibility of death or someone truly being injured, be it the strength games of the Minotaur or the archery competitions of the Soarin. The Riva Mortem is very different. There is a very fine line between honour and survival in such an event. You would not have been looked down upon for using what skill you have to beat your opponent."

"It's not like she gave us a guide of what we could and couldn't do, you know." Jason glared in disbelief upon what he had just heard.

"In such things, it is also important to know what will completely dishonour your opponent and what will not," Puc interjected. "Putting energy into your spear is one thing, but to teleport across the field is another."

Jason tried to follow what Puc was saying. "So would that have been allowed or?"

"Yes and no," the mage replied, "It is complicated subject matter, but think of it this way. You are in someone's home. It is not as richly furnished as your own. When the owner would ask your opinion about his living quarters, would you tell him the blunt truth, or not?"

"Well no, they did invite you so you should be courteous," the boy said.

"It is the same with using your abilities. You need to know when and what is appropriate. I suppose, however, this is something you will simply learn with age."

"Apparently, so they keep telling us," Jason grunted in reply to the end of the conversation.

ഇരുൽ

A few hours passed, and once Annetta was able to stand, the group made their way to a large clearing in a field, where a funeral pyre had been raised for Anuli. Night was beginning to gather all around, making the sky fade into a shadowy crimson. A group of Ogaien had already gathered at its foot, Natane and Amayeta among them. Both of them were dressed in black with a sash of red draped across their left shoulder.

Approaching them, Puc was the first to incline his head. "My greatest sympathies to you both in this hour of darkness."

The Great Mother tilted her head in reply slightly and gazed back up at the mage with her great emerald eyes. "She died with a spear in her hand. There is no greater honour."

Natane then turned to the masses as Amayeta handed her a torch, "Death comes for us all, be it in old age or in our prime, in the heat of battle or in the dark of night. Anuli knew this as well as the rest of us. It pains me to bury my daughter before her time, but I know the same thing she knew when her heart did once beat. It is the same thing which binds all life to the hope that all actions upon this world are of worth to Tiamet. That in the light of her flames shall we be born again."

With these words, Natane dropped the torch into the pillar, setting it ablaze in a display of orange and red flames which then changed to blue, green, yellow and purple until finally, all shades were visible in the dancing tongues which licked it.

Annetta watched silently as the pyre was consumed in a rainbow of flames. The bright colours seemed to soothe some of the sadness she felt. Something touched her arm as she stood mesmerized by the display. She looked to see that Link had placed his hand over her arm, the dark in combination with the fire making the creases on his face appear deeper than they were. She raised an eyebrow at the gesture and continued to watch the ceremony, giving it no further thought.

ഇരുൽ

They exchanged goodbyes once the last of the flames had died out at the funeral pyre. Carefully getting Annetta onto Firedancer, they made their way back to Severio castle. Night had befallen the world when they had emerged from the structure, the light of the stars greeting them like a thousand lights in a city upon the sky.

Completing the journey back to the Lab, they dismounted their horses, leaving the unsaddling to Link, Jason and Sarina, while Puc and Annetta made their way to the infirmary in order to have Annetta's shoulder properly looked at, a process the girl was not looking forward to as it meant touching the wound and igniting the pain anew. Still, she knew it had to be dealt with sooner or later and so, clenching her jaw, she let the elf do his worst while he examined her, running what looked like a hand-held mirror over her shoulder, which displayed an instant x-ray onto the screen attached to it.

"And how do pharmacies today not have this sort of equipment, again?" she asked once he explained what the device did to her.

"For the same reason, they do not have flying cars: Technology. The technology within Q-16 cannot be shared with the outside world, be it good or bad. It is not of this world and this world is not ready for extraterrestrial technology. It would do more damage than good," he replied bluntly as he continued to scan her. Concluding, he put the device down. "No splintering. However, it looks as if the bone fractured a little around the wound."

"Okay, what does that mean?"

"It means you got lucky," Puc stated, taking out three vials from a cabinet and handing them to Annetta. "Take that first one now to start the healing process. The bone was pierced clean through, so re-growth of the missing bone will need to occur. It may take up to a week, during which time you are not to place any pressure on that shoulder. In fact, I would prefer if you leave it in a sling and should anyone ask you sprained it."

"Doing what? Playing video games?" she snorted.

"Falling down the stairs, catching the bus, you daydream all the time, make something up," the elf retorted in an irritated tone, then added, "Take the other two before you go to sleep, they will numb the pain and help you rest."

"Okay, and last but not least, my folks," Annetta said, looking over at Puc.

"Annetta you are old enough to know your parents and what they are willing or not willing to believe," The elf replied as he finished bandaging her wound again and helped her slip on the sling. "If you wish my advice on the matter, however, I would not tell them of what took place this day. A parent's heart is ruled by forces not governed by morality."

"You mean like my episode today in the arena?" the girl asked with a chuckle, knowing full well the 'forces' Puc was speaking of.

"Something to that extent," the mage answered. "But multiply it by a thousand. I recommend you to get some rest now. I do not expect this accident to interfere with your education."

Annetta downed the contents of the first vial. "Sure, I can go to class, broken bones and all."

Puc sighed at the reply, his eyes staring down the girl. "You know full well what I meant. Good night, Severio."

Annetta turned around to walk away with a mischievous grin on her face, her point having been made, leaving the mage to his solitude.

೧೦೧

Saying his goodnights to both Sarina and Jason, Link made his way back to his sleeping quarters after making sure everything had been finished with taking care of the horses. His body was weary from the day's excitement and he wanted nothing more than to bury his face in his covers and pretend to be dead to the world. Accompanied by nothing more than the sword at his hip, the blue-tinted lights of the Lab and the sound of his feet shuffling along on the metallic floor, he was left to his own contemplations.

He no longer felt the strange presence he knew to be Annetta in the back of his mind, meaning she was asleep.

Pausing in the midst of the hall, he contemplated going to see Puc and finding out what condition the girl was in when he heard the distant sound of feet. Pivoting on his heel, he went to investigate, hoping it to be the elf. Heading in the direction of the entrance, the face he saw was one he had not expected.

Before him, stood a young man with ruffled brown hair, goatee and azure-coloured eyes, wearing a loose green military coat. From out of the sleeves protruded two thick gauntlets with silver finishing shaped like bear paws. Spotting Link, he did not move.

"Oh, Matt, it's you," Link said in a disconnected tone. "Didn't think I would see you alive again."

"I could say the same for you, Heallaws." The arrival gave a firm smile in return.

The two of them glared at one another for a good minute, before melting away their cold exteriors. Exchanging a quick brotherly embrace, they withdrew as a smile formed on both of their faces.

"Did you find him? Where were you all this time?" Link assaulted Matthias with questions.

"Give me something potent to drink and I'll tell you all about it. For now, where's the mage? I should probably let him know I'm back."

Before Link could admit his own reason for being out and about, the sound of a wooden staff thudding on metal echoed in the distance, paired with a set of fluid footsteps.

A voice preceded it. "There will be no need for that, Matthias."

Both Link and Matthias turned around to find Puc, clad once more in dark robes, observing them with one hand on his staff, while the other lay freely at his side.

"Nice to see you are alive and kicking as well, Thanestorm." Matthias flashed a grin at the mage before retracting his teeth behind his lips.

"How is Annetta doing? Is she going to be okay?" Link asked, interrupting the confrontation between the assassin and the mage.

"Lincerious, you should know our young and reckless leader better than that," Puc replied in a flat tone, only to be shot an eager look by the young warrior, at which the mage sighed and added, "She will be fine, no splintering occurred. It will just take some time for it to heal."

Matthias snickered, crossing his arms over his chest "What did she do now?"

"Spear through the shoulder," Puc answered, then changed the subject. "Have you anything to report of Amarok?"

The assassin sucked some air in through his teeth and patted his right shoulder in reaction to news of the injury. His face then became much more serious as he regarded the mage. "I would speak to you in private first before telling what I have seen to others."

"What's so bad that I can't hear about it?" Link asked.

"Nothing that concerns you," Matthias replied. "I will tell you in due time, but like every subordinate must report to their commander, I have to do the same. You should know, having been a soldier."

The grey-eyed youth glanced blankly at the assassin, feeling somewhat betrayed, before recollecting his wits and nodding. "I'll be in my room if you are looking for me."

Puc and Matthias inclined their heads in acknowledgement and watched as Link began to make his way back. The assassin then turned to the mage. "Got anything to drink?"

෨෬

A tall pewter stein filled with a dark frothing liquid slid across a table and was caught by a steady pair of gauntlet-clad hands. Taking the tankard to his lips, Matthias took a minute to gaze at his surroundings. The room the mage inhabited was dark, with only the candles present in it offering any source of light. Shelves upon shelves made of sturdy dark wood decorated every possible wall within the quarters aside from a tall dark red grandfather clock, whose golden pendulum swung back and forth in a monotone motion, and a great cabinet filled with potions and herbs. Tilting the tankard back, he tasted the thick and bitter brew as it left his mouth, leaving an aftertaste of oak and barley.

Puc seated himself at the other end of the desk, folded his hands and waited for the assassin to speak.

Drawing the stein from his lips and setting it upon the table, the assassin cleared his throat. "I won't even ask if this brew was handmade or not. Anyways, you've probably guessed by now that I was unable to track down Amarok. I spoke and met with all my old eyes and ears from service in Mislantus's ranks, but none of them had much to offer. My guess is either out of fear for their safety or because they genuinely didn't know."

"So your crusades through space proved a pointless mission, then?" Puc let his hands slide to the table top. "Was this reason to hide it from Lincerious and make him feel anxious?"

"No, but the other news I received and have heard much of these past few months is." Matthias took another swig of his drink before setting it down. "There have been rumours, and when I say rumours, I mean many of them. They were concerning the state of Gaia at present."

Puc narrowed his eyes upon hearing what was said but gave no other indication of his mood as he leaned back in his chair. "What sort of rumours were these?"

"Rebellion." Matthias's azure eyes reflected the flickering flames from the candles.

"That is not possible," the mage answered calmly. "There has not been any rebellion on Gaia in over twelve thousand years. Why would anything begin to stir now?"

"Same thing I kept asking myself." Matthias scratched at the hair upon his chin. "Their king is pretty solid, from what I hear."

"It was, as you said, a rumour," Puc responded, thinking more on the subject. "An ember, given the right circumstances, can become a forest of flame."

"I don't like it either way." the assassin wrinkled his nose. "I thought you should know and I didn't think it was a good idea for the kid to find out. You know how proud he is of his heritage."

Puc nodded his head in agreement. "You did the right thing by coming to me. But as I said, we cannot rely on rumours from spaceports, even if many of them coincide. We do not know the source of these ploys. For all we know, it could be Amarok trying to divide us. No, it is safest to assume they are poison from a viper's lips."

Matthias took another gulp of his drink, "And what if they aren't? What if truth rings within them?"

The mage did not move a muscle as he studied the face of the assassin. Giving a slight twitch of the jaw, he rose from his seat, turning away to reignite a candle upon one of the shelves.

"We will deal with their fallout when the time deems it necessary. For now, treat rumour as rumour and nothing else. Tell Lincerious nothing of what you heard in this regard. I would not have dark words of empty matter turn to fruitless actions."

Chapter 7

Annetta woke up the next morning to find her entire body numbed by soreness. Every muscle seemed to ache as she made her best effort to rise, pushing herself up with her good arm.

"Pain is weakness leaving the body," she muttered to herself as she climbed out of bed, her legs feeling like jelly from riding the Aiethon the previous day. Taking time to let herself adjust from one position to the other, the girl gazed over at her calendar adorned with pictures of waterfalls and noticed that she still had one day of the weekend left to herself. Exhaling in relief, she got up and proceeded to begin changing, only to realize the task was more daunting than it appeared at first with only the use of her one hand. Though her injured arm did not seem to hurt, she knew better than to test it out without Puc checking it again.

Finishing the lengthy process of getting ready, the girl went down the stairs carefully to her kitchen, where the smell of toast and scrambled eggs with green peppers, onions and mushrooms filled the room. Her mouth beginning to water at the smells, Annetta was reminded that she had not eaten since the day before. Coming around the corner, she saw her father, Arieus, hovering in a busy fashion over the stove. Hobbling over to the table, the girl seated herself in her usual spot.

Arieus turned, hearing the sound of the chair moving across the wooden floor. His usually neat copper hair lightly laced with grey and a thick bushy moustache to match were ruffled and made him look as though he had just woken up himself. His blue eyes instinctively turned to look at the girl's bandaged arm and made him drop the spatula into the frying pan.

"Annie, what happened?" he asked, coming over to her.

Annetta curled back a little in her seat in order to avoid her arm being touched. "It's not as bad as it looks. I sprained it when sparring yesterday. I just need Puc to look at it and make sure the potions he gave me last night worked." The lie came flying off the girl's tongue as naturally as though it had been the truth. She'd had a fair bit of practice over the last year, having to hide various injuries from her parents. She only hoped her father would not become suspicious and pry more at her, wearing away at the tall tale she had spun.

Brows furrowing, Arieus withdrew. Remembering the eggs on the stove, he frantically turned back to them. "You need to be careful. A sword is not a toy. It's a tool, and needs to be used appropriately."

"Yes, almighty Puc." Annetta rolled her eyes as her father placed a plate with toast and the eggs he had been making before her.

The man gave a chuckle as he went back to the stove. "That bad? Do I sound like a certain mage that much?"

Annetta took a bite of the eggs. "Just a bit. Where are mom and Xander?"

Arieus joined his daughter at the table, carrying a mug of coffee in addition to his portion of the meal. "They left to do some errands. The zipper in Xander's old coat went when he was trying it on, so they went to go get him a new one since winter is coming. I didn't see a point of fixing it either since the sleeves were looking short on him. So, what will you be up to today?"

The girl took a bite of her eggs, as she thought about how to answer him. Swallowing, she replied, "I think I'm gonna go check out some of the trails by the castle again since I don't think I'll be able to do anything else."

"You've taken a big interest in riding lately," Arieus commented as he continued to eat. "Sure you aren't part horse yourself? Or maybe a centaur?"

Annetta chuckled, wrinkling her nose. "No, dad. I just... I don't know, when I'm out there with Firedancer, I'm free. There are no rules about where I have to go or what I have to do."

"So you ride about and daydream," Arieus finished. Seeing Annetta's trapped-in-headlights look, he smiled. "There's nothing wrong with it, really. I used to do that all the time when I needed to get away. If you like, we could maybe go out riding together one of these days. Have you ever seen the caves behind the waterfalls guarding Aldamoor?"

Annetta shook her head. "I stay around the castle. Puc doesn't really want us running off through different portals without him knowing it. I guess we could go together at some point."

"Great, I can pack us some lunch, and we can go later." Arieus began forming the plan in his head.

"Actually, Dad, it's okay. It doesn't need to be today. I need a bit of time to myself," the girl cut him off as she finished her food, walked over to dishwasher and put her plate in. "I had a rough couple of days in school and in the Lab."

"Oh, I see." Arieus looked down a bit forlorn. "Well, if there's anything you want to talk about, you know I'm here for you. That's what a family should be for, after all. We brave the storms life throws at us together."

Annetta closed the dishwasher and turned around. "Don't worry, Dad. If I'm ever in trouble, I know who I can count on to come rescue me."

಴ඏ

After getting her arm checked out by Puc and given the order to lay off training for the day, Annetta slipped away into the stables as fast as she could. Putting a saddle on Firedancer and double checking to make sure everything was in place, she hopped onto his back and was off. Passing through the portal to get to the castle, she paused to gaze upon the world that lay before her, undisturbed.

The structure in the middle of the green plains of grass that surrounded its immediate area looked like nothing more than a toy. Cerulean-roofed towers peered upwards at the girl along with the warmth of the summer sun. It had taken Annetta some time, but she soon learned the castle only seemed to have one season in the land it laid, and it never seemed to change. Making sure no one followed her, the girl urged the horse onward as they made the descent down the winding hills.

She never took the same path twice when she came on her own, once she passed the initial path down. She did, however, take care to stay close to the paths that were already made, remembering Puc's cautioning about the possibility of new portals being hidden in the world around her. Severio Castle, or The Eye to All Worlds as most knew it, was located in a spot where the fabric of different universes was weakest, and oftentimes tore. Puc had explained to them that the castle had been put up by her and Jason's ancestors in order to protect portals which had already existed at the time. Though she had never come across any new portals on her own, some being more visible than others, she still heeded the warnings, for if there was no designated way of getting back from a world as there was in the ones located inside the castle, then there was a good chance a person could be stuck in another universe for the rest of her life.

Selecting a path which went past a cluster of broken logs and a couple of pine saplings, Annetta maneuvered Firedancer down the well-trodden route until they reached the foot of a rocky cliff. Descending out of the saddle carefully, the girl gazed up at the wall of white stone, making sure it was the same as before and walking over to a fallen log, she unfastened the reins at one side and tied them to one of the larger branches which were still intact. Patting the horse on the muzzle, she then closed her eyes and moments later found herself on a ledge located about thirty feet above where she had been standing.

Annetta would have usually made the climb up on her own, but with her damaged shoulder, she decided not to take the risk. Sliding against the wall of rock behind her, Annetta exhaled. Looking out into the horizon, she saw the sun was already half way through the sky. Sighing, she realized this meant she would be back in school, back to her regular life on Earth. She would have to forget about the weekend and focus on just being a high school student again. It was times like these she wished with all her heart that she would not have to go back. She then remembered, though tomorrow was not for her to dictate, the present day belonged to her. Closing her eyes, the girl stepped into a world she'd never thought possible before.

ෂාය

It always began the same way, the blinding light and the feeling of weightlessness which accompanied it. She had not understood at first the strange reoccurring dreams which had plagued her since the fall of Mislantus. For months, she had denied they meant anything more than an echo of her having crossed over and seen her grandfather in what many would say was the afterlife. When she had opened up to Puc about the nightmares that plagued her, he had insisted she try meditation as a form of facing what inner demons remained after the battle. It was in these attempts to calm her mind that she had discovered what it had all truly meant.

Adjusting to her surroundings, Annetta watched as her hands came into focus before her, and flexed her fingers, also seeing that her injured shoulder seemed to be healed. As the rest of her senses attuned themselves, the girl took a deep breath, watching a garden come into focus, followed by the sounds of wildlife.

Sure that everything was visible, the girl began taking a few steps forward but was interrupted in her venture all too soon.

"And who is this stranger that dwells in my abode?" a voice inquired from behind.

Knowing who it belonged to, Annetta could not help but crack a smile as she turned around. There, not five feet from her, was Orbeyus. The elder Severio lord sat upon a fallen log, dressed in his usual preferred garb of a tattered long brown cape, a loose light blue tunic with a wide belt, dark brown breeches and tall black boots. His bright blue eyes were fixed intently on the girl as a smile formed beneath his thick silver beard.

"Grandpa!" she grinned as she made her way to him, "I was wondering where you'd be hiding this time."

"Hiding? Never was my fashion if you should know, my dear," he chuckled, shifting his weight to make room for Annetta to sit beside him. "Tell me, what brings you here?"

The girl sighed and sat down. "I'm not quite sure where to begin... I mean...I thought I knew when I came here, but now..."

Orbeyus furrowed his brows and gently tilted Annetta's head in his direction. "Focus, love. You need to be able to resist the charms of this place. I told you before."

"I..." Annetta shook her head as her composition returned to her. "Sorry...the first few seconds are still rough, coming here I mean. I keep telling myself it's easy and nothing to it but... well, anyways. The reason I'm here is about the Riva Mortem."

"Natane had you participate. I saw." He nodded his head. "You did well, Annetta, but you were rash in not using your abilities at all."

"But grandpa, it felt like I'd be cheating if I did," the girl scowled.

"Not if you use your abilities in such a way that only levels the playing field," Orbeyus explained. "Annetta, even I used my abilities when I participated in such an event, and I didn't hide it as a young man. First time I rode, I teleported off of my horse in order to save a fellow rider."

Hearing this stung at Annetta's pride, but she knew her grandfather meant well by saying it. There were many things she had learned about the man they had once called the Lord of the Axe in her days of having discovered the ability to come visit him at will.

Exhaling in defeat, Annetta raised her eyes back towards him. "I'm sorry. I'm not like you."

"Like me? Dear girl, you are far more like me at times than you think, and at other times more like your father and mother, and even at times like your grandmother. Remember, none of us will ever be an exact copy of those who came before. We are all our own blueprints in life."

"It still doesn't change what happened," she muttered. "Anuli is dead because of me."

"Ah, what did I tell you about blaming yourself for the deaths of others?" Orbeyus raised a finger in her direction. "The Unknown gives us all a role to play in life and when he sees that role is complete, he takes us back into his fold."

"That still doesn't change it," Annetta mumbled.

Orbeyus ran a hand through his short, cropped hair, then turned to gaze at the youth as she peered off into the distance, trying to think of what to say to her.

"You're right it doesn't," he spoke, "and that is why you need to move forward and know that come what may, none of us are ever truly gone from all worlds."

છ⊙જ

Having finished grooming the last of the horses, Link dusted the hair off his hands. Taking one final look around to make sure everything was in its place, he then proceeded to leave the stables. His exit was interrupted by the sound of hoofs pounding on the stone ground from behind.

"Look, guys, I can't keep giving you treats. You had enough today and I can't-" the Gaian youth paused his rant upon seeing a hooded rider in a saddle looming over him, and reached for the sword at his belt. "State your business."

"Business? What if I'm not here for business?" The rider dropped his hood to reveal the face of a pale youth with short black hair and dark eyes. "What if I'm here to just see some old friends?"

Link's hand relaxed to his side upon seeing who it was. "Darius?"

"In the flesh, or so last I checked, Heallaws." The young elf beamed, slid down from his mount, and embraced the Gaian. "It's good to see you again."

"I can say the same." Link chuckled as he withdrew, taking a better look at Darius. "I barely recognized you in that cloak. You look like you've grown a foot since the last time we met! What are they feeding you at the Academy?"

"Beats me, but it seems to be working," Darius replied. "You're not doing much worse than I am. Your training seems to be paying off."

"You know Puc, pain is weakness leaving the body and all that," he replied, taking the reins of Darius's horse. "So what brings you back here? Kaian ran out of errand boys, so he's interrupting student's training because of it?"

"Not exactly." the young elf smiled weakly. "I've-"

Before Darius could continue his train of thought, more hooves could be heard in the distance. In a blur of motion, Annetta arrived atop Firedancer, halting the great horse to a standstill. It took her a second to realize who was standing beside Link.

"Darius?" She raised an eyebrow in question. "How are you?"

"To be honest, I should be the one asking questions, like why you're riding around with one arm in a sling?"

The girl went mute in the saddle as her brows furrowed, while she attempted to think of a concise answer to give. "How does a spear through the shoulder sound?"

"Brutal." Darius wrinkled his nose as he watched Link help her down. "Should I ask how and why? I'm going to assume it was not a freak training accident with my mentor."

"Riva Mortem, if that means anything," she replied. "So what's up? You don't write, you don't call... I mean, you've been pretty much invisible since the battle with Mislantus."

"It's complicated, Annetta," he said, looking down at his feet. "A lot has happened since that time. Many things have been changing and continue to change in Aldamoor. Amongst it all, I've just been so busy with my studies. I guess I didn't notice how long it had been. We elves don't age as quickly as humans."

"Boy, that's a lame excuse," Annetta grumbled.

"Lame, but it's the only one I've got because it's true," Darius said. "I'll explain everything when I can."

Link finished unsaddling Darius's horse and returned to the duo in conversation, "You better explain, but right now I'm pretty sure there's someone waiting to see you."

ഇറ

The trio travelled through the solitary hallways, recounting what had gone on over the last year. Before they knew it, they turned the final corner to where the living quarters were located. Annetta ventured ahead of the other two. Puc generally left his door ajar in case anyone wished to speak to him, and the scent of burning candles was also a sign he was there. She peered inside and sure enough, with piles of papers and books neatly placed in stacks, the mage sat at his desk, scribbling away on some parchment. Occasionally he would glance at an open book placed atop the others, showing a glimpse of organic movement to contrast his almost mechanical writing. She said nothing and continued to watch him work away, fascinated at the precision of the whole process.

"Miss Severio, the general rule of thumb is one knocks when they enter a room with another person in it or gives some indication of their presence," he answered, finishing up the last word on the page before looking up at her. "How may I be of service?"

"Maybe lighten up a bit. I brought someone to see you." Annetta smirked as she moved aside and made room for Darius and Link to come in.

At first, Puc did not realize who was standing before him, but once he was sure, the reaction was swift. Rising from his seat, the mage went to embrace his apprentice as a father would a son.

"Unknown's bane, I did not realize it was you." The mage chuckled lightly. "What are you doing back here so soon?"

Darius withdrew, and reaching into his robes he produced a scroll, which he then handed to Puc. "I came as soon as I got it."

Puc and the others knotted their brows, unsure of what to expect. Annetta and Link crowded around the mage as he unrolled the parchment and began to read its contents. The parchment rolled back up in his hands as the mage gazed at Darius.

"You are looking at the newest addition to the mages of Aldamoor," Darius stated. "I was allowed to take my trials early, and passed with flying colours."

"That's amazing! Congratulations!" Annetta beamed in happiness. "So do we get to start calling you Puc 2.0 from now on?"

"I'd kind of prefer if you didn't," Darius murmured under his breath, which only made the girl snicker more.

More noise came from the hall as Jason, Sarina and Matthias came in.

"Is there a party going on in here or something?" Jason asked, pausing his train of thought upon seeing Darius. "Is that... are you?"

"Darius Silver, now a mage of Aldamoor." The youth bowed. "How's it going?"

"Matt? I didn't know you were back as well." Annetta raised an eyebrow, having missed the assassin's entrance due to her absence. She pulled him aside briefly from the main conversation. "Did you hear anything? Anything at all about Amarok?"

Matthias shook his head. "There's been no sign of him. I contacted all of my old associates, but I couldn't pick up a trail."

Annetta growled upon hearing the news. "I don't like it. He's a loose end in this whole thing."

"I don't either, but part of me is still hoping that no news is the best news of all."

"Guys! Common room! I think it's time for a good old fashioned get-together," Jason called out over Matthias, interrupting their chat.

Seeing as the discussion had deadpanned, Annetta turned back to her friend. "Lead the way!"

ഇൻ

Having brought out a bottle of what Puc deemed to be a finely aged wine as well as non-alcoholic beverages for those still under age, the group gathered in the common room around a large wooden table with mismatched chairs that had been pulled out of the corners. Once settled, their glasses clinked in a toast to Darius's return and the finishing of his schooling. The companions then settled in as stories and banter were exchanged.

"To be honest, I had no clue what I was doing when they summoned me," Darius recounted his tale of the examination. "I mean, I had heard so many stories of how past students had been assessed that I really didn't know what to expect. There's no guideline they give you and I'm pretty sure those examining you just pick a task from a jar before you step in the room, so even they aren't sure what is going to happen."

"It is a lot more planned than that," Puc assured him. "But I do understand the trauma, having undergone the procedure myself."

"I thought you graduated normally." Darius turned to look at his mentor.

"We were at war with the Fire Elves," he explained. "The instant you had some basic knowledge they pushed you out into the field, more so because they needed cannon fodder and could not wait for an entire slew of mages to fully complete their studies."

"Man, that's like if they'd sent us to fight Mislantus only knowing how to use half our powers or like... no sword training." Jason took a sip from his goblet, feeling the fizzy substance that tasted like sour apples passed down his throat.

"Like I said, we were at war, and every able body was needed," Puc reiterated, "Which brings me to another issue specifically relating to Annetta and Jason, and that is what your plans are for postsecondary education, should you pursue anything."

Annetta nearly choked on her drink and keeping the cup at her mouth, waiting for the tingling feeling of a carbonated beverage having gone up her nose to dissipate.

"I'm thinking of going to university with Sarina, if that's alright," Jason said. "My parents never had a chance to finish normal school because of all of this, and I want to do right by my mom since she's letting me be here, even though she doesn't agree with it. I'm thinking of taking something with computers or engineering. I seem to have a knack for it, plus I figure I can maybe apply what I learn there to some of the things here and figure out how to build some stuff."

"I'm going to be taking history," Sarina added. "I'd like to learn more about Earth's past as it is."

"Bookworm till the end," Matthias smirked as Sarina rolled her eyes at him.

Puc nodded at what had been said. His eyes then found their way to Annetta, who still seemed to have the cup covering her face as though she wished not to be seen.

"And what are your plans, Lady Severio?" Puc shifted his position in his seat and rested a closed fist against his chin.

Annetta felt the sensation of a spotlight hit her as soon as the sentence was finished. She took another sip from her goblet before placing it down on the table in front of her.

"I wasn't going to pursue anything." The words seemed to take longer to say than they would normally. "To be honest, I don't see the point. I don't see the point in continuing on with the charade. I mean… with everything here, why can't I just stay in the Lab permanently?"

Though everyone was already silent, that silence now seemed deafening as everyone turned their attention in full focus to Annetta after hearing her declaration. Doing her best to defy the glares, Annetta straightened up and looked back directly at them all.

"What? I don't see what the point is." She shrugged. "I mean, we go up there, go to school and then come back down here right after. Wouldn't it make more sense for us to just stay here and monitor everything from the Lab? I mean, correct me if my line of thinking is wrong but if we get full-time jobs one day after school, it's not like we're just gonna be able to leave at a moment's notice to save the world or whatever it is we're going to need to do."

The eyes of those gathered in the room turned to Puc, who still sat in the same position, his eyes fixated on the girl. He seemed to have all but stopped breathing, and it was not until he began to move again that they were sure the elf had not died upon hearing Annetta's plan.

"It is a valid question," he said. "And one I can answer quite easily. Yes, it would make sense for you to simply stay within the Lab and not bother with life on Earth. However, we can only monitor so much from within here. Eyes are needed on the surface. It was why Orbeyus insisted, that he and your father stay on Earth and blend in."

"It's how Mislantus would gather information as well," Matthias added. "It's easier with someone actually there as part of the society than sending a probe in to analyze. You won't quite get the same data."

"Or how I was sent to watch over you and Jason," Darius uttered as an afterthought.

Hearing these things, Annetta reanalyzed her answer. Perhaps there was some sense in what Puc said, but it did not change the fact that she had no desire to participate in much of anything. Her time in the Lab had become the highlight of her days. All the minutes that counted down to when her body would be engulfed by the invisible waters that carried her down below seemed mundane in comparison to all else.

Puc noted the change in her eyes. "You still have time to think of something. Perhaps with this all in mind, you will view things differently. You can always take some time off and work before pursuing further education. There is nothing wrong with this."

"Yeah, I need to think a bit on it," she replied finally. "I just... I'm just not sure what to do is what it all comes down to I guess. Nothing really holds my interest as much as being here."

"Sleep on it," Puc suggested. "As us elves say, Aldamoor was not built in a day."

Chapter 8

Once the festivities ended and everyone parted ways, Puc and Darius lingered awake at the table in the common room reflecting on old times. Though the two had been separated for a year, it seemed an eternity. Stretching in one of his armchairs, Puc pushed his empty goblet away, feeling a slight buzzing in his senses. It was not often that he partook in luxuries, and it sadly showed in his tolerance.

"I am glad to be home, master," Darius said after a long pause as their laughter from the previous banter subsided.

"There is no more need for you to refer to me by such title," Puc stated. "Puc or Thanestorm will do just fine."

"Right...uh...Puc," the name came off Darius's tongue uneasily, as though he were testing how cold the water was in a bowl. "I have something I need to tell you, not related to...well... it's partially the reason for my return here."

"Please do not tell me you met someone at the Academy and things took their course in alternative routes so to speak," the older mage said with a smirk. "I had hoped you would at least send me a letter if such events occurred."

Darius blushed violently upon hearing what his mentor was thinking and laughed nervously. "No, no, no...nothing like that...uh...where's that letter."

Darius rummaged through the folds of his robes until he produced a small rolled-up piece of parchment, with a seal of red wax holding it closed. Puc accepted it, eyeing the seal, which he knew belonged to Kaian himself. He knew the First Mage was familiar with using the C.T.S. watches, so he did not understand what the letter was for.

Puc cracked the wax without giving it a second thought and proceeded to read the contents. The further in he got, the more his already-light complexion paled until finally he finished and dropped the letter onto the table. His gaze then turned to Darius.

"How long have you known this?" he asked. "And speak truthfully."

"I left as soon as I was handed the letter," Darius replied.

The older mage ran a hand across his face as though he were trying to wake from a horrid dream. He picked it up once more and stared at it.

The letter held the following words:

To my old friend and rival, Puc Thanestorm,

As we both know, each of us has a purpose in life, an age of destiny so to speak. From our youngest years we are taught this, for no one is meant to live forever. I have been bent over the contents of this letter for some time now and was never truly aware what it was that has been driving me to press ink to parchment, but now I do. Death is at my doorstep. We both knew it would come for one of us sooner or later, and so you need not mourn me. I have lived a full and long life, but before I go, there are things you must know, things that should not go left unsaid.

These things I speak of concern not only you but the fate of Aldamoor and perhaps all of the Water Folk. For years, it has been the best-kept secret, known only to a few. I am sure you know the names of Oberon and Titania Thanestorm, as they are the names of your parents. What you do not know is the following: Titania's maiden name was Summerknight. It is a name that has no mythic origin, nor any titles to go along with it, but what is important is who Titania's father was, and that is Damien Chironson, who went by Summerknight in order to avoid confusion, as he was my father's brother. It is a custom I know you are familiar with, as it was adapted by the Severio clan years ago in order to avoid confusion between the Severio and Kinsman lines.

If the reasons for the trespasses of my youth are now not made evident, then perhaps the words I spoke to you but a year ago are. Aldamoor will need your guidance in the coming days…

The letter continued in such a fashion. Puc withdrew his gaze from it and folded his hands, resting his chin on them.

"Then…" Puc glanced back at the parchment on the table.

"Kaian Chironson lives no more," the younger elf concluded, "and has summoned you back to Aldamoor."

Puc felt his jaw clench as he got up, the text from the letter still swimming in front of his eyes as he did his best to dissect what it all meant for him.

"I cannot go with you," he finally said. "I am sure Kaine will be more than thrilled to ascend to the post of First Mage."

"Kaine declined," Darius replied, "and as far as I'm concerned, there is no one better, even if they searched for others related to Chiron himself. I mean, Oberon Thanestorm is legendary-"

"A shadow I had to be in for many years," the mage interrupted, "and it was a long time before I could stand in the light. A feeling I am sure you know of very well. Besides, I am not my father."

"No one said you had to be." Darius sighed, starting to get frustrated. "But Aldamoor needs a First Mage."

"Then they can find one," Puc said through his teeth as he got ready to leave. "I want no part in it. There are bigger things at hand than sitting upon a throne."

"If you are referring to guiding Annetta," the younger mage interjected, raising a hand in his direction.

Puc spun around on his heel to face Darius once more. "Should a threat arise, Annetta and Jason will need all the help they can get. My help, to be more precise."

"And they can still have it, but Aldamoor needs a leader," Darius repeated. "Look, I get it, I get the whole be prepared thing, but nothing is going on here now. They can handle themselves while you go help and sort things out."

Puc ignored the continuous talking of his past pupil and proceeded to go to his chambers, the only sounds coming from him being his steady breathing, the billowing of his robes as he walked and the hollow wooden sound of his staff hitting the floor. Nothing seemed to matter. He would not stand for this, for any of it. As far as he was concerned, he wanted to be as far away as possible from the Council. It was not that he did not trust his leadership abilities. He had no desire to do so. It was part of the gift and curse that Orbeyus had bestowed upon him all those years ago when he had asked him to come and unite the Four Forces. Moving to the opposite end of his desk and setting his staff to rest beside his chair, he grabbed a quill and parchment and began scribbling something quickly. His work complete, he folded and sealed the letter with wax before handing it to Darius.

"There is my answer," he stated, as the younger mage accepted the paper from him. "Let it be known that Aldamoor was and is without a leader."

෧෮ର

The next day brought with it the first signs of winter. It was a notion Annetta was not particularly happy about, considering she lived for the summer. The small white flakes hit her jacket and bag without mercy as she crossed the gate to get into the school yard, followed by Link close behind her.

"I'll take another bout with Puc's training over this weather," she grumbled as she pulled her gloves on tighter and peered out into the distance from under the brim of her hooded sweatshirt that she now wore under her jean jacket.

"You're saying that now, but wait until tonight," Link chuckled, brushing the snow off his hair.

Before they could continue, Annetta noticed Sarina and waved to her, veering the two of them in her direction. Contrary to the usual scenario, Jason was not standing beside her.

"Hey, where's J.K.?" Annetta asked as they approached.

"Said he wasn't feeling well, so he stayed home," she said. "Pretty sure he snuck some of that stuff Puc had yesterday with Matt and didn't tell us."

"Doesn't seem his style." Annetta scrunched up her nose. "It could happen to anyone, though. I guess we can reach out to him later and see if he will be down tonight."

"It's what I told him," Sarina replied, then added as an afterthought, "Might have been something he ate."

Annetta and Link nodded their heads in agreement. The three of them stood quietly for a little bit until Link remembered something and began rummaging through his bag.

"I left the paper that's due at the beginning of class in my locker," he said. "I'm gonna go grab it now so I can beat the rush. I'll see you guys there."

"See ya," the girls said in unison and watched him leave.

Annetta rolled up her sleeve to check the time before the bell rang, and with a sigh she put down her bag beside her, leaning against the fence. Her mind was still swimming with thoughts from the night before.

"Is it wrong that I have no desire to continue school?" she asked out loud. "I mean... I get why Puc is adamant about it now, but part of me still just doesn't care for it."

Sarina, her nose as usual in a book, put it down and turned to face Annetta.

"I suppose because it is expected of you that you see it as a chore," she said, "but to me, I see it as a possibility to learn something new. I spent my entire life on board Valdhar. I mean, I did get to go off with my father and I had tutors, but I never had the option to decide what I wanted to do with my life. This chance to go to school is my choice. I see it as an opportunity I thought I would never get my whole entire life."

Annetta let the girl's words sink in. She had never thought about it like that. She looked over at Sarina once more to see her returned to the book, studying the contents of the page as though her life depended on it. Stretching and letting her hands rest behind her head, Annetta slouched against the fence even more, feeling the depression of the metal loops against her skin through the fabric of her many layers.

"Yeah, I guess," she answered. "I'm just tired of it is all. I still want something more out of life, but I mean when you put it that way it does make sense, more than what Puc said."

"You still have time," Sarina spoke as she turned the page of her book. "Think about what you would want to do. What you enjoy doing, or at least what you could handle doing for however many years work is required here on Earth."

"I don't think sword fighting and horseback riding are in any job description," Annetta snorted, shifting her weight from one leg to the other upon hearing the bell ring, "unless I'm at a renaissance fair."

"Think on it a bit," Sarina repeated as she packed up her book and headed off towards the school. "As I said before, you have time."

Annetta smiled, more to herself than anyone else. She had never expected to share so much conversation with Sarina. Ever since she and Jason had become a couple, Annetta had never found much to say to her. It was not out of rudeness, but simply that she did not know what to say, with Sarina's background and all. Shouldering her backpack and making sure everything was in place, Annetta turned in the direction of the school, her breath now visible on the wind as the snow continued to fall. She looked up into the grey heavens, as though looking for some further approval to her plans for the future. Picking up nothing, she headed towards the school with a single thought in mind.

"I've got time."

☙❧

The weather continued to worsen to the point that Annetta eventually caved and called home to get someone to drop off a winter jacket. To her surprise, it was Matthias that waited in the schoolyard for her, Link and Sarina to come out. Dressed in an olive green winter coat and high boots, he gave off the aura of an older brother returned from the military. His uptight stance as female students passed him did not help either.

"Should have dressed warmer, Severio," he chuckled as Annetta snatched the red parka from him and wrapped herself in it.

"What are you? My mother now?" she growled.

"No," Matthias replied with an amused look on his face as the four of them began to walk towards the exit of the schoolyard. "I was simply bored with the Lab. I happened to come up and your father threw the jacket at me, proceeding to order me to deliver it to you."

"You? Bored?" Link chuckled. "What ever happened to your vendetta with Amarok?"

"One needs a break every now and then," he answered. "It's not like I know where he is right now anyway."

Annetta and Sarina plowed on ahead of the two boys, their breath visible in the air as they exited the residential area and cut across the large park in order to get to the house. Coming up to the hill which oversaw the whole area, they stopped.

"Another summer come and gone," Annetta sighed, adjusting her backpack, the combination of the winter and jean jacket beneath making it uncomfortable.

"It's just one of the four seasons, though," Sarina reminded her.

"Honestly," Annetta turned to the other girl, "There's only two in Canada, winter and construction, and if I gotta be honest I prefer the latter even if it drives my folks crazy on the road."

"You need to look at the positive things, though." Sarina beamed. "I mean, we can go skiing and skating and snowboarding is fun too from what I hear..."

Annetta listened to the other girl and smiled a bit. She had forgotten about all of the fun things winter brought along with it. As the bitter cold wind nipped at her face, however, she retracted it into the folds of her jacket.

"I guess so," she replied, "But still I-"

Her train of thought was interrupted as something above caught her attention. At first, she paid it no mind as it blinked out of the corner of her eye, thinking it nothing more than a plane. Soon, however, she realized that it was not a consistent flashing of lights and then it hit her. They were no lights at all.

78

Annetta froze, feeling the hairs on her neck stand on end as she watched the light, only to see it getting bigger, worst yet, closer. She grabbed Sarina by the arm mid-sentence and began to run down the hill as quickly as her legs would take her. Tripping on an undone shoe lace, the girl fell face first into the grass, bracing herself with her forearms but continued to slide downward, bringing Sarina along.

Quickly scrambling to her feet and helping Sarina up, Annetta continued to proceed forward, only to be knocked down once more by an impact of what in her mind could only be an unearthly force. The two girls were swept off their feet from the shock and tumbled down the opposite end of the hill, rolling in a mixture of muddy snow and grass.

"What was that?" Sarina said in a half whisper, recovering from their trip down the hill once they had come to a stop.

Annetta did not bother replying and rising, began to scan the area around her. She stopped the moment her eyes reached the top of the hill, seeing it was now deformed from the impact. Curious, the girl lowered herself and began the crawl up on her stomach at a slow pace.

"Anne, what are you doing?" Sarina questioned again. Rolling over onto her belly, she began to follow the other girl up the hill. "These grass stains won't be easy to get out."

Not thinking about what was being said, Annetta continued on her way up until she reached the edge of the grass. As she came closer, she took note of the way the earth itself had been torn away, and it was a pattern she recognized from the media she watched all too well. Her eyes ventured down into the crater and the blood in Annetta's face ceased to flow. Where she had hoped and expected to see a meteor lay something else entirely.

At first, the girl felt certain the thing was a rock, or at least made of a similar substance. When her eyes had been given a chance to deceive her, all was lost as the thing melted and warped from one side. It would have been cylindrical in shape prior to the damage and was about the size of a minivan. The exterior looked organic, charred, much the way a meteorite would have had she not known better. Annetta lowered her head further and placing a hand on Sarina's back urged her to do the same. It would do them no good to give away their position.

The stone melted away from one side and left nothing to be seen on the inside but darkness. Annetta's eyes focused with all the ferocity she could muster, but to no avail. She was about to give up and stand but then she heard it. A thundering of boots echoed from inside the craft and sure enough, their owner emerged right after. What they saw came as a shock to both girls.

The humanoid creature stood at about seven feet tall. It sported a thick lion-like mane and had the face of a badger. The fur around its snout was cut shorter to give the illusion of bushy mutton chops on the sides of its face. At first, it appeared to only have one rabbit-like ear, pierced with multiple hoop earrings. Once it whipped its head to either side while surveying the area it revealed the other to be shortened, most likely in the same fight where it lost its eye, which was covered with an eye patch on the same side.

The creature, or the Hurtz as the girls thought it looked to be, was dressed in heavy chain mail with a crimson tabard worn over top of it, decorated with the crest of a white rampant lion. Strapped across its back was a hefty broadsword, which the Hurtz seemed intent on drawing at a moment's notice. Sure that no one was around, it stepped aside from the entrance.

A man in his early forties then stepped out from inside the craft. He wore his black hair cut short with sideburns that stopped at his cheekbones. He was not the tallest person, Annetta feeling he could not be much taller than herself, even if she was tall for a girl. His overall facial structure was sharp and grim, hinting at him having been a soldier his whole life, if his muscled physique did not already do so. He wore a black scale mail shirt, made of the tiniest scales Annetta had ever seen which seemed to be perfectly fitted to his torso, a wide black belt laced in gold and black pants that were tucked into high leather boots. From one shoulder a red cape draped and dragged behind him. None of these features however truly mattered to Annetta, aside from what she saw in the man's blue eyes. It was an aura that commanded both fear and respect. In those eyes, there was a fire which threatened to burn all opposition to the ground. Determination unbound.

A chill went down Annetta's spine as she watched the man look around the desolated ground, while the Hurtz stood vigilantly by his side.

"Did you scramble the local communication as instructed?" the man asked the creature.

"Yes, my lord, but we haven't much time either way," the Hurtz responded. "Earth's forces will soon be at the scene to investigate. We must flee."

"We didn't have much choice," the man reminded him. "We were low on fuel. Though I do agree, Skyris did not pick the best position for our descent. This area is far too densely populated and I-"

Before the man could continue, the Hurtz drew his sword and stood before him, planting the weapon into the ground.

"Ye who would hide in the shadows," the creature growled in a thickly accented voice, "know that I am Gladius the Hurtz, and should ye not show yerselves, know that I will be yer end."

"And how do we know you won't kill us if we do?" Matthias's voice rang from the other side of the hill. "What proof do we have that you don't already know our positions?"

"So ye admit to there being more of ye here?" the Hurtz growled. "Good, I haven't had a good fight in days and I-"

"Gladius, that is enough." The man raised a hand to hush him and took a step forward. "You have my word as a Gaian that no harm shall come to you if you choose to comply. I swear by the Sacred Tree of the Unknown."

It became clear to Annetta that Matthias was trying to create a diversion so she and Sarina could flee, but she was far too interested in the two new arrivals to be able to follow through with such a plan.

Matthias got up from his position on the other side of the crater and raised his arms in surrender, his gauntlet clad hands showing clearly from under his coat. He then began to slowly make his way down towards Gladius and the man accompanying him. As soon as he came to levelled ground, Gladius seized him and placed the massive sword close to his neck. Seeing himself in a tight spot, the assassin teleported some feet away and faced his foe, causing both the man and the Hurtz to go into a fighting stance.

"Two on one, why not." Matthias grinned as the claws hidden away in his gauntlets sprung out, "Bring it on."

"A psychic," the Hurtz grunted.

The man narrowed his eyes. "Who are you?"

"You'll just need to find out now, won't you?" Matthias grinned, flexing his hands at the challenge. "So, which one of you wishes to go first?"

"I will take on this one," the man in the crimson cape answered back as he walked in front of Gladius.

"But my lord, surely-" Gladius tried interjecting, only to have the man raise a hand in his face to silence him.

"This whelp requires respect be taught to him," he said, turning his gaze to Matthias. "But before I do so, I will give him the common courtesy of knowing who is about to end his life. I am Venetor the Ironfisted, the Crown Prince of Gaia and brother to Orbeyus of the Axe Severio."

Hearing the last part made Annetta forget everything that had just transpired. The muscles in her legs coiled as she stood up and shouted "Liar!"

Matthias's face went pale as he looked up, while the other two simply stared, at first in curiosity and then in wonder.

"Amelia?" the man named Venetor squinted his eyes.

"Anne, what are you doing?" Sarina whispered from the ground beside her.

Annetta felt a heat build on the back of her neck when she heard Sarina's voice. She hadn't exactly thought about what she was doing, but it seemed the right thing to do at the given time. Exhaling, the girl took a step forward to fully reveal herself. She couldn't exactly do anything else. Tapping into her own psychic abilities, Annetta used her telepathy while keeping a straight face as she moved down the hill towards the others.

'Sarina, I want you to get to the house and I want you to warn Puc that we may have trouble, you understand me? Get Link as well,'

Unable to reply due to a lack of abilities, Sarina simply nodded her head and crawled down the hill until she was far enough away to make an escape.

Sure that her friend had gone unseen, Annetta's pace evened and continued downward until she stood before them. Back straight and feet planted firmly on the ground.

"Orbeyus was no Gaian," she stated coldly.

Venetor seemed entertained by her arrival, a minor twitching of his lips indicating the slightest sarcastic smile. "And who are you that makes such bold accusations?"

"Why should I tell you?" she snapped.

The Gaian's smile widened slightly. "Well, it is a courtesy on Gaia that when you meet someone you introduce yourself, and if I am not mistaken about the customs of Earth, the practice is generally the same. Now, if you claim to know my brother I should very much like to know your name, especially since you remind me of someone I met a very long time ago."

Annetta looked over at Matthias for answers only to get a blank stare of disappointment for revealing her position. The girl then turned back to Venetor. "I am Annetta Severio, daughter of Arieus and Aurora Severio and granddaughter of Orbeyus Severio."

"Orbeyus and Amelia as it were," Venetor added, examining the girl from head to toe. "Oh yes, every inch Amelia as I remember her in our youth."

"That's great and all, but I'm not of Gaia," Annetta interrupted him. "I'm of Earth."

"This is where you are wrong," Venetor chuckled. "Did you actually in all this time not question why your grandfather was referred to as Lord Orbeyus? I can only assume if you know of him that you know of Q-16. Did you never question where the technology found in the base came from either? You more than likely also carry the genetic predisposition of being a psychic, another thing I presume you did not think to think about where you inherited from."

"Sire, we must flee," Gladius interrupted, his ears twitching. "I can hear sirens coming. We have twenty minutes at best before they reach us. If they discover us here we will have bigger problems on our hands."

While the scene unfolded, Annetta stood rooted to the ground. It was true that there were many things she had not even stopped to consider, things that this man who called himself Venetor had brought up in but a few seconds of talking to her. She wondered what else he knew. Despite her gut feelings, she did her best to keep a distant façade about her.

Sensing this, Venetor came closer to her. "If you thirst for truth, I can tell you what you wish to know. The things you have been fed up till this date have not been of honest intent. Everything they ever told you was a lie."

Before he could continue, however, there was a click and something metallic caught his eye. The Gaian looked down to see a cuff around his right wrist.

"You wanna talk, that's fine," Matthias said, coldly. "I know a place and a guy who will be all too interested to hear."

Gladius snarled and readied himself to attack, only to be stopped by Venetor's raised hand.

"Surrender your weapon to him," he ordered. "We both knew it could come to this."

The Hurtz spat and slammed his sword into the ground with a thud. "The runt can keep it."

Matthias ignored the comment and using his abilities, he summoned the sword into his hand before turning to Annetta. "Get the Gaian and meet me at the entrance in the woods. We don't want to lead these two to your home."

He then grabbed hold of Gladius's beefy shoulder and teleported away with him, leaving Annetta alone with Venetor. The girl felt a chill go down her spine, feeling the Gaian's eyes upon her back. She turned around to face him.

"You've made a wise choice," he said to her.

The girl ignored the comment and grabbed a hold of his arm tightly. She then added as an afterthought, "Wise or not, we'll just have to wait and see."

Chapter 9

His eyes darted across the screen in coordination with the characters on it, calculating every move his opponent would make. The nimble fingers pressed every button with animated precision, in anticipation of the end. Finally, success at hand, Xander Severio let out a long sigh of relief, allowing the game controller to fall into his cross-legged lap.

"One more down," he exhaled.

Sitting beside him, stretched out on the sofa was Liam Kinsman. Though he was Jason's younger brother, he was beginning to take on more of his mother's side of the family. He was far leaner in build, which also made him appear taller than he was. His brown hair was cut short and spiked in a similar fashion to that of Xander, whom he had been spending much time with of late.

The two of them still remembered when neither could see the other outside of school, due to some unspoken feud their parents had. Over the last year, this had changed since Xander had moved into his new home. Now, they were inseparable, almost like their elder siblings.

"Man, I'm done," Xander said, shaking his head. "I fried my hands."

Liam chuckled. "Well, yeah, with that much button mashing I'm surprised you didn't have them just burst into flames."

Xander handed the controller over to his friend, but Liam simply waved it away.

"I don't have a death wish," he replied. "Plus there's no way I could beat that high score."

"But you know you want to try," Xander teased, still holding the controller, dangling the cable like a carrot on a string.

There was a knock on the door to the room before the hand of Xander's father crept through the opening to reveal the man standing there.

"You boys alright?" he huffed, out of breath. "I mean, did you feel the earthquake from the meteorite that fell?"

"Meteorite?" the boys asked simultaneously. "What meteorite?"

"It's all over the news," Arieus said to them. "It fell not far from here. I'm surprised you boys didn't feel it. Then again, you were probably so distracted with your games you were dead to the world."

Xander quickly turned the gaming console off and turned the channel to the news. Sure enough, as his father had said, the headlines read "Meteorite hits Toronto" in bold red writing at the top of the screen. Below it was footage of people from the police and fire department sealing off the area from civilians with yellow tape. The boy narrowed his eyes as he took everything in.

"Does Annetta know?" he asked.

Xander and Liam had not been told much about where their siblings went every day after school or where Link, Sarina and Matthias had come from. They did know about the teleporter, having seen Annetta and Jason use it before. They also had a good idea that whatever was involved, it was something that needed to be very secretive. It was confirmed for Xander when Liam told him about the day his brother had made objects in their room float. Liam's mother had apparently gotten very angry and refused to say anything about it to him.

Arieus's face went very quiet for a few seconds and then he turned to the boys. "I'm sure Annetta and J.K. are fine, wherever they are."

"Can we go to the crash site?" Liam asked. "I mean, not to it but, like, where people will be? I wanna see what's going to happen."

"It would be kind of cool," Xander added, trailing off as he watched the television.

"I suppose." Arieus ran his fingers through his moustache. "I don't see why not, since the whole area where they don't want people has been closed off."

"Awesome!" Liam grinned. "I wonder if they're gonna bring in like the CSIS and CSA."

"The what?" Xander questioned as he got up off the couch, seeing his friend so excited.

"Canadian Security Intelligence Service and the Canadian Space Agency," Arieus clarified. "And they will most likely be there, so stay out of their way, okay? This is serious business."

"We will, Mr. Severio," Liam assured him as he went to go put on his coat and boots with Xander.

଼ଠଔ

Having freed themselves from the confines of Xander's room and the video games which inhabited it, the two made their way over to the park. A thin layer of snow caked the grass, green blades still poking through the powdery surface. In a hurry to get there before it was all over, they walked at a brisk pace, while still minding the unusually heavy traffic of cars as they crossed the road. They guessed it had to do with the crash.

"I wonder what it looks like," Liam said as they managed to get to the other side of the road.

"Like any old heap of rock from space," Xander guessed as he gathered some snow up into his hand, turning it into a ball.

Ever since he was little, Xander had enjoyed the feeling of snow on his bare hands. His mother had often scolded him when he was younger to put on some gloves when he did this. When she was gone, however, off they came again. He watched as the snow began to melt on his palm, trickling down his fingers. His observation was distracted when a snowball zoomed past his head and hit the utility poll by the street. Xander frowned and looked to see Liam standing some distance away, making another snowball.

"From how far away can you hit it?" he asked, tossing another ball at the pole from even further away.

"Why does it matter?" he inquired, wanting to continue their journey.

"We used to do it all the time," Liam remembered. "Don't you wanna see if your aim has improved?"

Xander looked down at the half melted ball of snow in his hands and sighed. He let it drop to the ground and gathered another ball to indulge his friend's competitive nature. It had been that way with them as far back as he could remember. One always had to challenge the other, though it was never in outright anger. It was a simple need to constantly better one's self.

His new arsenal acquired, Xander turned his attention to the pole, taking a few steps back so that he was way behind where Liam stood. He then waited. Levelling his eyes and focusing on his target he raised his hand and threw it only to be sent back by a light so intense, all else lost meaning to him.

ഇന്ദ

Puc stood vigilant at the front entrance to the Lab, flanked by Sarina and Link on either side. After being burst in on by the duo and being informed of the situation, the mage wasted no time with his next course of action. A white-knuckled hand gripped at his staff as he waited, impatiently for the cascade of events that was to follow.

"I don't think they should even bring them down here." Link voiced his opinion as he crossed his arms.

Not betraying his internal monologue, Puc shifted his gaze to the younger man. "Would you have preferred a conflict in the outside world then?"

"I think what he means," Sarina interrupted, "is that, remember what happened the last time someone from the outside was brought in so quickly?"

The elf gave a slight nod and turned back to look out ahead of them into the dark. "Understood, although if it is who you just told me then...well, we will just have to see."

Link raised an eyebrow at the last part of what the mage said and was interrupted by the familiar sound of bodies making their descent into the base. Pressing his hand on the hilt of his sword, he waited.

The first to appear was Matthias, holding a very large two-handed sword, accompanied by a one-eared Hurtz with an eye patch. Having fully materialized, he shifted aside, directing the creature to move along with him.

"Gladius?" Puc's eyes widened slightly upon seeing the creature.

"Aye," he answered with a twinge of defiance in his voice. "and if I remember correctly, ye be Thanestorm. My brother Brakkus spoke most fondly of ya. I trust he is well."

Puc felt a sharp twinge pull at him upon hearing the very last part. He wasn't quite sure what to say to the younger Hurtz, and was saved by the sound of more bodies descending. He turned back in the direction of the noise.

Annetta shook off the impact of being dropped by the sensation of invisible waves and quickly got to her feet, moving away from the second body that lay beside her.

The elf turned to her. "Are you alright?"

"I'm not quite sure what I feel right now," she grunted through her teeth.

He shook his head, knowing he would have a long night ahead of him as he turned back to see the man in the crimson cloak rise from the floor. Puc noted the cuff on his wrist and smiled slightly to himself. He then cleared his throat. "To what do we owe the pleasure of your visit, Venetor the Ironfisted, son of Balthazar?"

"Hang on," Annetta interjected, pointing at the Gaian on the far side. "You mean...is he who he said he was?"

The mage exhaled, attempting to decompress the building tension in the room. "Yes, Annetta, this is Venetor, your grandfather's brother."

"And it didn't occur to you for a moment to maybe mention..." the words stopped in Annetta's throat and she then turned to Link, "Or to you..."

"It wasn't my choice," Link replied, hanging his head low, his bangs obscuring his face.

"It was neither of our choice," Puc added. "Perhaps if you calmed down..."

"When did you plan on telling me?" the girl interrupted him. "Were you even going to? What else has been kept from me all this time? Are you even who you say you are?"

"Oh, he is Thanestorm alright," Venetor smirked. "I can vouch for that."

The girl sneered and throwing off her winter jacket along with her school bag where she stood, she stormed past everyone gathered.

"Where are you going?" Puc demanded as he watched her go.

"Away," she snapped. "And to get some answers. Don't bother following me. Any of you!"

All those gathered watched as the girl walked away, fading into nothing in the vastness of the Lab. There was a long and dead silence for some time, until Venetor began to clap his hands in a deadpanned manner.

"Brilliant display of enthusiasm and charm." He shook his head as his clapping stopped. "You've got a real gift with words, Thanestorm."

"Quiet, you," the elf hissed. "And what in the Unknown's bane are you doing here anyway?"

"My reasons are for her ears alone." Venetor pointed in the direction Annetta had sauntered off in. "I refuse to speak with anyone else. Until then, however, I would like to track the other pod which should have landed. It contains some rather precious cargo, if I can say so. You can help or obstruct me, gain no further information and perhaps risk the exposure of said cargo."

Puc felt his jaw twitch as he restrained himself from saying anything he might later regret. He motioned for Matthias to return the sword to Gladius, who slid it back his baldric.

"I have no further words for you, Venetor," the mage spoke. "Nor can I be of any use in this venture. Matthias, however, can be of aid. I have other more pressing matters I must see to."

With the whirl of his robes, the mage then took off.

ഐരു

Once she had saddled Firedancer, Annetta urged the horse into a full run, feeling the wind howl in her ears. Her mind was pounding with anger which could only be rivalled by the stinging sensation of the air currents that beat against her mercilessly as she rode onward. Veering the horse to a halt upon reaching her destination, she teleported straight off to her usual ledge, not bothering to tie Firedancer up or check to make sure the area was secure. She needed answers and she needed them fast.

ഐരു

The sensation of peacefulness hit her, muddling any previous emotions she had harboured but not allowing them to fully dissipate. The girl then found herself once more roaming the gardens she always did when she visited. Her senses clearing, she could feel the urgency of her coming to the place return in full swing, along with the rage that filled her.

"Annetta!" a familiar voice called to her from behind.

Annetta spun around on her heel to face the man she had come to know as Orbeyus. He stood in a clearing in the midst of a growth of tall sparse trees with a beaming smile on his face. She did not recall the scenery from previous visits and then reminded herself that the surroundings she saw when visiting her grandfather never stayed the same. She shook off the feelings of calmness and did her best to focus.

"Is it true?" she asked, pointing behind her as if to indicate the location of the Lab. "Is it true what I just saw and heard?"

What happiness there was beneath Orbeyus's bushy beard and the twinkle of mischief in his blue eyes faded. Where on his face moments before there was visible youthful prowess, now old age settled on the shoulders of the Lord of the Axe. Lowering his head in pensive thought, he walked past Annetta with his hands folded behind his back.

His contemplation on the subject completed, Orbeyus began speaking. "What Venetor told you is true. As I once was heir to the Gaian throne, so he is now and you are not of Earthly origins."

He then turned around to face Annetta, who was not sure how to react to anything she had heard. Part of her seemed to be screaming silently in denial as she looked at him. Orbeyus took this as his cue to continue. "When I was a young man, not much older than you are now yourself, I had become aware of how corrupt and selfish our society had become. How it had strayed from its ideals of helping those who were less fortunate, and how, with all its knowledge, it had turned its back on the one race that was closest to it, on humanity. For you see, every planet has a sister planet. A planet that is so similar in its geography, and even the species that inhabit it, that it is like a younger sister or brother. One is usually ahead of the other in terms of cultural and social development. In Unaverisim, the religion of believing in the Unknown, it is said that it is the will of the Unknown that sister planets should look out for one another, that the older and wiser should protect the younger and more vulnerable. For the longest time it was such an integral part of Gaian society that they made it their mission to seek out Earth, and once found, they even began to settle on it. Some Gaians, unfortunately, developed a bit of a god complex, sharing their technology with humans who had no idea of their origin and in turn began to worship them. The Intergalactic Federation saw this corruption and ordered for those Gaians in charge to be arrested, and some even put to death. For the longest time, Earth remained forgotten once more, until I came across the books of our ancestor, Adeamus Severio. I don't know what else to call it, but I fell in love with his writing. I fell in love with Earth and I felt it was my duty to seek it out again."

Annetta listened intently to the words of her grandfather, absorbing everything he said. While the tale intrigued her and her emotions had begun to cool, there were still many questions that remained.

"Why was I not told of everything when I came down to the Lab?" she inquired. "Why have Puc keep all these secrets? I mean... surely Link knew as well as Matt and probably Sarina. Not to mention Mislantus."

Orbeyus stroked his beard, smoothing out any tangles. "Mislantus knew, he was well aware of who I was. However, I gave all claims to the Gaian throne to Venetor when I left for Earth. I was never again to be known as a prince of Gaia, but simply as Lord Severio. I instructed Puc not to tell you until much later, because I did not want to overwhelm you, nor for you to seek out Gaia. Lincerious knew full well your origin, but was sworn to secrecy by the angels that led him to Q-16. As to why Matthias and Sarina said nothing, it most likely never came up in conversation when they were hunting you both with Jason initially or they didn't make the connection. Once they got to the Lab and found you, I wouldn't have been surprised if Puc has a spell that casts itself on anyone who comes down like a trap that is triggered upon entry. He is quite a trickster."

"Yeah, I can see that," Annetta muttered, feeling somewhat betrayed.

"I meant it for your own good, Annetta," Orbeyus confessed. "A person who fights for home fights more fiercely than a hired hand. Home sometimes simply means the people you love and not where you come from. I wanted you to have that choice and that chance."

The girl nodded, understanding what he was trying to say, even if part of her was still mad for having to find out the way she had.

"Thank you, grandfather," she acknowledged. "Thank you for telling me."

"You're welcome, my dear." He smiled back at her. "This all having been said, there will be choices ahead of you in the coming days that will not be easy. Stay true to yourself and remember, severed be he whom forgets."

ಬಿೂಲ

What sun there was had begun to set as Link waited at the edge of the stables in hopes of sensing Annetta's presence. Even when she was sleeping, he could subconsciously know she was there, but there were times where she disappeared without a trace, especially when she went off on her own to the castle to ride around the trails. It unnerved him.

The excitement of the day and the arrival of the Gaian prince had taken its toll on him, causing his eyelids to grow heavier by the second. He was almost asleep against the wooden doorframe when he heard the sound approaching hoofs. He opened his eyes to see the reddish blur of Firedancer coming closer into view.

Annetta halted the great beast to a stop and patted his neck gently in a soothing manner. She then slipped out of the saddle, grabbed the reins and led the horse to his stall.

"Annetta." The name escaped the Gaian youth.

She turned around and saw him standing in the doorway. An instant flare of anger brewed within her, knowing he had lied to her in the way he did. She then remembered what Orbeyus had told her and did her best to push it to the back of her mind.

"Hey, stranger," She greeted him as she removed the saddle and bridle from the horse so she could groom him.

Link paused, hearing the hint of sarcasm. He'd known this day would come sooner or later. He could feel the hidden anger inside her. Focusing on what to say next, he ran a hand through his hair and down his neck.

"Annetta...I'm sorry," he began. "I really am. I wanted to tell you so many times before."

"You don't need to apologize," the girl interjected as she continued on with her task. "I know it wasn't your choice."

"It wasn't. But I still feel like I should have hinted at it or something," he protested. "You deserved to know. You should have known all this time who you really are."

The girl finished putting away the riding equipment, and then turned around to face him.

"Who I really am?" she surmised. "Has who I've been this whole time not been the real me? Last I checked, I was pretty sure I knew who I was, and the fact that I'm not human doesn't change who I am inside. Maybe there's some stuff I have to learn and figure out now, but as far as I'm concerned, I'm still Annetta Severio, who's being forced to go and do post-secondary school on Earth. Nothing has changed about that."

Link was taken a little aback, not expecting such a rational reaction from Annetta, who he knew to have a temper hotter than the sun when something infuriated her. Sure that it was safe to approach her, he took a few paces forward. Hearing the last bit of what she said caused his face to light up.

"And that there is exactly what makes you who you are," he said with a grin.

Annetta smirked and turned back around in order to give everything a second check to make sure it was all in place. When she pivoted again to leave, she saw Link watching her from the other side of the stall. His grey eyes seemed to have an ambience about them that she seldom saw in anyone. Had she not known any better, she would have suspected it was admiration.

"What?" she asked, feeling self-conscious, as she walked towards him.

"Uh…nothing." Link shook his head as though he were coming out of a daze. "I mean… I agree with what you said completely. It doesn't change anything, but…"

The Gaian youth paused and took one of Annetta's hands into his own. He then gazed into the two sapphire orbs that looked back into his own.

"I swore that I would protect you," he continued. "And I feel that my not telling you in a way was the complete opposite of that. I feel like I betrayed you, like I, in some way, contributed to putting a knife in your back when I should have been the one to guard you against it. I promise I will never do such a thing again."

There was a second when the two of them felt as though a magnetic force was trying to pull them together. It was something deeper than any words in any language could explain. The moment was lost, however, when the sound of wood on steel could be heard in the distance. Annetta and Link turned away to see Puc and Darius emerge through the doors leading the Lab, both dressed in dark blue robes.

"What's going on?" Link asked, letting go of Annetta's hand.

"Ready my horse, Lincerious," Puc instructed. "I must travel to Aldamoor. There has been a series of events I need to tend to, which could potentially shape the future of the Four Forces."

"Wait, now?" Annetta stammered. "We have a pretty big situation on our hands here, don't you think?"

"I should not be long," the mage declared, "and you will not be alone. Darius will remain behind in my place to counsel you."

"What happened?" Link asked as he finished saddling the horse for Puc and led it around to him.

The elf mounted it in a single swift movement and adjusted his robes before addressing those gathered. "Kaian has died, leaving the seat of First Mage vacant. A new First Mage must be chosen. Depending on who that is, it could affect the state of the Four Forces. While not many in the High Council, there are a few that opposed our involvement. I need to be there to make sure everything stays intact."

"That's great and all, but what about Venetor and Gladius being here?" Annetta complained. "What about our training?"

"They are who they say they are," Puc assured her. "As for your training, who better to learn from that the Crown Prince of Gaia himself. The title of the Ironfisted is not without reason."

The mage said no more. Prodding the horse into a canter, he was off as quickly as he had come into the stables, leaving the trio on their own.

Annetta watched as Puc disappeared from her line of sight. While she was still somewhat upset at him for having hidden the truth about her origin, he was a familiar person she could speak with. Despite the hell he put her through in the training arena, Puc was someone whose advice she was beginning to trust more and more. Now, in a time of crisis, that advice would have been invaluable to her and to her friends. Sighing, she ran a hand through her bangs and turned to her two remaining companions.

"Great, now what?" she fumed, throwing her hands up in the air.

Darius, his hands folded inside of his robes glanced over at Link, who also wore a grim expression upon the loss of the mage.

"We press on," the younger elf remarked. "We don't have much of a choice, do we? First thing though, we need to find Jason and fill him in, if Sarina hasn't already done so."

"Yeah, I guess so," Annetta concurred. "I can't imagine how he's going to take it. Not much better than I did, I suppose."

"Probably not," Darius agreed. "And you remember what happened the last time he found out news like this, right?"

The girl inhaled a deep breath through her nose as her mind recounted the events Darius spoke about, her hand running to her arm where a few of the scars still remained.

"Let's go," were the final words she spoke before taking off into the depths of the base.

Chapter 10

Jason arrived in the Lab upon receiving the call from Sarina on his C.T.S. watch. He was feeling much better, having rested most of the day at home instead of being bent over schoolwork. Despite feeling better, however, he had needed to slip out of the house in case his mother caught him steering away to the teleporter leading to Q-16.

Materializing in the base and getting up after having been floored by the pull of gravity, he looked up to see Sarina standing but a few feet away.

"Hey," he greeted her, only to see the stern look on her face. "What's wrong?"

"Come with me to the lake biosphere," she said. "There are some things I need to tell you."

Pursing his lips, the boy did not question her and did as he was told, keeping quiet the entire way until they entered the area. Something about her tone and actions did not sit right with him. Upon reaching their destination, Jason stood close to the doorway, watching Sarina as she continued forward to where the river dividing the two sides of the biosphere appeared. Certain that she would go no further, he caught up to her.

"So," he started again, "Are you going to tell me what all of this is about?"

A gust of wind passed by them, causing the grass and leaves of the trees to rustle louder in the silence. A loose strand of Sarina's hair fell out of place, but she made a quick effort to fix it.

"I never told you about my father, did I?" she began. "Not how he was, but who he was."

Jason scrunched up his eyebrows. "Okay… you hated him and he's dead, isn't that all that matters?"

"It's not that simple, Jason." She shook her head. "Partially because this also affects your own history. You are not human, but a Gaian."

"I'm a what?" the boy exclaimed.

"A Gaian," she reiterated, "much the same as I am. My father and my grandfather were as well. Our last name is Freiuson, deriving from our ancestor Freius, who was said to have been the Gaian that enslaved Korangar the Great Destroyer, sometimes known also as just The End. There's a legend that if Korangar was not enslaved, then the multiverse would be annihilated. My grandfather and his followers got the notion that it was he and his descendants who should rule the multiverse because they were the descendants of someone who managed to stop the end from coming about. He believed in himself and them being the masters over life and death. Fashioning his ancestral home into a flying fortress, he then began conquering as many planets as he possibly could, propagating this belief forward. His followers, driven by the fanatical devotion of whom they were serving, soon began to outnumber the Gaian forces. But they met their match upon Earth, where a Severio lord had gathered an army of his own."

"Why didn't you tell me this sooner?" Jason asked, feeling the sensation of ice draped across his skin. "Why didn't Puc tell us? Or-"

"When we first met there just never was an opportunity to tell you," she informed him. "It wasn't part of the role I was given to play when we were trying to gain your trust for my father. He feared if you knew with Annetta, you may try to contact Gaia for aid somehow against him. I wanted to tell you sooner, but something kept preventing me. I'm not sure, maybe Puc had some kind of spell up so we didn't-"

"So Puc knew and he decided not to say anything?" the boy snapped. "Anything else you want to confess while we're on the subject?"

"J.K.," the voice of Annetta came from the entrance, causing Jason to spin around and see her, along with Link and Darius.

"How long have you known?" He gritted his teeth as he looked at her.

"Uh, not much longer than you have," she stated. "Don't you think I would have told you about something like this?"

"I'm not sure what to think." Jason inhaled unevenly. "So what you're telling me is we aren't even human?"

Without warning, Annetta marched over and in a fluid movement, punched Jason in the shoulder.

The boy recoiled with a shocked expression. "What was that for?"

"Does it hurt?" she asked.

"Uh, yeah," he answered.

"Would it have hurt the same before you knew all of this?" she queried again.

"Probably," he uttered.

"So, what does it matter?"

Frowning, Jason rubbed his shoulder. "It doesn't, I guess."

"Exactly," Annetta affirmed. "Now that we have that out of the way, we have bigger things to worry about. Firstly, Puc leaving for Aldamoor with no actual return date in mind because of Kaian's death and the need to appoint a new First Mage. Secondly, my would-be great uncle from Gaia dropping in for a visit and occupying the Lab with his own Hurtz bodyguard in tow."

"Wait, what?" The boy's eyes widened. "Great uncle?"

"Long story short," Darius said, stepping forward, "Orbeyus had a younger brother who is now the Crown Prince of Gaia and he's here, in the Lab, looking for another pod from his spaceship that fell to Earth."

"And this pod isn't going to go unnoticed by other people how?" Jason raised an eyebrow, voicing the first question that popped into his head.

"New Gaian pods are designed to look like meteorites," Link explained. "Not only from the outside. The pods are fashioned in such a way that once its passengers leave, it self-destructs by turning into an actual meteorite, so if picked up by local life forms, they will never distinguish it as having been a spaceship of any kind."

Jason and Annetta both stared at Link upon hearing what he had just said, as their minds raced a million miles an hour in an attempt to rationalize everything.

"It's fairly new technology," he assured them. "Mostly military would use it, and those pods are generally for escape only. They would be attached to a ship that would launch them. The ship itself would then camouflage to look like an asteroid. Anyways, once you get off, there's no way back up unless a shuttle gets you."

"Right," Jason thought as he summarized the information in his head. "So… what's this great uncle of yours here for, Annetta?"

"I'll be damned if I know," she replied. "I was so angry that I left without giving it a second thought."

"If I can suggest something," Darius added, "It may be wise to go check on Matt. He is with them."

The group nodded in agreement. Annetta and Jason, in particular wanted to hear what Venetor had to say. Collecting their thoughts, they left the biosphere in search of answers.

හᏀ

Having locked themselves in Xander's room as soon as they crossed the threshold, the duo quickly came to realize that the house had no power as daylight began to fade into dark. Grabbing a large flashlight, they placed it in the centre of the room, using it as a pretend campfire while they huddled around it. Neither of them spoke for a longer time, trying to register what had transpired.

Unable to keep quiet any longer, Liam spoke. "It was probably just a loose wire, anything could have done it."

Xander looked over at his friend, a half-frown present on his face. "You don't actually believe that do you? You saw the same thing I did, there was a spark coming from my hand and it hit the pole. To top it all off, I didn't get electrocuted!"

"It could have just been the way the spark bounced that made it look that way." Liam argued.

"Liam I'm telling you, it wasn't natural-" Xander hissed through gritted teeth.

The door handle moved and in peered Xander's mother Aurora, holding an ornamental oil lamp that both boys knew as one of the random knickknacks from one of the shelves in the kitchen.

"Oh, there you both are." She smiled. "Xander's father thought you were both still at the crash site."

"There wasn't much to see Mrs. Severio," Liam told her. "They picked up the hunk of rock and there was a bunch of police telling people to keep their distance so we just turned back and left thinking there would be more on the news but when we came home there was no power."

"The meteorite must have hit some power lines when it came down." She told them. "Well, hopefully, they manage to fix it soon. A power outage in the summer is one thing, a power outage in the winter is a whole other."

Liam and Xander both nodded, not wanting to think of what it would be like to have to be inside with no furnace running. At least in the summer if it was hot, there was the basement to hide in.

"When you are ready to go home, let us know Liam so we can drop you off." Aurora informed him. "It's going to be very dark if they can't get the streetlights fixed."

"Thanks Mrs. Severio, I will." He replied.

Sure they were alright, Aurora then left the room and closed the door behind her.

Liam waited until he heard her footsteps creaking down the stairs before he continued to speak again.

"I'm telling you dude, you did something back there and you just don't want to admit it."

Feeling defeated and unable to defend himself any further, Xander took a deep breath and felt himself deflate when he let it go.

"Whatever it was, if it was anything, it's not like I can replicate it at all." He finally said.

"No." Liam agreed. "Not yet at least."

ഇരു

Annetta and her four companions entered the control room to find Gladius, Matthias and Venetor spread out among the glass screens. The trio was intensely at work, scouring what looked to be satellite images of Earth. A mixture of hand gestures as well as verbal commands was used by them to change the content of the screens. It served as a reminder to Annetta how little she knew about the technology found in the Lab.

Sensing the five sets of eyes staring into his back, Venetor turned around to face the youth.

"It will take some time for the scanners to find the second impact site," he said, "but it is vital that we retrieve the others on that ship."

"Who are you looking for?" the girl asked.

"There were three others travelling with Gladius and myself," the Gaian replied, "My sister and your aunt Skyris, who was our pilot on the main ship we used before escaping in the pods, her handmaiden Atala Shade and my son, Titus."

Venetor then fell silent as his eyes went to Jason who stood beside Annetta.

"You are Arcanthur's boy, aren't you?" he stated, motioning for the boy to come forward.

Jason furrowed his brows but did as was wanted of him and moved past his friend. "I am."

"I take it then that you are also a psychic warrior?" the Gaian prince probed further.

"We both are," Annetta interjected. "Puc's been training us since we found out about the Lab."

"That over-cocky elf has been teaching you?" Venetor scoffed. "By what right? It is the duty of a psychic warrior to teach the young to harness their abilities. I can guarantee you don't know the half of it when it comes to how to use your powers."

"Well, there hasn't been anyone else that was qualified so to speak." Jason raised his arms to indicate all those present. "I mean, Matt did try to teach us some but he's been gone for most of the time trying to locate Amarok."

"Mezorian lives, then." Venetor frowned upon hearing the name, then turned his attention back to the youth. "Very well, I suppose since I am more capable and Thanestorm is gone, then perhaps I can assist you. However, I'll need to see what you're able to do first."

"I don't see that as a problem," the boy replied.

The Gaian prince nodded and turned back to where Gladius and Matthias were still at work. "Show the other three how to operate the controls. I'm going to take these two for a test run in the arena. It's been a while since I've had a good fight."

"Aye, but I wouldn't count on much of one, my prince," Gladius said from among the screens as he motioned for Darius, Link and Sarina to join them. "They're young no matter what way ya try and frame it."

"I'll keep it in mind, old friend." Venetor gave the Hurtz a sly grin and turning around, marched past the youth.

Darius, Link and Sarina had long since joined Matthias at the front, while he instructed them to use the screens, leaving Jason and Annetta where they stood. The two of them faced one another.

"Here we go again," Jason muttered sarcastically as familiar feelings from their first days resurfaced in his memory.

Annetta smiled in return, then turned her attention to the door where she could still see the disappearing visage of the man who was known as the Ironfisted.

⁍⁍⁍

Entering the Calanite diamond-walled training grounds, Annetta and Jason found Venetor with his back turned to them. The Gaian had stripped off his crimson cape, which he then tossed to the side of the arena. As soon as they were fully inside, they stopped and waited.

"I used to train with your fathers here once," Venetor said, with his back still turned to them. "They were no older than you are now."

"How old are you, then?" Jason inquired as he tried to do the math.

"Another thing I don't think the elf told you," the man chuckled. "A Gaian matures at the same rate a human does, but their life cycle is much longer than their Earth cousin. We can live up to and sometimes over three hundred years if the Unknown is willing. I assume then also that he never told you that being a psychic is hereditary. You both come from bloodlines filled with psychics and have the predisposition to one day have offspring that are as well. This gene's prominence depends on species. Mislantus would go around the universe and gather psychics to create an army, one of the reasons he was so dangerous. As to what causes it, no one has been able to crack the case, though some theologians say it has something to do with the Unknown. Now, as to how old am I? A question one such as myself rarely answers, least of all to someone like you. I've been around a long time. I've seen nations rise and fall. I've travelled the stars and have seen things you could scarcely ever imagine. I've made friends and enemies alike. I have loved and I have lost. I've fought in wars and I have won them, and that, my young friend, is all the answer you shall get."

"I've heard of being sensitive about your age, but that one just took the cake," Jason retorted.

"You think you're being cheeky, are you, boy?" Venetor growled. Widening his stance, he readied himself. "Let's see if you fight as well as you talk."

Jason glanced over at Annetta, who only shrugged and moved aside. The boy said nothing more and summoned Helbringer from its dormant state, holding the mace tightly in both hands.

Venetor watched him with an amused smile on his face. "You know, it's seen as unfair to bring a weapon to a fist fight."

"Who said Puc taught us to fight fair?" Jason remarked and with a roar of anger, charged towards Venetor, teleporting halfway in order to avoid being detected.

The Gaian seemed not to move from where he stood and closed his eyes at the oncoming attack. Jason reappeared some distance away from him, ready to strike. Venetor teleported away at the last second, the blades of the mace missing him by a hair. He then reemerged on the other side of the area.

"Sloppy," he commented. "You'll need to do better."

Jason gritted his teeth. "I'm just getting warmed up, old man."

"Old man?" Venetor intoned. "Who are you calling old man?"

"I think you know him quite well." Jason charged again and teleported.

Venetor, as if knowing, pivoted exactly to where Jason turned up next. The Gaian prince then grabbed hold of the mace and teleported it into his free hand. He then snatched Jason by the scruff of his shirt, flipping him onto the ground on his back.

"Were you referring to your fighting style?" Venetor scoffed, as he continued to hold the boy. Letting him go after he was sure Jason had had enough, he turned to Annetta. "You next."

Annetta swallowed hard after having seen how quickly her friend had been put down and entered the arena. She locked eyes with the man as Jason scurried out, still catching his breath.

Venetor went back into his fighting stance, every muscle coiling on his body underneath the skintight scale mail shirt. There was not an ounce of fatigue on him as though this was just the first round again. "Well? Are you going to attack me or am I going to have to coax it out of you, girl?"

"Is there really a point?" she asked. "I mean, you just took down J.K. like it was his first day at this."

"I would know how far along both of you are before I gauge how much work must be done," he explained. "Now, do I need to ask again?"

Annetta rolled her eyes and did not even bother going into a fighter stance, teleporting instead.

Venetor spun around in time to catch the blade of Severbane in between his hands, feeling the impression of the words etched into the blade under his palms. The girl had drawn it from its dormant state once she was out of his view and as soon as he had it, Annetta teleported away once more. Dropping the sword to the floor, Venetor turned again to see psychic fire coming his way and barely had time to teleport from the spot. Annetta recalled Severbane from the ground with her abilities and furiously scanned the arena for Venetor. Her quest was ended when an elbow slammed into her back, causing her to lose control of the weapon in her hands and fall to the floor.

"Pathetic," Venetor sneered. "A first-year militia would have more cunning than either of you. I don't know what the elf has been doing with you all this time, but you both clearly know nothing."

"Well, I don't know what you were expecting," Annetta growled as she got up, massaging her back with her hand. "Besides, we took down Mislantus and his goons well enough."

"Mislantus was a disgrace to the Gaians," Venetor barked. "I will have his name removed from all writing when I am king."

"Why?" Jason muttered from the side, "So some halfwit can commit his mistakes someday instead of learning from them?"

"No," Venetor turned to him. "So that he will not be remembered by the commons."

Annetta recalled Severbane once more to her and slid the blade into its scabbard. It unnerved her how quickly Venetor had disarmed them. What angered her, even more, was the fact that it was nothing Puc had not taught them before. He had simply been quicker. She looked over at Jason on the bench and could tell from his disgruntled face he was thinking the same.

"Whatever," she spat as she began to walk off. "You're not on Gaia anymore. Come on, J.K."

"And where are you both going?" Venetor demanded.

"Away," she stated and then added with a sarcastic overtone, "To let off some steam if we may, oh prince of Gaia."

Venetor watched, clenching his teeth as he prevented himself from lashing out. Once they had gone, he allowed himself to exhale a rough deep breath in order to empty his lungs of pent-up air. His frustrated wheeze was then accompanied by loud, obnoxious applause. He turned around to see the one-eyed Hurtz clapping his hands in a monotone fashion.

"Magnificent show, yer lordship," Gladius complemented as he walked further into the training arena. "I couldn't have said it all better myself, if I may."

"Quiet, you," Venetor growled. "I spoke the truth no matter what way you put it. It's a wonder they won against Mislantus as is."

"Aye, but they did." The Hurtz came to a standstill beside the Gaian. "I think ye forgot the most basic of lessons ye learned as a young man."

"I suppose this is where you enlighten me then," he retorted, going over to gather his cloak.

"If I can be so bold to say, my prince," Gladius continued, "All that is to be great starts from humble beginnings. A cub grows to be a lion."

Venetor's scowl did not leave his face as he listened to the Hurtz, fastening the crimson cape around his shoulders. "Perhaps I was a bit too harsh on them. Perhaps my expectations were too great. They were, after all, left in Thanestorm's hands."

"Thanestorm or not," Gladius said, "one goes by Kinsman and the other wears the name of Severio. Yet you know neither."

"I've no time-" Venetor began.

"You've time enough," the Hurtz interjected, "If ya are to need their aid in future events. Get to know 'em and see 'em for who they are."

The Gaian prince huffed upon hearing this. "I don't see how this will help in their training, but I suppose I owe them the common courtesy, seeing as I just crashed into their lives with nothing but revelation upon revelation."

Gladius chuckled and slapped a paw onto Venetor's shoulder. "And that, my prince, is how you win the heart of the people."

ಶಂಡ

Deciding to split up, Jason wishing to go see Sarina, Annetta made her way back to the lake biosphere. It had become her alternative spot for quiet when heading to the trails around Severio castle proved to be too long of a process. For the time being, it seemed like a good idea not to go far.

Entering, Annetta went down to the riverbank and walked along the shore until she came to where the stream finally spilt into the lake. Finding a large enough boulder to sit on, she climbed up and settled herself there. Her anger at Venetor had already started to dissipate somewhat as she stared into the blue waters before her, beating down on the brown murky sands. Closing her eyes, she allowed for the cool breeze to wash over her.

"Annetta!" the familiar voice of Link called from the location of the entrance.

The girl opened her eyes and turned around, but not seeing him, she sent a message through telepathy. *'I'm by the lake, come find me.'*

The youth came running as soon as she finished transmitting her thoughts to him. Shortly after, the sounds of crunching sticks and the swishing of long thin grass against fabric were accompanied by his unsteady descent down the hill towards her.

Smiling, Annetta moved over from her spot, allowing for the young Gaian to climb up beside her. "Took you long enough."

Link settled himself on the rock before glancing in her direction. "Hey, I got here as soon as I could. I had to wait till Matt figured out how to set everything up so it would scan automatically instead of having us all scan manually. Turned into more of a mess once he got Sarina, Darius and myself involved."

"Oh, I see," she said, bringing her knees to her chin and wrapping her arms around them.

"I could feel something was up though," he replied. "You went from shocked, to hurt to just down right angry."

Annetta raised an eyebrow at him. "You keep saying that, and it's kinda creepy."

Link chuckled. Stretching out on the rock, he lay down. "Don't ask. It all started after Brakkus made me swear that oath, or at least I think it did. Or maybe it has something to do with me accepting my feral form, but that's just a theory I have."

"Feral form?" the girl asked.

"Yeah," he began to explain. "Each Gaian has their own feral form, an animal native to Gaia which they can change into. We think that at one point, this form was used to hide from those who would try to use psychic abilities to read the minds of others. Some scientists think that before even that it was to avoid being killed by other Gaian tribes. There are many Gaians who no longer practice the art of learning to phase into a feral form with all the laws prohibiting mind reading and, well, the existence of an actual civilized culture. For those in the military or with noble status, it's considered a symbol of power if you're able to do so though."

"What kind of animals would people change into?" Annetta inquired, feeling intrigued by what she was learning. "How different were they on Gaia from the ones found here?"

"Many would be familiar to you," he assured her. "Gaia is the sister planet of Earth. Our two planets share an almost identical origin with only a few differences, like a Gaian's ability to phase into a feral form. We have creatures like horses, lions, bears, wolves, eagles and lizards, but some things you wouldn't know, like beta dragons, sabertooth dogs and ridge-maned lions. As for what people would change into, well, it depends on factors in their life, like what their parents changed into and what sort of person they are."

Annetta listened intently as he continued to talk. Though her grandfather had explained that Gaia was the sister planet of Earth, she gave no hint of it when Link spoke. She also noticed how easily all of the information fell out of him like he had wanted to tell her these things all along. Feeling cramped from having been in a balled-up position, she lay down beside him, watching the blue sky overhead. It still bewildered her how she was actually in a base, miles beneath the ocean.

"So, what were you?" she asked again when he had finished talking.

The boy looked at her. "I was a wolf, just as my father was before me and most likely my grandfather before him. Though. I only ever got to see my feral form once before the curse took hold."

"Well, you could have been a sabertooth dog for all I knew." She smirked.

The boy laughed. A year ago, such a comment would have insulted and even shamed him if he were to talk about it. Now, it was just another thing in his day. It was all thanks to Annetta and her friends being able to accept him even with the scar that was meant to mark him as an outcast on his home planet.

Annetta cracked a grin, her joke having hit its mark. She then caught herself looking into the grey eyes that belonged to her friend. She marvelled at how they reflected the sun, causing them to be alive in pale blue hues instead of lifeless shades. The girl then felt that magnetic force once again. A feeling she could scarcely begin to understand aside from a need to move closer. As she did so, she studied him, the broad hardened face that was now lined with light brown hairs around his chin and lips. She then gently brushed back the hair that was obscuring the scar that ran across his eye, in order to see it better. Annetta realized she was so close, she could feel his breath against her cheek. Still, she wanted to move closer and she could see that he wanted it too.

"Annetta!" another voice called, and once again the moment was lost.

The two of them turned around to see Venetor, standing upon the hill that overlooked the lake. Annetta blushed lightly, remembering how close she was to Link as she quickly moved away from him.

"Now what?" she groaned upon seeing the Gaian prince.

Venetor noted the two of them upon the rock, his eyes narrowing as he scanned the horizon. Then, in the steadiest pace he could muster, he made his descent.

Link immediately jumped off the rock and moved to the side upon seeing him approach and straightened his black shirt out as best as he could, checking to make sure his jacket was also smoothed out. Annetta found the gestures funny, but said nothing and remained casually on the rock. She was still, after all, annoyed with him.

"I come to make peace with you," he announced, stopping beside the rock. "That is, if you will listen to a thing I have to say."

The girl craned her head to the side to see Venetor standing beside her. Due to his shorter stature, he barely stood level with the rock she sat on.

"You know," Annetta mused, "That last bit there... sounded almost like a threat. Not very peaceful if you ask me."

Off to the side, Link kept his head lowered and did his best to not make eye contact with the prince. Though he knew full well his relationship to Annetta, the man still made him uncomfortable, more so than anyone else he had ever met in his life.

Venetor's jaw twitched slightly upon hearing the girl. The muscles and tendons in his arms coiled as his body prepared to lash out. Closing his eyes, however, the older Gaian said nothing in return. He had not come to her in order to start a fight. He tilted his head slightly upwards to see the pair of defiant blue eyes glaring back at him with an almost venomous hate. He knew those eyes. They were his eyes and the eyes of his brother, Orbeyus.

Annetta turned her head back to the lake, watching the waves roll in and out from the sandy bank. Her hopes were that Venetor would just go away if she ignored him, but it was not to be.

"You are lucky you are not on Gaia right now." Venetor's voice pierced her thoughts directly from behind.

The girl nearly jumped from where she sat and instinctively turned around to see Venetor towering above her. She then realized that he was not standing at all, but floating. The hairs on the back of her neck stood up as she recoiled a bit and stood up.

"How are you?" the words stopped in her throat as she pointed in his direction.

In a fluid movement, Venetor hovered upwards and landed on the rock in front of her.

"That is for me to know," he said with a smug look on his face, "And for you to find out, should you choose. Flight is perhaps one of the most fundamental things for a psychic to know how to do."

"Wait, you mean like actual flying through the air?" Annetta felt her jaw slack. What anger there had been festering in her before had all but dissipated.

"Don't act so surprised," he smirked. "I meant it when I said Puc hasn't taught you everything there is to know about being a psychic. Perhaps more harshly than I should have, but it is a truth. Stick with me and I will show you all that I know. It is the least I can do for my brother's granddaughter."

"How do I know you won't just blow up at us again?" she asked, somewhat suspicious.

"I had to see where you were at," he reiterated. "I could only do so by not holding back. You know the fundamentals, and so, one could argue that we are all equal, but there is one thing that sets us apart: experience."

Annetta bobbed her head in understanding. She still did not like how he had begun his training with them, but having heard what he said, it made sense in the aftermath. She then remembered that neither she nor Jason had ever been thrilled with the things Puc had made them do. With that in mind, she did her best to let the encounter from earlier on slide. Glancing down at her watch, she then realized the time.

"I need to get going home, actually," she said. Walking over to the edge, she jumped off the rock. "My parents don't like it when I stay down here too long, especially on a school night. They will come looking for me otherwise."

"At least you don't disrespect all your elders," Venetor snickered. "Very well. I expect to see both you and Jason down here tomorrow then. If you behave, then perhaps I will show you how to fly."

The girl smiled with her back turned to him. Perhaps training under Venetor the Ironfisted wouldn't be so bad after all. "I'll let him know."

The girl then began to make her way back up the hill towards the exit. Link, who had been standing off to the side in silence, also began to make his way to go after her. He was paralyzed, however, when the elder Gaian cleared his throat.

"And just where do you think you are going?" Venetor's voice boomed behind him, his arms crossed as he loomed over the boy from the rock he stood upon.

Link lowered his head slightly and turned around. "I was just going to walk Annetta back to the teleport station. Puc always had us walk in twos in case we stumbled across anything that had gotten in during the blackout."

"Oh, please," Venetor huffed. "You don't actually expect me to believe that after I just found you both on that rock. Do you think I was born yesterday, boy?"

Venetor jumped off from where he stood and landed on the ground with a thud. He then made his way over to Link in a brisk pace.

"This whole time, you have not faced me once," the Gaian prince spoke again. "You think I would not find such a thing suspicious?"

Cupping Link's jaw in his hand, he lifted his head up and moved aside his bangs, revealing the scar upon his face.

"Heallaws," he snarled as he let him go. "You are the son of Rannulf, aren't you?"

Link took a step back and rubbed his chin, feeling the imprint of where Venetor's fingers had held him. "I am, my lord."

"Then you know well what his crime was in his youth?" Venetor crossed his arms across his chest as he eyed Link up and down. "I should also not need to remind you of whom the girl you were lying with on a rock there was."

The youth lowered his gaze until his eyes met with the black running shoes on his feet. He shifted his legs awkwardly as if attempting to walk in the direction of the exit and away from the man before him. He wanted to run, but his better judgment prevented him from doing this.

"I do," he finally acknowledged, then added, "I also know that if she knew we were having this conversation she would not be happy."

"Don't you dare try to mouth back to me," Venetor snapped. "I am your prince and one day to be king! Her happiness is not of your concern. She is a Severio. In the long run, she will be happiest without one with traitor's blood in his veins at her side. If I see you with her again in such a manner, you will regret the day you ever came into this world."

Link opened his mouth as though to protest, but nothing came out. Despite being on Earth and in the safety of the Lab, he was still a Gaian, and nothing it seemed would ever change that. He then knelt before Venetor.

"Yes, my lord."

Chapter 11

Night having approached and the children having gone to bed, Arieus and Aurora stood on the steps of their patio in the backyard. The raised design had been Arieus's idea. When they had moved in, all that they found in the backyard were some slowly rotting cedar planks that had not been cared for in years. With the help of Annetta, Link and Xander, Arieus had demolished the old deck and created a new one.

The two of them stared quietly into the dark sky, watching the stars peaking through the wisps of navy blue clouds. The weather having gotten colder already, they both wore their winter coats over top of their clothing.

"Did Annetta say anything about the meteorite when she came home?" Aurora inquired.

"No," Arieus answered her. "In fact, I don't think I saw her at all today, to be honest, aside from when she came back up before bed. I'm not even sure she had dinner."

"Puc has been working them to the bone," Aurora grumbled. "Perhaps we should go talk to him?"

"A lot of good that will do," Arieus chuckled.

While the two of them spoke, Talia faded onto the patio, causing both Aurora and Arieus to jump back with fright. She was dressed in snow boots, pyjama bottoms and a long brown winter coat topped with a fur-lined hood.

"Talia? What are you doing here?" Aurora asked and then looked around frantically to make sure her neighbours were all inside. "Did anyone see you just now?"

"Dead of night. I highly doubt it," she assured her. "Besides, we have bigger problems to worry about."

"What are you talking about?" Arieus questioned her and then looked to his wife.

"Uhm...A meteorite in the middle of Toronto?" Talia stated, "As well as a very upset and angered son that came home and demanded to know if he was human or not."

The colour then drained from both Arieus and Aurora. They had both dreaded when this day would come.

"You can't mean..." Aurora began.

Talia could barely contain her rage as she forcibly ground her teeth in order not to speak too loudly. "Apparently, there is a certain Gaian prince within the confines of the Lab."

ဆၢ

His peace having been made with Annetta and his confrontation with Link having concluded, Venetor prowled through the confines of Q-16. He had many things which needed to be taken care of in a short span of time and it felt as though he was slowly being buried in a pit of quicksand. Every second counted, yet at every turn an obstacle became apparent.

Coming to a stop in the corridor leading to the living quarters, he ran a hand through his short hair, feeling it bristle roughly against his palm. He remembered these halls. He remembered how busy and vibrant they had once been with the sounds of Gaian and otherworldly armed forces alike. He even remembered which soldiers had occupied what rooms and their exact order. What he tried not to remember, however, were his final days during his last stay. He tried not to remember the tears of his sister when he told her the news of their brother's death and the inevitable collapse of the Four Forces. He had been there through it all. He had survived.

Venetor had carried his current crusade to Earth with a heavy heart. It had been a last resort. Seeing the young girl standing upon the hill had brought some hope back to him. Perhaps the work of Orbeyus Severio had not been in vain.

A pair of heavy boots echoed through the hallway, and soon, the form of Matthias Teron beckoned from under the pale blue halogen lights. Dark circles ringed the assassin's azure eyes and the rest of his facial hair had begun to come in from a long night.

"I checked once more on the screens, but nothing," he reported to Venetor. "The latest, we should know is by tomorrow afternoon."

"Good." Venetor nodded. "I'm sure also once we recover Skyris, she can have a look at the system and optimize it for speed. I doubt anything has been upgraded since last she set foot in here."

"More than likely," the assassin agreed. "I can't see Puc or Brakkus ever having tinkered with the hardware."

Venetor returned a stiff smile to him, studying the younger man intently from head to toe. "Of what origin are you?"

"I'm not quite sure, to be honest," Matthias answered. "I was just a boy when I was brought on board Valdhar. Once there, no one ever thought to tell me my species or where I actually came from. I only remembered years later that I had a little sister."

"How is it that you came to be here?" Venetor queried.

"I was originally charged to gain access to the Lab and to end Annetta and Jason." Matthias recounted.

Venetor eyed the man suspiciously as the muscles in his back tensed. For all he knew, Matthias was still working for the now dead tyrant.

Sensing this, Matthias spoke again, "When Annetta and Jason went to go and recruit the Ogaien back into the Four Forces, we were all forced to partake in the Visium. It was there that I learned my parents had been killed on Mislantus's command along with the sister I remembered."

"I see." Venetor nodded, relaxing somewhat.

There was a pause between the two of them for some time, neither knowing what to say to the other.

Venetor then voiced his thoughts. "And in all that time, you never bothered to find out where it is you come from? I'm not quite sure whether to marvel at your lack of passion on the subject or to feel sorry for you."

Matthias opened his mouth and paused. His mind wandered to when he had phased into the bear creature while fighting Link, something he had not been aware of being able to do, then to an older memory when he had tried to learn his origin. "On Valdhar, we fought as one unit. Your species and race were considered unimportant. I tried once, I believe, and after being given that as an answer, I no longer cared."

Venetor bobbed his head but then added as an afterthought, "Perhaps it is for the best, and yet, I find that knowing one's past helps us understand who we truly are in the greater scope of things."

"I might look into it again one day." Matthias yawned, covering his mouth with his hand. "For now, I'm going to get some shut eye."

Moving past the Gaian, the assassin did not look back with any further words.

Venetor watched as his silhouette disappeared into one of the rooms. Alone again, he resolved to continue his walk and became enthralled by his thoughts once more. Before he knew it, he found himself within the common room area. He stopped to look around at the small group of couches that had been pushed together, while all the other seats remained off to the sides. He remembered a time when all of them had been scattered around the room, and at times there was no space to sit. He smiled inwardly at the thought. Further musing on his past was interrupted when he heard the sounds of more feet approaching. He turned in their direction. Coming towards him were three people he had been certain he would not see again.

Arieus, Aurora and Talia froze in their tracks as soon as they were able to make out a clear image of the person directly in front of them. He was a hard man to forget, dressed in his crimson cape and emanating soldier-like bravado to match.

"Venetor Severio." The name escaped the lips of Talia as she crossed her arms. "I had a feeling you'd be the one making a grand entrance."

"You're too kind, Talia." He flashed a wicked grin. "And dare I say, the years have not changed you or your temperament at all."

The woman did not answer and continued to stare him down until Arieus got into their line of sight. "What do you want?"

"Why is it that I am always wanting something?" Venetor queried. "What if, perhaps, I just happened to be flying by and decided to pay a visit to what is left of my extended family here on Earth?"

This time, Aurora stepped in. "I think the only one you are fooling with that answer is yourself."

"Such hostility in this room." The Gaian prince shook his head. "In a room that was meant to unite all as one during the time my brother lived. Could we not revert to a more peaceful manner of greeting?"

"Depends on your definition of peace," Talia snapped.

Venetor chuckled inwardly and crossing his arms, leaned against one of the couches. "Fair enough. As to my reasons for being here, they do not concern any of you, seeing as you have all given up on this aspect of life."

"With good reason." Arieus furrowed his brows as he glared at the man. "It cost us too much."

"And yet, you allow your children to participate," he pondered. "It's strange, given the fact that a parent's first line of duty is to protect their child."

None of those gathered spoke back. The only indication of their mood was the tension which danced through the air like an electric current.

"It doesn't mean we will not worry," Aurora finally retorted, in an effort to keep the conversation going.

"And you have a right to do so," Venetor acknowledged. "It will not change the fact of what I said. My reasons for coming are for them, and them alone to know. Despite what you may think of me, Annetta is also my niece. You may want to consider that I do care for her well-being in my own way, as well as that of Jason, seeing as he is a Kinsman and we share a common ancestor."

Aurora and Talia seemed somewhat satisfied with what the Gaian said. Arieus, on the other hand, was not. He continued to glare at Venetor with the ferocity of a wild animal. Seeing no point in arguing with the man any further, he finally exhaled, allowing his own anxiety to disperse.

"This does not mean I will stay out of it," Arieus sneered. He then turned to make his way back without anything else to say.

Venetor kept his position and watched as the trio disappeared again. Once gone, he relaxed and lowered his arms to his sides. He was beginning to grow tired, the fatigue of space travel finally catching up to him. Shaking his head to keep himself awake, he turned back to the living quarters, leaving memories in the past in order to dream of a new tomorrow.

ഇരൽ

The next day after the final school bell rang, Liam waited outside, huddled in his slightly-too-big navy blue winter jacket. The late autumn wind ruffled his brown unkempt hair as he scanned the opening and closing doors of the school with his green eyes for any possible glimpse of his friend. Finally seeing Xander emerge among the commotion of students, he smiled.

"Alexandrius!" he called him by his full name and waved.

The other boy stood dazed for a moment and upon seeing his friend he waved back and jetted in his direction before greeting him. "I thought you already started to head home."

"Nah." Liam shook his head. "I wanted to see how you were doing after...you know..."

The smile evaporated from Xander's face as he nodded. "I think I'm okay... I just still don't get it, you know?"

Liam inclined his head in reply, and then looked up. "I think I may know what's going on. You think you can head over to my place for a bit before going home?"

"I guess so," the other boy replied, straightening the backpack on his shoulders and followed his friend.

‰

Before they knew it, they had made it to Liam's house and soon found themselves in his and Jason's room. His older sibling rarely making an appearance, Liam had all but claimed the room for himself, his clothes piled on top of both beds as well as his other belongings. Putting his bag down, Liam set to go through his closet.

Xander took the opportunity to move some of the clothing aside from one of the beds and sat down. He nearly parked his rear end on a discarded action figure before placing it on a nightstand. He smiled, knowing full well his own room would not be much different were it not for his mother constantly coming in and checking on it.

"Okay, there we go," Liam finally said as he pulled out a large box from the depths of his closet and slid it across the floor until it stopped right beside Xander.

The second boy curiously lifted the lid to reveal the contents inside, "Comics?"

"Graphic novels," Liam corrected him as he plopped down beside his friend. "It didn't start making any sense to me until I remembered that I had these from when my brother used to collect them."

Xander lifted one of the thin papery booklets with a colourful cover as he examined the animated characters on the front. "What do comics have to do with us?"

"Everything!" Liam exclaimed, "Don't you see that everything that just happened to us is a superhero origin story? We went to go check out a meteorite, and then you electrocute a ball of snow and like... short circuit half the neighbourhood. Good thing people around just blamed it on the meteorite and we got away."

"I don't think that's how it happened." Xander screwed up his face and flipped through the book.

"Who you gonna trust?" Liam asked, "You were half out of it. I was there to see the whole thing."

Xander groaned as he put the comic book back in the box. "I just think that if it's anything, maybe we should tell our parents. I mean... Anne and J.K. are obviously up to something similar. We've both known this for some time now. We've both seen them use the teleporter at my house. We might not know where they go but, something's definitely up."

"That's like breaking the first law of superhero origins," Liam protested. "We can't tell them! Are you kidding me? No superhero ever told their parents from the get go that they had superpowers. That's just insane."

"Our families aren't exactly normal," Xander tried to reason with him. "I mean, didn't you see J.K. make things float in your room like a year ago?"

Liam then got up and walked to the other side of the room, closing the door. He then paused and stood with his back turned for a good long time.

Xander knotted his brows upon seeing his friend's behaviour and would have almost missed the box of comics beginning to hover up off the ground, the books themselves floating away from their prison. He jumped back, caught unaware by the sight unfolding.

"Maybe it was him, or maybe it was me," Liam stated as he turned around.

"How long have you known you can do this?" Xander questioned, feeling the hairs on the back of his neck stand up.

"Does it really matter?" the other boy asked in a nonchalant tone. "A month, maybe more. My point is that if Anne and J.K. are up to something or know about this and we were meant to be part of it, wouldn't they have said something about it to us sooner?"

"Maybe," Xander answered, poking at one of the comics as it glided by him. "There's always the chance they don't know we have any sort of powers."

"There is that chance." Liam nodded. "But I wouldn't take risks. For all we know, they may hunt people like us... maybe they work for CSIS or someone like that."

Xander frowned hearing the accusation. He was willing to believe a lot of things. He remembered the night of lightning after all, but somehow the notion of his sister being a secret agent seemed doubtful. This was Annetta they were talking about, his big sister. He still remembered when she was going through her first year of high school, dyed her hair purple and wore punk band shirts. It was a short lived phase, mostly due to Annetta realizing half the other girls in school were doing it and she didn't want to be like everyone else. She would still listen to the music, but the days of punk-rock Annetta were very much gone. Perhaps it was a strange thing to think of, but to Xander, it painted the picture of his sister not being very different than the average teenager.

He then looked over at his friend who was convinced that keeping it all secret was their best option. In a way, Xander agreed. Everyone around them seemed to be keeping secrets. Why shouldn't they have something to call their own?

"All right," he finally agreed. "What do we do now?"

"Isn't it obvious?" Liam snickered as he lowered the box gently to the floor. "We give ourselves secret identities and we go out to kick some butt. We'll need to train before we're ready for that, though."

Losing his concentration, the comics fell to the floor, scattering everywhere like raindrops. Xander removed the comic that had artfully landed on his head and looked around, seeing the plethora of paper which covered almost every inch of the room.

"Before any of that, I think I need to clean my room, or I'm grounded for eternity."

Chapter 12

The last bell for the day having rung, Annetta and her friends made the journey down to the Lab in their usual manner. There was a silence that surrounded the group this time around, however, and it was not a byproduct of a long night out. It was of knowing that nothing would be the same when they would arrive. Each of them felt this hollow pain in their own way, dealing with it on different scales of variance.

Making the descent, they went their separate ways, Sarina to go help Darius, Link to go tend to the horses, Annetta and Jason to go face what would be awaiting them in the training arena.

The duo's shoes felt as though they had been suddenly lined with iron as they trudged down the hallways to their destination. Neither of them was looking forward to being humiliated again.

"I don't see why we have to listen to him," Jason finally spoke. "I mean, we did beat Mislantus and his whole army no matter how you look at it."

"Oh, trust me, I've looked at it," Annetta retorted, "Looked at it so much that I've run out of ways to look at it."

"He had to have used some spell or something," Jason continued to rant. "I mean...there's just no way. I won't believe it. It's not possible."

"You can live in denial all you want, J.K.," the girl sighed. "We got our butts handed to us and that's that."

"Doesn't mean I have to like it." He gritted his teeth as they came to a stop.

"Nor should you," the voice of Venetor came from the training arena.

Annetta and Jason both gave each other a quizzical look before they quickened their pace to where the voice had come from. There, Venetor was standing with his back to them, his arms folded across his chest. He had cast off the Gaian uniform he had worn the day before and traded it in for combat boots, dark grey jeans and a white t-shirt.

"Isn't retrieving like...super bad?" Jason furrowed his brows, raising his hands in a questioning manner.

"You are correct, Kinsman." The shorter man spun around on his heel. "However, I was not reading any of your thoughts. I merely amplified my own hearing so that I can hear what you were saying from further away."

The two youth glanced at one another yet again in confusion. Neither could fathom how their abilities could allow them to do such a thing.

The Gaian prince chuckled, seeing their perplexed looks. "You forget that you are both Gaian as well. I can only assume this means you have not yet tapped into your feral forms."

"Feral what?" Jason inquired.

Venetor cleared his throat and then began, "Every Gaian holds the ability to transform themselves into a single animal with which they associate themselves with, or has some historical significance to their family. All warriors on Gaia are required to learn how to phase or to at least have a mental link with their form, achieved through meditation. This allows them to tap into the feral form's abilities, which they can then use on the battlefield. These abilities include but are not limited to a heightened sense of hearing, smell, sight, speed and strength. They can become especially handy when dealing with someone who happens to have a charm or spell that makes them immune to psychic abilities. Under my instruction, you will learn to harness these, but first, you will need to discover what your form is. I will also further your knowledge and skill in using your psychic abilities, seeing as your current level of use is almost infantile."

Annetta and Jason did their best to hold their tongue upon hearing the last part of what he said. They remembered all too well when a certain elf had spoken to them in a tone that did not vary much from the current one. Granted, Puc had not humiliated them in their first training session.

"Alright then, teach, what's first?" The girl threw up her hands before letting them fall limply at her sides.

Seeing as no one else had anything to add, Venetor nodded and continued, "I will want you both to take an hour each day to meditate in order to uncover your feral form. There is not much we can do here in the arena before then about learning to hone those abilities. Now, let us focus on your psychic skills. As I mentioned last night to Annetta, the only thing which truly sets you and I apart is experience. Psychic abilities are focused on strategy and in being able to read your opponent. If you've ever heard the words 'all is fair in love and war,' it certainly applies here to war. If you can mould something to your needs as a weapon, it works. If you can surprise your opponent in some way, it works. If you can think of it, chances are they will as well and you need to be one step ahead. You need to analyze everything and be aware of all things all the time. Battling a psychic is not a duel of honour, it is fighting at its most cunning. You will either emerge victorious or you will die. Such is the way of this world."

"So how exactly are we supposed to get better?" Jason inquired.

"Simple," Venetor replied. "You fight and you explore. Exploration is your greatest tool in understanding your abilities. While Thanestorm did provide you with the basics, I assume aside from your use of psychic fire that you have not looked into them more."

"We learned to amplify the force of a blow in a weapon," Annetta said after giving it some thought.

"A good start," the Gaian acknowledged. "It is safe to presume after the conversation I had with Annetta last night that neither of you has attempted to fly before."

"Not since I was a kid in a cape jumping off the top dresser." Jason smirked, remembering the look on his mother's face when she came in and caught him.

"I won't even ask," Venetor exhaled.

The Gaian prince then straightened his posture. Taking another deep breath, he began to rise off the ground until he hovered some few feet above it.

"The concept is not much different than lifting another object off the ground," he explained. "Focus in the same way, but instead of focusing on something else, your body is the object. Let's see if you can both catch up to me."

He then shot up, stopping short of the lights that hung overhead. Annetta and Jason glanced at one another and giving each other the nod to go, focused as told. They were rewarded as their bodies began to float upwards.

"So... is this the point where we both say we can fly and go to Neverland?" Jason cracked a grin only to have Annetta roll her eyes at him.

When they arrived at their destination, Venetor continued with further instructions. "Easy enough, wouldn't you agree? Such a small alteration to a skill you already knew, and yet it makes all the difference. Now, one more question remains, and that is... can you catch me?"

Before either of them could say anything, Venetor shot past the youth as a blur of colours to end up on the other side of the arena.

Jason thought nothing of it and launched himself in the direction of Venetor. It seemed simple until he was forced to stop himself, causing his body to jerk forward awkwardly and nearly lose his dinner in the process. He clenched his stomach, feeling queasy as the juices roiled in his guts.

"A process which requires some fine tuning," Venetor assured him. Watching out of the corner of his eye, he grabbed Annetta, who was about to collide into him. "And practice."

The Gaian then descended to the bottom, waiting for Annetta and Jason to follow him before speaking again, "From what Matthias has told me, you both still attend school. Each day after your classes, you will report here to me. We will first practice flight, and then you will spar with one another as well as myself."

"What about weapons training?" Annetta asked.

"You will speak with Gladius about that," Venetor stated. "He is more skilled than anyone I know in the art of swordplay and marksmanship."

Before further words could be exchanged, Matthias teleported into the room a few feet away from them both.

"I think we found what you were looking for," the assassin said abruptly, without any underlying context.

Venetor gave no reply and instead teleported out of the room. Annetta and Jason turned to Matthias questioningly, not sure what to make of any of it.

"Meet us in the control room," he said to them and was off himself.

∞⊙∝

Teleporting themselves into the control room, Annetta and Jason found Matthias, Venetor and Gladius, who were huddled around two of the glass screens, while Venetor moved the angle of what was being seen using his hands. Noting the presence of the youth in the corner of his eye, the Gaian turned to face them.

"The other pod has been located," he declared. "I will be leaving tonight in order to retrieve my sister, son and Atala."

Turning around from his current position, Venetor grabbed a leather jacket he'd stashed earlier and threw it on as he moved out of the room. Peering over at the screen where he had been standing, Annetta and Jason saw what looked like another crater, snow mostly having covered the depression where it had fallen to make it look like nothing out of the ordinary among the snow. Gladius quickly hastened to Venetor's side.

"My lord, ye shouldn't be going off on yer own like this," the Hurtz commented.

"This is Earth, Gladius," he answered. "I'm sure I can hold my own."

"Ye don't know the lay of the land," Gladius added, "I know full well ye can take yer own hits."

Venetor stopped in his tracks and turned to regard him. "Then what course of action are you proposing I take?"

"I can go with him," Annetta offered.

"And do what?" Matthias queried, "If anyone is to go, it will be me."

"The hell is that supposed to mean?" The girl shot him an angry glare.

"It means you are not qualified," Matthias began, only to have Venetor clasp a hand on his shoulder, causing the assassin to turn around and face him.

"If she wishes it, she can accompany us," the Gaian told him. "I see no harm in greater numbers. This isn't a stealth mission, after all."

Jason, who had observed the whole conversation, pulled Annetta off to the side. "You gonna be okay going off on your own with this guy? I mean… what if it's a trap?"

"Then I have Matt with me," she assured him. "Plus I feel like I should go. He is family, even if he was a huge jerk about all the training before."

"Yeah, but family don't mean he isn't out to get you. Look at Sarina and her dad's relationship or even mine. I just don't like it," the boy admitted. "But do what you gotta do, I guess."

The girl bobbed her head in thanks, before looking back at the others.

Venetor approached the screens again and began zooming out of the image as he assessed the area around it. "Looks desolated. We should be able to teleport in and out easily enough."

"But Puc always said we needed to be careful not to be caught with our powers," Jason protested.

The Gaian snorted upon hearing the remark. "We will not be caught in the middle of nowhere. There isn't a living soul in sight."

Just as quickly as he had responded, he was gone, and appeared upon the very screen he had been observing just seconds before. Annetta and Matthias frowned at one another but said nothing and followed, leaving Jason and Gladius to observe from within the base.

⁖⁗

The cold hit her almost instantly upon teleporting. Feeling the frost bite at her hands and face, Annetta withdrew into her jean jacket. Getting a feel for her surroundings, she noted the entire area was covered in coniferous trees that were decorated in snow. There was also no sign of any human activity to be seen, not even the distant humming of cars on a freeway. She could see why Venetor had disregarded the rule about being seen. A chilling wind blew past her, reminding her of her primary problem.

"Man, I know we're in Canada, but-" her teeth chattered as she spoke, not bothering to finish the sentence.

Matthias arrived moments after, having a similar reaction, not having expected the weather as it was. The only one who seemed unaffected was Venetor, who was already down in the crater, inspecting the craft from the outside.

Annetta ran down the hill to meet with him. "And?"

"They've gone," he informed her, before raising a piece of parchment-like paper for the girl to see. "I found this on the outside. Typical Skyris. She never was one for staying in one place."

The girl reached for the paper only to have it snatched by Matthias, who had snuck up behind her. The assassin scanned it and then lowered his hand. "What now, then?"

"We find, and I quote the text, the closest and loudest bar," the Gaian mused.

"And how do you propose we do that?" Annetta asked.

"Just follow me," he said plainly and began walking without so much as an explanation of where they were going.

The girl wanted to protest but stopped herself when she noticed that Venetor was following sets of half covered tracks that had been left in the snow by whoever had come out of the pod in the first place. Not missing a beat, she fell in line with him, Matthias following her without a word.

"So... what do we do when the snow ends?" she probed.

"I'll worry about that when it comes to it," he stated.

"You're telling us you have no plan?" Matthias shook his head.

"No," Venetor interjected. "I am simply saying don't worry about it because I can smell the trail."

"What are you? A bloodhound?" Annetta quipped.

"A Gaian trained at accessing their feral form's abilities at will," Venetor retorted. "Honestly, did the elf teach you so little about your heritage?"

"Well, to be honest, we were under the impression that we were human," the girl replied.

"That would be typical of Thanestorm to say nothing," the Gaian spat.

"Why do you hate Puc so much, anyway?" Matthias asked, trying to change the subject.

"I have my reasons," he said simply. "Reasons you will one day find out, but right now they are unimportant, seeing as we need to get moving and figure out just how far my dear old sister dragged the others out to."

As if in answer to their conversation, the group stopped atop a hill. Down below gleamed the lights of a settlement in the distance. An assortment of dark wooden buildings, laced through with more modern ones suggested to Annetta they had ended up on the outskirts of a small town. She glanced over at Venetor in question once more but was ignored as the short, stocky Gaian continued on his path down towards the town.

"The sooner you get a move on, the sooner you get to be indoors again," he said as if he knew how cold the girl was.

Annetta growled, wrapped her jacket around her tighter and trudged on through the snow to their current destination without another word.

They walked for what seemed like hours to her until they set foot on the salted-down concrete sidewalks of the town that she had noted from the sign was called Alova. Annetta scrunched up her face as she tried to remember if she had heard anything about it in her geography class, but drawing a blank, she simply shook her head and turned around to see Venetor already a street and a half away with Matthias. Bolting, she rushed over to them, their pace decreasing as Venetor raised a hand to signal for them to stop.

"What now?" Annetta huffed as she caught her breath, watching it rise on the wind before her under the light of a street lamp.

The Gaian did not answer the girl and wordlessly walked around in a circle. Annoyed, the girl was about to snap another remark when she heard the faint sound of music blasting in the distance. Slack-jawed, she looked over at Venetor again.

"Oh dear little sister," he mused, "What have you been up to now?"

೧೦೧೩

Turning and twisting down the maze of streets, Venetor soon led Annetta and Matthias to a building lined with wooden logs, giving it the feeling of a cabin in the woods. Yellow light bulbs hung loosely from the roof, further giving the building a cozy country feel, complete with a wooden sign hanging overhead with the name McNavern's carved into it. Rock music could be heard blaring from inside the building, accompanied by the smell of fried foods, beer and smoke from the few patrons brave enough to venture outside to have a light.

"And you are sure this is the place a Gaian princess would go to?" Matthias asked.

Venetor chuckled lightly and turned to the assassin. "Trust me when I say this. Skyris is everything but conventional royalty."

Not adding anything else, Venetor strode towards the door and pushed it open, allowing the music to blast through the entrance into the outdoors. Annetta looked over at Matthias to see what his thoughts on the matter were, only to have the assassin glance in the direction of the entrance and then back at the girl with a sarcastic 'ladies first' look. The girl sighed and followed suit.

The interior of the locale was darkened for the most part with dim blue and purple lighting available to the patrons. The bar itself was the only area where bright yellow lights beaconed to those who would want to order another beverage, a busy bartender conversing with one of the bearded plaid-wearing locals in a bomber hat. Annetta glanced around in a perplexed manner as she tried to see where Venetor had gone off to, only to have a gruff, thin man slam into her, causing the contents of his glass to spill onto the sleeve of Annetta's jacket.

"Watch it!" he growled. "You gonna pay for that?"

Before Annetta could respond, a hand from behind gripped her shoulder, moving her slightly back.

"I think it's you who should be watching where you're going." Matthias gave the man a sly smile, to which the local only grumbled something under his breath and proceeded to go back to the bar. The assassin then turned to the girl. "Stick close to me, this isn't exactly a trip to Aldamoor."

"I figured as much," Annetta grumbled.

Her attention then moved to the other corner of the room. There, on one of the solitary vertical beams coming down from the ceiling to the floor and holding up the building, a woman in her thirties danced in rhythm to the music being played. She was surrounded by a group of at least ten men. In general, Annetta would not have wasted any time in looking at what was going on, but something about the woman made her continue to do so. Copious black hair cascaded down her back and past her chest, swaying back and forth, enveloping her shapely, well-muscled form. Her thick red lips were parted in a grin revealing a set of white teeth, and her icy blue eyes twinkled with a mischievous streak in them as she continued her routine. She was dressed in a black tank top and jeans that were tucked into high black boots. There was a confidence that radiated from her, the likes of which Annetta had never seen from anyone she knew. This illusion was broken when the girl saw the woman grab a shot of whiskey from one of her admirers and down it.

"I see you found her." Venetor's voice caused Annetta to jump up and turn around. "Not exactly how I pictured your introduction would go."

"That's Skyris?" Matthias raised an eyebrow curiously.

"The one and only." Venetor's eyes continued to scan the room until they fell upon a table not too far from the woman. He waved and then began to walk over to it.

Annetta noted a young man sitting there along with another woman, both of them caressing a single glass of beer on the table.

"My son and your cousin, Titus," Venetor indicated to the tall young man with a narrow face, shaggy dirty blonde hair and sideburns wearing a thick grey winter coat. Annetta could see the resemblance between father and son, though Titus was far narrower in the chest than his father, his build closer to that of someone who was a runner. His blue eyes fixated on the girl, he extended a hand to Annetta. Venetor then turned to the woman who wore her hair in a long thick braid and was dressed in a red coat. She wore a grim expression, her golden eyes and dark complexion further accentuating this, giving her at times the appearance of a great jungle cat that was observing her prey. "Atala Shade, sworn shield to my sister Skyris."

"Thank the Unknown you found us," the woman named Atala sighed. "I was worried I'd have to drag her out soon and look for other lodgings."

"How long have you been here?" Venetor inquired.

"A couple of hours," Titus answered, "But aunt Skyris already managed to finish two pitchers of beer, and I believe she is on her eighth shot of whiskey."

"Did she at least adhere to the rule of beer before..." Venetor used his hands to finish the sentence as Titus bobbed his head in response. "Well, she managed to remember that, if not her limit."

Further conversation was cut off by Skyris's laughter as she left her pseudo-stage once the song that had been playing finished. She then flopped into the lap of one of the admirer's closest to her, draping her sweat-beaded arms around his neck and resting her feet on the table.

"I ain't ever met a woman like you," the man blurted out, handing her another shot from the table.

"And that love is because there are no other women like me," she giggled, taking a sip from the glass, savouring the liquid inside of it, "At least not here."

"Oh? Where do I gotta move to then?" he asked with a grin on his face.

Venetor took this as his cue to move in. "Skyris, there you are. I think it's time to go home, sister."

Skyris, downing the rest of her drink, looked over at Venetor with glazed eyes. "Oh...you made it. Well...you see, I'm just not ready to go yet, and-"

The next song began to play. Skyris cracked an even wider grin upon hearing the opening and jumped from her human perch onto the table next to her. The men began cheering upon seeing their entertainment restored to them.

An annoyed twitch of the lips passed Venetor's visage. He got ready to withdraw in order to call the others to move, only to collide with the same patron Annetta had run into earlier. There was a shattering of glass that could be heard over the ambience of the bar as the load the man carried dropped. The next thing Venetor knew, a fist sailed through the air and the Gaian only managed to escape it by seconds. Pivoting on his foot out of the way, he watched as his assailant stumbled and fell onto another table, taking the contents of it down with him. The occupants of the table glanced down in shock only to see the man rise in a staggering fashion and turn around to throw himself at Venetor once more. By this point, the bouncer that had been keeping close to the door was making his way over along with a soberer regular in tow as a backup.

"I think that is our signal to leave," Matthias said to Annetta as the two of them rose from their seats, followed by Titus and Atala.

While Matthias, Annetta and Titus shuffled towards the exit, Atala moved towards where Skyris was still immersed in her dancing. Standing at over six feet tall, Atala cut an imposing figure as she passed through the crowd of men with ease and gripped Skyris's wrist.

"Alright, that's enough Sky," she said in a firm but calm tone, pulling the drunken woman down from the table.

"Awe, come on," Skyris groaned, "I'm just getting warmed up."

Before she could say anymore, the man Venetor had been fighting crashed into the table, sending Skyris toppling to the floor. Seconds later Venetor arrived and grabbing Skyris's arm he pulled her up.

"We're leaving," he barked the order and half led, half dragged his sister out.

Annetta and the others were already outside at this point, the girl's teeth chattering from the cold air once again as she huddled in her jacket, savouring the last of the heat from her venture into the bar. Snow had begun to fall again, leaving a crisp new layer of white on the ground around them.

As soon as they emerged, Venetor let go of Skyris, allowing her to stumble towards the nearest streetlight to steady herself. The woman continued to giggle for what seemed like no apparent reason.

"Did that just…really happen?" she chuckled, taking a loose strand of her hair and pushing it behind her ear, nearly losing her balance in the process.

"We need to get you inside." Atala rushed over to her, putting Skyris's arm around her shoulder to support her.

"But we just came from inside. I wanna be out now," Skyris pouted.

Before anything else could be said or done, Venetor came up behind Skyris and pinched the side of her neck, causing the woman to fall asleep and go limp in Atala's arms. She looked curiously at him for an explanation as to why he had just done that.

"She was being a liability," he said sternly. "We both know how Skyris gets when she indulges and we don't have much time if they notified the authorities of our presence. Now, I don't know about any of you but I would rather not spend my night in a human prison cell."

Atala nodded in acknowledgement and hoisted Skyris over her shoulder as though she were nothing more than a sack of grain. She then followed Venetor.

As this all unfolded, Annetta, Matthias and Titus stood off to the side, the assassin and the girl with quizzical looks on their faces. Titus seemed the only one who was taking it all in stride.

"My aunt, our aunt I suppose, likes to party." Titus turned to the girl. "She's been like that ever since I can remember, really. It will really deceive you right now, but Skyris is a force to be reckoned with, possibly more than my own father."

"I definitely find that hard to believe," Matthias scoffed, crossing his arms. "Back on Valdhar, we had female fighters but, even the most elite of them did not become that inebriated."

Before the assassin could continue his rant, he found himself staring down the barrel of a colt revolver. Matthias's gaze wandered past the weapon to see Titus on the other end, his eyes glaring at him with cold rage.

"Uh... you realize I am a psychic, right?" He raised an eyebrow along with his hands.

"Good, then you should realize I'm not human," Titus retorted as he removed the safety from the gun.

"Whoa! Time out!" Annetta waved her arms in protest. "Titus put it down."

"Why do you associate with this one?" he demanded, not moving.

"What do you mean why?" the girl questioned angrily. "Matt was part of the reason we blew that fortress sky high in the first place. He helped rescue Jason from Mislantus's dungeons and helps in training us in the psychic arts."

Titus lowered the arsenal, his face returning to its neutral look. He locked the safety once more and proceeded to conceal the weapon on the belt he wore beneath his jacket, his eyes never leaving Matthias.

"I wouldn't trust him," he stated in the aftermath. "Once a servant of the seven-headed beast, always a servant of the seven-headed beast."

"I suppose your little code doesn't include those whose family was murdered by said beast," Matthias sneered.

As the two of them exchanged insults, Annetta looked around at their surroundings to see Venetor, Atala and Skyris nowhere in sight.

"Uhm…guys…bigger problem," she began. "We lost them."

The assassin clenched his jaw and looked to where Annetta was turned, seeing the tracks in the snow.

"Not yet we haven't," he spoke after analyzing the prints. "Though if we waste any more time, we may."

Matthias still felt Titus's eyes burrowing themselves into his back, and so he turned to face him. "To be continued, where we can't get stranded in a hick human town."

"As you'll have it," Titus scoffed, "Servant of the beast."

"Whatever floats your boat." Matthias rolled his eyes and proceeded down the road where the tracks led.

Chapter 13

With the quest for retrieving the missing members of Venetor's travelling party having concluded, life within the base resumed. Or at least, it attempted to resume as best as it could given the new set of circumstances.

Awakening early the next morning after the events, Link found himself trudging down the halls towards the stables. His mind still weighed heavily on the encounter he'd had with Venetor. While he understood the prince's concern for Annetta, part of him screamed at the thought of having to stay away. It was as if someone was taking a hot iron rod to his wrists and commanding him not to move. He knew he needed to leave, to get away, but he couldn't. Mulling things over as he walked, he realized it was the part that allowed him to sense the girl's presence. Silently deciding to confront Venetor when he had a chance on the subject, he stepped into the stables and began his morning routine.

All this was interrupted when the Gaian youth heard footsteps approaching some distance away, along with the jingling of metal. Sword hand at the ready, he turned to meet the source of the noise. His stance relaxed somewhat when he saw Gladius enter. The one-eyed Hurtz strode in without a single word, his blind side the only thing visible to Link at the angle he stood. The Hurtz then craned his head around slowly, turning to look at him with an air of authority.

Link swallowed hard and spoke. "Is something the matter?"

Gladius stood in silence for a moment as he regarded Link. His single good eye gazed into him, piercing his flesh with predatory persistence.

"I want to know the whole story of me brother's death," the creature informed him as he took a step towards him. "I also want ta know why ye be the one bonded to Annetta and what significance ye had to Brakkus."

"Bonded?" Link raised an eyebrow, not very familiar with the term.

"Aye, bonded." Gladius shook his head. "When a warrior is mentally linked to another, as I am bonded to Venetor and his descendants and just as my brother was bonded to Orbeyus and his."

The young man continued to look at the Hurtz as though he were making things up on the spot. He knew however exactly what he was referring to and had hoped that it had not been true.

Seeing the spark of recognition in him, Gladius smiled wryly. "Brakkus made you swear an oath before he passed on, didn't he?"

Remembering the encounter with the wyvern and the last moments of Brakkus's life, Link gritted his teeth, "He did. As to why, I'm not sure. I was training under him before he died... he was a good friend of mine despite not having known him long."

Gladius flattened his good ear along with the damaged one when he heard the confession. There was no immediate response from him, his animalistic eye surveying every inch of the boy, unflinching. His verdict finally made, the ears retracted to their neutral position.

"Perhaps my lord was wrong to judge ya as he did," he concluded. "Only time will tell whether it was my brother who erred or Lord Venetor, but in the meantime ye have my support."

Link felt the last of his tension release, only to have the heavy paw of the Hurtz land upon his shoulder. "Now come, I must know what fate was it that claimed him that was once called Brakkus."

ഇരുൽ

Hazy shapes came into focus as Skyris felt herself come to. The exhaustion of the night before clawing up every inch of her as her body complained due to the need for hydration. Becoming acutely aware of what she did remember, she raised her head ever slightly to get her bearings. She appeared to be lying in a king-sized bed that was fitted with white cotton sheets. Or perhaps cream. Everything seemed too bright, so she wasn't sure. Deciding to brave the world finally after a few more minutes under the covers, she rose and had a better look around. She did remember the descent to Earth and having come to the bar in the small town, but she was not sure exactly how she had left, or worst yet, with whom. Bare feet padding on the tiled floor, Skyris found herself looking for some indication of whose home she was inside. When she noted the refrigerator on the opposite end of the room, along with what looked like a very familiar set of card keys on the dark oak dresser beside her, she knew instantly. Opening the fridge, she noted the endless supply of orange juice containers.

"Made it home after all," she said with a grin.

ഇരുൽ

Freshening up, Skyris donned a clean set of clothing. It consisted of a similar outfit to the night before, but with the addition of a brown leather bomber jacket that was lined with lamb's wool, giving it the distinct look of an old pilot's coat. In tow with her was a large jug of orange juice that she held carelessly at her side as she walked.

It had been a very long time since she had last set foot within Q-16, or the Lab as her older brother had dubbed it. The thought of Orbeyus made other memories surface inside of her, causing the woman to take a swig of the juice in order to take her mind off of it. The sour taste invaded her mouth and she grimaced, putting the cap back on. She continued to travel down the winding monotone steel corridors until she came upon an opening. When she noted the sets of sofas and chairs all around the room, Skyris was able to gain her bearings precisely as to where she was. Coming into the room, she slid into one of the couches comfortably. Resting the juice container beside her, she closed her eyes. Aside from the buzzing of the halogen lights, she could hear nothing.

The silence was soon interrupted when the sound of the teleporter activating and bringing someone down could be heard, followed by feet. Skyris opened her eyes, looking over in the direction of the sound to see a young girl with reddish-brown hair and a jean jacket appear on the far side of the room. She froze, uncertain of what to expect of Skyris. Sensing no threat from her, Skyris remained where she was.

"You know," Skyris began, "I don't bite, at least not when I'm sober."

The girl eyed her strangely upon hearing the proclamation and began to move towards her. Skyris sat up straighter as she got a better look at her. She looked much like Orbeyus's wife, Amelia.

"Now remind me what your name was," the older woman continued, uncapping her drink and taking the container to her lips.

"Annetta," the girl replied. "Annetta Severio. You're Skyris, right?"

"In the flesh." Skyris wiped the corners of her mouth with her thumb. "Or what's left of her, yes."

Annetta raised an eyebrow, not sure what to make of the answer she received, causing Skyris to chuckle.

"When you are old enough to partake in the drinking of spirits, you will understand." The woman smiled infectiously. "Annetta, you say. I'm going to take a stab and say Arieus's daughter."

134

"That's right," Annetta replied stiffly.

Skyris noted the girl's discomfort and through the haze of the night before, she remembered glimpsing her amidst the roller coaster of imagery. Feeling somewhat guilty, the woman placed the container she was holding on the couch and focused.

"I'm assuming Venetor was the one that led you to me last night," Skyris began to speak once more. "Well, with that in mind, I'm not sure what he did or did not tell you about me. Understand, however, that I am still, in fact, the younger sister of your grandfather Orbeyus, which I suppose makes you my great aunt. You may refer to me as Aunt Skyris, or just Skyris, I'm not the proper title-loving sort. I realize that perhaps our introduction was not of the most graceful kind, and though I wish it had been otherwise, I will not apologize for it. You will learn very quickly in this life that we all carry our demons. Some of us just choose to externalize them more than others."

Annetta stood rooted to the spot as she absorbed the information, giving a firm nod once Skyris had finished speaking. While she was still not sure what to make of the woman, some of the feelings of unease were starting to dissipate.

Skyris smiled, seeing her point was made and took another drink before rising to her feet. "From what I've seen, it looks like you guys had to do a full system reset. Am I correct?"

"If you mean the power having been out and us having to start it up again with J.K.," the girl said, "then yes."

The woman pursed her lips as she looked around at the ceiling and the surrounding area, her mind slipping into work mode.

"Figures," she muttered, more to herself than Annetta, and then began to walk off.

Curious as to what the woman was on about, Annetta followed her down the corridors until the two of them ended up where the workplace benches were situated, covered in tarps.

"Home sweet home," Skyris proclaimed as she ripped off one of the tarps and booted up the flat rectangular glass surface of the table by pressing her hand against it, the uncovered another and did the same to it.

Instantly, the surface sprang to life, displaying 3D-mesh drawings of various objects, some which Annetta recognized from having seen them lying around in the Lab, while others seemed foreign. Skyris flipped through these by swiping her finger across the table, then proceeded to exit the screen and go to another one of the tables, which appeared to have nothing but lines of gibberish displayed on it. Looking at it made Annetta's head spin.

"Uhm....what is all of that?" the girl questioned.

"The programming of Q-16's various defences, life support, infrared scanning, DNA recognition...you name it. This is the outline of the Lab's brain," she explained to her, "Created by yours truly among a host of others who worked on it."

"You wrote that stuff?" Annetta gestured to the screen. "I mean...you can read it?"

"Of course I can," Skyris chortled, "I wrote it. I was the one in charge of all programming, computer sciences and robotics within the Lab when Orbeyus was around. Now...that reminds me...I wonder if it's still in here somewhere..."

Setting down the jug of orange juice and using both hands, Skyris began to skim through other schematics on the table, completely forgetting that Annetta was beside her.

Seeing the time on her watch, the girl turned to the woman. "I should get going. I'm supposed to meet Venetor and J.K. for a lesson. It was nice talking to you."

"Likewise, kid. See you around," Skyris replied, not bothering to turn around, her mind lost in the array of blueprints and lines of code.

ↂↃ

Coming to the entrance of the training grounds, Annetta noticed that Jason had not yet arrived and slowed her pace. Before her, in the heart of the arena, Venetor was engrossed in his own training. He was dressed yet again in his armour from when he arrived, his cloak nowhere in sight this time. Immense stones three times the height of him surrounded the Gaian prince as he engaged them in a series of melee combat moves. His body seemed to be engulfed in psychic fire from head to toe as he fought, the flames forming a protective barrier around him. At times, he seemed to move so fast that all Annetta could see was a blur. What intrigued her, though, was that he wielded no weapon at all. Every hit was aimed with a rehearsed precision and seemed more of a dance than sparring.

Finally, the battle coming to an end, Venetor recoiled, withdrawing from his invisible foe. Then without warning, his fist flew for the rock before him and shattered it on impact.

136

Annetta recoiled, the sudden destruction of the stone taking her off guard. The dust clearing, Venetor glared at her from where he stood with his usual grim demeanour. Feeling the icy stare seep into her bones, she shifted uneasily.

Seeing his point made, Venetor looked away, and using his abilities, moved the stones to the far side of the arena, clearing it of any obstacles.

"I'm guessing that's why they call you the Ironfisted," Annetta said finally as she walked in, still keeping her distance from him.

"If a Gaian is to attain anything in his life, it should be by the strength of his own two hands," Venetor stated. "Words I was taught from a very young age by my father and words I have lived by since then, even in battle if the need arises."

"But if someone has a weapon, how can you fight them?" the girl probed further. "I mean...a blade can cut you."

"That is their purpose, yes," Venetor acknowledged, "but if you know how to harness psychic fire as a shield, you will have nothing to fear. No blade, nor projectile, so long as they are not laced with magic can hurt you. Even if they are, however, with precision and training, you can learn to fight them. It takes a long time to learn, but it can save your life."

"Can you teach us how?"

"You are still both far from such things," Venetor scoffed. "Perhaps one day, though."

The girl nodded, lowering her eyes a little, until they stopped at Venetor's scale mail shirt. She found it odd still how it was so well fitted, as though it was not armour at all, but simply a tight piece of clothing.

"Beta Dragon mail," Venetor told her, causing the girl to snap out of her train of thought. "Forged only on Gaia, it moulds to the body of the user. For Gaians, when changed in our feral form, it changes with the body, preventing us from changing back without having anything to wear. It is lighter than Gyldrig mail and just as strong, making it ideal for psychic warriors."

As he explained this to her, Annetta saw for a split second something in his face other than the battle-hardened fighter when he had first arrived. She couldn't put her finger on it, but perhaps it had something to do with him not trying to force everything upside down in her life and instead of trying to explain the changes. Before she could say anything further, however, Jason came into the room, a scowl clearly visible on his face as he glanced at Venetor.

"Good of you to join us, Kinsman," the Gaian prince greeted him. "Now that we are all present, let us begin."

ဢၓ

Their training with Venetor having concluded, Annetta and Jason sat on the sidelines of the arena, both of them feeling lethargic from the amount of focus that had to be put into learning to control their ability to fly. While the two of them were used to training their abilities with Puc, Venetor's way of instruction differed greatly. Where Puc had been stern and to the point, Venetor's method seemed much more unpredictable. There was nothing that they could ever do which the Gaian prince would find impressive.

"Now remember, I want you both to meditate for an hour on your feral form," Venetor reminded them as he begun to make his way to the exit. "I want you both to empty your minds when doing this. Picture a natural setting, the first thing that comes to mind. I want you to picture yourself in it and how you would interact with this world. Start from there for now. I will add to your exercises when I feel you are both ready. We will discuss what you have seen when next we meet."

The two youth simply glanced at the man without uttering a single word and watched as Venetor left their line of sight.

"Finally," Jason groaned, sinking more into the bleachers as he leaned back. "I didn't think he would leave us alone."

"You're telling me," snorted Annetta, rising and feeling the muscles in her legs flare up as she stretched them out.

"Can't we just lie and make something up?" the boy griped. "I mean, how is he gonna know if all we have to do is meditate? You daydream half the time anyway. Improvise."

Annetta couldn't help but crack a grin at her friend upon hearing the plan. "I'm sure he has some way of knowing if we didn't."

"Like what? It's not like he can mind-probe us," he continued. "It's illegal and all, right?"

"And for all we know the Prince of Gaia has a special privilege like the First Mage of Aldamoor," Annetta reminded him, causing Jason to frown in resignation. She then added, "It can't be that bad. We aren't doing anything with our bodies or using abilities. Come on, let's try this."

The boy growled under his breath and followed Annetta to the centre of the arena. They both then flopped down onto the floor, crossing their legs. Annetta pulled off her C.T.S. watch and flipped to the timer, setting it for exactly one hour.

"Alright, when the timer goes off it should be loud enough to snap us out of it." She formulated a plan in her head.

"You're sure about this?" Jason grumbled. "Maybe we should have Darius or Sarina here in case we don't come out of it."

"I don't think my uncle would tell us to do something like this without supervision," she reasoned.

Jason sighed, having wanted to get this off his chest for a while now. "Look, Anne, I know he's your uncle and all, but don't you find it suspicious that he just shows up out of the blue with no real explanation? I mean... he just waltzes in and starts helping us with our powers. What's in it for him?"

The girl opened her mouth as if to say something, only to be cut off by Jason again. "The last time someone came to the Lab to help us with our powers, it was Matt when he was still working for Mislantus. For all we really know, this guy is working in league with someone or something we don't know about. Also, and I can't believe I'm saying this, Puc is nowhere in sight and he's usually the one we count on to be sceptical of new arrivals."

Annetta thought long and hard on what Jason had said. It was true, yet at the same time, she recalled Puc having identified Venetor. There was also the fact that the mage had left despite the Gaian prince's appearance. Jason's paranoia becoming null and void in her mind, she closed her eyes.

The boy muttered again under his breath, and despite his reservations, set his own watch, following the girl's stead.

೦೦೧

It did not take long for the girl to focus, mostly due to her other meditation she had been doing. Annetta's breathing became steady as she felt her consciousness float off into its own world, going from seeing darkness to forming a mental picture in her mind's eye. She was not sure at first what she was seeing, aside from a bright golden orb that appeared to be the sun rising upon a green horizon before her. Grabbing hold of the moment in her mind, she delved further into the image, allowing for the individual blades of grass to come into focus all around. She could feel them tickle her hands and legs as they brushed past her while she walked.

As she continued, she noticed the blurry shapes of trees some distance away. Her gaze was distracted when a sparrow shot right past her, joining with a flock of others in the grass ahead before they took off in a display of tiny wings fluttering in the sky above.

In spite of everything appearing as though it were something out of one of the biospheres within the Lab, she could not pinpoint which one exactly she was in. There were neither mountains nor a lake. Perhaps it was one of the biospheres that still lay hidden in parts of the base she had not explored. Yet, if that was so, how would she know about it?

Trying not to lose focus, Annetta remembered the task she had been given by Venetor, and continued forward. The trees ahead were now coming into focus and she realized that she had simply stepped into a clearing. Looking further in the distance, she began to see what appeared to be hills, and beyond them, mountains. It then dawned on her that it was no place in the Lab that she was seeing, but one of the trails close to the castle that she would so often set out to explore on her own.

The scenery around her then shifted, and she found herself staring down from one of the rocky shelves she occupied on her excursions. Observing the world below, she noted how small and insignificant everything was, how everything came together and created a whole. All had its place in the grand scheme of things.

The scene was interrupted when the sound of beeping blotted out her focus.

§୬ରେ

Annetta and Jason both opened their eyes simultaneously upon hearing their watches go off. Grabbing hold of the small devices, they turned them off, unable to stand the sound for an extended period of time.

"Well?" Jason looked over at his friend questioningly. "What did you see?"

"I was outside of Severio Castle," Annetta replied. "I mean, at least I think I was. You?"

"It's hard to describe, to be honest." Jason scratched the back of his neck. "I wasn't sure at first. Everything was a blur, then just towards the end things became a bit clearer. I think it was a field. It was really warm."

The girl furrowed her brows as she tried to picture what her friend was saying, but all she could see was the track and the schoolyard when a field was mentioned.

"What do you think it means?" she asked.

"Who knows," Jason shrugged his shoulders. "I guess he'll tell us tomorrow. Anyways, I'm gonna go find Sarina and hang out with her for a little while. Night, Anne."

"Night J.K.," Annetta watched as her friend got up and walked off.

Slouching in her cross-legged position, she took a second to replay the whole scene of what she had witnessed in her head. The more she thought about it, the more she tried to rationalize what sort of animal her feral form would take. It then became a guessing game until the girl found herself nodding off. Her sleeping spell was interrupted when she heard the sounds of feet approaching in the distance. Instinctively, the girl rose from her spot. Her eyes then met the form of Skyris, who stood beside the door, leaning on the frame.

"Looks like you could use a cup of java," the woman beamed, causing Annetta to chuckle a little.

"I uhm...I actually don't drink coffee." The girl smiled back sheepishly.

"What?" Skyris exclaimed. "I thought that was all the rage with you kids nowadays. Staying up late and then sleeping in till the middle of the day. Don't tell me Earth youth don't do it."

"Pretty sure that's a teenager thing everywhere," Annetta answered her. "Still, that doesn't mean I drink coffee. Isn't it bad for you?"

"Pfft! Who told you that?" The woman laughed and then sighed. "Well, all in due time, I guess. I have someone I want to introduce."

Annetta tilted her head slightly to the side in curiosity as she peered around Skyris to see no one there. Perhaps the woman's jug had been filled with alcohol the whole time. She would not have been surprised with how their initial meeting had gone.

Before she could voice her thoughts, however, a sphere no bigger than a large yoga ball hovered into the room. It appeared to be made of black metal, with a single large red glass eye which protruded from the front of it. The girl tensed up upon seeing it, not sure what to make of the thing.

"Hello, I am Dexter, or Digital Escort X-droid and Technical Exploration Robot," the thing said in a monotone computerized male voice as its one red eye blinked while observing her. "You must be Annetta Severio. It is a pleasure to meet you."

Annetta felt her jaw slack open a little as she walked around the machine, marvelling at it. She had been part of the Lab for almost two years, yet never in her time had she had a chance to see an A.I. of any sort.

"How did you-" the girl tried to formulate a sentence.

The woman smirked as she leaned on the doorframe. "Old project I had been working on before I left. Orbeyus wanted me to create an X-droid, an index A.I. to help those around who weren't very tech-savvy. Kind of like you guys, but of course when I had to leave, the project never got finished."

The girl continued to look at Dexter in astonishment. "Why did you guys leave to begin with? I mean, I know Venetor is prince of Gaia and all."

"Politics." Skyris shook her head. "It was all politics. There was a time I would have given everything to stay on Earth, but being who I was I had to go back when the time came."

"How come you never came back to visit after that?" Annetta inquired.

"For the very same reason I had to leave so long ago." Skyris smiled weakly. "Politics."

Chapter 14

One month later…

Meeting after school as was now their custom, Liam and Xander set off towards Liam's house. The days were already becoming shorter, resulting in the sky being past its zenith by the time they reached their destination. Exchanging a quick hello with Talia, Liam and Jason's mother, the two of them proceeded to barricade themselves in Liam's room. Pulling out an assortment of Halloween costumes that both of them had procured at the party store they had visited the day before, they set to work. At first, it was just both of them trying on the costumes in various combinations to see what looked best. This not seeming satisfying to the boys, they began to cut up bits and pieces of other costumes and glue or staple them together.

Finally, their works of art completed, the pair stood in front of Liam's mirror, admiring their creations. Liam wore a wizard's cloak with a dark blue bandana that had holes cut in it for his eyes. Underneath he still wore his jeans, and on his hands he had black gloves which he had taken from a skeleton costume that had bones painted on them in white with fabric paint. Xander stood beside him wearing a ninja costume with a soldier's camouflage coat thrown over top, a cut-out lightning bolt glued onto it.

"This is so cool." Liam beamed.

"We look ridiculous," Xander groaned and proceeded to take off the mask, only to have Liam slap his hand away.

"No way. Man, this is awesome!" he exclaimed. "We just gotta think up some names."

Xander, seeing how seriously his friend was taking this, simply rolled his eyes underneath the black mask and sighed as he slumped his shoulders. "Fine… I can be… Captain Bolt."

"Ooo, I like that." Liam grinned as he brought his thumb to his mouth and bit down on his nail, burying himself in thought. "I guess I need to come up with something, don't I? You got the easy one with your lighting stuff…what to call myself…ah! How about… The Levitator?"

"Kind of sounds like elevator, doesn't it?" Xander wrinkled his nose, to which Liam scoffed.

"Well, I don't know what else to call myself."

"How about Psi Boy?" he suggested.

Liam's eyes lit up upon hearing the name. "You're so good at this! How did you-"

"Video games," Xander chuckled.

ഇരുണ

It didn't take long for it to get completely dark outside, and before they knew it, both Xander and Liam had snuck out of the house without Talia realizing it. The duo wandered the lamplit streets under the cover of night, avoiding the golden light patches as much as possible.

"Man, this is so awesome, I can't believe we're doing this," Liam whispered in a hushed tone to his friend.

"I don't even know what we're doing, to be honest," the other boy replied.

"What else? If we see crime then we fight it," Liam explained. "That's what superheroes do. We were given these powers to help people. It's our responsibility."

"Somehow I get the feeling that it isn't, but okay." Xander frowned, following his friend.

They walked in this manner for some time, deciding to use the route that they would normally take from one another's house, their justification being that it was their neighbourhood that they were protecting by doing so. Lights from the windows of the various houses greeted them along the street. The shuffling of feet on salted icy pavement was the only other sound aside from the occasional car passing by. Further in the distance, the noises of busier streets indicated that they were still in suburbia.

"This is getting boring," Xander finally said after a lengthy stretch. "I thought stuff happened in comics, this is just making me sleepy."

"It doesn't happen right away," Liam argued.

As if in answer to the younger Kinsman's protests, the sound of slightly raised voices could be heard coming from the park across the street from them. Both boys froze upon hearing it. Adjusting their masks, they began the slow trip in its direction, making sure to be as quiet as possible.

"You go first, I'll back you up," Liam whispered, slipping away from Xander, who was left to approach alone.

Coming closer to the source, he noted that it was three young men, all in dark hooded parkas and a woman in a light-coloured fur-lined jacket. Stumbling over a half-buried stick in the snow, Xander lost his momentum and instantly had all four pairs of eyes on him.

"Yo, check out this freak," one of them nodded in his direction, causing the other two to snigger. "We got ourselves a masked man here."

Xander growled under his breath and he straightened up to face the group, noting the woman leaving.

"Hey where you going, girl? Come back!" one of the other men yelled, only to shake his head afterwards.

Annoyed, he turned to Xander who stood before them, not moving a muscle. "Great, Tricia left, and we're stuck here with this clown. You at least gonna tell us a joke or what?"

"I'm not a clown," Xander retorted with an air of coldness to his voice, causing the trio to whoop and chuckle at his behaviour.

"Boy, you're definitely a clown to be out at this hour of the night alone," the first one stated. "Either that or your head ain't screwed on right or something."

At this point, Xander wasn't sure what to say back. His reservoir of cool sayings that he had accumulated over the years of hanging out with his sister and her friends had run dry upon being put on the spot. He was left to the pure meddling of his own intellect, the likes of which was limited even for a boy of grade seven. Nonetheless, he was prepared to battle it out until the end. Raising his arms to either side, he then slammed them together, causing sparks to crawl all along them in a dazzling lights display.

"Ooo, we got some pyrotechnics going on," the third youth said. "You gonna show us some fireworks?"

"Fireworks this!" Xander grabbed the stick from under his feet he had tripped over before and tossed it in their direction, causing the whole thing to be covered in sparks as it sailed through the air.

Finally aware of the seriousness of the situation, the trio jumped from their seats on the park bench, just in time to see the branch burst into flame and hit the bench. Seeing the scenario unfold before them, they made a run for it without further words.

"Whoa! That was so cool!" Liam reappeared from the shadows once they were gone. "You didn't even need my help for that one."

Xander smirked, seeing his handiwork. "Yeah, I don't think they'll be coming back anytime soon, not here anyway."

"I knew it! This is so what we should have been doing from the start!" Liam squealed with glee. "Just you wait. There's gonna be newspaper articles and news broadcasts and-"

Before Liam could finish what he was saying, a pair of headlights appeared upon the horizon. A car then materialized in the dark and stopped but a few feet away from them. They both recognized the make and model without a doubt.

Arieus exited the vehicle and began inspecting the damage made to the bench, which had begun to catch fire due to the stick thrown at it. He then picked up a nearby bottle and sniffing the top, ripped off a piece of cloth he had lying around in his car and stuffed it inside, only to then throw it into the embers. His gaze finally landed upon the boys.

"Both of you in the car with me," he ordered, "Now."

The duo looked at one another, shocked and unsure how to formulate a protest against Xander's father. They shuffled into the vehicle and closed the doors behind them.

Arieus got into the driver's seat and sped off as quickly as he'd come. His eyes darted from the road to the rearview mirror every few seconds to make sure no one was following them.

"Liam's mother called asking where you both were when she noticed you were awfully quiet in the room," he explained. "When you didn't show up at our house, I went to investigate and then I saw the lightning. What were you two thinking?"

"You mean you know?" Liam blinked in disbelief.

Arieus exhaled roughly as he continued to drive. He had expected as much and Liam had just confessed the entire thing to him without realizing it. It was enough for him that he had to worry about Annetta being down in the Lab. Now it seemed Xander and Liam had by some sheer dumb luck tapped into their abilities. Perhaps the seal to bind abilities until the first descent into Q-16 that Puc had once placed on Annetta and Jason had not carried over to their younger siblings.

"You are both about to become engaged in a very different world from the one you know about," he stated while silently contacting Jason and Annetta with telepathy to meet him in the living room of his house, "And you must know the seriousness of what you will be part of. How long have you known how to use your abilities?"

"Uhm...a month or so." Xander hesitated with his answer. "It happened after the meteorite fell. We went to go see it and-"

"A few months for me," Liam replied. "I just started trying to lift objects with my mind like J.K. did the one time when I was having a bad day."

Arieus listened attentively to what the boys were telling him and nodded as he pulled up in front of the house. "We're going to need Thanestorm for this."

෫෨ඟ

A pair of paws padded past the thick grassy trail as an amber sun set on the horizon, leaving all in an orange hue. In the distance, the sound of birds could be made out as they chirped, undisturbed by the new arrival. Flicking its ears, the creature raised its maw into the air, taking in the scent. The smell of rich soil and abundant vegetation filled its lungs, providing vibrancy to the world that had not been there before. It also filled it with hunger.

Turning its head to the side, the creature froze. There, on the far side of the plain, a deer had made its presence known. Chewing on a few strands of grass nonchalantly, it looked around absentmindedly without a care. Little did it know of the predator which now stalked it, its liquid steel muscles shifting underneath its fur, preparing for the kill.

Soundlessly pacing through the grass, it closed in on its prey. As it got closer, however, the deer seemed to change, shift somehow in its appearance, white and black markings adorning its face and body, while two thin twisted horns protruded from its head. The creature then became conscious that the deer was, in fact, a gazelle. Lowering its head, it then let out a deep rumbling growl.

෫෨ඟ

Jason watched from the side as Venetor and Annetta both sat cross-legged on the floor of the training arena with their eyes closed. Their psychic lessons with the Gaian having come to an end for the day, they had been asked to project the latest result of their feral form meditation to him. Having completed his, the boy waited impatiently for his friend to finish so they could both go back home. He furrowed his brows, seeing at how long the whole process was taking her, though perhaps it was just his fatigue distorting time.

Snapping out of the trance, Venetor opened his eyes and almost immediately a scowl appeared across his face. Whatever he had seen, he had not been pleased.

Annetta opened her eyes as well, only to be faced with her uncle's brooding expression. Watching him rise wordlessly, she followed suit, unsure of what was going on.

"So...what's up?" she inquired.

Not replying, Venetor turned on his heel and gathering up his leather jacket from one of the benches, he put it on over top of his scale mail shirt, adjusting the collar to his liking. The contorted look on his face, still present, only caused the two youth to continue to glare at him in question. Finally, seeing no point in prolonging the silence, he turned his attention to them.

"You are confused," he concluded.

"I think anyone would be by the way you're acting," Jason reasoned.

The Gaian turned to fully face them. "I did not mean you, Kinsman, I meant Annetta. Your feral form projections are clear, concise. You know what you are and where your form inhabits. Annetta, on the other hand, is wavering between two."

"What do you mean wavering?" the girl protested, "I think by now it's clear that my form inhabits a grassy area with trees. The place looks similar to where the Eye to All Worlds is and it's a hunter."

Hearing what his friend had said, Jason realized the problem.

"Wait...so you haven't seen what you are yet?" he asked.

"No." She looked over at him. "Have you?"

Jason looked over at Venetor. The Gaian had asked the boy not to say anything to her. It had not happened long ago, but Jason knew Annetta's nature and it seemed Venetor was quick to pick up on it as well. Biting his lip, Jason looked down at his running shoes as he traced a scuff mark on the floor with his toes.

"Look, if it makes you feel better, it only happened like last week," he confessed. "And I didn't actually see it, not really. I saw a striped tail and that's it."

"So then there's a bunch of possibilities for what it could be," Annetta concluded.

The boy glanced over at Venetor, who shook his head. Not having anything else to say, he left, leaving an aura of red behind him.

Before he exited the final set of doors however, he called out, "If you truly knew your place in this world, or who you are loyal to, the choice would be easy."

෨෬

Leaving the training grounds, Annetta and Jason headed over to where Skyris was busy at work on her latest invention. The woman's quirky love of technology came as a welcome change to the two of them, particularly Annetta, who had found another female to speak with in the Lab aside from Sarina. Unlike her brother, Skyris was much easier to converse with, and there seemed to be little which could make the woman angry, aside from someone having moved her whisky or orange juice bottle. Having seated themselves on some of the extra chairs, the duo watched as Skyris, a metal band around her head with sensors attached to it, poked away at some contraption she had discovered unfinished on one of the multiple tables, while projections on glass surfaces beside her showed an array of code scrolling downwards. From time to time, she would turn to it and swipe and or add something to what was scrolling.

"The choice would be easy? The hell is that supposed to mean?" Annetta fumed.

Skyris did not answer immediately. Focused on her venture as she muttered to herself, she typed something into the board by hand and then turned back to the device before giving her attention to the girl. "Well... is there something that you feel needs to be chosen between?"

"No, why should there be?" Annetta raised an eyebrow.

"He said she was wavering," Jason clarified.

"So...you mean like going between two forms?" Skyris concluded. "I did that for a while, drove our mentor mad."

"How did you choose?" the girl questioned.

The sound of feet could be heard approaching and soon, Titus came around the corner.

"Telling stories again, aunt Sky?" he said in a form of greeting.

The dark-haired woman turned to the younger man. "Annetta seems to be having the same problem I did when it came to finding a feral form, and if I am correct, so did you."

"Oh, you mean not being able to choose?" The light-haired youth widened his eyes a bit.

"Seems to be a common enough problem," Jason summarized, seeing the reactions of the other Gaians. "So why is Venetor all worked up about it?"

"Do you know what you are wavering between?" Titus asked.

"Uh..." Annetta only managed to articulate the sound as she searched her mind. The truth of the matter was that she had no idea.

Seeing the dilemma, Skyris shut down whatever was running on the screen. Moving her hand over another screen that was now littered with icons, she tapped on one and took off the device from her head, handing it to Annetta. "Put this on."

The girl accepted the band and gingerly placed it on her head, "Uh... so what now?"

Skyris fiddled with the screen a bit before turning to her. "I want you to focus as if you were projecting what you saw to Venetor."

"Okay." She frowned, closed her eyes and began to recall everything she saw.

Taking a step back from the screen and folding her arms across her chest, Skyris watched beside Titus and Jason as the image on the screen fizzle before it became clear and showed everything Annetta had shown Venetor. The video coming to an end, Annetta opened her eyes and handed the circlet back to Skyris.

"Well?" she asked.

"If I am correct in what I think it is, you are wavering between a wolf and a lion," Titus said, "Which would explain why father reacted the way he did."

"A wolf and a lion... how did you get all that?" Annetta raised an eyebrow.

"A program created so non-psychics could see the projections of those who are," Skyris explained. "It's a work in progress, and I agree, that would explain why."

"You gonna enlighten us on the significance of it all?" Jason interjected.

"The lion is the sigil of Gaia," Skyris huffed. "In past generations, many Severios had their feral form be this creature. It's even foretold, though I find it to be a bunch of prophecy booha, that when the doom of Gaia strikes, a white lion will rise to lead the people to victory. Both Venetor and Orbeyus had the form of a lion, even Arieus."

"Wait, my dad can change?" Annetta stopped her.

"Among his other talents, yes," the woman continued. "Now, the wolf...well... I'm guessing Lincerious never told you the whole history of his curse?"

"What does any of this have to do with Link?" Annetta growled.

"His grandfather fell in love with my grandfather's sister," Titus said. "When my great grandfather refused to give him her hand in marriage, he raised a rebellion and tried to overthrow the throne of

Gaia. His feral form was that of a wolf. His rebellion did not succeed and he was cursed so the rest of his line would forever be unable to change into their true form, only a grotesque monster, a hybrid beast."

"But if they loved each other..." Annetta interrupted again.

"Our society is very structured," Titus continued. "Nobles marry nobles to further alliances, or if they happen to find love within their ranks. It's why aunt-"

Before he could finish his sentence, Skyris shot him the vilest glance she could possibly muster.

"That is a story for another time," she hissed, then turned to Annetta. "Venetor just holds a grudge, but you are of Earth and not Gaia. Whatever you choose as your form, make sure it is what you want. Don't rush into it. It's obvious you have feelings for this Link, and if so go with it. Don't look to the past to uncover old truths. Life moves forward, not back."

೩೦೦೪

Finishing a count of their herbs inventory, Darius and Sarina did their best to tidy up the storage room. It was a plain area within the confines of the Lab. Shelves covered every wall, each stocked with assortments of jars and containers filled with a variety of ingredients. For this reason, it was also dimmed, and the temperature set slightly lower in order to prevent things from spoiling. While Darius had been away to complete his training, Sarina had taken it upon herself to help Puc whenever possible. In exchange, she had learned a great many things from the mage, who she was sad to have seen leave last month.

"That was everything, right?" Darius asked, cleaning some sticky residue that had been on the jars he was handling from his hands.

"I think so." Sarina glanced over to the neatly-written lists on parchment that Puc had used to keep track of everything. "Nothing urgent that needs to be acquired, so we're good for now."

"Key words, for now," Darius muttered, whipping the rag over to where he had found it by the sink. "I should probably make a few batches of potions for blood clotting and replenishing, since we only had like two of each."

"We used up that much when we went to go see the Ogaien?" the girl asked in disbelief. "I mean, I know Annetta was beaten up pretty badly, but still. I could have sworn Puc and I made a bunch not too long ago."

Darius made his rounds around the shelves once more, picking out the ingredients he would need as he spoke, "Knowing him, he probably took a few for the journey to Aldamoor. It's sort of standard for a mage to have with them. Like the equivalent of a human first aid kit."

"I guess I never thought of it that way," Sarina replied. "I keep forgetting that this is not like Valdhar."

"I hear you," the young mage replied as he placed everything on the table at the far side of the room.

Before further conversation could commence, a large black metal ball hovered into the room, a red eye gleaming at the two gathered. The youth froze. While the A.I. Skyris had created had become a common sight in the last month, it was still taking time for them to get used to the cryptic mechanical being.

"Hello, Sarina Freiuson and Darius Silver, I am glad to have found you both well," it greeted them as was its usual habit.

"Uh…hey," Darius stuttered. "What's up?"

"As you know, I was created by Skyris Severio to aid those dwellers of Q-16 that are not familiar with all of its technologies," the thing continued once more in its mechanical voice. "My ulterior programming is also meant for me to act as a monitor of all comings and goings within the base. I came here now to inform you that there is a new arrival waiting at the stables. The being's biochemical composition suggests that he is a Water Elf. Shall I let him in?"

Darius quickly closed his mouth in order to prevent it from hanging open as the thing spoke to him. "I…uh…yeah, let him in. Can you tell him where we are, as well?"

For a moment, there was no response. Dexter seemed to stare blankly at Darius and Sarina, its emotionless eye narrowing as if it were having second thoughts about its nature. This brought a chill to both of them, each having heard their fair share of A.I.'s having gone rogue.

"I will see it done," Dexter finally replied in the same cheery tone, "I will bring him here shortly."

"Wait, uh-" Darius realized that he had not asked who it was that was waiting at the stables, but it was too late, the thing had already sped off into the distance, faster than Darius thought it possible for the ball to move.

"It's probably just Puc," Sarina told him. "We had a similar system onboard Valdhar. It was just… less mobile."

The young elf nodded in reply, still feeling wary of the A.I. being present. He had grown used to the limited use of technology, despite the base being first and foremost made of it. His fears were somewhat lowered when the hum of Dexter's engine could be heard incoming once more, accompanied by the sound of feet.

Following the robot in was not Puc as Sarina had deduced it would be, but Kaine. The son of the First Mage of Aldamoor sported the blue military coat that the soldiers of the city wore, along with a rapier at his hip, indicating his station as a pilot rather than a militia. High leather boots tucked neatly into his pants announced his arrival as he approached.

"Kaine," Darius greeted him and coming forward, embraced his former schoolmate. "What are you doing here? Where is Puc?"

"Back in Aldamoor," he replied. "Are Annetta and Jason around?"

"I don't think so," Darius thought. "I can check if you give me -"

Before Darius could type anything on his C.T.S. to get in contact with either of them, Kaine handed a folded piece of parchment with a wax seal on it to him. The young mage glanced at what he held in his hands, questioning.

The pilot looked over at the contents on the table. "Standard blood clotting and energy potions?"

Darius nodded blankly without a word, joined by Sarina, who was curious about what was going on.

"Good, you're going to need lots of them in the coming days."

෫ාൾ

Leaving Skyris and Titus, Annetta and Jason made their way back up to the surface when they were contacted by Annetta's father. Leaving the girl's room, they were confronted with a bizarre sight. On the couch in Annetta's living room sat Arieus, Aurora and Talia, along with Liam and Xander dressed in an odd assortment of Halloween costumes.

"Whoa, what's going on?" Jason asked. "You guys decide to rob a bank or something?"

"Oh, it's a little more serious than that," Talia replied curtly, then turned to the two boys. "Well...show them."

Liam and Xander shifted uncomfortably in their seats. The younger Kinsman finally stood up and reached his hand out in the direction of the coffee table, where a stack of coasters lay. As soon as he did so, they began to float up into the air as though a soft wind were

153

taking them along for a ride. Both Annetta and Jason went a little pale in the face.

"Wait, so..." Jason pointed at Liam and then Xander, unable to finish his sentence.

"I'm not like him," Xander stated. Stretching out his hand, he caused sparks to circulate his palm.

Annetta felt a cold chill go down her spine upon seeing both of the siblings exhibit their abilities. She then turned to her father. "But how? Puc said our abilities were blocked until our first descent to the Lab."

"For you they were," Arieus answered. "It appears, however, that for Xander and Liam they were not."

Jason bit down on his thumbnail, only to have Talia shoot him a glare, indicating to stop. He turned to his friend for some form of guidance and then back to the two boys and trio of parents. Seeing that she did not have the answers, they both took a seat on one of the couches that were available.

"Liam needs to be taught about his abilities," Arieus explained. "As for Xander, I think it is best for Puc to determine what his powers are and go from there."

"That might be a bit of a problem," Annetta said. "Puc is still in Aldamoor right now, and we don't know when he'll be coming back. He's still sorting the issue with the First Mage appointment from when Kaian has passed away."

"May the Unknown watch over him," Aurora spoke quietly and shook her head. "Poor elf, it never seemed like anything would touch him."

"They seem to be taking a long time with choosing and leaving you both without his counsel," Talia muttered.

"Either way, the boys need to know," Arieus interjected and turned to the two teenagers, "Which is where you both come in."

Jason sucked in some air and clasped his hands together, looking over at Annetta. "Well, I guess that means show time."

The girl simply nodded in reply and glanced back at the two younger siblings, "Yeah...okay...where to begin. Uhm...well, you both know about the teleporter in my room, the one that was in both mine and Xander's back in the apartment right? Uh..."

Annetta felt at a loss for words. She wasn't sure what to say to either of the boys. Was there really a beginning for a conversation like the one she was about to have with them? She took a step back from it all in her mind to give herself a centre of focus. She remembered the way her father had presented it all to her and Jason just a few years ago, the way he had walked them through it. She then attempted to put herself in their shoes.

"What I am about to tell you," she began anew, "there is no easy way to say or easy place to start. Our families have always been different, gifted, and there is a much deeper reason behind this than a few powers. The place Jason and I always go to after school, down the teleporter, it's a place called Q-16, a base that mine and Xander's grandfather created. This base guards a castle, the very same one that is on the painting over the TV set. It is called Severio Castle, the Eye to All Worlds. This castle contains portals in it which lead to other worlds, alternate universes. For generations, it has been the duty of both those from the lines of Severio and Kinsman to protect this castle and to lead an army known as the Four Forces."

The two boys seemed entranced by what Annetta was telling them. The more she spoke, the straighter they seemed to sit on the couch, as though something may escape them if they did not.

Jason then saw the pause as his way to take over, "Over a year ago now, a warlord named Mislantus tried to take over the castle so that he could use the portals inside of it to take over the other worlds. Annetta and I, along with some of the friends we met down in Q-16 had to call upon the Four Forces to fight him. We beat him, but it wasn't easy or fun. The first thing you need to know about these powers of yours is that no one outside of those of us here and the people you meet in Q-16 can know about what you can do."

"I guess that makes sense." Liam bobbed his head. "But wait, you guys go to a secret base in that thing? That's impossible."

Annetta and Jason both got up simultaneously, causing everyone else in the room to rise. Without another word, they proceeded back up the stairs to Annetta's room. Opening the door adorned with a poster of two dragons, one red and one white that were ready to do battle with one another, they gathered around the mirror which contained the teleporter hidden behind it.

The girl slid her card key down it and turned back to the boys as the keyboard and teleporting pad materialized. "There really isn't another way about this than to simply show you."

Jason was already at the keyboard typing before he spoke up. "We're gonna let you guys go first before we go down with Annetta. First trip can be a bit rough, but don't panic."

Liam and Xander nodded and then turned around to look at the trio of parents standing in the doorway but a few feet behind them. None of the adults present seemed to have anything to add. There was neither scolding nor words of encouragement. The feeling of indifference to the situation confused the boys as to how they should feel themselves. Dwelling no more on any of it, Liam came up first and stepped onto the platform.

He then looked up at his older brother. "What do I do when I get down there?"

"Just wait for us," Jason told him. Pressing the enter button on the keyboard, he took a step back as his brother faded from sight.

೩೦೮೩

Panic gripped Liam as he felt himself being swallowed up by waves of water from all sides. His body's instincts called for him to scream, yet he was paralyzed, unable to respond. Before his panic could turn to fear, however, he found himself lying on a metallic floor, completely dry. Rolling over onto his back, he groaned, allowing the large halogen lights overhead to come into focus. Seconds later, Xander materialized beside him, coughing as though he were trying to purge his lungs after nearly drowning.

"What a ride," he breathed heavily as he got up and tried to walk it off.

"I'll say," Liam replied, still on his back. "How the heck did Annetta and J.K.-"

Before Liam could finish what he was saying, Jason and Annetta appeared one after the other on the floor beside them, not in much better shape.

"...get used to it," Liam finished.

"You don't," Annetta replied. "You don't get used to it, at least not as long as we have been doing it. Although Puc said we should soon."

"Who's Puc?" Xander asked, and then caught sight of the doors. "Whoa!"

The boy felt his feet melt into the floor as he gazed upon the twin behemoths towering over him, with block lettering spelling out Q-16 across them. He felt small and insignificant in comparison to them.

"Pretty impressive, right?" Annetta smiled, walking up to her sibling, and then proceeding to answer his earlier question. "Puc was the first person Jason and I met when we came down to Q-16. He taught us how to use our abilities. He was grandpa's advisor once, and I guess he's ours now too."

She paused before speaking again. "He's also a Water Elf from another world, and the most sarcastic thing to walk the Earth since Quixote's comebacks in grade ten. Hey J.K., you want me to do it, or?"

"Nah, I got this." Jason looked in the direction of the doors and without warning, they began to creep open, the sound of metal grating against metal announcing the arrival of those at the entrance.

Before either Jason or Annetta could say anything else, they were greeted by the perplexed faces of Darius and Sarina, who were both but a few feet away on the other side. Beyond them, large tarp covered shapes seemed to be lined up on either side as if hailing in greeting to the new arrivals.

"Darius? You know about this place too?" Xander felt his jaw hang open upon seeing him.

"Uh... hey Xander," the young mage managed to say as he looked over questioningly at Annetta and Jason.

"Long story short, we got another psychic and..." Jason motioned to Xander, who curled a fist and made sparks crawl up it. "A guy with some other powers he can use...what's up with you guys?"

"Do you want the good news or the bad news?" Sarina asked.

"Good?" Annetta shrugged her shoulders.

"Well, we are out of luck because there isn't any," Darius informed her and pulling out a piece of parchment, handed it to her. "Fire Elves have been storming the borders of Aldamoor. They've been pillaging and torching anything that comes their way. There are reports even that they are amassing an army for a full on assault on the capital."

"What?" the girl's eyes opened wide as she scanned the letter, which for once was written in plain English so that both she and Jason could read its contents.

"It started happening after Kaian's death," Darius continued. "Ever since the death of the First Mage became common knowledge. With Aldamoor being without a leader and in the process of trying to secure a new one, they are vulnerable. It looks like the Fire Elves are taking advantage of that fact. Puc has asked us to rally the Four Forces in aid of a possible battle."

"We were going to go see you when you showed up here," Sarina added.

"A battle? Cool!" Liam exclaimed. "Man, this place is awesome and we've only been here like five minutes."

"If you think you guys are participating then you got another thing coming," Jason said. "A battle I can handle, but explaining to mom why you got hurt...no thanks."

"Aw man," Liam groaned. "But we can use our powers to help!"

"You are untrained, Liam," Annetta stated. "As for Xander, we don't even know what his abilities can do."

Before any further discussion could continue, a spherical object floated towards them, its gleaming red eye glaring at each of them individually.

"Hello. I am Dexter," the thing introduced itself to Liam and Xander. "My name stands for Digital Escort X-droid and Technical Exploration Robot. I was created by Skyris Severio to aid those dwellers of Q-16 which are not familiar with all of its technologies. It is a pleasure to meet you, Liam Kinsman and Alexandrius Severio. I look forward to helping you both settle into your roles in Q-16."

"Are we going to have to hear that spiel every single time someone new comes down?" Jason grumbled to Annetta.

"I don't think we have much of a choice," the girl replied before she turned back to Darius. "What do we need to do to rally them? Last time we were sort of in space when it happened."

The young elf ran a hand through his short hair before replying to the girl as if he were trying to organize his thoughts. "From what I know, Puc just went to Kaian last time and told him to begin sending out messengers to the other three races, but there is no First Mage this time, so..."

The group of youth stood transfixed in their places as they looked down at their feet. For the first time since Puc's leave, they all understood how much responsibility the mage had shouldered. Jason was the first to reply, and flipping open his C.T.S., he began punching in some numbers.

"What are you doing, J.K.?" Sarina asked.

"What needs to be done," he responded briskly as he finished the sequence on the device and waited.

"This is 05 here," a very tired sounding Puc came through the speaker.

158

"02 here with 01," Jason spoke back into it. **"We got the letter. We don't know what you need on our end, but we'll do what needs to be done."**

There was a pause on the device before the elder Elven mage spoke again. **"I will organize the messengers. Be here on the morrow. There is much work that needs to be carried out. Avoid using this as a means of communication, I fear there is someone spying on the inside. 05 out."**

The C.T.S. went still once more and Jason closed it, turning back to the rest of the group.

"I guess it makes sense now why he didn't just contact us sooner. I take it we're gonna need time off school then?" Annetta crossed her arms, not thrilled as she thought of the mountain of homework that she would have because of it.

"I'll get it arranged," Darius said in an attempt to calm her and then remembered the two siblings who were still standing there in the midst of all of this., "Seems like you guys chose one hell of a time to manifest your powers."

"This is like the greatest thing ever!" Liam shouted with glee and looked as though he might fall over with joy.

Xander, on the other hand, simply stood beside him with his hands shoved into the pockets of the coat he wore. He had known something was going on with his sister and had even witnessed the strange night years ago when the sky went dark. He wasn't sure how to react to any of it and it was as though his emotions had shut down due to the overload, waiting for everything to cool down. It was too much to take in.

"So... do we send them back up?" Jason pointing at the two siblings.

Before anything else could be said, the sound of feet advancing towards the group was heard. Then Venetor and Titus came into view.

"I thought I heard a lot of voices." The Gaian prince confirmed his suspicions, then turned to Liam and Xander. "And what have we here?"

"My brother Liam and Annetta's brother Alexandrius, but we all call him Xander," Jason replied.

Annetta glanced over at her uncle and cousin. "Puc sent us a letter, Aldamoor is being raided by Fire Elves. He wants us to rally the Four Forces in case of an attack."

"Typical of the elves, they never could keep their own kind in line," Venetor uttered, noting from his peripheral vision the tightening of Darius's hand, but ignoring it. "And what do you plan to do in response to this letter?"

"We already did it," the girl answered. "We told him to send out messages to the other races and begin assembling them. I mean, what else were we really to do?"

"Wait until I get here so you could send someone over in person to make sure it is not a trap," Venetor retorted. "For all you know, you are sending all of those soldiers to certain death. I assume you got the letter and replied by your C.T.S., am I correct?"

Both Annetta and Jason felt their jaws go slack, neither of them having anything to say back to him. Neither of them had even thought of the possibility of it all having been a trap.

"I thought as much," he spat. "Very well, then. I suppose the only decent thing of me to do is to go and assist you. Seeing as you clearly both still need adult guidance."

No one in the room seemed to challenge the notion and Venetor's eyes fell back to Liam and Xander. "Now then, aside from being your siblings, what are you both doing here? I saw no records of you having been down here before, which is what prompted the A.I. to come greet you. I have to hand it to Skyris, it was a smart move on her part to add that into the programming."

"They tapped into their powers." Annetta kept the explanation short, seeing as she was growing tired. "Liam is a psychic and well...my brother..."

Seeing as he was being beaconed on once more to show his abilities, Xander sighed and focused again to produce the sparks around his arms.

"You're an elemental," Venetor stated, seeming unfazed, "a person with the ability to manipulate the natural elements he comes into contact with."

"I've only ever done it with electricity," the boy added.

"Then you are either an Aerokinetic elemental or your powers are not yet there," Titus cut in.

Titus then pulled the Colt from the holster at his hip and turning around aimed it at one of the nearby tarp-covered objects. Once he was certain he had his target, he pulled the trigger, causing a bolt of

160

lightning to pass out of it and hit the object, forming sparks all over and leaving a gaping hole where the would-be bullet had hit its mark.

"Oh, your aunt is going to hate you when she sees that," Venetor chuckled.

"Aunt Skyris does not need to know," Titus smirked and spinning the Colt on his finger, placed it back in the holster. He then turned to Xander. "I can teach you how to use your powers, but it's gonna have to wait till this business with Aldamoor is finished."

"I still don't see why we can't go with you," Liam grumbled, crossing his arms.

Upon hearing the comment, Venetor faced the boy, his sharp blue eyes seeming to penetrate him. "Have you ever killed another conscious being?"

"What?"

"Have you ever killed another conscious being? Seen the lights go out in their eyes?" the Gaian prince inquired, to which Liam shook his head briskly in response. "Then you have no business on a battlefield of the magnitude we are about to walk into."

Annetta trailed off into her thoughts as she watched the scenario, more particularly, watched Venetor interact with Liam. There was a commanding air around him again, the likes of which she had only witnessed among the leaders of the Four Forces. The sureness with which he barked orders and explained his decisions left no room for questioning among the group. Finally, when all was said and done, Venetor simply retracted his physical presence a step back, showing he had said all he meant to.

"Once Annetta and J.K. return from Aldamoor with the rest of us, the two of you will begin to report in for training along with them," he added as an afterthought and began walking in the opposite direction with Titus at his side once again as Dexter following close behind them.

Seeing them disappear into the Lab, Annetta looked to the remainder of the companions. "Well, I guess we can show Liam and Xander around briefly before we have to send them home again. Seeing as that problem is...uh...somewhat solved."

Darius nodded, his eyes still lingering to where Venetor and Titus had vanished. His mind, however, was already a thousand leagues away, in a city above which zeppelins floated and in which a certain mage now resided.

Chapter 15

Though it had been over a month after speaking with Venetor, Matthias walked the vast halls of the Lab still consumed by the topic. He could not help but feel a tinge of guilt for never having questioned where it was that his family had come from. He vaguely remembered the small house his family had inhabited, but everything after was tinted in a red haze that was his years of service under Mislantus. It had seemed natural to fall into the role he had been given once aboard Valdhar and he had never questioned it. Not until he had gone through the Visium that is and the transformation while fighting Link. No one had really thought twice either about what had occurred during that fight, thinking it as being one of his abilities, but the truth was that he had known nothing of it before then. Perhaps if he had fought harder to rediscover the truth of who he was then it would all make sense. His mind played this inner turmoil over and over again until his meditations were interrupted by raised voices in the distance. Recognizing who they belonged to, the assassin felt the need to stay undetected. Slipping into the shadows, he made his way forward to be within hearing distance of the quarrel.

"Just how much longer are you going to let this thing drag, father?" Titus inquired in a tone bordering on anger. "We had a reason to come to Earth. A reason-"

"And all will be fulfilled," Venetor retorted indifferently. "Everything must run its course."

"People are dying, father," the younger Gaian argued.

Matthias narrowed his eyes at the last part. He'd heard the rumours of what they spoke of when he was travelling in space searching for Amarok. Now it seemed that those rumours had been confirmed by mere coincidence if they were speaking of what he thought they were. He waited in the dark for a few moments more before making his presence known by simply walking out into the light.

"My, my, I was wondering what all the fuss is about," he said. "Such a brilliant delivery of that line, Titus. Although, now you have me curious as to what people you might be referring to."

"How dare you," Titus snarled as his hand went straight to his gun.

Still unimpressed by what he was seeing, Venetor clasped a hand on Titus's shoulder while his gaze focused on Matthias. "Peace, Titus.

How are any aliens to gain a good reputation if we go shooting all of the locals?"

"A question I'm sure Annetta and J.K. would love to debate with the both of you right after you explain to them and to the rest of us what exactly in the Unknown's bane is going on," Matthias spat, pointing both his index fingers at them, "Because it had better not be what I thought I heard on my last trip into space."

Venetor exhaled, dropping his arm to his side in defeat as Titus withdrew from his hostile position.

"You know then of what has befallen Gaia," Venetor said with his eyes lowered to the floor, "Of the horror that has been unleashed on my people."

"The horror?" Matthias asked. "I heard it was a rebellion."

"Not of the sort you think it would be," he replied. "Those that follow are blinded by a false prophet. The rebellion is but a front put up by those who would have you think otherwise. There is a darkness which has captivated the homeland of my people, a shadow which the armies of Gaia have failed to keep at bay."

Matthias frowned upon hearing the cryptic speech, not sure what to make of any of it. He looked to Titus then for clarification.

The youth met the gaze of the assassin. "The lord of the tower has risen, and he is angry."

෨൬

Shimmering in the afternoon sun, pearl white armour pieces floated through the air as if suspended in zero gravity. Their course was not in vain, however, as each individual piece made its way towards its owner, clicking into place one after another overtop of a white Beta scale mail shirt. The procedure coming to an end, a crimson cape draped itself around the shoulders of the owner.

The task of dressing having been completed, the owner, a tall man with shoulder-length golden hair, sapphire eyes and a neatly trimmed beard strode towards the mirror in his vast, dark room. There, on a dresser beside it lay a brutish looking metal crown with sharp points and a red gem encrusted into the centre. He took a moment to look at the craftsmanship of the thing, how simple and yet complex it appeared to be. It had been his by right for so long, too long, and now his patience had paid off. Placing it atop his brow, he turned to exit the room.

Passing the doors into the hall, he came face to face with a man in a mask resembling that of a misshapen broken star.

"The lords and ladies are ready to receive you, my king," the masked man spoke.

"They are in the main room as I asked, then?" the king queried.

"All the representatives of noble houses as per your request Lord Razmus," he assured him. "It was not an easy task to complete with half of them having been in hiding after your ascent to the throne. Nonetheless, as my king commanded, I made it happen."

"Good, then let us get this meeting underway, Amarok. I will weed these traitors out one way or another and even if I must spend all day doing it."

Coming to their destination, Razmus opened the hulking wooden doors and strode inside before his presence could even be announced.

In the room was a large round stone table, upon which were carved various animals. Around it were gathered men and women dressed in rich medieval garbs. The style had never gone out of fashion on Gaia, particularly among the noble houses on formal occasions, and was meant to denote their status as apart from the common people.

Taking his seat, Razmus motioned for those gathered to seat themselves as well. He then took a long pause, observing each and every person gathered in the room. He found it fascinating how many of those present looked so much like their predecessors. One man, in particular, stood out to him with an uncanny resemblance.

"You are of house Brant." Razmus pointed a clawed hand at the one he was addressing.

The Gaian noble being pointed at, a tall man of medium build with short cropped dark brown hair with a long well-groomed beard, stood up from where he sat.

"I am," he answered. "Bretus, or Lord Brant as I am referred to."

"Yes, yes, I knew it." Razmus beamed as he motioned for the Gaian to come to him. "You have the same facial structure Pinarus had when he was alive. Did you know that?"

"There is little record of what he looked like at the time," Bretus said as he came before the king. "From what I have seen of him in paintings and in sculpture, though, I do see a resemblance."

"It's incredible," Razmus marvelled at the Gaian as he stood up and moved around him, examining each detail of him. "Do you know then, perhaps, what it was that Pinarus Brant was remembered for?"

"Well, he extended research into the use of psychic abilities, and also led the charge in the Hurtz civil war, my king."

Razmus stopped before the Gaian again. "Historical footnotes, but do you know what I remember him for?"

Bretus seemed puzzled by what the king demanded. He was answered seconds later when an armoured set of clawed fingers sliced his throat.

"For betraying me and being responsible, along with a score of others, for locking me in the tower," Razmus intoned as the Gaian noble died at his feet. He then sat down and regarded all of those who looked on in fear of what they had witnessed. "Listen here and listen well. I am the white lion who has come to bring you out of darkness, a darkness that for too long you have been led into by false leaders and traitors. For too long have you all grown fat on the power that was given to you. Today I take it back. Gaia has only one king, and you will serve me, not I you. If there is anyone who opposes this, you may find your place on the floor next to Bretus and before you judge me any harsher than you already have, know that Bretus himself aided in the escape of your would-be prince and his companions, neglecting to destroy his fleet of space vessels till the last moment. This meeting is dismissed!"

Those in the room parted without having anything else to say to their king save for bowing as they left. Guards soon after rushed in to remove the body, while servants had begun to scrub the floors clean.

Amarok then took this as his chance to slide into the chamber and take his place beside the king.

"My lord, I am not certain I understood the purpose of that. Would it not have been better to imprison him or send him to work in the mines?" Amarok said.

Razmus turned to regard the assassin. "Sometimes a melodramatic display is needed to instil subservience in one's subjects. I could have sent him to the mines, but then I risk others disobeying me."

"I see." Amarok's mask glinted as he nodded his head.

"I have a job for you," Razmus informed him as he watched the servants at work. "I want you to find the spawn of Magnus and bring him to me."

"I will find him, my lord," Amarok responded.

"Good, and do not return until it is done."

෨ඏ

The next day, Annetta and Jason met up at first light, their parents having called into school saying that both had come down with strep throat. Once in the base, they headed towards the stables, only to be stopped by all of the Lab's current occupants sitting together in the common room. Venetor had seated himself in one of the armchairs, dressed in his outfit from when he had first come to Earth, with Gladius and Titus standing to one side, and the Gaian female named Atala at the other with Skyris. Link, Sarina, Matthias and Darius stood off to the side of this sight, their eyes meeting the duo once they came within hearing distance. The scene seemed eerily like one of a courthouse.

"Uh...hey, guys." Annetta greeted them. "What's going on?"

"There's something you both need to hear, Anne," Darius replied, his eyes shifting to Venetor and then back at her. "Something you should have been told a while ago."

Hearing the second part got Jason suspicious. He had not trusted Venetor from the get go, not like Annetta had anyway. It suddenly felt like his gut instincts hadn't been far off from their mark.

"What do you mean?" The girl took another step forward.

"It will be best if you sit down for this," Venetor spoke and using his abilities, moved one of the sofas so it was right behind them. "It will take some time to explain."

"Always a conspiracy with you offworlders," Jason grumbled as he sunk into the seat.

"It makes for a more interesting existence." Venetor flashed a set of white teeth at him, before resuming a neutral face and turning to the both of them. "I know I should have spoken sooner, and perhaps that is what has led to us meeting in this way, but so it must be, and so I shall begin without further delay. We have travelled far to get here, through foreign solar systems and through the depths of space not yet known to humankind in one particular quest: Aid for Gaia. I understand neither Jason nor yourself are aware of the rumours of the fate which has befallen your ancestral homeworld and so I will fill you in. It all began nearly twelve thousand years ago, which may seem like a very long time in Earth years, but the average Gaian life span is three hundred. The current lord of Gaia at the time, Markus Severio, had twin sons named Magnus and Razmus. Both boys showed exceptional leadership skills and good temperament for ruling, and so year after year, the king could not choose which was to be his heir. As they approached adulthood and the king still could not name an heir, his advisors grew tense, fearing a war would break out should a decision not be made soon. Hearing the words of his councillors, the king came up with an idea. He went to his sons and bade them both to begin construction of a tower. The son with the highest tower would win the throne. There was a catch, however. Neither son could use any psychic abilities to aid in the process. This way, both would have to use other skills to settle the matter, for both were accomplished psychic warriors. And so they set off upon their father's orders, both planning and preparing what would be their masterpiece in honour of the Unknown. The work began with each brother sporting a team of the finest builders they could recruit into their ranks. Enthusiasm flew high, and all who knew awaited with anticipation of the results the competition would bring. But days turned into weeks, weeks into months and months into years. Neither brother would give up chisel and hammer while the other still built. The king and his councillors watched on helplessly as the two behemoth towers continued to grow without end. What they did not know was that the pressure of the project was beginning to cause Razmus to go mad. In his madness to obtain the throne, he had begun to hatch a plan which would alter the course of Gaian history forever. The creation of the Hurtz."

Annetta and Jason took the pause to have their eyes wander to Gladius, who stood unmoving on the spot, his massive chest rising and falling with his steady breathing. They both felt a tinge of betrayal as they remembered Brakkus telling him about his race. They had been told that the Hurtz were similar to Bugbears and Hobgoblins. How they had been hunted to near extinction in the middle ages. Had everything he'd said to them been a lie as well?

Venetor noted the shock on both of their faces but continued the story. "The Hurtz were stronger than any living Gaian, even those who could tap into their feral form's strength and speed. The Hurtz were Gaians who were perpetually stuck in a half-transformed state, and more often than not it consisted of more than one animal. With his army of Hurtz, Razmus continued to build, and soon was outpacing Magnus, but all of this was to change, for Markus's councillors were furious with what his son had done. Overnight and without the knowledge of Razmus, Magnus was given control of the Gaian army and ordered to march on his brother to put an end to it all. It was a bloody affair that almost ended in both brothers dying at each other's hands, but when it was over, Magnus emerged victorious. As punishment for his crime, Razmus was placed within the base of his tower and sealed within it with a spell to keep him alive there for all eternity. His father did not have the heart to see him executed and knew that he could not be kept in the dungeons for fear that his supporters would try to free him. A series of spells and rituals were performed to encase him in his tomb, the Gaian who would be known forevermore as the Lord of the Unfinished Tower. All traces of the spells, or so we were led to believe, were destroyed to prevent anyone else from freeing him. His story faded from our history after four and a half generations to become just a legend, a bedtime story, a thing spoken of in past tense, until now. Just over a year ago, he was freed from his prison and rallied many Hurtz and Gaians to his side. He took control of the planet, proclaiming himself the prophesied one, the white lion of Gaia. I managed to escape with Titus, Skyris, Gladius and Atala in order to seek the support of the Four Forces."

The duo stayed silent, neither of them knowing what to say after having heard the story. Jason was the first to speak. "So, first of all, you didn't even bother mentioning this in over a month and you came to Earth wanting an army that technically Annetta and myself command?"

"We came to ask for your aid," Atala responded. "That is the primal reason the Four Forces exist, isn't it?"

"Well, yeah, but we got our own problems too, lady," Jason retorted. "I mean, the Water Elves are in trouble and they're part of that army you need."

"He's right, Atala," Venetor spoke to the other Gaian, who huffed back in reply with a strained impatience visible in her body language. He then turned back to them. "Atala is the general of the Gaian forces. She travelled under the guise of being Skyris's handmaiden in order for us to avoid unwanted questioning as to why she was with us."

"And don't think for a second I'm going to clean up after her to fit the role," the darker-skinned Gaian spat before she turned back to Venetor. "So then, Lord Venetor, what exactly is the plan in this case?"

The Gaian prince rose from his seat. "My course of action has not altered, but Jason is right. The Water Elves form the alliance and so must be helped. I will ride with Annetta and the others as I stated the previous night."

Annetta, feeling her level of impatience rise decided to speak. "So, is there anything else you haven't told us about why you came here? I'm really starting to get fed up with all of this secrecy."

There was an iron-like resolve in the girl's words which made her seem that much older when she addressed Venetor. He saw for an instant a little something of another Severio pass through her blue eyes, but it was gone before he knew it and before him stood the teenage girl once more.

"No, that is everything as it stands," he stated and walked past her.

The meeting having concluded, the group began to dissolve. Link, Matthias, Skyris, Titus and Atala retreated back to their quarters in order to prepare themselves, while Darius and Sarina left to gather any supplies that may be needed for the journey. Annetta and Jason rose from their seats, seeing only Gladius left.

"He was to tell ye sooner," the Hurtz spoke, observing the two youth with his one good eye. "He wanted things with the Water Elves to be sorted first. He knew ya'd need full strength to go to Gaia."

"Well, he could have said something like, hey, I'm your uncle and I'm here because I need your help since my planet got taken over by some dude we are all related to that was walled up in a tower for all eternity but somehow managed to get out," Jason snapped. "I mean...do the words out of the frying pan and into the fire mean anything? And you know what? Where was Gaia when Mislantus came and wanted the Eye to All Worlds? And don't even play the family card on this one."

The Hurtz sighed in response to what the boy had said and replied, "Venetor wanted to aid ye, he saw what was going on, knew Arieus had given up his post and for all we knew ye weren't here to do anything about it. It was the Intergalactic Federation which forbade him, the same Federation which now will not allow other worlds to come to Gaia's aid. At least not the ones who be inducted into it, and Earth is not."

"If Gaia is in so much trouble then why aren't they allowing anyone to help?" Jason asked. "I mean, all we have ever heard was how great the Gaian army is."

Gladius flattened out his good ear, causing the many earrings to jingle on it. "It is the Federation's form of punishment for Gaia's pride. Years ago, when Mordred, Mislantus's father, pillaged across worlds, gathering his army, the members of some of these planets came to ask for Gaia's aid when they were being attacked. Gaia never refused to help, knowing Mordred was one of them, a problem they had given birth to and had not stopped when it could still be contained. The lives of the Gaian people were always ready to be lain down in the service of other planets. They were the protectors of the known worlds. The other planets in the Federation soon began to rely on Gaia, calling them forth when any danger lurked, abusing that alliance they had made. It was in such an encounter that Venetor insulted the Greys."

"Wait, you mean Greys as in like…," Annetta stammered. She'd heard the conspiracy theories about the Grey Aliens but had never thought them to be an actual species that existed. Then again with everything she had learned the last little while, it was not something she could expect not to be real.

"The one and the same you be thinking." Gladius nodded his head. "And also the now elected leaders of the Intergalactic Federation. So when Venetor came grovelling before the Greys a year ago, seeking the permission of the Federation, ye can see why they declined his request and forbade Venetor to come. Ye help all of us or none of us, not even yer sister planet, they told him. Later when the issue with Razmus arose they told him that if Gaians can fight so well then they can resolve their own quarrels."

Annetta exhaled roughly, her head spinning from the overload of information she had just received. It seemed like every day since Venetor had arrived the world she had just become accustomed to was beginning to shrink to nothing more than a spoke in an even greater wheel. She rubbed her temples, feeling the pressure begin to build from the stress of thinking. She didn't want to think about it all, not today. She would have to focus on her spoke and not the wheel.

"It still doesn't change the state of things," she finally said and turning heel, marched off to get ready.

♋

Assembling in the stables, the companions set out for the portal towards Aldamoor. When they finally arrived upon the grassy Plains of Erper, the group found themselves surrounded by war tents of every size and description being hoisted up. Soldiers from all the races of the Four Forces had begun pouring in from various portals, causing a colourful array of beings to run about. As they rode towards the city, trumpets and horns sounded their arrival to those who were in the camp, causing soldiers that were present to salute both Annetta and Jason. The duo rode at the front of the group, dressed in their gyldrig armour and tabards, which displayed the Severio and Kinsman lions on them. Annetta's hair had also been tied into a braid by Skyris, who had insisted to her that it would prevent it from getting caught in her armour. So far, the Gaian woman had been right. Behind them rode

Venetor and Atala, dressed in their Gaian armour, then Link and Gladius, followed by Sarina, Matthias, Darius, Titus and Skyris.

Approaching the front gates, the party halted. A lone figure with a brown beard in a blue uniform loomed over the stone gates of the city, peering down at them.

"About time you showed up," Iliam Starview, Puc's close childhood friend, called as he motioned back to the guards to unlock the gates, causing the large structure to creep open.

Riding inside, the group were soon joined by the now vice-general of Aldamoor. There was weariness in the elf's face which suggested a lack of sleep once they saw him up close. This, however, did not stop his friendly demeanour.

"Puc is with the other members of the Council in the tower," he informed them. "Once you are there, I'll send word to the other leaders so that you may hold a meeting. I must say, your group has grown a lot bigger since the last time I saw you here."

Annetta turned and motioned to each of the members of the group as she introduced them. "This is my uncle, Lord Venetor, the Crown Prince of Gaia, Atala Shade, general of the Gaian forces, Titus, Venetor's son and my cousin, Gladius the Hurtz and my aunt, Skyris, Venetor's sister."

"Oh, I know who they are," Iliam stated, his eyes lingering on each one of them. "I'm going to assume, however, that the rest of the Gaian army didn't just join the cause, did they?"

"It's complicated," Atala replied. "The Intergalactic Federation forbade Gaia to get involved with any of the dealings the Four Forces have."

"Right, so you are just here to watch," Iliam remarked.

"We are here to help in whatever way we can," Venetor retorted, his icy stare regarding the elf. "Gaia is at war, one which the planet is losing."

"I have no idea what you are talking about, but I see." Iliam beamed a sarcastic smile in the direction of the Gaian prince and continued walking without another word.

"I get the feeling Venetor isn't really well liked by these guys," Annetta whispered to the side to Jason.

"You think?" he raised an eyebrow.

They soon arrived at the front doors of the tower and dismounted. Seconds later, they found themselves within the same audience chamber Kaian once inhabited as First Mage. It was a bit more crowded than the companions remembered it from before, with Puc sitting on the other side of the desk with Kaine, Kaian's son, standing over one shoulder and two other elderly mages over the other. They seemed to be in some kind of heated discussion and it was not until Iliam cleared his throat that any of them bothered to pay them any mind.

"I brought you some new friends to play with." Iliam grinned at Puc and motioned to Annetta and Jason. "Be nice, Thanestorm."

"Make sure the defences are in place, Starview," Puc instructed as Iliam shook his head in reply. The mage then turned to those who had just entered the room. "I am glad you have arrived. There is much I need to inform you of."

His eyes then turned directly to Venetor. " I am surprised to see you here, considering our past."

"What quarrels we had before, Thanestorm, we need to set aside for now," the Gaian spoke. "Your people need you, and need the Four Forces."

There was stiffness to Puc's disposition as he observed Venetor. It was only after a few moments that the elf managed a bob of the head to show his agreement. He then looked at Jason and Annetta, who stood in the midst of everything. "I am sure it has been mentioned to you by now that the Fire Elves have been spotted raiding our borders, an event not uncommon for the Water Elves to have to deal with. Our two races have been at odds with one another since our beginnings, a conflict with no end. The Fire Elves have waged war against us in the past, desolated cities and destroyed the lives of countless people who have found themselves within the path of their flames. Now, reports have come in over the last while that the Fire Elves have been doing more than just raiding. They are amassing an army, one which they intend to march upon Aldamoor."

"What Puc has failed to mention," one of the elderly mages, a tall elf with wild flowing locks and a short-cropped salt and pepper beard, spoke, "is that there is no First Mage. The Fire Elves are taking advantage of this fact."

"Wait, so you mean you never took your vows?" Darius blurted out.

"For the last time, I will be taking no vows." An edge of anger could be heard in Puc's voice. "I am not a Chironson and it is a Chironson which must reside as First Mage. It has been so since the inception of the Council and I will not be the one to break this. My place was and always has been as the advisor of Orbeyus and his kin for the Four Forces."

"Well, good luck finding a Chironson," Kaine remarked as he lifted his arms in the air to draw attention to himself. "Because last I checked, I flunked the Academy and am not qualified to lead."

Puc let out something resembling a growl from his throat as he raked a hand through his hair in frustration. He felt trapped, and though his main intent when his eyes went for the door was to sate a need for escape, they also searched for a person he had hoped to see, but was not there. He then turned to the two mages and Kaine standing at his back.

"I will only be acting First Mage for the duration of this crisis. Afterwards, I wash my hands of it. My place is with the heir of Orbeyus and the son of Arcanthur."

"Once the Fire Elf forces are defeated we will figure something else out," the second elderly mage, who was much shorter and wore spectacles said. "For the time being, Aldamoor needs you, Thanestorm."

Puc curled his upper lip in protest and then breathed heavily. "I will do all I can, but my mind is made up."

"A choice we understand," the first of the two mages said.

"Good," Puc retorted as he folded the parchment he had been studying, then turned to the shorter mage. "Tobias, I want you and Alaric to see to the inner walls. I want no shortage of spells that have been cast upon them. They are the last defence of the city if all else fails."

"As it is willed, so it shall be done." The shorter mage named Tobias made a shallow bow and exited with Alaric.

Watching them go, Puc was thankful for there being fewer people in the room and turned to the remaining crowd. "A tent is being prepared for us on the field as we speak. I'm sure by the time we get there, Ironhorn, Natane and Entellion will be waiting."

The mage rose from his seat and pushed his chair in. He grabbed hold of his staff and began making his way for the door.

"Looks like you had your hands full here," Jason mused as he followed suit.

"Believe me when I say this Jason, you have not seen the half of it," the elf grumbled as he left the room.

Just as Puc had predicted, a large tent had been raised in the midst of the others. Inside, candles were being lit and an assortment of wooden tables brought in, upon which the elven mage had spread all of his battle plans. Annetta, Jason and Venetor, still in their armour, along with Puc and Kaine took their respective places around the table. While Annetta and Jason had insisted that Sarina, Matthias, Darius and Link join them, Puc forbade it, saying there would be enough confusion as is. His words became truth when the other leaders of the races which made up the Four Forces found their way inside and a heated discussion came under way.

"You will want a labyrinth erected around the city," Ironhorn, the king of the Minotaurs explained as he showed Puc one of the sketches he had brought with him, featuring a map of the city with what looked to be a maze around it.

"There won't be time to build something like that, though, will there?" Annetta interjected, doing her best to keep up with all of the ideas being thrown around.

"We can have the mages assemble and throw one up with ease," Puc reminded her, "But if they have airships of their own then the wall may be for naught."

"You've the entire fleet of Aldamoor at your command," Kaine reminded him. "We have three hundred fighting vessels ready to take them on. If we get desperate, we can even outfit some of the faster trade galleys as well as the heavier scouting ships like we did when fighting Mislantus."

The mage nodded and then turned to Natane and Entellion. "Have the scouts been sent to warn the other cities of an impending attack?"

"The swiftest of the swift were sent out," Natane stated, "and they shall be back in time for the fighting, methinks."

"The Sky Wolves did not spare our troops, either," Entellion assured him.

While the planning continued, Annetta and Jason could not help but feel the stare of an individual pierce their backs. The duo turned to see Venetor, standing some distance away in silent observation. The youth felt themselves recoil internally but showed no outward emotion to the psychological singling out that the Gaian was trying to evoke.

Seeing his antics have no effect, he addressed them. "And in all the might and accumulated power, what do the leaders of the Four Forces bring to the table, I wonder?"

A deafening silence filled the room which was not broken until both a sword and mace landed upon the table. The Gaian prince looked down at the weapons and then at the duo which dropped them.

"Our lives," Annetta replied, "In service of those who are our strength and wisdom."

෬෬

The meeting had come to an end, Annetta and Jason emerged from the tent with exhausted looks on their faces. They had both been absent the last time such a meeting was held when Mislantus planned to invade Severio Castle, so there was much they had to learn on the go in terms of strategy. Thankfully, Puc was there.

"Man, did you catch half of that?" Jason asked once they were out of earshot. "If you did, I got the other half."

Annetta laughed upon hearing him. "Guess that's why they say two heads are better than one."

The boy nodded and smiled. "I'm gonna go see what Sarina is up to. You wanna come with?"

Before Annetta could open her mouth to answer him, Venetor emerged from the folds of the tent. While the Gaian had not said much during the gathering, she could tell he was calculating every move in his head, seeing every possible angle and outcome. It brought a chill down her spine when she remembered how easily he had defeated both of them on their first day of training with him. She then also recalled her conversation with Gladius and watched as the Gaian prince walked past both of them in his usual warrior swagger, with his crimson cape snapping on the wind behind him.

"I'll catch up later," she said to Jason. "I gotta do some stuff first."

"Okay, later Anne," Jason replied, seeing the intent on her face and went off in the direction of where Sarina and the others were helping with preparations.

Annetta bobbed her head in acknowledgement and sprinted after Venetor. Her armour was making it difficult for her to move any faster due to all of the layers. She'd nearly bumped into a few of the soldiers by accident in the pursuit, but made sure not to lose sight of the shorter Gaian's cape. When she finally caught up to him, Venetor had seated himself some distance away from all of the commotion on a boulder which jutted out from the otherwise grassy area.

"And what brings you out here, heir of Orbeyus?" The words sounded mocking, coming from him.

The girl stepped back a foot, still not able to get a read on him fully. In fact, she was confused as to why she had even bothered to follow Venetor at all. Gathering up the courage, she finally said, "There are some things I wanted to know."

Venetor exhaled gruffly and pointed to another rock which lay hidden among the grass just a few paces away from him. Annetta quickly accepted the proposition and sat down, taking a moment to collect her thoughts as she looked at her feet.

"Gladius told J.K. and me about the Intergalactic Federation," she explained, "How they didn't let you come to Earth when Mislantus was heading our way and how now, they aren't allowing any aid to come to Gaia from the outside. He told us about how the Gaians were used by the planets of the Federation when they needed military aid."

The Gaian's mighty shoulders slouched with another sigh as he looked over in the direction of the busy camp.

"I spent my life in Orbeyus's shadow when I was younger," he stated, "When he left, or rather I should say fled to Earth, he forfeited his title as the Crown Prince of Gaia. As next in line it passed to me, a task I never thought I would have to carry out. And the Unknown knows I never wanted it anyway. He was slightly younger than you when he left. I was not reunited with him for many years. We were both men by then, of course, him the leader of the Four Forces and I the future ruler of Gaia."

Listening, Annetta felt a tinge of nostalgia to the words he spoke. It seemed another lifetime for him, and yet he did not look much older than her father. She then asked, "Did you fight in the Great War?"

"As soon as news reached me, I had rallied Atala with ten thousand of her best soldiers and set out for Earth without thinking twice," he answered. "My father doubted Orbeyus and the legitimacy of the legends surrounding the resting place of the Eye to All Worlds. I never did and I knew he would find it, just like Adeamus did all those centuries before. When I finally saw him standing beneath the banner of the Four Forces with that great axe of his, I knew I had been right."

The girl nodded again in reply, not sure how else to respond. As she studied Venetor's face, she began to see common features that he shared with Orbeyus. It was something she had not had a chance to notice before with everything that was going on and with Venetor continuously ridiculing them in their training.

"As you grow older," he said, interrupting her train of thought, "you will come to understand the importance of family, especially in the Severio clan. Orbeyus was my brother and I would have followed him anywhere if he asked. He was a great warrior and a champion for those who had none. He was also in my father's eyes the golden son, even if he did adopt a black lion for his sigil when he came to Earth. I know that I failed to get to Earth when Mislantus came and I've been angry with myself ever since for it."

"It wasn't your fault," Annetta said.

Venetor seemed, however, to be lost in his fury as memories continued to pile up. He curled up his hands into fists, the blood draining from his knuckles. Reminding himself of where he was, he let them go limp, "I should have been there."

"Like I said, don't worry about it," she repeated. "I have to ask, though, what did you do to the Greys exactly to have made them forbid you from coming here to begin with?"

"I refused to lend them the Gaian troops to a fallen outpost," Venetor told her without hesitation. "And why should have I? People's entire homeworlds were under threat, and the Greys, who are considered one of the oldest and wisest races quaked in their boots when Mislantus put a colony to the torch. Gaia is a warrior race and we will not bow to such whims when actual worlds in need of aid. The Greys behaved like spoiled youth, and I simply called them out for it. I'll be honest, I never did think they would be elected as the leaders of the Federation for the next four federal decades at the time so when the votes were cast in a few years ago, I knew retribution was coming."

"I see," Annetta replied, shifting her position on the rock. "There's also something else that I wanted to know about. You mentioned the Hurtz having been created by Razmus. What happened to them after his downfall?"

There was no immediate response this time from Venetor. His gaze seemed spaced out as he looked back to the camp, watching soldiers scramble in preparations.

"For many years after, the Hurtz were used as slaves," he finally said. "Many were used and still are today as gladiators in the fighting pits."

"You practice slavery on Gaia?" Annetta seemed shocked.

"Did, past tense," Venetor corrected her. "There is still tension among the two races, but we do our best to suppress it. The Hurtz who participated in the fighting pits now are free and fight for the money that can be earned. Some of them even enlist in the military or the private services of lords and ladies, such as when my father brought Brakkus and Gladius to be mine and Orbeyus's sworn shields."

Annetta shook her head to show she understood him. Deep down, however, she was still not fond of the idea that one race had enslaved another, even if for a brief period in time. Venetor noted this.

"Gaia is not perfect," he spoke, "But we are a proud race, a warrior race. Our history is laced with the blood of our own and of the Hurtz whom we share a world with. That cannot be denied and it is also not to say that we haven't been learning as we go along. Much like the humans of Earth, from what I hear."

The Gaian stood up and walked a few paces to stretch his legs. "Gaia is, after all, the sister planet to Earth. How can we not be similar if we are, to a degree, family?"

Annetta watched as the Gaian who was her great uncle, her grandfather's brother, began his journey back to camp. The more she spoke to him, the more of a puzzle he became. It hurt her head to think about it. Perhaps this was what studying for exams in university felt like, a feeling she was willing to pass up, even if according to Puc it meant not fulfilling her purpose in life.

಼ಂಡ

Having completed the last of his tasks, Puc left the camp and headed into the depths of Aldamoor. He needed time to think, away from the prying eyes of other mages of the council and away from the bustle of the war camps. In truth, his time in his homeland had left him weary, strained. He longed for nothing more than everything to be over so he could return to Q-16 and resume his life as it once was. He rode as far as the natural rock walls that protected Aldamoor from the north, and dismounting his horse, left it tethered to a post nearby. He continued on foot in the direction of the waterfalls that fell unevenly all along the walls of stone. To those out of the city, they would seem a wondrous site, to Puc and other elves that had grown up around them, they were as ordinary as the trees and shrubs which populated parts of Aldamoor, carefully planted in an orderly fashion among the cobblestone streets. What many of them also did not know was that there was a multitude of caves on the other side of the falls, and this is where the mage was headed for.

Braving the slippery steps etched into the side of the stone, Puc tread with care until he had reached his destination. It was a small cave, hidden behind one of the larger falls. The steps had been his own addition in his youth, an easier way of accessing the remote area. It had been his place of study during his years in the Academy. A place he could rely on where he would not be bothered by Kaian or any of the other students. It was ironic now how he would have given anything to hear the Chironson's voice once more. Crossing the threshold and shielding his head from the water, Puc gazed into the empty cavern.

Everything was as he remembered it. The large rocks he had used as a desk and chair still stood untouched. Feeling his way around the walls, he moved the corners of his lips up in a slight smile. Muttering an incantation, lights illuminated the interior in an orange glow as if little candles had been placed within the crevices of the upper walls. Finally feeling more comfortable, the mage inhaled, his lungs filling with the scent of ancient stone mingled with water. Closing his eyes, he allowed himself to be lost in the thundering ensemble of the falls.

Suddenly, he felt something rest upon his shoulder above the folds of his robe and snapping out of his thoughts, he pulled a dagger from his sleeve, pointing it at his assailant. He turned around. Staring back at him in the rusty glow was a face he had not expected to see ever again.

"Skyris." The name rolled off his tongue in a foreign manner as he lowered the weapon.

The Gaian female took a step closer to him. Her inquisitive eyes studied his face as she brushed a stray strand of black hair from his brow.

"After all this time," the mage spoke yet again as he attempted to make conversation.

"You doubted I would come back." The words came sure and steady.

The two of them withdrew, taking a step back as each party studied the other. In truth, neither of them knew what to say. This silent questioning persisted until Skyris finally broke it.

"You stayed, just as Orbeyus asked."

"I did as commanded," the mage stated bluntly as he continued to look at her. "And you came with Venetor."

"Escaped with my life more like it," Skyris smirked, running a hand through her hair. "If you only knew what was going on right now on Gaia."

"I am aware of its current state," he replied, "but as you can see, my hands are tied in Aldamoor."

"I don't blame you for it." She clarified her position.

Turning away from her, Puc sighed as he looked out into the falling water that veiled them from the rest of Aldamoor. Memories seemed to tumble out from deep within him, things he thought he had buried for good, left behind in a past life. They were the things that had made him who he was today. He needed to let her know before she assumed anything else.

"Skyris...I-" before the mage could say anything he was met with a pair of lips that locked in with his own. For an instant, he froze, not certain how to react, feeling her arms wrap around his neck, causing him to nearly lose balance. As quickly as they had collided, however, Puc pushed her away and recomposed himself. "I'm sorry, but I cannot do this."

"Thanestorm, we are alone. Venetor won't know I was here," she reassured him.

"And that worked out so brilliantly the last time," the mage said, voice laced with sarcasm. "Just what were you thinking in coming up here?"

"The same thing I'm guessing you were," she said. "Reminiscing about old times."

What joy there was in Puc's face when he had initially seen Skyris was now replaced with anger, old wounds having been torn open.

"Spare me the romanticism of it all, Skyris," the mage sneered.

"Don't even try to act all high and mighty," the Gaian chuckled. "I like to think I know you better than you're willing to admit."

The mage huffed. "And what if in the last two decades I have changed?"

Skyris snorted as she sat down on one of the rocks and pulled out a flask from the brown woollen cloak she wore. "You and me both."

Puc watched her as she took a swig from the container and hid it again. "What happened to you, Skyris?"

The Gaian female closed her eyes as she allowed the contents of the flask to warm her insides. "Simple. I adapted to deal with the past."

Puc watched Skyris from the corner of his eye and feeling surer of the situation, he sat down beside her. "Then I suppose there is no point in me asking you if you are happy with your current life."

"If by happy you mean capable of outdrinking many a Gaian, then sure," she scoffed. "If you mean settled down and enjoying marital bliss with some political match my dear brother deemed worthy of me, then the answer is no. I refuse to be a game piece for his gain."

"Skyris, what we had…" The words seemed to stop in Puc's throat, "It was not meant to be."

"Damn it, Thanestorm, it was!" The Gaian growled and stood up. "Even Orbeyus approved it."

Stillness fell within the cavern, the only sound of life being the waterfall in the background as the mage and the Gaian locked gazes with one another. There was so much both of them wanted to say that all they were capable of was unwavering silence, blocked by the limitations of speech. It was Puc who finally strode forward. "Skyris, you are a Princess of Gaia and I a mage of Aldamoor, even if I was Orbeyus's advisor. No matter what way we try to look at it, your station outranks mine."

"Unknown's bane, Thanestorm, I have spurned every suitor Venetor has sent my way in hopes that some day I would come back to Earth, to you." Skyris's fury was beginning to reach its peak. There was a pause before she spoke again. "We had a son, you and I."

The blood drained from Puc's face, leaving it a shade paler than usual. "A son?"

"A baby boy," she reiterated. "I wanted to tell you sooner, but Venetor forbid me to send any communications back to Earth."

Feeling something remotely resembling joy creep into his limbs, Puc could not help but smile a little as he took Skyris's hands into his own. "How old is he? What is his name? Is he well?"

The Gaian's face told an entirely different tale, a story so old that she had no more tears to shed. Skyris looked down at her hands, freeing them from his grip and she turned away. "He didn't make it. He was taken from me just after he came into this world."

As quickly as the news had built up a whole new reality for Puc, it came crashing down. Feeling the weight of his years catch up to him, Puc leaned heavily on his staff, trying to discern his next move. There before him was a woman who in his younger years he would have fought and burned entire armies for. While to some degree the feelings were still there, they had become numb, subdued through time, overtaken by his sense of duty. Moving closer, he drew her into a one armed embrace which she returned with both of her own. Pulling away slightly he then kissed her gently on the forehead before fully letting go.

"I cannot love you as I once did," he said, "but know that my heart will always beat in time with your own."

He then left her in the depths of the cave.

Chapter 16

It had been too long since Matthias had been out on the hunt. He'd received strict orders by Puc not to let anyone know he had left the camp, in case those who could be spying for the enemy got wind of it. He welcomed the challenge. After all, it was a test to see if life in the Lab had made him soft. He didn't like the idea that it could have.

Having been shown a map by Puc, he set out on a course to where the Fire Elves had struck last. He left his mount some distance away in order for it not to get detected and continued on foot from there. It was a small village on the outskirts of Aldamoor, or rather it had been. His destination no longer resembled a place where life had once flourished. Burnt skeletal structures greeted him on the horizon, with not a soul in sight. Furrowing his brow under the cowl of his long black hood, the assassin trudged onwards, making sure to be cautious of his surroundings. As he arrived in the vicinity, the smells of scorched timber filled his nostrils while his eyes scanned the blackened wood to try and tell a story of what had once been.

He had been warned by the mage what to expect once he got there, so the fact that nothing remained did not faze him in the least. He remembered having to pick up trails with less when serving under Mislantus. This was child's play.

Coiling the muscles in his legs, the assassin continued to stride forwards, examining the patterns of destruction, analyzing the proximity of each blow and the strength of each attack.

"I tell ya it ain't here," a male voice from among the ruins spoke abruptly, causing the assassin to hide behind one of the more intact buildings. "You must have dropped the damn thing during the charge."

"And I'm telling ya that I had it with me," a female voice snapped back. "Honestly, Julian, I don't lose my head to bloodlust that easily."

As the two new arrivals chatted, Matthias took the opportunity to sneak around the building in order to get a better look. At first glance, they looked no different than the Water Elves he had encountered. Both beings sported long platinum hair that appeared to be braided, and wore crimson leather armour. It was not until he caught sight of their feral red eyes that he knew them to be on the other side. Further behind the duo stood two creatures which Matthias could only describe as large black lizards with orange and yellow spots on them. They appeared to be saddled.

"Come on, Rommy, Tamora is waiting for us with the rest of the ships. Yer trinket necklace can wait," the one named Julian said as he mounted his lizard. "Once we sack Aldamoor, ya can make thirty more of them and still not know what to do with the rest of the gold you'll get."

"Fine," the female elf huffed as she slung into the saddle. "By this time tomorrow, it all won't matter anyway. That stinking city will be in flames and we'll be the richest elves there ever were on Terrailim."

"That's if the siege weapon works," Julian snorted. Urging their mounts, the two were off as fast as they had arrived.

Remaining in the shadows, Matthias smiled under his breath at the information having been handed to him. While he had taken into consideration the fact that the information he had just heard could have been fabricated on purpose, he could tell from the body language of the two that it was not so.

"Sometimes, I really question the intelligence of certain species," the assassin chuckled as he vanished from the scene.

ഇരജ

Having returned to the tent that had been assigned to her, Skyris peered through the fold to find Gladius seated at the far end of the room, inspecting his metal armour as he donned it piece by piece. It was a lengthy process for the Hurtz, one at the end of which he would be covered from head to toe in thick plate mail that little could get through. Even less could get through when he would swing a sword.

"Back from yer romp, m'lady?" he asked, taking note of her presence.

Skyris lowered her hood to give him a slight nod in return. Removing the cloak completely, she folded it neatly and rested it on the back of one of the chairs which were placed around a large round table in the middle of the space. There was not much else in the tent, and it was obvious that it had been arranged for them in a hurry, given the lack of cots to lie down on. The elves it seemed did not expect a long wait before the attack.

"If you are back, then we need to talk," the voice of Venetor spoke from behind her as he stepped inside.

"Okay." She frowned. "About what, exactly?"

"Don't peg me for a fool, sister." The Gaian gritted his teeth. "I know exactly where and who you went to go see."

"Lord Venetor, if I can be forward," Gladius interrupted.

"No, Gladius, I will not hear it," Venetor retorted and then turned to Skyris. "You went to him, didn't you? I knew from the start that it was a horrible idea to bring you here. I only brought you along because father begged to take you off of Gaian before things got any worse."

"Please." Skyris rolled her eyes. "Who would fly your ship if I hadn't?"

The words temporarily silenced Venetor. While he was not a bad pilot himself, Skyris had always excelled, and they had needed all of her skyward prowess to get off of Gaia in the state it was. Still, the rage boiled within the prince.

Skyris ignored the building anger and joined Gladius in dressing herself in her armour, starting with the padded gambeson over which she would place her gyldrig chain mail.

"You cannot love the elf," he finally said. "You are a princess of Gaia."

Annoyed by his childish behaviour, Skyris turned on the heel of her boot. Continuing to button up the gambeson, she marched straight towards him, only pausing once she was a few feet away.

"What does it truly matter if I will never sit upon the throne?" she snapped at him. "Orbeyus never saw anything wrong in our union. He encouraged it. He loved Puc as a brother. We loved each other."

"He is an elf," Venetor stated. "An elf. You have a responsibility even if you do not sit upon the throne to strengthen the alliances of the great houses on Gaia."

"Well, a whole lot of good that will do with Razmus there now," Skyris huffed. "Unless that is part of your brilliant plan. Perhaps you will marry me off to him. Or why not Atala?"

"Oi lassie, that was uncalled for." Gladius flattened his good ear as he observed her.

"Maybe, but it's the truth," Skyris replied as she went back to putting on her armour, glaring at her brother. "You have no regard for anyone. We're all just pawns to you. I bet you don't even care about those kids out there, do you?"

Before Venetor could answer her with anything, Skyris had finished with her chain mail. Grabbing the red Severio tabard with a black lion upon it, she threw it over her head, snatched her belt which held two short swords, and left.

ഃഃൟ

Annetta, Jason, Link and Sarina all sat within their tent. It featured four cots with white sheets, a desk with some parchment and a quill as well as some chairs and another larger table with some wax candles, a silver pitcher and four water goblets. It reminded them all of the tent they had waited in while participating for the Riva Mortem and the anticipating atmosphere among the four was much the same as it had been then. All of the battle plans that had needed to be discussed had been done so in the meeting, so all that remained was the actual battle itself.

Each of them had their own method for dealing with the wait. For Sarina and Jason, it was sitting together on one of the cots with their hands entwined. For Annetta, it meant sharpening the blade of Severbane while seated on a chair that had been placed backwards so her arms rested on the back of it while she ran the whetstone along the edge. For Link, waiting signified time to catch a nap on one of the other beds, despite how uncomfortable everyone else found them. All four of them had undressed from their armour and were once again in their civilian clothes in order to give their bodies a chance to rest for a little.

Annetta watched as Link's chest rose and fell with each breath he took, completely oblivious to everything around him. She recalled their last encounter by the lake. It had been the last time the two of them had any time alone to speak with one another. It was not that Annetta did not enjoy her outings with the rest of the group, but sometimes she felt like she needed to spend time alone with one person at a time. It was then, she felt, that she got a clearer picture of the person she was engaging with. That was also when she truly understood who they were.

"You think if the fighting started, he would wake up?" Jason wondered. "I mean... I still remember the story he told of Brakkus flipping over his bed when he didn't wake up on time."

"Pretty sure he would," Sarina responded. "They certainly had enough trumpets and horns when we were riding into camp."

Annetta smiled as she remembered the Hurtz. It felt like ages ago that he had been with them. His voice seemed almost a distant memory to her as she tried to recall him speak. She also tried to remember the way in which he would bicker with Puc and chuckle when he had gotten the better of the mage. It all seemed a million miles away to her, as did the person she had once been when she had first learned of all of this.

Sighing, she put down the whetstone. Examining the blade, she stood up, gave it a good swing and slung it back into its scabbard on her belt. Anxious, she then walked over to the opening of the tent and peered outside, watching soldiers buzz about like busy bees.

"Will it ever end?" she asked.

"Will what end, Anne?" Jason looked over at her curiously.

The girl searched within her to find what she had asked about before replying. "The changes. I'm starting to get tired of them. It's like… nothing can ever be stable, everything is just constantly spinning out of control just as we manage to get a grasp on it. Ever since we found out about the Lab it's just kept going on and on… I feel like I'm on a merry-go-round sometimes."

"But that's what life is supposed to be, isn't it?" Sarina interjected. "It's always changing."

"Yeah, I guess so, just not to this degree," Annetta grumbled as she pulled back the curtains. "I guess the novelty of living out what I thought was the dream is starting to wear out on me."

"Is the unbeatable Annetta Severio throwing in the towel from being Earth's great defender?" Jason teased, only to have one of the pillows thrown at him by Annetta.

"Can it, J.K. You know what I mean," she muttered. "I'm talking about my uncle coming in out of the blue with all of these other things we didn't know about, and now this snag with the Fire Elves."

"I hear you," the boy said. "I just try not to think about it all at once and take it one step at a time. Otherwise, I'd be a walking time bomb mess of emotions like you are."

"Oh thanks, like I didn't have a complex already." She snickered.

Their chattering came to a stop when without warning, Matthias materialized in the midst of the room. Dropping his hood, the assassin revealed his messy brown hair.

"Glad to see you are all here. Where is Thanestorm?" he demanded.

"In his tent." Sarina pointed to the entrance.

"What's got you all in a fit?" Jason added, crossing his arms as he observed him. "Where have you been, anyway?"

"Doing what I do best," Matthias replied as he eyed the boy and turned back to Sarina. "I need to see him, there's something I need to-"

Before the assassin could explain anything further, the low baritone sound of a horn filled the air. The vibrations from the instrument were so intense that the group felt them in the very marrow of their bones.

The only one who seemed unshaken by it all was Link, who had woken from his sleep. Sitting up, he looked to the others. "The Fire Elves are here."

ജ‑ഓ

As soon as the horns sounded, Puc was in full armour and stood upon the newly-erected labyrinth which surrounded both the camp and city. He had traded in his regular mage outfit for the one of the First Mage. It had been insisted on by Tobias and Alaric, who were convinced the gesture would give heart to the Aldamoor troops. Tracing the hilt of his sword with his thumb and gripping his staff in the other hand, Puc looked out into the plains as a host from the east made itself visible upon the horizon among the sea of grass. The Fire Elves had earned their name. Everything around them seemed to ignite into an orange-reddish glow like an all-consuming flame as they advanced.

"Uglier than I remember," the voice of Iliam proclaimed. "A lot meaner looking as well."

The mage furrowed his brows as he looked forward, doing his best to estimate the numbers of the approaching army. His train of thought was interrupted when he heard the onrush of armoured bodies heading his way.

Conquering the last set of stairs, Annetta appeared, followed by Jason, Matthias, Sarina and Link.

"What's happening?" the girl blurted out prematurely and turned her head towards the slowly growing mass in the distance, "Oh…"

"Well then…" Jason's gaze followed Annetta's. "That can't be good."

"No, it most certainly is not," Puc replied coldly.

"Perhaps I shouldn't sour the mood then, and yet I feel I must," Matthias spoke directly to him. "I spied on a few scouts that rode ahead. One of them let slip about them having a siege weapon of some kind."

"A siege weapon?" Iliam regarded the assassin. "What kind of siege weapon?"

"They did not say," Matthias responded.

Iliam looked to Puc as if hoping for a solution to the problem. The mage, however, only turned his eyes once more outward.

"That gives us nothing," he said. "For all we know, their siege weapon could simply be a fortified battering ram."

"Either way, what do we do?" Annetta inquired.

Narrowing his eyes yet again as he continued to gaze at the growing mass on the horizon, Puc could feel the pressure from those gathered begin to seep into him, past the armour he wore and into his very being. He could not bring himself to signal for everyone to take up their positions. Behind the ageless eyes, scenes from his childhood played out. A city covered in flames and destruction clouded his vision, as did the cries of a boy who had lost everything he had ever known. Shaking off the shock, Puc turned to his companions.

"Ready the horses. I will ride out to meet the vanguard with Annetta and Jason," he said and began making his descent. "Iliam, I will leave you in charge here with the wall. Sarina and Lincerious, I would have you find Darius. Join us in the vanguard once you have done so. Matthias, take no more than five mages with you aboard one of the ships. Have them cast a storm spell. We may yet need the rains to quench the fire and the lightning could be a valuable distraction."

"And what would you have us do, Thanestorm?" the voice of Atala cut him off upon the steps. Beside her stood Venetor, while further behind were Gladius, Titus and Skyris.

"Ask your prince. I have an army to lead," the mage stated as he walked past them. "You Gaians have always had a knack for finding your place when it comes to war."

The group separated to their respective posts. Before they knew it, Annetta and Jason rode out alongside Puc, the banner of the Four Forces snapping viciously on the wind from the saddle of Firedancer. The tension of the impending fight was thick among the soldiers, lining their grim faces. While the front lines of the vanguard consisted mainly of Elven soldiers, Minotaurs and Ogaien alike could be found within their ranks as well. It had been decided that no race would shy away from any of the positions. The Sky Wolves, having the advantage of natural flight, had been placed among the airships which now held their places, their great propellers softly turning in the air above.

Knowing her place in all of this, Annetta urged her horse forward. "Warriors of the Four Forces! Your courage was tested and remained true in the fight against Mislantus. Now you are called upon again to defend the lands of your fellow allies, to defend Aldamoor from the Fire Elves."

The clashing of weapons against shields could be heard as a response to her words. Annetta took the pause to collect her thoughts and turned to Puc. "I know you want us making the speeches, but this is your home and you should probably say something to them."

The mage regarded the girl through his helm before clearing his throat and speaking. "As I am a native of Aldamoor, born and made to live in the devastation of a city that had befallen the Fire Elves before, I know of their ilk. Make no mistake, they will claim our lives if they can, and I have no plan for such things. Today we live! Today we fight! Today, we will send them all to the abyss. What say you? Will you ride once more with the heir of Orbeyus and the son of Arcanthur?"

The ranks roared even louder. The point being made, Annetta raised Severbane high into the air and Jason followed suite with Helbringer. By this point, the shapes of individual units could be made out on the horizon.

At the front rode a most peculiar figure. In a chariot drawn by two of the spotted lizard creatures was a female. She looked like an albino, her pale alabaster skin adorned with tribal markings in red war paint. She was clad in dark brown patchwork leather armour that was decorated with trinkets, some metal and some that looked to be bone. Gleaming red eyes bore their way into those ahead and her platinum white hair swayed in dreadlocks round her head, crowning her thin face like a lion's mane. In one hand, she held the reins of the impressive machine which drew her across the field and in the other, a cat o' nine tails dangled freely at her side.

"Tamora," the name escaped Puc's lips.

Annetta regarded the mage, seeing the recognition of the figure on his face. She turned to Jason in question, only to receive a blank stare back from him in reply. In all their time with Puc, he had never mentioned anyone by that name.

"Thanestorm," the woman's voice rang out like a roaring flame. "I see you have brought some pets with you today. I will give you one chance to surrender, just as I gave your father before he met his end."

"If it is begging you want, then you will be sorely disappointed," the mage retorted. "You will get nothing here."

"Suits me just fine." The woman smirked. "Just means more for us to burn!"

Before either Annetta or Jason could ask Puc about the origins of the woman, chaos broke out. The ranks charged at one another, like waves upon the ocean, fighting for dominance in the sea. Spears and swords came at them, snapping like rabid wolves, leaving very little time for further thought, only action.

Separated from Puc, Annetta and Jason did their best to stay close to one another. Still seated on horseback, the duo parried enemy attacks from the oncoming swarms of pale-faced and red-eyed elves. Regaining focus, Annetta snarled and used her telekinetic ability to lash out with her sword, throwing ten of the closest soldiers back, giving her and Jason some breathing space.

"So... old girlfriend you think?" Annetta glanced over at Jason.

"Girlfriend? Puc?" Jason raised an eyebrow as he dodged an enemy spear. Parrying with his mace, he snapped the enemy weapon. "You think he'd be capable of that? I always thought he just made like an amoeba and split."

"Never thought of it that way," the girl replied through laboured breaths and moved out of the way quickly as a berserk Fire Elf raced right past her in an attempt to skewer her on his spear, only to be met by other members of the vanguard. She then turned back to Jason. "Matt mentioned a siege weapon. You have any idea what we should be looking for?"

"Beats me." the boy answered, "We're just gonna know it when we see it and until then..."

Jason was interrupted by an elf swinging an axe at his face, only to have the weapon caught in the lion head-shaped blades of his mace. Pulling the weapon from the opponent's grip, he buried his own in the fiend's chest and watched him fall to the ground, cringing at what he had done.

"Uh... as I was saying," the boy said as he cleared his throat, "Until then, we just need to stay alive."

∞∞

Separated from their friends, Sarina and Link were caught completely off guard during their attempts at finding Darius in the crowds of soldiers. Without warning, the ranks began rushing forward in a chaotic rampage. Elves, Soarin, Minotaurs and Ogaien alike charged in a blur of colour past the two wary teenagers.

"That didn't take long," Sarina mused as she drew her sabre from its scabbard. "Now what?"

"We need to find Darius still," Link reminded her, drawing his own sword. "We should hurry, we need to get back to Annetta and Jason."

"Right, and how are we going to do that on the battlefield, genius?" the girl grumbled as she followed the long strides of the Gaian youth.

"You're just going to have to trust me." He turned back to her briefly before continuing onward.

"Like I haven't heard that one before," the girl groaned and followed.

ಐಐ

Further along on the field still, another group of fighters made their presence known as Fire Elf soldiers fell or were seen flying through the air as though they were made of mere parchment.

Venetor Severio roared with a fury not known to mortal men. The Gaian prince held no weapon in his hands, yet he was the eye of the storm. His savage blue eyes glowed with anticipation as he picked out his next prey. Dodging an enemy spear, he snatched the shaft of the weapon and pulled towards himself, causing the enemy to lose his balance. Once within range, down came his elbow, slamming into just where the skull connected to the spine. Lifting the projectile, he then flung it at another fiend, the weapon finding its mark in the victim's chest.

Close by, a behemoth in plate armour swung his massive sword, never giving his enemy the chance to get close. Even the projectiles they threw could not pierce Gladius's suit of armour as he blocked and countered with his blade, his good eye keen enough for two.

"Remind ye of something, m'lord?" the Hurtz rumbled with laughter as he cut down his opponent and began fighting another.

"I don't know what you speak of, Hurtz," Venetor grunted as he head butted an unaware soldier and then uppercut him, causing the fighter to soar through the air before hitting the floor.

"I will give ye a hint," Gladius replied. "We be two warriors short here, though."

"I assume you mean my dear old brother and your own," Venetor stated, finishing off the final adversary before him.

The one dubbed the Ironfisted then wiped the gore from his knuckles, seeing the field cleared for the time being as he watched the bloodshed unfold around him. To Venetor, fighting was what he lived for. From his youngest days, he had been trained to lead armies, to be

Orbeyus's right hand. It was all a shock for Venetor when his brother approached him one day with nothing more to say than he was leaving. That he had to go, and it would be Venetor who would one day rule Gaia. To many, such a revelation would be all they could ever hope for as a second son. To Venetor, it had been an insult. On Gaia, any status one gained was either through birthright or through battle. Venetor had fought no battles for the throne and he had not been born into it. His placement there, in his eyes, was a farce. As such, he wielded no weapon, for he had vowed that his hands would be what he would build his reign upon. The battlefield would be treated no different.

The corded muscles growing tense beneath his armour, Venetor curled his fists anew, lifting them before his face in a defensive manner. A new group of enemy soldiers, having braved the turf, turned toward him, thinking the unarmed Gaian a madman. Little did they know the carnage they would evoke by tangling with him.

"Come and try to take down the Ironfisted, boys!" he hollered and threw himself into the fray.

∞○∝

Elsewhere, Skyris and Atala stood back to back with their weapons drawn. The two women were not strangers to warfare. Atala, dressed in her traditional Gaian garb, wielded weapons of her own design, short war scythes. While the original weapons were meant to be used on a staff or pole, Atala had cut the wood on each to the length of her forearm. An additional shorter piece of wood had then been added so she could grip it with ease.

Skyris had opted for a more traditional arsenal, her two short swords. Though she was an innovative mind, she understood and trusted the pair of blades. Sometimes, as someone had once explained to her a long time ago, it was not about being creative, but understanding what worked for a given situation. It had been a lesson the Gaian female had taken to heart and never forgotten.

Encircling the pair were three female elven foot soldiers, one brandishing a sword and shield, another a hand axe and the third a dagger and sabre. They all sported the same wild, unkempt platinum manes and vicious red eyes which now shone with bloodlust. Giggling for no apparent reason other than their own amusement, they stared down the duo on the inside of their ring. Growing bored with their taunting, the one wielding the axe and the one with the dagger and sabre sprung forward at Skyris, the other lunging at Atala.

A fierce colliding of armaments ensued, none of them seeming to slow or deter in their devotion to striking at their foe. Blow upon blow, the combatants exchanged attacks without mercy.

"They seem bolder in their resolution than I remember," Atala shouted to Skyris through the ringing of steel, "As though the Unknown has quite literally pumped them full of fire."

Skyris did not respond. She was far more focused on her targets. Her eyes darted back and forth past her mane of loosely-tied dishevelled black hair in an effort to keep track of both of their movements. Hooking the edge of the axe with one of her blades she finally pulled her opponent close and drove her second sword into her chest. Killing did not come easy to the female Gaian, this she was certain of, and so watching the female Fire Elf slide off her blade in remorse had cost her precious time. A boot collided with her back, causing her to fall straight onto the corpse she'd just created.

Rolling over and bringing her swords to shield her face, Skyris heard the familiar sound of a firearm. Moments later, a second body littered the ground beside her. She looked up to see Titus standing some distance away, placing a pistol back in its holster.

"I thought we agreed you'd be staying close to your father," Skyris grumbled as she got up.

"A thank you would have worked too, aunt Skyris," Titus replied. "And I was until he told me to go find you."

"Scrofulous baseborn half-wit," she growled under her breath as she turned to him. "Is he at least with Gladius?"

The young Gaian nodded. The third of the elves having fallen, Atala turned to her companions, "We should go and rejoin with him. I know Venetor is a capable warrior, but he is still the Crown Prince of Gaia. Which way was he, boy?"

Titus pointed in the direction behind him. Before either he or Skyris could get their two words in, Atala had already taken off, charging head-on into another group of soldiers, shortly after being joined by a score of Water Elves, Ogaien and Minotaurs. Glancing at one another, nephew and aunt gave each other a curt nod and followed suit into the fray.

೪೦೦೪

The smell of rain was thick in the air as Matthias watched from the helm of the airship. He could tell the five mages he had brought aboard had begun weaving their spell. The assassin's azure eyes surveyed the chaos below as tiny figures from either side clashed.

Beside him, Maria Gladiola appeared. The captain of the Tessa wore a brooding look as she gazed down where Matthias was focused on.

"Makes you feel lucky to be up here, doesn't it?" she spoke, trying to ease some of the tension.

"I would rather be down there with my friends than hiding up here," he replied. "No offence."

"None taken," Maria said as she looked ahead at the storm clouds. "We will need to pull back soon, the mages seem to be almost ready."

Matthias turned to reply, only to notice a large projectile hurtling towards them from an enemy vessel that had been hiding behind the clouds. Grabbing hold of the captain, he quickly lowered them both as the large bolt soared overhead and crashed into the railing, causing splinters to fly everywhere.

Rising to his feet and creating an orb of psychic fire, Matthias shot the blast at the enemy ship, the flames catching hold of the ballista onboard the vessel.

"Still think we are safe, captain?" Matthias questioned her.

Maria looked over the destroyed edge of the deck as droplets of water began to dot the wood on the ship's planks. "I suppose not."

ℝ℞

Having found Darius, Link and Sarina managed to locate Annetta and Jason amongst the chaos of the battlefield. Annetta and Jason had left their horses in the care of elven soldiers near the outskirts of the field. The standard flag of the Four Forces needed to be guarded with care. With it attached to Firedancer, Annetta did not have the freedom to move as she needed, for this battlefield was proving to be much different than the one against Mislantus. Rain had begun to fall at a steady pace, drenching all around them.

The five companions soon found themselves entangled in the fight as a troupe of soldiers came upon them. Swords, javelins, axes and all other manner of weaponry clashed in the frenzy of battle. When the last fighter had fallen, Annetta, Jason and the others crowded in around him. The fiend still struggled to live, clutching at his slashed stomach as he tried to reach for the blade, only to have Annetta step on his foot.

"Where is the siege weapon?" she inquired, getting straight to the point.

"Wouldn't you like to know?" the soldier grinned through bloodied teeth, causing Annetta to grind her heel into his hand more, the Fire Elf squirming as a result.

Jason and the others looked on, feeling uncomfortable. In all the time he had known her, Jason had never seen his friend react in such a way. She'd stood up for people in the schoolyard and wasn't afraid of bullies, but this elf was defenceless.

"He's not gonna tell us, Anne," Jason stated, in an effort to get her to stop. "We're wasting time."

"He's right, Annetta," Sarina chimed in. "The weapon could be at the walls by now for all we know."

Annetta, however, was beyond listening. She then drew Severbane from its scabbard and pointed it at the prisoner.

"If you think I fear death, you have another thing coming," he cackled through his coughs. "I will be greeted a hero in the afterlife. The work we came to do is already done."

"What are you going on about?" the girl inquired, the grip on her sword not faltering. The elf only continued to beam a Cheshire cat grin, causing her to grow impatient. "Answer me!"

The Fire Elf's smile continued to grow ever wider, filling each corner of his face with maniacal glee. It was as if he had truly gone insane within the last moments of his life, due to the lightheadedness from blood loss.

"You foolish children," he guffawed. "There never were any siege weapons."

ಬೋಐ

The tide of warring soldiers had swept up Puc in a torrential chaos. Where before, his target had been clearly within sight, now she was nowhere to be found, but the elf would not so easily give up. Slashing and hacking away at enemies while his mount trampled those who fell underfoot, Puc's keen eyes searched among the havoc. His persistence paid off when he finally caught sight of the wildly swinging mane of locks upon a chariot.

"Tamora!" he hollered, to the point of rendering his throat raw.

The object of his chase turned her head towards him, a wicked smile crossing her lips as she leapt from her chariot into the crowd, drawing a sabre from her belt.

His attention having been diverted, Puc had little time to notice as an enemy spear punctured the hindquarter of his horse, leaving the animal lame. Abandoning the creature to fate and jumping from the saddle, he wasted no time in drawing Tempest from its hiding place within his robes.

"How many years has it been since last we met, Thanestorm?" the Fire Elf chimed.

"Not long enough," the mage gritted his teeth.

By this point a ring was visible around them as the other soldiers seemed to push out, giving the two the space they so craved.

"I remember it like it was just yesterday," she continued. "You were but a lad who was barely out of the Academy, partnered up with that boy Orbeyus and his army of misfits, which I see has endured quite well. Although where is Orbeyus, I wonder?"

Puc's eyes glinted with a reserved rage as he watched her from beneath his helmet and raised his sword into an attack position. "Enough talk, Tamora. I have no words to share with the likes of you."

"Oh, but that wasn't the tune you were singing when we were both growing up in the Academy, was it?" she sneered. "Or have you forgotten?"

The mage's face remained neutral as he glared at her. Whoever she had been once was dead in his mind, another spectre like all the people he had left behind.

Seeing his disdain, the Fire Elf smirked, and without warning lashed out like a viper with her sword.

Blocking the attack with the edge of his own blade, Puc used the staff in his other hand to push Tamora back. Prepared for the assault, the Fire Elf dug her blade into the ground as soon as she was sent flying, tearing at the trampled grass. Retracting the weapon, she gave it a whirl with the flick of her wrist and lunged again at the mage once more in a series of quick, arching strikes.

Though anger and betrayal pulsed through his veins like a poison, Puc did his best to maintain his level-headed demeanour as he hindered each attack from reaching its mark. Having calculated every move and the aftermath of it, the mage was well-prepared. He would have her know he was not playing a game.

"All business, just like your sire," she scoffed.

Uninterested in conversation, Puc continued to drive his sword forward, alternating with his staff where he saw an opening. Tamora did not miss a beat, her blade whirling and colliding with his own as though they were both engaged in a waltz. When all seemed as though it pointed to a kill, however, the Fire Elf withdrew her blade, grinning at the mage in a teasing, contorted alabaster smile.

"I'll give you one thing, Thanestorm," she sniggered, "You're a greater fool than he ever was, for the wolf has been at your doors all along."

Before Puc could say anything, a familiar stench filled the nostrils of the mage. It was a scent he knew from his youth, and it was not one that was native to Aldamoor. Not even the smell of the rain mingling with the surroundings could mask it. His fears were confirmed when Tamora's crimson eyes and pale complexion began to glow in an orange hue.

"Fire!" one of the soldiers cried out, causing Puc to turn back.

Beyond the newly erected walls, the tower where the Council held court was slowly being swallowed up by a serpentine of flames. Zeppelins with mages had already begun to move in the direction of the blaze. Puc could only stare with his mouth slacked open.

࿐

On the other side of the battlefield, Venetor saw the flames within the city. He had felt from the very beginning of the fighting that something was amiss, that it had all come together, too perfectly orchestrated. His gut feelings proved right.

"What is that?" Gladius's good ear pricked up.

"Fire, and a big one," Venetor confirmed.

The duo was shortly joined by Skyris, Atala and Titus.

"Is that what I think it is?" Atala gaped at the city.

A plan already forming in his head, Venetor turned to those who stood with him. "Seems the Fire Elves found a way into the city after all. How about we show them how Gaians fight?"

"I heard Annetta mention something about a siege weapon. Could that be it?" Titus inquired.

"Won't know if we don't go in," the Gaian prince declared as he extended his hand. "Better grab hold so I can teleport us in, and hope there's gonna be enough of them for all of us in there."

誾

"How?" Puc managed to say.

"You are not the only one with friends in high places, Thanestorm," Tamora imparted. "You've a traitor in your midst, and the rewards of such a thing have been mine for the reaping."

His grip tightening around Tempest, Puc turned back to the object of his earlier wrath. "A fire will get you nothing, Tamora. For you forget water quenches flames."

Lunging once more, the blade of the mage clashed with Tamora's sabre. Growing bored of the tempo of their bout, she dropped the cat o' nine tails she'd carried in her other hand. As quickly as the action occurred, a second blade came up from a hiding spot on her boot, slicing the mage across the hand that held his sword.

"Whoops," Tamora smiled. "Now, if my calculations are correct, I just nicked the spot where the flexor tendons are located, which will cause your grip on your sword to weaken...like so."

With a powerful strike, Tamora's sabre came down on Tempest, which after some resistance fell from Puc's hand.

"An injury I'm sure you could fix with ease if you had your precious potions with you," she sneered.

"Is there a point to all of this, Tamora? I grow weary of your rambunctious games," he glared at her.

"That's no way to address an old classmate and friend, I would say," she retorted, raising the tip of her blade to his throat. "It's funny to think that this is the way the mighty Puc Thanestorm will go down."

Stone faced, the mage watched the tip of the blade, void of any emotion. He then looked back up at Tamora in whose eyes the reflections of the flames still danced. There was a hint of disappointment in her body language as her jaw tightened along with the grip on her sabre. She longed for him to show fear.

His lips then finally curved slightly upward. "You are quite right, it would be funny."

Then, faster than Tamora could anticipate, Puc used the bottom of his staff to toss his fallen blade into the air. He knocked away the sabre's tip from himself with his staff and switched the hand he was using to hold it just in time to catch Tempest with his good one.

He pointed the sword at her. "Especially considering I am ambidextrous."

සාශ

"What do you mean no siege weapon?" Annetta demanded of the fallen soldier, only to watch his eyes roll into the back of his skull.

Before she could further question, she felt an intense heat on the side of her face, causing her to look back and see the flames inside Aldamoor. Panic surged through her.

"They played us," Darius confirmed what they were all thinking. "Those soldiers Matt probably saw were placed there to spread a rumour that they had a siege weapon so we would concentrate most of our forces here."

"Great, so now what?" Sarina growled.

Off to the side, Jason regarded Annetta. Her soot stained brow was furrowed as she looked over at the soldier that she had been trying to get information out of earlier.

Unable to stay silent any longer about what he had seen, he spoke, "Just what were you getting at back there Anne?"

Annetta looked over at Jason, "What do you mean?"

"Anne, don't pretend to ignore it, you were ready to torture information out of that dying Fire Elf, that's not like you."

Annetta didn't answer, not right away at least. Her eyes lingered on Severbane's bloody edges, her face still contorted in concentration. Had what she did really been all that horrible? It had felt right at the moment to her. Hearing what her friend had said, however, made her less sure of that now.

"War brings out the worst in people I guess." Was the only answer she could give him.

Her mindset then changed as she tried to come up with a quick decision to their more immediate problem, Annetta looked to the sky and whistled. Moments later, two Soarin dropped before her.

"I need to rally at least fifty fighters to go inside Aldamoor," she said to them, to which they nodded and took off as quickly as they had arrived.

"Anne, what are you planning?" Link asked as he looked at the girl.

"Everyone is busy fighting out here," she explained, "But we need more soldiers inside. Chances are if the tower is on fire then there will be enemy soldiers, a lot more than what we originally left in place in Aldamoor to defend it and they are going to need backup. We have to go in."

"Puc would have left troops inside the city," Sarina stated, "He wouldn't have placed everyone here."

The girl shook her head in response to her comment. "Remember what this guy said, though? Someone infiltrated them. Someone set this whole thing up so the city is ripe for the taking."

"Betrayal 101." Jason nodded his head in agreement.

An assorted group of Soarin, Ogaien, Minotaur and Water Elves then assembled around them. Among them was Iliam.

"We saw the flames and heard you might be in need of some assistance," he said. "You got a plan, Severio?"

Annetta turned and looked up at the tower, airships racing towards it in hopes of quenching the flames. She frowned as she tried to think of what to do, but adrenaline was clouding her judgment.

"I don't," she answered him bluntly. "We need to get inside and we need to make sure the people in the city are safe. I don't know if this is a trap and I don't know how many troops there are. I do know that you know how it feels to be one of those people inside there and that's all the reason that we need to help them."

There was a silence among those gathered, particularly the Water Elves. Many of them had been affected by past battles with the Fire Elves and many had not forgotten. To this, they drew their weapons, followed by the other races.

"Good enough plan for me." Iliam confirmed his thoughts and then turned back to his troops, "You heard the lady! Let's give them hell!"

A unified shout erupted among the troops. Annetta and her companions moved forward with their weapons drawn, striking down any foes that got in their way. The Minotaurs leading the way through the maze that had been constructed, they finally arrived at the ancient gates of Aldamoor. The soldiers on the walls opening it for them, they poured into the city.

Materializing inside with his companions, Venetor found himself gazing up at the burning tower that now stood but a few feet away from him, being eaten alive by flames. As he had predicted, the area below was overrun by Fire Elves which had turned their eyes to them.

Cracking his knuckles and neck, the Gaian prince quickly set his sights on the nearest target, and with a roar, charged at them, fists first. Stunned by the berserker approaching, the enemy had little time to discern his next move and found himself without a weapon shortly after Venetor was within fighting range.

His hands set to executing an elaborate routine, dodging enemy blades all throughout while his hands weaved back and forth past them. To those not trained, Venetor would seem a blur as he fought. A spinning mass that knew where to strike and where to avoid. This illusion of perfection was diminished each time the Gaian warrior was struck by the blades, a hazard of using his hands. These cuts, however, only fuelled him further as he continued. Finally, throwing his opponents off, he disarmed and ended them.

Beside him, Gladius was a force of rage. The Hurtz hacked and slashed without remorse. His thick plate armour was nearly impossible for the Fire Elves to penetrate as they crowded around him only to be swept away by an arching swing from his blade. At the same time, aware of his bond, the creature kept an eye on Venetor, making sure the prince was not in any immediate danger despite his reckless fighting style.

Alongside them, Skyris and Atala held their own, making quick work of those who came at them, backed by Titus. Staying in the rear, he used his ranged arsenal to take out those that would pose a problem to his aunt and the military leader of Gaia. The youth's keen eyes focused in on his targets, fingers on the trigger of his two colts as he allowed the energy to pass through him into the weapons.

Skyris exhaled, pushing loose strands of dark hair from her face with the back of her hand. Her grip still firm on the twin blades, she looked over at her brother as he finished off another foe. Feeling the warmth of flames, her head then turned to their source, the Gaian seeing the blazing inferno which had spread from the tower to one of the nearby buildings. The natives of Aldamoor had already begun to quench the fire, but the thing seemed to have a mind of its own and continued to blaze. She was about to turn her attention back to the fray when she heard the voice of someone inside.

"Cover me!" she beckoned to Titus, and turning heel, she ran towards the building.

"Skyris!" Atala shouted after her, noting the Gaian's actions.

Hearing the name of his sister being called, Venetor glanced sideways and saw her charge into the flames. The Gaian's instincts to protect being triggered, he teleported away from his enemy and allowed Gladius to naturally fall into his place. Landing on his intended spot, Venetor quickly pivoted out of the way as debris from one of the airships overhead fell to the ground. His eyes, however, never left the silhouette of Skyris. Reaching the foot of the building, Venetor used his cloak to cover his mouth and nose, his eyes beginning to water from the sting of smoke.

"Skyris!" he yelled, doing his best to gain her attention.

Were it not for a wooden beam falling a few feet from where she stood, Skyris would not have heard his call. It was sheer luck and coincidence which caused her to look over in his direction.

"Venetor?" she gasped.

"Skyris, what are you doing?" he asked.

His concerns were answered soon after when Skyris slipped past the debris and helped a woman up which was clutching a baby in her arms. She proceeded to lead the pair around the burning beam, carefully checking to make sure nothing else would fall on top of them.

"There was still someone on the upper floor," Skyris stated when she came closer to him, "I have to go up there."

"You will do no such thing," Venetor informed her. "You get this elf and her child out. I will go up myself."

"But Venetor, you are the Crown Prince," she protested, only to have him raise a hand to silence her.

"I am also a psychic warrior and a Gaian," he replied. "I can handle it. I will get whoever it is up there out in no time."

Frowning, knowing she would knock no sense into him, Skyris simply shook her head. Keeping a hand on the back of the terrified elf, she led her outside as quickly as possible.

Alone and with his sister out of harm's way, Venetor tightened the cloak around his mouth and strode further into the structure. The building was becoming more and more consumed by flames. Knowing his time was limited, Venetor ascended the stairs to the upper level with care, making sure to steer clear of the raging fire. His diligence and patience were rewarded upon reaching the top, where he heard the voice of a young child calling out. Tapping into his feral form's senses, he made his way towards the cries.

"Hang on! I'm coming!" he called out, scaling the side of a wall as he avoided part of the already caved-in floor that had burned through.

The Gaian then headed for the room he heard the child call from, only to be stopped dead in his tracks. Beyond the flames glistened a silver broken pointed mask and no child anywhere in sight. The hair's on the back of the Gaian's neck stood erect as he was faced with someone he had long thought gone. Before he could utter a name, however, the ear-splitting sound of collapsing wood could be heard thundering all around. What little coherence the Gaian prince once had was replaced with chaos, and all faded to black.

Chapter 17

Puc continued his dance of death with Tamora, their swords locking at each step. The switching of his hands to use Tempest had done little to slow him and his words were proving true. Gritting his teeth and pushing against the enemy blade with all of his might, he found an opening and sent his foot into Tamora's gut, causing her to stagger back.

Having mere seconds to exhale the pain, the female elf looked up with a crooked grin at him and at the battlefield around, including the burning buildings beyond the wall. There was a maddening delight in her eyes as she beheld the flames in the distance and she laughed in a wild glee.

"You might beat us back this time, but it means nothing in the long run," she stated through raspy breaths. "We are flame incarnate. We consume all in our path one way or another. This was but a taste of what is to come. You cannot withstand the storm."

The adrenaline beginning to let go and allowing him to feel the soreness in his body, Puc used his damaged hand to grip his staff as best as it could while his good one still clutched Tempest. He could see the reflection of the raging fire within his blade, making Tamora's words hit him harder. Despite this, he was not about to show it. The once advisor of Orbeyus Severio had witnessed too much to allow such a thing to be his undoing. His jaws tightening along with his resolve as he glared back at her.

"Wrong. I am the storm." The mage charged at her with a renewed fury.

Their weapons collided once again, and this time it was Tamora who caught him off guard. Spinning away from his sword's embrace, the Fire Elf raised her blade above her head in a defensive stance.

"Only time will tell," she hissed and was instantly consumed by flame.

His eyes widening, Puc strode towards where she had stood. He heard a crack and moving his boot away, he noted an elongated vial. Picking it up, he examined it, only to be distracted when he saw the other Fire Elves begin to disappear in the same manner.

Witnessing this, many of the soldiers began to cheer, thinking their enemy defeated. Puc sighed. It was a sigh of relief, but also of worry.

Little did many of them know that this was just the beginning of something far more complex than what they had originally planned for.

 හාශ

Matthias watched from the helm of the ship as the figures burst into flames below, leaving nothing but a pile of ash behind them.

"What's going on down there?" Maria questioned him.

"I could ask you the same thing." He looked over at her and then added, "I'm going to go check it out."

Before Maria could protest, the assassin was gone.

 හාශ

Teleporting below, Matthias found himself surrounded by a slew of dead and wounded soldiers. The once-green grass now lay in yellow muddied tatters around him, having been subjected to the beating of hooves and feet alike. Some distance away from the remains of an airship still burned in an orange afterglow. His azure eyes scanned the horizon for any sign of his friends, but among the masses of Water Elves, Soarin, Minotaur and Ogaien he could see none.

His eyes then caught sight of the Severio war banner still mounted atop Firedancer, and he rushed towards it, only to find a lone elf leading the mount along.

"Where is she?" he inquired.

Before the elf could respond, another voice came from behind. "I was asking the same thing."

The assassin turned around to find Puc but a few feet away from him, the hand holding his staff, covered in blood. As relieved as Matthias was to see Puc alive, his immediate thoughts turned to Sarina and her well-being. He hoped the rest of the group had managed to stay together. A second later, a gust of wind was felt overhead, and down came Entellion.

"To where did the foe get to?" he inquired.

"They have retreated," Puc answered as he sheathed his sword.

"Retreated?" Matthias furrowed his brows. "But why?"

"Because Tamora knew if she continued, she would be overrun," Puc explained. "Fire Elves are guerrilla fighters. They do not attack head-on like that. What Tamora tried to do was create a distraction while she managed to get a smaller group into the city, into Aldamoor."

"If you manage to get into the city, why not sack it?" the assassin asked. "It makes no sense. If Mislantus was taking a planet, he would never back down, especially if the odds were in his favour."

"Have you ever heard the words," Puc interjected, "Show the world a god can bleed?"

Those gathered remained silent, not sure what the mage was getting at. Puc exhaled roughly, seeing that none of them understood what was at stake.

"Aldamoor is the stronghold of the Elven world," he began. "It has stood so since its very beginning. For a Fire Elf such as Tamora to get inside, it shows others that we are weak. Now more than ever is this apparent since there is no First Mage holding the office."

"Then this battle..." Entellion trailed off.

"Was a demonstration," Matthias concluded.

Hearing the words come from another, Puc closed his eyes upon hearing it. The worst of it all was that the mage knew the solution to the problem. It was a solution he had done his best to run from. Yet it seemed that all of his efforts had been in vain. His mind refocusing on the stinging pain in his hand, he turned his attention back to more immediate matters. "Where is Annetta?"

ↄↃ

Annetta and her companions, along with the group of soldiers she had brought into Aldamoor, resided among the wreckage in the city, helping the wounded and putting out the now dying flames. While the rain the mages had summoned helped to prevent the fire from spreading, there were still some buildings which not been as fortunate.

Pushing back her soaked hair, the girl walked through the city streets assessing the damage and casualties. She had been taken aback when the Fire Elves all seemed to go up in smoke and disappear. She could not fathom it no matter how hard she thought and with the adrenaline from the fighting still pumping through her, that was diminished even further. Snapping out of her contemplations, she made out the distinct raised voices of Skyris and Atala. Hastening her pace as much as she could in the drenched armour, she made her way to them.

Among the ruins of a structure, Gladius seemed busy at work as he tossed mighty pieces of burnt timber to either side as though they weighed nothing at all. Titus, Atala and Skyris also seemed to be scouring the smaller pieces. As Annetta got within hearing range, she finally understood what they were saying, causing her face to go rigid.

Coming closer to them she asked, "What happened?"

The girl then noticed the tears which streaked Skyris's face and understood. Summoning up the remainder of her strength, she began moving the debris to the best of her abilities while in her armour.

"Uncle Venetor!" she called, hoping to hear something, even if it were just a groan.

As if on command, Link showed up and began helping Annetta lift the charred wooden planks. He was soon followed by Jason, Sarina and Darius, who also did their best to help in the recovery effort. When it seemed apparent that nothing remained beneath the structure, they took a step back as they tried to process what had just occurred.

"It should have been me in there," Skyris whispered quietly, to no one in particular.

"He's still alive," Gladius announced, furrowing his brow as his good ear dropped to a flat position. "I can feel him through the bond. Where is the real problem."

"How can you be sure?" Atala questioned the Hurtz in an uptight tone.

"Ye know as well as I the workings of the bond," he replied. "Were Venetor dead, I would be the first to know."

"If he's knocked out, though, how can you feel him?" Link probed further, aware of how his own bond to Annetta worked.

The Hurtz, feeling agitated, glared at the youth. "Ye would know. There would be no mistaking it."

"Maybe he teleported out," Annetta added. "Maybe he thought the building would collapse and went further away because of it."

"If he were in the city, I would have felt it," Gladius explained. "I've been bonded to him so long that I know when he is near and when he is far."

"That's great, but where is he?" Jason inquired, "I mean... he didn't get abducted by Greys from the house for coming to help us. I'm pretty sure we would have noticed it and if he didn't teleport out, then what happened?"

"You think if the answers were so easy to find we would have already come up with a conclusion, boy?" Atala snapped, folding her arms over her chest.

"Is there really a need for hostility at a time like this?" Sarina interjected.

Before further banter could come of the situation, Puc arrived on the back of Entellion, followed by Matthias on the back of a second Soarin.

"Thank the Unknown we found you," the mage greeted them, noting the distraught looks on their faces as he inquired further. "What's wrong?"

"Venetor's gone missing," Darius told him. "He was in the building helping someone and then it collapsed."

"I'm sure he is fine. He must have teleported out somewhere," Puc assured them, and turned to Entellion and the other Soarin. "Take one or two of your kind who are in good form, and see if you can spot the Gaian prince outside the walls of the city."

"I will see it done," he replied, and they were off.

"I still don't think ye will find him out there," Gladius protested, slamming the massive double-edged sword into some burned wood beside him.

The mage turned to the Hurtz. "What makes you so sure of that?"

"There may be some validity to the Hurtz's claim," Darius stepped in.

Those gathered turned to see Matthias standing beside him holding an object in his hands he had recovered from the wreckage. It took them all a few seconds to realize exactly what it was, as he polished off the soot to reveal a wicked looking five-pointed mask which was damaged.

Annetta and Jason glanced at one another, both companions getting a sinking feeling in the pit of their guts. They knew the mask all too well, and it was for this reason they were in disbelief that it would reappear at so inopportune a time.

"Amarok." The name escaped Sarina's lips as she stepped forwards to touch it. "But why and how?"

"I thought it a blur when I saw him on Gaia but now it all makes sense," Atala stated. "I thought I saw Amarok Mezorian's mask glinting in the background when Razmus attacked and there were even rumours later that he might be the one who set him free to begin with. I wouldn't have believed it if I hadn't seen this. Now it all makes sense."

"Razmus is free?" Puc's eyes widened upon hearing the news. "Since when? And why were we not told sooner?"

"What difference would it make, Thanestorm?" the Gaian hissed. "You got your hands tied here anyway."

While the bickering escalated, Gladius watched from the side with Skyris and Titus close at hand. Giving the duo some time to sort their differences of opinion out, he then withdrew his sword from the ground, sheathed it, and strode towards them.

"If Amarok truly is the culprit, which I believe he be, then he'll keep Venetor alive," the Hurtz silenced the pair. "But that don't change the fact that we gotta get him back."

The words brought a slight wave of relief to those gathered, but the tension was far from over. Their eyes turned to more immediate concerns, such as the now-burned High Council tower. While it still stood, it was but a skeletal remain of its former self. The round clock face which decorated the top had mostly been eaten away by flames, along with the rest of the upper portion of it. Around them, the soldiers and natives of the great city had begun to gather.

The scenery lingered most with Puc, who seemed to be visited by ghosts of his past on all sides. Wrapping a loose strand of his battle-tattered cloak around his injured hand, the mage strode forward.

"Citizens of Aldamoor! My people!" he shouted, making sure he was heard. "You have been done a most grievous injury this day! And though I could simply say that time shall heal all wounds, I will not stoop to so low a level, thinking that this road is easy to attain. Time implies a passage of it, a quantity, but what of tomorrow? What of those we have lost? This is what we must concern ourselves with. The Fire Elves will come back, and if given the chance, they would see our great city burn completely. But there is one thing they forget, that this is my city as well!"

Those gathered seemed taken aback by Puc's words. The stillness seemed infinite, and it was not broken until one of the unnamed many raised his fist from among the crowd. "Long live the storm of Aldamoor!"

Others followed suit, cheering the title. Where hope had been lost, it had been reborn again in a single shout. Annetta and her companions watched as the fervour in the group rose, only to be calmed again by Puc. The girl was astounded at the ease with which he was able to command the presence of all those gathered, as though he had been doing it his whole life.

"I am no Chironson," he continued. "I was never born to walk in the steps of the First Mage. My father was Oberon Thanestorm, leader of the forces of Aldamoor. A warrior. I will not lie now and say that peaceful is the blood that runs through my veins. I am as you have named me, the storm."

The assembled looked at one another in confusion, trying to figure out what it was that Puc was trying to say. The mage kept going. "Aldamoor's fate has always been spoken for, this time I would have you choose. There are many mages, capable of leading you just as I am, some I would say better suited for it than I. I give you this chance to decide, who will lead you, my people?"

Observing intently, Annetta crossed her arms over her chest, attempting to loosen the stiffness from her limbs. She did not understand the purpose of what Puc was doing. A small part of her did, however, and she did not like where it was going. She did not appreciate what change it would bring. It took everything inside of her to not say anything and to simply allow for events to unfold.

Another voice, this time female, rose from the crowd. "The storm of Aldamoor!"

The chanting was invoked anew, and the fate of the city was sealed.

Chapter 18

A thundering feeling becoming present in his skull, Venetor Severio opened his eyes and gazed up at his surroundings. Through the darkness, he could scarcely make out anything worth noting. He could feel his face was caked with soot and blood, which quickly led him to remember his last moments before losing consciousness. His body jolting to act, he felt restraints digging into his wrists, causing him to focus on them and see the thick metal cuffs that now encircled his hands. Pulling at them to free himself, he caught a glimpse of shimmering chains, which only gave further fuel to his need for escape. Concentrating on trying to teleport, he found he could not do this either, and felt the weight of a psychic-blocking collar around his neck.

"I'm afraid you will be going nowhere, son of Balthazar," a voice spoke among the darkness of the room.

His throat dry from dehydration, Venetor turned in the direction of the sound, attempting to swallow the dusty taste from his mouth and replying, "Only temporarily."

"Oh, really? We've just been acquainted, you and I," the voice chortled in a taunting tone.

Grimacing, Venetor tried to stretch, causing the chains to rattle some more. Squinting his fatigued eyes, he could make out a silhouette some distance away. By the figured stance, he could tell it was not bothering to elude him. The Gaian smiled through the grit on his face and straightened his back as best as he could.

"Why should I bother acquainting myself with the likes of you, Mezorian?"

As if on command, the silhouette strode towards him. There was no mistaking the identity by its gait, and the closer it got, the more visible beneath the cowl of its hood was the trademark broken silver mask. A white-filmed dead eye stared into the distance, while the other twinkled in mischief as it gazed upon the captor. Behind him from the dark emerged two hulking Hurtz guards in black plate armour, with a massive twin-bladed sword strapped to each of their backs. Both had a mix of feline and canine features on their faces.

Venetor curled back a little, his suspicions of where he was being kept having been confirmed. Still, he could not make sense of how he had gotten there to begin with.

"How did you find me in Aldamoor?" He demanded an answer.

"That is irrelevant," Amarok stated. "There is another who would see you now, and he has waited a very long time to meet you."

ഇരുര

Taken down from his chains, Venetor had his wrists bound and was escorted by the two Hurtz guards, with Amarok leading the procession.

Though he was half dragged, half prodded to move, Venetor still took the time to look around the grey marble halls and recognize he was in his father's fortress, Castrumleo. Though much of the tapestries and finery had been stripped away, there was no mistaking it.

What shocked the Gaian prince most, however, was not the state of his home but what he saw happening below from the large open windows. The capital, once green and teeming with life, now seemed a dark and sullen wasteland, a shadow of its former self. Buildings that once housed the many that had lived at court, now stood barren, abandoned. Hurtz patrolled every corner and occasionally could be seen leading a string of Gaians from one end of the city to the next. Beyond all of this, climbing above every structure was Razmus's tower.

It seemed three times as large at the base, the smooth black stone rising well above the stronghold Venetor found himself in, reaching almost to the clouds. A sickness gripped the pit of the Gaian prince, for he knew exactly who was building the tower. This sickness was quickly replaced by anger as he was made to walk through the final set of doors before reaching the audience chamber.

Dropped to the floor without any regard, Venetor groaned, feeling his bruised ribs collide on the marble. Cringing, he did his best to rise, only to be pushed down into a kneeling position. Before him on an elevated platform stood a Gaian male with his back towards him, looking out a window. Dressed in impressive pearl white plate mail with lion-face-shaped pauldrons on both shoulders and a crimson cape to match, the figure seemed oblivious to those that had entered.

"Isn't it beautiful?" the Gaian spoke.

Barely able to orient himself around the room, Venetor watched as both Hurtz guards and Amarok dropped to their knees before him.

"It is a sight to behold, Lord Razmus," the masked assassin replied.

"It will be even greater once the work is completed, I assure you," he informed them. Turning his head, the cascade of blonde hair which was kept in place by a war-like crown wreathed in sharp points and a red gem gave way to his face that sported a short cropped beard. While not seeming more than forty Earth years old, it was an ancient face, a face that Gaia had not known for over twelve centuries. Behind the teeming blue eyes beat a single-minded desire to climb ever higher. His gaze was fixated on Venetor as he descended the stairs. "So, you are of Magnus's line? The dynasty that was never meant to be."

"I am Venetor, son of Balthazar," he introduced himself. "Called the Ironfisted."

"Ironfisted, you say?" Razmus scoffed. "Then you will make a wonderful addition to those working the mines. As my family could not kill me, so I shall not kill you, not by my hands at least. Call it a mercy if you will, or a curse. Good work in finding this one, Amarok."

"A pleasure to serve, my lord." Amarok inclined his head.

Razmus nodded lightly in acknowledgement and looked back at Venetor, whose eyes seemed to ooze venom at him. "You think you are up to the challenge, son of Balthazar?"

"No challenge at all," Venetor spat.

The Lord of the Unfinished Tower cracked the same insane smile as before. It was as though Venetor's words had just passed right through him without any recognition. It disappeared seconds later, only to be replaced with a very conscious glare.

"You have no power here," Razmus beamed, "Yet still I admire your constitution in trying to show otherwise. Guards, take this one to the mines. I have seen all I need to see of where my brother's bloodline has gone to. Let us see how the prince fairs when placed with his people."

Paw-like fists digging into his shoulders, Venetor was lifted off the ground. Attempting to struggle earned him a well-placed punch in the gut by his handlers. Cringing, the Crown Prince of Gaia was dragged from the hall without a further exchange of words.

⊱⊰

Her armour having been removed and her wounds treated, Annetta set out to have a look around the camp. Back in her favoured jeans, t-shirt and jacket combination with Severbane swinging at her hip, the girl stuck out like a sore thumb among the array of medieval and fantastical creatures. She was used to it by now and they to her, so no exchange of awkward glances were shared as she made her way past the assortment of tents, stopping every so often to check in on those who were injured, offering a kind word where she could. Spotting the tent where her friends were, she walked towards it, only to be stopped from behind by someone calling her name.

"Lady Annetta!" a young man's voice shouted.

Not recognizing it as anyone she knew, Annetta screwed up her face in a silent question to herself. She was anxious to get to her companions but knew it would do no good to ignore whoever it was, seeing as she had already stopped. Neutralizing her expression, she turned on her heel and responded in the same manner she had been taught by Puc to address troops, "How may I be of service?"

Standing but a few feet away from Annetta was a slight-looking Minotaur with light golden-brown coloured fur, dressed in gold armour with a blue tabard over it. A wide belt over his midsection held two single-bladed axes. There was something familiar about him, but Annetta was not sure what it was.

"Have we met before?" she asked.

The young Minotaur bowed, before looking back at her. "I was smaller in our last encounter."

Annetta squinted, still not registering who it was she was speaking with, and then it hit her. "Snapneck?"

"Prince Snapneck, and yes, that would be him," Lord Ironhorn's voice came from behind the girl, causing her to turn around.

"Oh...I ..." She managed to choke out of herself in her perplexed state. "That's...some growth spurt."

The younger Minotaur chuckled. "I'm not done yet, but yes it, was a fairly large one. Lady Annetta, if there is anything I can do to help with finding your uncle, I will be glad to assist. After everything you have done for father and I, there could be no other course of action on my part."

Moved, but not sure what to say, Annetta replied, "See to your warriors for now. I'm not certain what's going to happen next. I'll make sure to keep everyone up to date though."

Giving a short nod as a goodbye, she made her way towards the tent and entered it to find Matthias, Puc, Gladius and Atala engaged in heated conversation over a wooden table with maps sprawled out on it. Jason, Sarina, Link and Darius stood off to the side, listening to what was going on, while Titus and Skyris were nowhere to be found. Her entrance ignored initially, the girl lowered herself into an empty seat before making her presence known.

"Hey guys, what's up?" she inquired.

"We cannot spare that many troops," Puc stated, taking no note of her. "And how, pray tell me, would you get them to Gaia in the first place?"

"A ship. Isn't it obvious, you overly pompous elf?" Atala growled. "I get the feeling you don't really want to help get Venetor back. Given your past history with him, I don't blame you."

"My past with Venetor has nothing to do with it," the elf rebuked, "But it has everything to do with what the attack the Fire Elves demonstrated today, or has everyone forgotten that in this feverish madness to charge head on into another battle?"

"If this Razmus guy is such a problem, why don't I just slip in and take care of him," Matthias offered. "I mean, I've done it before."

"Easier said than done, lad," Gladius said. "Anyone Gaian who's not loyal to him be in chains, and the Hurtz be under Razmus's influence. Something to do with his tower."

"And remind me again why you never turned?" Matthias questioned. "Or aren't secretly waiting to murder us all in our sleep?"

"You're one to talk," Link added from the far side of the room, only to be shot a glare of disdain from the assassin.

"Tis true that Razmus be using a frequency to target Hurtz," Gladius remarked. "The only explanation I can give is I be deaf in one ear. I lost it during the Great War and never bothered getting an implant of any sort."

"He's using a stereophonic sound wave," Puc suggested, "Which could explain why you were unaffected."

"So the sound is coming from two different areas." Jason summarized the information. "Like stereo headphones."

"It could be." Atala rested a fist against her chin. "What little we do know of Razmus, it seems like the sort of thing he would do."

"The question then is, where is the other one located?" Sarina inquired. "And how do we find out where?"

"That's simple, you send someone in," Matthias restated. "I still don't see why I wouldn't get away with being there. I mean, is Razmus some kind of all-knowing psychic? I mean, last I checked that sort of thing was illegal."

"What I think Gladius is worried about is you not knowing Gaia," Link cut in, "Which is why I should go."

"You're not serious, kid." Matthias widened his eyes in protest.

"I am of legal age, thank you, and yes, I am," Link retorted.

216

"There is validation to what Lincerious says." Puc raised a hand to end the feud. "He would know the world best and would know how to blend in."

Annetta continued to watch the conversation go back and forth in this manner, her eyes slowly beginning to droop. Despite the high amount of energy in the room, she was exhausted and could feel that exhaustion creeping further into her bones by the second. It was the same feeling one got from exercising, the kind that felt good to have but made it that much more difficult to fight off. Looking off to the side, she could see Darius nodding off, as well as Jason and Sarina.

Puc took note of their behaviour and turned to the others. "This meeting would best be taken up on the morrow. I need to be sworn in as First Mage, and I think I speak for everyone when I say that we will all feel better after a night's rest."

Picking up his staff, the mage exited the tent.

ଛୀଙ୍

Outside, Skyris stood by the entrance of the tent with Titus. The youth sat on a discarded log, polishing his pistol, while the Gaian female leaned on one of the wooden beams supporting the structure. The weariness of searching for her brother in the ruins had taken its toll on her. She'd been present for part of the meeting inside, but when Atala had begun to argue with Puc, she slipped out, followed by Titus. Neither of them had the heart for listening to squabbles over Venetor's fate. Her hand venturing into the breast pocket of her bomber jacket, she produced a small silver hip flask and opened it to take a swig.

"Really, Aunt Skyris?" Titus looked at her disapprovingly.

"Helps me think, you know this," she replied, putting the canteen away. "I'm going to need all the brain power I can get on this one."

The young Gaian said no more to her and occupied himself in his task, his own distraction from a now-missing father and the responsibilities which would fall to him. While Titus had always known what his destiny would be in the future, he was not ready for it yet. The thought of ascending to be the Crown Prince of Gaia when his father had not even been king sickened him. Perhaps his aunt had the right idea.

Puc emerged not long after from the tent, a look of fatigue tinting his features in the fading sun.

"Thanestorm," Skyris called after him, causing the mage to pause in his tracks.

"Yes, Lady Skyris?" he asked, turning on his heel.

Skyris felt the chill from his formality but did not flinch. "What conclusion was reached?"

"None. It is to be continued on the morrow at Q-16," he confirmed. "I know not how many troops I can spare to the venture, however, due to the Fire Elves."

"And what of your plans to be sworn in as First Mage?" she probed.

"To be carried out as intended," Puc replied.

"I see." Skyris looked down at her boots, readjusting her stance. "Thanestorm, I know you and my brother did not get along well."

"That is light coming from you," he mused. "Is that another trick they teach you when becoming a princess of Gaia?"

"How did you just address my aunt?" Titus snarled and rose from his seat, only to have Skyris block him with an outstretched arm.

"He meant nothing by it, should you know the whole story." She defended Puc, then turned to face him. "Look, you and I both know that if nothing is done with Razmus, things will escalate. When he has built his tower, don't you think he will turn to Earth?"

Puc said nothing in reply but stood stone-faced as he listened to her.

"That does not change the fact of the present situation," he retorted. "What good is a leader if he cannot defend his home first?"

"You have armies in other cities," she continued. "They will come to your aid as you once did for them."

Having had enough of listening to her, Puc turned back around and went in the direction he was originally heading, giving no hint that the words she had said held any weight to them.

After a moment, he called out, "I will see you at the meeting tomorrow."

೮೦೮೩

With the tower where the High Council met having been burned and in need of much repair, the residents of the city, along with members of the Four Forces gathered in the central square. A large seven-tiered fountain marked the middle of it, decorated with patterns of foreign-looking fish and animals. At the top, the statue of a maiden poured water out of a jug, the contents of which seemed to change colour as they dropped to each tier at random. Before it stood three mages, two of them being Alaric and Tobias, while in between them was an elder female elf with a pale rounded face and short cropped silver hair, holding Chiron's Toolbox with the front cover facing towards the crowd. All three were dressed in long robes of light grey, piped in a sapphire thread.

Annetta and Jason stood among those gathered, waiting for what was to happen next. Even though they were tired at this point from all of the fighting and the meeting before, they knew this one last thing needed to be done.

Puc emerged from the crowd shortly after, dressed in his usual navy robes piped in gold, his staff in hand. There were no signs on him of the earlier conflict, save for his bandaged hand and the darkened circles around his eyes which indicated a lack of sleep. These of late had become a permanent addition to his face. Coming to the forefront, the mage knelt before the trio.

The female elf took a step forward, her eyes upon Puc as she began to address him. "Puc Thanestorm, son of Oberon and Titania. For what purpose do you come here this day?"

"To take up the mantle of First Mage," he replied, void of any emotion.

"And what to this role do you offer to bring?" she questioned further.

"I bring my knowledge, experience and my loyalty to this great city that is my home," he intoned. "May the Unknown and his hosts deem me worthy of this task and may those gathered bear witness to my calling."

Satisfied with his answer, the female elf nodded to both Alaric and Tobias in a quick exchange and turned back to Puc. "The brotherhood has deemed you worthy, and the people have called your name. You may swear the oath. Rise now and do so."

On command, Puc was up and placed his right hand upon the tome before him. Clearing his throat, he began. "I, Puc Thanestorm son of Oberon and Titania do hereby swear to uphold the office of First Mage with all the integrity of my being. To be the shield to those who have none, to give wisdom where it is needed and to take up arms in the name of the land that is my home. As Chiron before me, I vow to build upon what has been given. So help me in this, Unknown."

The words having been said, Chiron's Toolbox began to glow a pale shade of blue for a split second before returning to normal. Puc took a step back and turned to face those around him.

"The tome has accepted the words," the female mage proclaimed to the crowd. "Here is your First Mage, long and prosperous may be his reign!"

A wave of cheering erupted in the crowd, and Annetta and Jason clapped along with those gathered. Having been mere spectators to the event, they enjoyed the time being out of the spotlight. Looking over at one another, though, they knew this time would not last long, for it seemed another battle was just on the horizon.

Chapter 19

The ceremony of Puc's induction to becoming First Mage having concluded, a short war council was held within the main tent, despite talks of waiting until the next day. Annetta and Jason stood in the midst of the leaders of the Four Forces, both teenagers at the point of using the last of their willpower to stay awake. Had it been a year ago, Jason would have snapped and complained about being tired, but they both knew better now. It would do no good, and so they stood patiently beside Puc, Iliam, Natane, Lord Ironhorn and Entellion, listening to what each of the leaders had to say beneath little more than the orange glow of a few candles dispersed within the vicinity. The smell of hay and sawdust was thick in the air.

"If this was but a skirmish, then we do not even know their full numbers." Lord Ironhorn expressed his concern.

"If the army we saw is even remotely an indication of their numbers, then my scouts counted a host well over twenty thousand strong," Entellion added. "It could be more if that was but a taste of what they were holding back."

Jason then broke his silence. "Couldn't it have been a trick, though? I mean, maybe they were bluffing and pulled out all their soldiers just to make us think they have more."

"Exactly what I was gonna say," Annetta interjected. "I mean, wasn't it a bit odd that they decided to all just disappear when it seemed like they had basically taken the city by getting inside?"

"It's true," Iliam chimed in. "In days past, Fire Elves did not back down until everything in their path was cinders. If anything, this shows their lack of forces and a want for conservation."

Puc listened to the debate around him, his jaw twitching from time to time as he weighed what everyone said. His mind was going a thousand miles an hour as he tried to comprehend every possible calculation and the outcome of each. He was not only responsible for the lives of Annetta and Jason now, but for all those in Aldamoor as well. While everything being said seemed logical, something else still prodded at the back of the mage's mind like a light scratching against a plaster wall which distracted one from their current task.

After some more thought, he finally said, "It may all be more complicated than we like to think. When I fought with Tamora, she divulged a secret to me and said she had a spy within Aldamoor. Of whom she spoke, I do not know."

Everyone stopped what they were doing and gazed directly at him.

"A spy in Aldamoor?" Iliam's jaw dropped. "Who? I mean, yes we have merchants come and go from other cities, but for the most part, everyone has been the same."

Puc faced those gathered, his eyes focusing on Annetta and Jason. "Tamora. Who currently leads the Fire Elves, was a child of war. She was left behind by her kind in a skirmish on the city and taken in by the Academy, who believed if raised by them she would be of no threat. Iliam and I befriended her once we got there. However, as we grew older, it became apparent that she was shunned by those around her, and in time this isolation grew into hate. Finally, she fled to rejoin her kind, and with the advantage of knowing the magic of our people. There is a good chance she planted a spy long ago in Aldamoor without any of us noticing. It could even be someone we grew up with or someone who has been here even longer. The truth of the matter is that we have no way of knowing."

"What are you going to do?" Jason asked. "I mean, what if she's just trying to cause paranoia?"

"He has a point, Thanestorm." Natane glanced at the mage. "What proof is there to her claim other than the want to create more confusion and mistrust among you and your comrades? Have we not seen this tactic used before?"

Annetta then weighed in. "I agree with Natane and J.K.. We have no proof of any of this, aside from Tamora words, including her claim that she has more troops. Maybe J.K. and I are too optimistic but in my opinion, half of her moves make no sense. What did she have to gain by telling you exactly how many troops she had and what would she gain by telling you she has a spy in Aldamoor? Nothing, aside from us being better prepared to deal with her and being on the lookout for a traitor."

The full attention of those gathered drew itself to the girl as she continued to address them. "If I can be bold enough to say so, we don't need to be on high alert here, and I think we should take most of our forces to Gaia, especially if things are as bad as people say they are there. That could become a bigger problem if we don't do something about it."

222

"What?" Jason's eyes widened as he pulled the girl aside. "We can't do that, Anne."

"We have to. Gaia needs us," she retorted.

"You sure this is about Gaia?" he questioned her. There was an edge of anger in his voice.

All eyes in the room then wandered to Puc and Iliam. The First Mage and vice-general of the Aldamoor forces held grim expressions. Both had been victims of the attacks of the Fire Elves in the past, both had known the devastation of their flames and both found it hard to part with any upper hand they could possibly hold. Finally, it was Puc who moved to speak. "While it is difficult for me to hide my disdain for Gaia and their absence when Mislantus tried to take the Eye to All Worlds, I know Orbeyus, like Annetta, would not choose to abandon it. There is merit in the assumptions that Tamora may be leading us astray. The problem is that we do not know and we have no way of knowing. I can lend one hundred airships to the cause of going to Gaia and ten thousand soldiers. I cannot spare more than that. I need to keep part of Aldamoor's resources here in case Tamora tries to breach the city again."

"You shall have three thousand Ogaien at your disposal here as well, under Amayeta's leadership," Natane assured him.

"Aye, and five thousand Minotaur with Prince Snapneck in command," Lord Ironhorn added.

"And another four thousand Soarin," Entellion added afterwards. "I shall leave Doriden in charge with them."

"I am truly grateful for your support." Puc inclined his head.

"Mention it not, Thanestorm. You'd have done the same," Lord Ironhorn chuckled, giving the mage a hefty pat on the back. "Now, if this concludes the meeting, I shall be turning in for the night. Fighting tires the soul, after all."

"Finally, someone else on our wavelength." Jason threw up his arms in an exaggerated manner, causing the other leaders to laugh quietly as they began to disperse.

Lord Ironhorn, Natane, Entellion and Iliam having vacated the room, Annetta and Jason were left alone with Puc, who still stood over the table. The light of the candles seemed to darken the features of the elf, causing him to look more gaunt and frightening than the youth knew him to be. The familiarity of the scenario to the Lab brought a sense of peace, despite the tension that the duo had just created between the two of them.

"It seems an eternity since last we were in one space together, alone." The mage broke the silence.

"Tell me about it," grumbled Jason. "It's like the world has gone upside down since all the stuff with Venetor happened and it seems like it's not going to stop anytime soon…is this what being an adult's like?"

Puc let out a half-hearted snicker as he began to put out the candles, "I suppose you could say that and to answer your latter question, yes, minus the continuous battles."

Jason growled in frustration. It was not frustration at his fatigue, however, but at the words Annetta had spoken before, what had caused the Four Forces to be broken up. How was this fighting as one unit?

Before he could voice his opinion to her, Puc interjected. "You should both get going as well. You will require your wits for tomorrow."

"Don't have to tell me twice." Jason nodded. "See ya later, Puc."

The boy headed for the exit of the tent, but Annetta remained rooted to the spot. Her mind had been swimming since Puc's induction into becoming First Mage and now the splitting of the Four Forces. She could not hold her thoughts much longer.

"Puc, I need to ask you something," she began, formulating the words as best as she could through the fatigue. "What happens now?"

"What do you mean, Annetta?" he asked.

"To us," she continued to expand. "I mean, with you being First Mage and all…"

Understanding what she was trying to say, Puc regarded the girl, seeing the genuine concern etched across her worn face. He remembered well the first day he had laid eyes upon her in the Lab, a youth who knew nothing of the many worlds he had seen over his long life. She had been untouched by war then, knew nothing of the struggles which happened beyond the reach of her own home. Now, just only over a year later, her face held a much different demeanour. The weight of responsibility had seen to that.

"Annetta," he began, "My appointment as First Mage changes nothing to what I promised Orbeyus many years ago. It will mean that perhaps some of my time will need to be spent in Aldamoor, but it does not change who I am to you. Should there be a time when I am not available, Darius will be there as well to give you counsel."

Annetta nodded, hearing her question answered, her nerves about the situation quelled. Still, something else nagged at the girl and she spoke anew, "Hey, can I ask what the deal between you and Venetor is anyway?"

"Whatever do you mean?" he inquired.

Annetta let out a lengthy yawn, which she caught with her hand before elaborating. "I don't mean to pry, but ever since Venetor showed up, it's obvious that you don't like him, more so than anyone else I've seen you come into contact with. Did he do something I should be aware of?"

Puc stopped in his tracks. The mage then withdrew from his task of putting out the candles and gazed directly at Annetta. From what the girl could see in the faded light, the usually neutral face of the elf seemed to be battling an internal turmoil he was doing his best to hide, but it was peering through regardless. After a few seconds of this lost composure, he cleared his throat and addressed her. "There is a complicated history between Venetor and I, one which I do not wish to divulge into. I can understand that it may appear that my hesitation to help Gaia now is further feeding this fantasy in your head. I tell you now that that quarrels Venetor and I have, are between us. They have nothing to do with the people of Gaia, and were there another way I would not hesitate to come to their-"

Before Puc could continue, an out of breath Jason ran into the tent, his hand was smeared with blood.

Adrenaline renewed, Annetta sprung back to life, "What happened?"

"It's Iliam," Jason managed to say, to which Puc did not wait to hear more, and nearly knocked the boy over as he bolted past him.

೩෮೪

Outside, in the dead of night, a crowd had already begun to gather in a circle not far from the tent, torches creating a lit inner circle. Muscling his way through it, Puc was confronted with the sight of his best friend on the ground, lying in a pool of blood. Beside him was Skyris, barking orders to Atala while she suppressed a large gaping wound on his side with a cloth.

"I need blood replenishing potions!" were the first coherent words the mage heard from her.

Breaking past the last barrier of bodies, Puc knelt beside Skyris, handing her what she had asked for from the folds of his robes. The

Gaian accepted the vial and forced the contents down the throat of the fallen elf.

"What happened?" Puc managed to choke out of himself.

"The one named Tobias nabbed him," she informed him as she continued focusing on her task. "Matt and Titus went after him, but in the night, who knows where he went."

"Tobias?" Puc's eyes went wide at the realization of Tamora's warning ringing true. "The spy... he was the spy?"

"Thanestorm, I don't know what you are on about, but a little focus here would help," she growled as a young mage pushed past the crowd with another set of vials and bandages to give to her. "Apply pressure while I give him the clotting potion and then switch out the cloth for the bandage."

"Was there a poison used?" Puc probed further.

"I don't know," she growled, taking the potion from the young mage and thrusting the bandages into Puc's hands.

The spell being permanently etched into his mind since the day Orbeyus passed away, Puc moved his free hand to the wound. Pressing down on it, he began muttering the words quietly under his breath. His suspicions becoming apparent, he withdrew the one hand, leaving the other to keep pressure on the wound.

"It is poison, some mix of rainbow serpent venom," he confirmed and then paused. "I cannot identify the other component."

"If we get him to the Lab, I can use the nanotechnology in the emergency ward to purge it from him," Skyris told him, "If he makes it that far."

His temples throbbing from exhaustion, Puc did his best to stay level-headed. Coming up with a solution, he gestured for Skyris to take a step back. Pressing both hands over Iliam's chest, the mage spoke a few gruff words. The soldier's unconscious body was surrounded by a wave of greenish light which then disappeared, leaving him as still as before.

"I slowed his vitals," he said to her, watching Atala bring a sturdy warhorse through the crowd towards them.

Skyris, with the help of Atala, mounted Iliam onto the beast, then got on herself. Puc handed her the reins, hesitation visible in his actions.

"He will be alright, Thanestorm," Skyris assured him as she adjusted herself in the saddle.

"Wait!" Annetta's voice rang through the crowd. Seconds later, Firedancer burst through with the girl atop him. "I can teleport to the portals. It will help us get there faster."

The mage glanced up at the girl. "Are you sure you're up to this, Annetta?"

"Well she's not exactly doing this alone, is she?" Jason appeared from behind her, approaching on his own mount.

Annetta looked over, shocked to see her friend there to help. She was about to thank him as he came closer, only to see the scowl on his face. Coming to a halt, he whispered, "We still need to talk when this is done."

Hearing the words, Annetta knew it was about what she had said in the tent earlier regarding her desire to go to Gaia.

"Right." Annetta nodded back with a stern expression.

Puc's worries answered for, the mage said no more and standing aside, watched as the trio disappeared from sight.

Chapter 20

Half escorted, half dragged, it was not long until Venetor found himself thrust into the back of a small metallic vehicle. Recognizing the interior design, the Gaian was at once able to determine that he had been thrown into a produce carrier, the type that had once been used for bringing edible vegetation from one end of the city to the other. He snickered at the irony of what it was being used for now as he felt it take off.

Not long after, it came to a stop and two Hurtz guards opened the doors, allowing for the sunlight to shine in the enclosed environment, blinding Venetor temporarily. Grabbing hold of the Gaian prince, they flung him out onto the dust-caked ground.

"Let's see how long ye truly last, yer highness," one of the Hurtz chuckled, followed by his comrade as they walked back towards the carrier and took off.

Growling something incoherent under his breath, Venetor got up, stretched his sore limbs and gazed at his environment. From what he could tell, there were no signs of civilization present. Rocky cliffs dressed in a russet hue surrounded him from all areas and all plant life seemed to be stripped from the ground, trampled out by some greater force. Nothing lived here. He shifted his body weight as he tried to think of where he was, for no area of Gaia had ever looked this way, not in the time of the king, his father. His gaze then rose skyward. He was greeted by an orange sunset and the silhouette of a structure that had once been a ruin. There, just a few miles from him stood the unfinished tower. Up close, he could truly see how large the base had become and the toiling Gaians which were at work even now. They dragged massive slabs of black stone to their final resting places and set mortar in between them to keep it all together.

Being so engrossed in observing, the Gaian prince had little time to discern that he was being watched until it was too late. Feeling the burning heat on his back, Venetor turned around to see men, women and children emerge from beyond the rocky terrain. They were not the most fearsome group he'd ever seen, each one with a collar around their neck, much like his own, and dressed in rags he assumed had once been the very clothing they had been taken in. What the prince found most unsettling in them was the look in their eyes, for it was a hungry look.

It was the kind that led men to strip lesser men of their flesh, or at least that was what he had read in his military books as a boy.

Not allowing for his persona to waiver, Venetor turned around to face them. His defiant composure filled his frame as every muscle and fibre in his body flexed with the anticipation of an attack. He had no idea what to expect from these people, his people, and so he was prepared for the worst. His anxiety continued to build when nothing happened and those gathered continued to take him in.

"Well," Venetor's gruff voice made his presence real, "Go on with it. I know what you are all waiting for, have been waiting for. On with it!"

No response came from them as they continued to gaze upon him. Just as Venetor prepared to speak again, one by one they began to drop to their knees, bowing their heads. A chill ran down the spine of the Gaian prince as he observed what was going on.

"Long live the Prince of Gaia," the voice of an elder Gaian spoke from the back beyond the rocks.

"Long live the true and rightful future king," a female Gaian kneeling a few feet away added.

Venetor was taken aback by the proclamations as one by one, all of those gathered spoke similar words. He had expected different reactions, especially with his leaving of Gaia in its gravest time of need.

"Rise," he said and they got up on his command. "One of you tell me what has gone on here."

"Razmus has taken control of much of the planet," a Gaian male standing some distance away with an auburn-coloured beard said. "Those who refused to acknowledge him as king and the white lion have been captured and forced to work on the tower."

The Gaian prince cocked his head sideways towards the source of the voice, and taking a few strides towards the Gaian asked, "What are your name and rank?"

"I am called Marianus Spero, my lord," the Gaian said, taking a low bow. "I was a professor of Gaian history at The University of Pangaia."

Venetor nodded and pointed to the female who had spoken second. "And you?"

He continued in this manner with all of those gathered around him, identifying each Gaian's name and rank. Finishing, he voiced his conclusion. "As I suspected, no discerning of rank or position. Yet I wonder where the soldiers are?"

"Many have been sent to attend to the actual building of the tower, my lord," Marianus spoke. "That is to say, those that did not escape."

"And what of my father?" he questioned.

"There has been no word of the king since the castle was stormed," Marianus confirmed.

A void-like feeling filled Venetor upon hearing the news as he turned away to contemplate his plan of action. While part of him wanted to believe the king of Gaia still lived, he knew there was a very slim chance of that. Razmus would not want any contenders for the throne. Yet he had thrown Venetor into the mines. Perhaps he had hoped that the people of Gaia would have torn him limb from limb upon seeing the one person they had trusted would protect them. Protection for his people was the duty of the monarch, after all. In this, he had failed them, and he knew it all too well.

Turning back around, Venetor gazed at those gathered, "I cannot give you any promises of freedom won. My predicament is not much different than your own."

He could see the hope fade from their eyes with his declaration, like a thousand candles all going out in a darkened room before him. Still, he knew it was best to be honest and so he continued. "But I can tell you this, we still have our pride, for that is something Razmus cannot take from us so long as it resides within the heart of each Gaian here. My leave of Gaia was also not in vain."

"What do you mean my lord?" Marianus asked.

Upon hearing this, the people gathered closer to listen to what the prince had to say. Seeing the crowd riled, Venetor gave a small smile.

"The heir of Orbeyus walks the Earth."

※

Having brought Skyris and Iliam to the Lab, Jason and Annetta both waited outside the emergency ward with their eyelids growing heavy. It was only a matter of time before the two of them, still in their armour, passed out in their seats without knowing it. The initial exhaustion having worn off, Annetta was stirred awake by the sound of voices coming from the room Iliam was in. Looking over at Jason, who was snoring on the seat opposite of her, she punched his arm lightly to wake him.

Jolting from his sleep, Jason looked over wide-eyed at his friend. "Jeez Anne, you trying to kill me?"

"I think enough people have tried to do that already," she said as she turned her attention to the room.

Inside, Skyris sat on a stool at the far end, monitoring two screens, with Dexter hovering quietly beside her. It was not the biggest enclosure in the Lab, the bed on which Iliam lay asleep taking up the majority of the space. It reminded Annetta a lot of the room she was in when she'd had to have stitches put in after having had a nasty fall from a tree around Jason's house when she was ten. The smell of bleached material filled her nose, making it almost uncomfortable to be close to it. Despite this, the girl did not move, especially upon seeing Puc standing on the opposite side of the bed, his injured hand having also been properly tended to. He was engaged in a heated conversation with Skyris and Atala, who stood by the door.

Hearing her and Jason enter, the trio turned to regard them, cutting their conversation short.

"Annetta, Jason, you are both still awake," Puc spoke.

"Kind of hard to sleep when you're trapped in a tin can." Jason looked down at his armour and then back up. "Everything okay in here?"

"Iliam has been stabilized," Skyris assured them, "All traces of the poison were extracted and an in-depth analysis is being run on it to determine the rest of the components."

"Okay, so why the long faces?" Annetta motioned to those gathered.

There was a brief silence in the room. Atala, seeming the most angered out of the three was the first to speak. "Well, go on, Thanestorm, you say it."

The weight having been thrown onto his shoulders, Puc turned to the two youth. "In light of this attack, I will be unable to travel to Gaia in order to aid you ...I am truly sorry, but I need to stamp out the warfare of the Fire Elves before I take on another foe."

Hearing the words come from the mage, Annetta felt her body set alight as she processed what this meant for her. Puc had always been there for them, had always been the one force of stability in a world both Jason and her did not fully understand.

"Puc...you can't mean that," she managed to choke the words out of her.

"I am sorry, Annetta, but I must," he replied. "With the attack on Iliam, I am not even certain who I can trust. I have called upon the aid of the other Water Folk cities of Terralim. This threat is far bigger than what I had expected when I returned home."

Hearing the finality of the words coming from him, Annetta felt a sense of doom emerge. How could they possibly go on without Puc to Gaia? How they would even get there was another question entirely. It was then that she realized how much faith they had put in the mage during all of their time within Q-16.

"Darius will aid you in my time of absence," Puc said as an afterthought. "He knows just as much as I do, and will be a great asset if you let him."

The illusion of helplessness fading for a split second, Annetta felt comfort in this knowledge. Still, though, she knew she would miss the elf, even if at times he was a thorn in her and Jason's side.

"Sarina and I will go with you," Jason then stated.

"What?" Annetta blurted out loud.

"Jason, I cannot ask this of you," Puc began, raising a hand as if to stop the boy from his future course of actions.

"Anne." He turned to the girl. "I wanted to talk about this later, but it can't wait. The Water Elves are part of the Four Forces, and they need our help first. The fact that you're even considering splitting up the army to go to Gaia baffles me, but if the Four Forces have to be split up, then I think it only makes sense that we are, too. How else are we going to show our support for all four races? I know you want to help your uncle, but we can't be blinded by family ties. Besides, where was he when we had to fight Mislantus? I thought you would be the one person here who would understand my reluctance to go help him."

Annetta felt everyone direct their eyes at her. It was true what Jason said, even if part of her disliked it. Were it the other way around, she would have been the first to confront him.

"You don't know all of the facts, J.K.," she retorted, agitated by his accusation. "But fine, Jason and Sarina will go to Aldamoor for this campaign."

She then glanced in Skyris and Atala's direction. "I will go to Gaia with the other half of the army, once we know the situation."

Jason felt a tinge of betrayal upon hearing what his friend said. How could she not see how important it was for them to stay together right now? Still, he knew there would be no changing her mind, even if it angered him, and he nodded silently.

A yawn then formed in the back of the girl's throat, which she tried to suppress, but it ended up escaping regardless. "Also, not until I get some sleep."

Puc nodded and reaching into his robe, produced two vials, handing one to each of the youth. "Take these tomorrow once you begin to feel tired. I think you will be in need of them."

"Why do I get the feeling that this isn't liquid Tylenol?" Jason said, shaking the bottle lightly.

"It is the same kind of energy potion I gave to Annetta on your first descent to the Lab," he explained. "It will restore your energy where the amount of sleep you will get will fail to do. I will summon the other leaders here tomorrow and we will convene our gathering as planned."

"Something tells me this is going to be a regular thing for a while," Annetta sighed examining the vial.

ଯଉଷ

Bright and early next morning, as it was a school day, Annetta was up and about. The night before, she'd stripped out of the armour, returned to her room and crashed into bed like a fallen tree. It was little wonder that when she awoke, she was filled with fatigue, and every inch of her body ached from the fighting the previous day.

While she really wanted to call in sick, she knew she'd already had one too many this semester, and had a sense there would be much more to come. Finishing getting dressed and draping the heavy winter jacket over herself, she grabbed her backpack and went to leave the house. She'd seen no sign of Link anywhere and had assumed that he'd gone ahead to school without her, or was needed down in the Lab to prepare for his journey back to Gaia.

She was surprised to see him waiting at the bus stop already, dressed in a bright red parka. His ruffled hair was obscuring most of his face from the side. For some reason she could not explain, the sight brought a wide grin to her face that she was forced to wipe off before speaking with him.

"Morning," he greeted her. "How are you feeling after last night?"

"I think you mean what am I not able to feel?" She smirked, causing the youth to smile lightly before turning around and seeing the TTC bus coming towards their stop.

"Point taken." He pursed his lips, showed his student pass to the driver and got on. Finding a place to stand beside the door, Link waited for Annetta to join him before continuing in a low tone. "We caught Tobias with Matt. He's confined to the prison in Aldamoor until further questioning."

The girl nodded, not wanting to draw attention to their odd topic of conversation on a very packed bus. While she knew most people would care less what two teenagers were talking about, part of her was cautious due to Puc's consistent warnings about being found out. She sighed, remembering the elf would not be present with her in this next fight, nor would her best friend. A pang of anger coursed through her, causing her to squeeze the pole she clung to a bit tighter than normal.

Link saw the reaction. "Everything alright?"

"Depends what you mean by alright," she grumbled.

"I can sense you're upset," he reminded her. "Also, it's hard to miss with you clenching that pole like it was a broadsword."

Realizing her grip, Annetta loosened it before glancing at him. "It's stupid and selfish. I wish Puc didn't have to leave or you either for that matter."

"Oh." Link ran a hand through his hair to push back the bangs. "Wait, what do you mean Puc is leaving?"

"To go after the Fire Elves," she replied. "Puc is going after them and Jason said that he and Sarina are going to go with him in order to show the support of the Four Forces. He said that going to Gaia instead of helping the Water Elves is a bad move because the elves were there to back us up and Gaia was not."

"Does he know why?" Link probed as Annetta shook her head. "I can see why you're upset."

The bus came to their stop, signalling for them to get off. Hopping off the bus, Link continued. "But at the same time, I can see what he means. Gaia is not a member of the Four Forces. Some Gaians fought alongside Orbeyus during the Great War, but they never officially declared allegiance of any kind."

"They need our help, though," Annetta protested. "I thought you as a Gaian would have my back in this."

"I do." Link frowned. "I also understand where Jason is coming from. The Four Forces are an alliance, not a personal army and splitting it up will weaken it."

"And I get that, too." Annetta exhaled as she adjusted her backpack. "But people's lives are in danger on Gaia and Razmus can become an even bigger threat if we don't do something about it."

"You sure that is the reason you want to go there and not to rescue Venetor?"

"Well, that's part of the reason, but not all of it. I mean, he is my uncle," she answered.

Before Link could reply to her, a blur of black and grey zoomed past both of them, pushing them apart so hard that Annetta ended up falling on her already sore rear into a pile of snow. Seconds later, another shape darted past them and collided with the next, followed by a third. When all was said and done, the two youth looked over to see two police officers, tackling a young man dressed in a puffy black jacket, loose jeans and heavy black boots with a black beanie on his shaved head.

Throwing aside one of the officers as though they weighed nothing at all, he got up and was about to run, were it not for the female officer who got in his way.

"Out of my way, pig!" he snapped and took a swing at her.

The woman, a brunette with an olive complexion, dodged the attack with ease and grabbing hold of the assailant's arm, twisted it back in a disabling position. The man swung another arm at her, only to have the woman restrain his other arm.

Just as the action came to a stop, the sound of distant sirens could be heard and a police vehicle pulled up to the curb, producing two more officers which went to assist the woman, along with her partner.

Annetta stared at the scene with mixed feelings, only to have Link tap her on the shoulder to bring her back to reality.

"Let's get out of here before they see us," he said to her. "Otherwise they may question us as witnesses."

"Won't it be a crime if we do?" she raised an eyebrow.

Link looked around and noted the crowd of curious onlookers which had gathered, then looked back at her. "I don't think we will be missed."

Seeing his point, Annetta nodded in reply, and they quickly vacated the area.

&0G&

A blazing red sun had begun to set upon Gaia, outlining the silhouette of Razmus's tower perfectly against the orange sky. From his balcony, the Lord of the Unfinished Tower gazed into the horizon. It had become a ritual for him to come outside and watch each day as the sun set upon his ever-growing monument. To Razmus, the tower was more than just a structure. It was his legacy.

He remembered his father, trying to convince him that the towers that he and his brother had built were not everything there was to life but merely contemplation, a test to showcase which of them would be fit to rule. With that, Razmus had been close, he would have beat Magnus had he been given a little more time. His father, however had stripped him of this chance when he put Magnus in command of his army to arrest him in the dead of night. His father had been a fool on that account as well as for not having had him executed. Now, twelve centuries later, when his bones and the bones of his brother Magnus were dust, Razmus, with the help of his prison, had endured. Venomous rage fuelled him and he would see the line of Magnus erased. One of the perks of having been locked up with the spell that had been cast to seal him was that it had kept Razmus frozen, not aging despite the world outside continuing onward through time. He would see the tower complete, a structure that would lead to the heavens as he would rule Gaia, establishing a new dynasty. This he was certain of. He was the one who had come to rescue Gaia in its time of need. He was the white lion.

From the far end of the chamber, Amarok observed his master, not moving a muscle. He had been standing there for quite some time, unsure of whether or not to interrupt the hypnotic stare of the Gaian king. Finally, as the last of the sunlight vanished from the horizon, he strode forward.

"Lord Razmus." He announced his presence, causing the Gaian in white plate mail to veer around and face him. "If I may have a word with you."

"What of Amarok?" Razmus asked as he strode into the inner chamber, the doors to the balcony sealing behind him. "Well, assassin? Speak!"

There was a melodic yet violent tone to Razmus's voice, but this did not faze Amarok in the least bit. His good eye simply watched as the blonde-haired Gaian moved around the large round metal table in the centre of the room and fixed the various piles of scrolls, scribbles on parchment and assorted pieces of scrap paper with writing and sketches on them, each dealing with some aspect of the tower.

"It concerns the matter of Venetor Severio," Amarok spoke once more. "Do you think it wise to leave him unattended in the mines as is? He is a royal hostage. He could be used to our advantage, with his father having perished."

Pausing what he was doing, Razmus looked over at Amarok with his glinting blue eyes. There was ravenousness in them, the likes which Amarok recognized from his previous master. Everything seemed to slow to a halt around them as the two locked eyes. Knowing his place, Razmus was the first to look away, not caring what the assassin's opinion was.

"Have you ever truly known isolation, Amarok?" the Severio lord spoke. "The impenetrable silence of a sealed-off chamber? The chasms of such a prison are only filled with wishful fantasy. Such was my reality for twelve thousand years. No, I do not think to use Venetor Severio as a bargaining chip. What for? When I have control of the planet? What uses have I for the descendant of Magnus, who cheated me out of what by my right, by my intellect should have been mine. I will have him rot as I rotted and I will have it be so among his people, those who had forsaken me."

A second bout of silence ensued. Amarok's silver mask shone in the last rays of the fading sun. Shifting his stance, the assassin cleared his throat.

"Did you know that there is more of Magnus's line?" he asked.

Razmus's ears pricked up upon hearing this. "Where and of whom do you speak?"

The assassin regarded the king. "On Gaia's sister planet, Earth, there is a youth named Annetta Severio, the granddaughter of Orbeyus Severio, who was the elder brother of Venetor. He abdicated the throne for Earth and adopted the sigil of the black lion for his own as a sign of his disobedience to his father."

"The legendary keep of the Eye to All Worlds, where the veil is weakest?" Razmus confirmed, recalling his folklore lessons.

"Yes my liege, and I can assure you that the Eye to All Worlds is very real," Amarok nodded.

"And what of this Orbeyus?" he questioned.

"Dead, by my own hand for many years now."

Razmus calculated his thoughts on the matter. "Then I will deal with Annetta Severio when the tower is complete. She is no threat to us this far away. For what good is a single black cub against the white lion of Gaia?"

හ⊙෬

Downing one of the energy potions given to her by Puc and remembering its revolting palate, Annetta strode into the common room area of the Lab. Despite the few hours of sleep she'd had and the whole day of school she had just endured, she was waking up with the help of the marvellous concoction. She noted as she came closer that an enormous round wooden table had been placed in the middle of the room, the couches all pushed to the sides. Gathered around it were Puc, Darius, Skyris, Titus, Gladius, Atala, Natane, Amayeta, Entellion, Doriden, Amelia, Lord Ironhorn, Prince Snapneck and Matthias. They seemed dressed for war, causing her to feel out of place in her casual school wear and to feel intimidated by the large gathering. Though she knew all of those present, it was the situation they were about to discuss which unnerved her.

Soon after, Link walked up beside her, having made his descent. Stripping out of his jacket, he was left in his usual attire of a black t-shirt and jeans.

"You ready for this?" he asked.

"Like we got a choice." She muttered and walking closer, greeted those gathered. "Hey everyone, I guess we're just waiting on J.K. and Sarina, right?"

"Aye, that would be it." Gladius bobbed his head, causing the silver hoops on his good ear to jingle. Turning his head, he then saw Jason and Sarina's silhouettes come into view. "Oi! Before we turn grey here, lad and lassie."

Hearing the booming voice of the Hurtz, Jason's eyes seemed to widen and grabbing Sarina's hand the two dashed over to the table, still wearing their winter gear.

"Sorry. We came straight from school," Jason explained.

"No matter. We are all here now." Puc shook his head. "We have much that needs to be discussed."

Puc's gaze then turned to Annetta, followed by everyone else present. "Lady Annetta, if you would."

The girl's nose wrinkled her upon being called 'lady,' which Jason apparently noticed as he stifled a snicker under his nose. Knowing it was out of place to say anything, she ignored him, reminding herself

238

mentally to hit him again when he was in his armour or tease him about being whipped by Sarina. Either way, she planned to get even.

Taking a deep breath, she began. "We find ourselves in a situation where it looks like we'll need to split up the armies of the Four Forces in order to give aid to both the Water Elves and to liberate the people of Gaia."

Chattering began almost instantly among the leaders gathered. Though they had all heard what she meant to do the night before, they had been exhausted after the day of fighting. Now with clear minds, they heard what the young girl was proposing to be done and only with half of the forces they would normally use. The sensation of ears flattening against her skull took over Annetta as she witnessed the scene.

"An army? To free a planet?" Lord Ironhorn mused. "I mean no disrespect, Lady Annetta, but the odds would not appear to be in our favour on that one."

"You would only need to worry about one city, and that is Pangaia, our capital," Atala explained. "The true root of the problem is Razmus. If we take him out along with the two towers he is using to control the Hurtz, the battle should be over before it even begins. The one named Lincerious Heallaws will be sent ahead of us in order to get a good read on the towers and give us more information on the current state of things."

"A battle for a city seems more reasonable," Entellion added, "Though I dare say getting to Gaia will pose a bit of a problem."

"We have ships in Q-16 that we can use," Gladius stated.

Skyris nodded. "It's true. Though I will need to inspect them to make sure they are usable in order to get a more accurate count."

Annetta only listened and nodded when needed, seeing the conversation unfold itself. There was not much else for her to do. Hearing what Skyris said, however, she jumped in. "I'll leave you in charge of that if that's alright, Aunt Skyris."

"I'll be on it," the Gaian confirmed.

"Right," Annetta huffed, then collected her thoughts again. "I think that brings us to our most pressing issue, and that's how we're going to divide up the Four Forces in order to take care of both the Fire Elves and go to Gaia. Now, as you all know, I have little experience in this, and so I'll leave this matter in your care. It's only fair I think that you all be involved in this. I know Gaia is not of the Four Forces, and

I know they didn't even come to help us with Mislantus when he came, which there was a reason for, but again, I know how that looks. What I also know is that the Gaians are at our mercy, because no other help will come. The Greys have cut them off from everyone, not allowing a single fighter from their so-called Federation to help. Now, correct me if I'm wrong, but not everyone on Gaia is a warrior. There are civilians as well, who are suffering with no one to help them, people who can't protect themselves. When I was asked to come down here I did so, so that the people of Earth would have someone protecting them. I can't turn a blind eye to people that I can help. What I'm trying to say is that when I was told Gaia is the sister planet of Earth, it made it just as much a part of me as my own home. This is why I feel I need to go. That being said, the Water Elves are a part of the Four Forces, too, and I count many of them as my close friends. I can't abandon them."

Everyone present continued to remain silent. It was not that no one knew what to say, but that they were waiting for someone to speak first before voicing their opinion.

Puc was the first to do so. "I agree with Annetta on this. Both causes need us, and I say this both as Orbeyus's advisor and as First Mage that neither fight should be treated with less effort. Lives are at stake and the enemy will not hesitate to spill blood. Gaian, Elf, Minotaur, Soarin or Ogaien for that matter."

"What are you proposing be done then, Thanestorm?" Lord Ironhorn probed.

The mage looked over in the direction of both Jason and Annetta before continuing. "I have called upon the aid of the other cities of the Water Folk to go in pursuit of the Fire Elf forces. Scouts have already been sent out as of this morning to go to past Fire Elf regrouping locations to investigate. In terms of the division of the armies, I will need to cut my previous offering of provisions in half."

Annetta winced upon hearing what was being done with their already-dwindled force but said nothing. She looked over in the direction of the other leaders in order to get a read on what they were all thinking.

"You must do what needs to be done." Natane inclined her head as the serpentine tongue flickered in and out. "I stand by with what I could offer you before. The rest of the Ogaien go to Gaia with Lady Annetta."

"As do I," Lord Ironhorn added. "I will also call in the banners from other cities to aid with Gaia. We say it is taking one city, but who knows what we will find once we reach there. I will not take any chances."

"Lord Ironhorn, what of the protection of your other lands?" Skyris interrupted. "If I may be so bold as to ask, would that not leave them exposed?"

"Every Minotaur is a trained warrior, Lady Skyris," Lord Ironhorn replied to her. "And I will still be leaving the militia behind. Fear not for the safety of my people, when it is yours which are in peril."

"I suppose then the answer of the Soarin can be no different." Entellion finally chimed in. "Doriden shall go with Thanestorm to Aldamoor with those forces we promised, while Amelia and myself shall go to Gaia."

Seeing as all those gathered did not have anything additional to say, Jason stepped in. "Then it's settled. I'll go with Puc to Terralim to represent the Four Forces. Sarina has also offered to go with me."

"As do I, if that is the case," Matthias spoke up.

"Matt," Sarina hissed in opposition.

"Very well," Annetta concluded. "If we all know our places, then I suggest we dismiss and begin preparations. I will make sure each of you is kept up to date with when we launch for Gaia."

With that, the various leaders began to disperse. Annetta felt as though all the air from her lungs had deflated when this happened and rested both hands on the table while looking at her feet to steady herself. She was still learning about being a leader, but she knew even with her little experience she had that they were going to be severely strapped for resources in both fights and she didn't like it. Perhaps she should have listened and kept everyone together.

"You okay, Anne?" Jason asked, coming over to his friend.

"Yeah." she glanced over at him. "I'm just tired is all."

"Seems like a bit more than tired." He furrowed his brows.

"Well, what? You want me to jump for joy over us having to divide the army?" she growled, the potion beginning to wearing off and her fatigue coming back full swing.

"You did this yourself," Jason snapped, his own weariness beginning to show. "I told you it would go down like this."

"As far as I can see, we didn't have a choice," she growled back.

"Yes we did Anne, help Aldamoor and if we have the resources, go deal with Gaia after all is said and done."

Seeing the spat between the two, Puc interjected. "Fatigue can be our own worst enemy."

Annetta and Jason both turned around to face him, the first face they had laid eyes on when coming down to the Lab. It was strange to think it had only been a little over a year since they had come to know him. It felt as though they had both been here their whole lives.

"Puc, I want your honest opinion." She looked the mage directly in the eyes. "Do we even stand a chance on Gaia as our forces are divided now?"

"Annetta, you know I cannot offer you a proper answer for this," he said. "There is no such a thing as an easy win in war. If, however, you are asking me if in the current state of things the Four Forces can hold their own, then it will depend on many factors, some as simple as whether or not the element of surprise can be used."

The girl sighed. It was not the response she had hoped to hear from the mage but he was being truthful with her. There were too many factors. Looking off to the side, Annetta saw Link watching her from the corner of his eye as he spoke with Gladius. She hoped he would be the one to find some of those answers for them, even if she did not agree in sending him off alone to Gaia.

"I guess Sarina and myself are gonna need some kind of note of absence for school, won't we?" Jason's words pierced through her train of thought as he continued to address Puc.

"I will see to it that Skyris takes care of it." The mage inclined his head. "Your mother will need to be notified as well, and I am not sure how you want to go about doing that."

Jason wrinkled up his face as the comprehension hit him. His mother was not overly fond of him spending time in the Lab as it was. To have it interfere with his studies and cause him to be missing for an extended period of time would be a whole other issue. The more he thought about it, the more he realized he did not care.

"There are far more important things going on right now," he said. "I know she won't be happy, but I'm also sure that she knew something like this might come up."

The mage nodded upon hearing this. "See to it that you are both ready for tomorrow. We will leave sometime in the afternoon, once you have both finished class. I will use that time to mobilize troops as well as to see to Iliam's condition."

Puc then took off in order to begin preparations, the sound of his staff hitting the metallic floor being the only form of farewell.

Watching him go, Darius approached the duo. "It's going to be strange without him on this one."

Annetta regarded him with a frown. "Oh? You're not going to go with Puc and the rest of the elves?"

"And miss out on the chance to babysit you?" He snickered. "No, someone needs to remain behind and be the adult."

"Thanks for the vote of self-confidence," she grunted.

Darius chuckled, "I'm only kidding, but I am serious about staying behind. Puc did say before that should anything happen to him, I need remain here to advise you, and that is exactly what I intend on doing. Besides, this is my home, even if I was born in Aldamoor."

Annetta gave a short bob of the head as a form of acknowledgement. She glanced around again, taking in those that remained. With the amount of beings there, it no longer felt as expansive as it once had, or perhaps it was that she was imagining things, reminiscing on what had once been. She remembered all the times she had come down after school to find Brakkus or Puc awaiting her and Jason. She remembered when it was just her and Link sitting on the couches, waiting for everyone else to arrive. She remembered what it was like before. She realized then that one day she would remember all of this too and that try as she might, she had to move forward. Pushing back her shaggy bangs, the girl sighed, focusing on what now lay ahead.

Chapter 21

The red blazing giant that was Gaia's sun rolled out on the horizon of jagged stone. From his stoop on a pile of rocks in the encampment, Venetor watched a new day be born. He had barely slept the night before, his mind having been turned to the tower which rose further away from the mines. His warriors were all there. At present, the Gaian prince knew that he stood little chance against Razmus's mind-controlled Hurtz, nor the soldiers that had decided to back his claim. It was a sad truth, but one that Venetor had come to see while he pretended to slumber, watching as the exchange of guards took place around their camp. He did not blame his people for not all being loyal to him. Many had families to protect, and for all he knew, many were simply in hiding. Still, it angered him to see defectors, and he silently promised himself that justice would be dealt accordingly when this was over. From what Venetor could tell, Razmus had a pretty good grip on things as they stood. He had single-handedly taken over the planet by controlling the Hurtz and his claim of being the white lion of prophecy. It still boggled his mind how such a feat had come to be since Gaians were not a superstitious lot.

When he had first heard news of Razmus's return, he recalled both his and his father's reaction of dismissing it all as a rumour. Before they realized it, however, Razmus was at their doorstep with all the Hurtz he needed to successfully take over the capital and noble houses that had rallied to him. Perhaps that was the power of a legend. No one knew the Lord of the Unfinished Tower was a threat until it was too late. A chill passing through his spine, he wrapped the flimsy blanket he had been given around him.

"Up, ye lazy scum!" the raspy voice of a soldier echoed from behind.

With his back still turned, Venetor listened to the ambient sounds surrounding him as the others in the camp awoke on command. The shuffling of shoes on dirt could be heard as they got ready. He, however, did not move.

"Oi! Did you not hear me? I said up!" the voice boomed directly at him, only causing Venetor's fists to tighten beneath the fabric.

"I think he's deaf," another soldier spoke. "Maybe shake him awake?"

Focusing on his hearing and waiting just until the feet of the first guard was coming to a stop behind him, Venetor sprung to action. Grabbing his opponent by the neck, a Hurtz guard with the head of a feral cat and elongated canine ears, he threw him down to the ground, locked his legs around his throat, and proceeded to hammer his fist into the guard's face.

The action was over before it began, however, as two more guards grabbed Venetor under each arm and dragged him off the Hurtz. Wriggling in their grip, Venetor managed to throw the smaller guard off, only to land a fist in the gut, which crippled him.

"Don't think I won't kill ye, prince," the Hurtz guard growled. "Ye'll learn soon enough there be only one monarch in these mines, and that is I, Sentius."

Sentius then turned to one of the guards that had attempted to hold down Venetor. "No rations aside from water for the rest of the day for this one. If he tries it again, stick him in the hole."

Grimacing, Venetor began to rise to his feet, the sun havng been momentarily obscured as Sentius loomed over him. "Now, up with ye and get to work."

The Gaian prince said nothing in return, rising as he was bidden to do. He watched the Hurtz and his guard companions stalked off, going to make sure the other prisoners were awake.

"That was reckless, if I may say," Marianus spoke as he approached Venetor.

"Reckless but necessary," Venetor smirked as he wiped away the blood from his split lip with a single finger. "That bumbling idiot just proved to me that the collars do not restrict our feral form abilities, just the psychic ones."

"Feral form abilities?" Marianus looked at Venetor questioningly. "What good will that do? Most of us don't even know how to harness our form."

Venetor chuckled at the Gaian's lack of foresight on the subject. A small devious smile crept onto the face of the Gaian prince, "Why... level the playing field, of course."

ಬಃಆ

Annetta, Jason, Sarina and Link got off at the bus stop that was closest to Annetta's house once school had ended. While the school was still within walking distance, the cold always put a damper in the commute. It was easiest on those days then to simply hop onto public transportation and endure the cramped ride for a few stops before getting off.

"So, what excuse were you given for missing school?" Annetta asked, still in disbelief over what she had heard that morning.

"Family trip," Jason reminded her. "Apparently I'm going to sunny Florida for a whole month. Crappy thing is, they gave me all the homework I was missing and expect me to hand it in by email."

"Best hope Aldamoor has WiFi," Link chuckled.

"Yeah, don't remind me," Jason groaned.

"Bad reception is always a valid excuse," Sarina assured him, "From what I understand at least with this primitive form of technology."

"The world wide web is far from primitive," Jason retorted. "You should have seen it when it was dial up a few years ago. That...that was primitive."

Sarina simply glanced over at Jason, raising both eyebrows to say he was indeed mistaken. She then continued on to Annetta's house without a word.

"Well, maybe it is a bit primitive with the whole signal thing," he mumbled as an afterthought.

Catching sight of this, Annetta made a whip-like motion with her hand while stifling a laugh and glanced over at Jason.

"Very funny, Anne," he growled, only to cause the girl to laugh louder.

౭౦౧౹

Their descent to the Lab was made after an awkward confrontation between Annetta and her mother. The subject of the encounter was when Xander would be taken down to have his abilities honed. There was not much the girl could say, of course, in order not to risk exposing what was going on, but she promised soon.

Once Jason and Sarina had everything they needed packed and ready, they set off to the stables. Puc, Darius, Matthias and Skyris were all present. Much to the surprise of the four, Iliam was also there. He was leaning against one of the fences and while he seemed paler and more drawn around the face than usual, it looked as though the elf would be fine.

"About time." Matthias greeted them. "I was going to start placing bets on whether or not you would show up."

"We had a holdup with Anne's mom," Jason stated.

"Yeah, she wants Xander and Liam to start learning to use their abilities," the girl added. "Not that there's going to be anyone left to teach them."

"Hey, I like to think I did an okay job with teaching you guys to retrieve back in Aldamoor," Darius interrupted, "Even if it was technically illegal."

"Sometimes being placed in a corner creates the better teacher," Puc said as he did a secondary check on the saddle of his grey mount, "And you will not be alone, Darius. There will be another to help you along the way."

"You can't possibly mean who I think you do," the younger mage scoffed and peered over at Annetta.

Seeing both Puc and Darius cast their glances her way, Annetta raised her hands in protest. "You've got to be joking me?"

"You know everything I had to teach you," Puc explained. "Remember also how long it took you to grasp the basics."

Annetta growled in frustration at the thought of the task, running a hand through her hair, "Even if I agree to this, I can help Liam, but I don't know anything about Xander's ability except that it's similar to Titus's."

"I'll have Titus work with him," Skyris assured her. "It will be a good distraction for him with everything that's happened."

Puc nodded, hearing the exchange and turned to Skyris. "How are you holding up?"

"I can take care of myself," she assured him with a half-smile.

His gaze then turned to Iliam. "And you?"

"I will stay back a day or so," Iliam informed Puc. "I doubt I'm ready to sit in a saddle, or even be of any use on the battlefield."

"You rest easy, friend, and when you get to Aldamoor, oversee the repairs on the city," he replied. "I will make sure to tell Maria you are on the road to recovery."

The mage said nothing more to them and turned back to the others. "I suggest we leave now. It will take some time for us to organize the camp."

Annetta and Jason both bobbed their heads in agreement. They then stood in front of each other for a few minutes while each of them tried to figure out what to say. Deep down, they both knew this would not be a one-day excursion, and yet they could not avoid what had transpired. The disappointment each felt at the other for taking a different stance on the subject of the Four Forces. The subsided anger was still present inside each of them like a slowly dying fire eating away at their cores.

"I guess this is it," Jason said. "I know I can't talk you out of this, to keep us all together instead, so you take care of yourself, Anne."

"Likewise," she replied and then turned to Sarina. "You keep an eye on him. He still doesn't pay attention to his right when defending."

"I'll do my best," Sarina assured her. Inclining her head in a goodbye to the others, she mounted on her horse.

Off to the side, Matthias had his own exchange with Link. "Stay out of trouble on Gaia until I get there."

"I make no promises," he answered as the two of them clasped hands.

Further off, Puc spoke with Skyris before getting on his own horse, ready to lead the others. With a final wave goodbye they were off, leaving Skyris, Darius, Annetta and Link alone.

೫೦೧೩

The earthy scent of dirt filled Venetor's nostrils. With the fading sunlight still beating down on his back, he could feel his muscles recoil in dehydration, unwilling to stretch further than they needed to. Having had time to accustom himself to his surroundings as he worked, he found that he recognized the area. With Razmus's tower looming overhead, he was able to discern it as once having been a luscious plain. Now only a few patches of grass remained, the ground having been torn apart in search of the dark stone used for the tower. The stone itself was only found inside the russet cliffs in the area, the texture was similar to that of limestone but black instead of white. Venetor noted somewhere mentally having heard in his studies as a youth that it had something to do with ash having been mixed into a body of water millions of years before resulting in the strange combination.

Grunting, the Gaian prince heaved another of the large slabs into the cart which would then bring them over to the construction site. Feeling his strength flee him, he regretted his decision to attack the guard in the morning, which left him with no rations for the day. Looking over to the side, he saw a young Gaian with a mop of bushy light brown hair and chiselled jaw as he continuously struck at the rocky mountain face with a pickaxe. He wore nothing but cloth breeches and wrappings to cover his arms from injury, leaving his broad chest exposed to the elements as he worked furiously. He seemed to be no older than Titus.

Venetor continued to watch him for a little while before he addressed him. "And why did you not enlist in the Gaian forces, pray tell?"

The youth turned to face him with a glint of arrogance in his eyes, slamming the pickaxe heavily into the ground as he did so. "Someone needed to stay behind and help maintain my parents' farm, m'lord."

"A farmer." Venetor pursed his lips as he stood up and examined him. "And not an only child, I take it?"

"The youngest of three, m'lord," he replied abruptly.

"My sympathies then," Venetor chuckled. "It seems we, the youngest, always get the short end when it comes to dealing with family legacies."

"If I can be bold enough to say so, m'lord, I don't see what the short end is when it comes to being the future king of Gaia," the youth spoke again before turning to place a hand on the pickaxe and resumed working.

"You truly know nothing then of Gaian rules of noble succession?" the Gaian prince asked, resting a hand below his chin as he watched him.

"And you, m'lord have no knowledge of how your people work," the Gaian growled as his tool struck solid rock again, "For the common folk care not for how someone came into their power, but what they choose to do with it."

Hearing these words, Venetor fell silent as the venom of them sunk their way into his flesh, resonating with him like an echo in his mind. He did not have long to dwell on them, though, when a cry came from behind. Veering his body around, Venetor was faced with the scene of an older female Gaian with long greying blonde hair, dressed in torn garments lying on the ground some distance away. She had been carrying buckets of water slung over her shoulders, the contents of which now lay spilt and absorbing into the thirsty soil. Two Hurtz guards were making their way over to her in haste.

"Second time this week, this one," the first of the two growled, hoisting her up by the arm. "Maybe we should talk to Sentius and have her put down?"

"I'd say stick her in the pits," the second one chimed. "No sense in having good mortar going to waste."

Before anyone could reply, there was a flash of silver as the pickaxe of the youth found its way into the shoulder of the first Hurtz, setting the female free of its grip. The weapon, having lodged itself into the meaty flesh, became of no use to its attacker, who soon found himself thrown to the ground by the second guard.

Venetor cursed himself as he watched, weighing his options. The ache from his empty gut served a reminder of his earlier trespasses, making him more reluctant to get involved. Seeing the youth kicked down to the ground and continue to be pummelled, however, triggered a shift in his empathy.

"He's just a stupid boy," Venetor called from where he stood, causing both guards to stop.

"He must be," grunted the first one, "Considering birdboy here just assaulted a Hurtz guard which is punishable by death."

"The pickaxe slipped from his hand." Venetor wove the story as he went along. "It was dumb luck that caused it to land where it did at that precise time. He's no fighter, he's a farmer. Though I dare say he'd have good aim if it were otherwise."

The injured guard ripped the pickaxe from his shoulder and tossed it to the floor in disdain, then turned to his companion.

"We'll let it slide this time," the second grunted, "Only because we don't wanna deal with Sentius and explaining why this here runt was beaten to a pulp. Wouldn't wanna rid the chief of his favourite amusement, too."

"Aye, it's nightfall anyways," the first one added but turned back to the young Gaian. "Next time ye might not be so lucky, birdboy."

The Gaian prince kept a straight face as he crossed his arms and continued to watch the Hurtz both stalked off. Once out of hearing distance, he exhaled deeply, feeling a wave of nausea due to hunger pass over him. He then proceeded to go and help the female.

"My lord, thank you." She bowed before Venetor, only to have him motion for her to stop as he proceeded to go help the youth.

"Why did you do that?" the young Gaian questioned him, grabbing hold of Venetor's hand.

Helping the lad to his feet, Venetor took a step back. The youth towered over him by well over a foot, as most Gaians did. What Venetor lacked in height, however, he made up for in his presence. His sapphire eyes examining the young Gaian, he asked, "What is your name, boy?"

250

"I am Janus," he said. "That's my mother, Flavia."

Nodding his head, Venetor acknowledged the exchange of names before continuing. "Janus, you defended your mother because you felt it had to be done, correct?"

"I guess so," Janus shrugged, wiping the blood from the corner of his mouth.

"So too a leader must defend his people or fear the prejudices you have marked against me earlier," he replied and then added, "What did the guards mean by when they called you the chief's favourite amusement?"

Janus frowned as he looked at the ground, not wanting to answer.

"Show him, Janus," Flavia spoke. "He's a gifted young Gaian, my prince. Always has been, but he refused to join the army."

"Mother, I shouldn't," he hissed, only to see the nagging look upon her face, which caused him to sigh. "Very well, but only quickly."

Looking around to make sure none of the guards were watching, Janus closed his eyes. His form melted away, shifting and changing until in his place was a white falcon. The creature flapped its massive wings, taking to flight and swooping down where the pickaxe lay, transforming back into Janus just in time for his hand to make contact with the tool. Slinging it over his shoulder, he glanced back at Venetor.

"There, now you know," he huffed.

"You can use your feral form?" Venetor stared at the youth, slack-jawed. "Who taught you?"

"I taught myself," he replied. "When we were captured, I tried to escape and to find help in that shape, but the Hurtz caught me. Since then, I've been a toy to the Hurtz overseer Sentius, a pet. He likes to bring me with him when he goes hunting from time to time."

"Can you not flee?" the prince further pried.

"All of the collars are traceable and will cause us to seize up if we get too far," Janus explained as he tapped at the device around his neck. "They also change to fit whatever form you take so you can't get out of them by changing. You can't run from the Lord of the Unfinished Tower."

Venetor chuckled, hearing the dramatic delivery from the youth. "Oh, but I don't plan on running, boy. I plan on fighting him."

"You have no army," Janus reminded him.

"An army will be worth nothing against those banded together to fight for their homeland," Venetor argued. By this point, a small crowd of Gaians had assembled to listen in on what he had to say. "Hear me, all those willing. As I am your prince, so do I vow that I will lead you out of this, even if it is to be with my last breath. I spoke of the heir of Orbeyus before, but the truth is we only have one another to rely on, and from what I have gathered, that might just be enough. Meet with me at midnight in the camp."

ⅎ⅏

After Puc, Jason, Sarina and Matthias had departed for Aldamoor, Link had set off to prepare for his own journey. Entering his room, he dropped the large backpack Brakkus had once had him train with on his bed. Smoothing out the creases in the dark green canvas, it reminded him of all the times he had spoken with the Hurtz and of all the memories he shared with him. He then set to work, packing clothing, medical supplies, food and water. There was only so much he could carry with him without the risk of being caught. Even the flimsy bag seemed like a lot, if the state of Gaia was as bad as Venetor had told them. His task finally completed, Link went to his closet and retrieved his militia outfit. Having changed into it, he then hoisted the backpack onto his shoulders, secured his sword and left the room.

As he walked down the hallways, he felt a great weight pressing down on him, and not from the load he now carried. It was something in the very back of his mind, something he could not quite pinpoint. Turning the final corner to where Skyris had her workspace, Link paused, seeing the female Gaian intently at work once more while Dexter hovered some feet away like an oblivious blimp. He remembered seeing the woman a few times on occasion when he was on Gaia, participating in celebrations and such. It was still strange to him at times to be interacting with her as he did with Annetta or the others, yet she hated the formalities the few times he had tried to address her by title in private.

Taking note of his presence, the A.I. sprang to life. "Hello, Lincerious Heallaws, also known as Link. Did you find everything you were looking for in your living quarters for your journey?"

"Uh...yes...yes I did." Link shifted his footing, the robot still making him squeamish whenever it spoke.

"That is wonderful to hear." The large single eye seemed to smile as the words came from it, causing Link to cringe even further.

Skyris then glanced over at Link. "Hey, you ready?"

Before he could respond, Skyris was up and having checked to see her glass was empty at her work station, she threw on her fur-lined bomber jacket.

"I've been having Dexter run diagnostics on all the crafts we have," she began to explain as she walked past him, the A.I. flying in tow behind her. "I found a small cruiser which dates back about two decades, but it's in running order. Everything else we've got would cause suspicion since it's even older. Orbeyus had a thing for collecting vintage crafts. The engine in this particular model is in immaculate condition, maybe run twice or three times…"

While Skyris continued to list off the specs on the ship, Link could not help but continue to feel the weight creep up on him like someone had placed a bag of bricks on his chest and was adding to it continuously. Perhaps it was the anxiety of the mission, of going back home. He shook off the thought. Q-16 was home.

Coming to a stop, they entered a large area with multiple tarp-covered objects. Among these was what looked like a small sleek bullet-shaped vessel coated completely in a reflective silver material. It had no windows and no visible way in. Had Link not known any better, he would have thought it to be an abstract art piece.

"Meet Vesta 6118." Skyris beamed as she pointed to the ship. "Try not to break her too much."

Link examined the craft, walking around the metallic structure, which held not a single flaw in its smooth design.

"To open it, place your palm anywhere on the ship," she instructed him. "I've coded it to your DNA sequence, and it will only obey you."

Nodding, Link pressed his hand against the side of the ship. Taking a step back, he watched as the wall beside him melted away and reformed into perfectly symmetrical stairs.

"How do we get it out of here undetected?" he asked.

"Dexter and I will scramble the signals. As for liftoff, your friend Darius seems to know how to make it happen, from what I hear," she answered him.

The youth sucked in some air to steady himself. "Well, it looks like everything has been taken care of then."

"You gonna be okay to fly?" Skyris probed further, crossing her arms.

"I was never good at many things while training," he said. "Flight was not one of them, thankfully."

Skyris bobbed her head in acknowledgement. "I'll go start on the scrambling and get Darius to meet you here. Might as well make yourself comfortable. I'll be in contact with you through the C.T.S."

"Okay," Link replied as he peeked inside the ship, taking in the white sterile environment visible from where he stood.

"Best of luck, kid," Skyris remarked, giving him a gruff pat on the back. "You're gonna need it, and remember, all of Gaia is counting on you so no pressure there."

His focus still on the ship, Link did not even notice when Skyris had left the room. Adjusting his sword and backpack, he was about to go up the stairs when the weighted feeling intensified. Frozen in his tracks, he turned around. There, at the entrance of the room, stood Annetta. Seeing her there, the youth understood where the feelings were coming from, and that they were not entirely his own.

"Annetta," the name escaped his lips.

"I wanted to come see you before you left," she said, taking a few steps towards him as she looked up at the ship. "At least they're sending you back in style. Think Puc would let us take one of these to prom?"

Link chuckled, hearing the girl. "Maybe."

Annetta grinned, seeing his reaction. The smile faded quickly, however, as the two of them regarded one another. It was the first time in a while that they were both standing in a room without another soul among them. It felt serene, peaceful, like the times they both spent by the lake. Link took a step closer, studying the girl, the lustre of her dishevelled reddish hair contrasting against her glistening cobalt blue eyes.

They stood this way for some time, entranced by the presence of one another until Annetta took another step towards him. She could feel Link's breathing against her cheeks as air came in and out through his nostrils. Moving in even closer, she felt the same force of gravity as before pulling her towards him and this time, try as she might, she could not stop it. Closing her eyes, she leaned in and kissed him.

The Gaian youth's first instinct was to pull her closer. He had been anticipating this for quite some time. Now as it occurred, he couldn't be happier. The moment was lost, however, as Link remembered his oath to his prince and the words he had exchanged with Gladius.

"I'm sorry Annetta, I can't," he apologized, pulling away.

Annetta raised an eyebrow as she observed him. "Sorry, for what?"

Link hesitated as he shook his head and took another step back. "We shouldn't do this, Anne."

"What are you talking about?"

"We just can't." Link growled in frustration. "It wouldn't be right."

"Look, can you explain in plain English what you mean?" Annetta folded her arms across her chest, awaiting an answer.

"I…" Link tried to collect his thoughts, "I'm just not sure I feel the same way."

"Oh," Annetta let the word escape as she also took a step back, the sensation of ears flattening against her skull following. "I just thought that…"

"Hear me out before you say anything else." He motioned with his hands in a calming manner. "Do you remember when Brakkus had me swear that oath before he died?"

"Uh…yeah," she shook her head.

"What if I told you I could feel your emotions?" he continued. "Ever since that day, I've been able to sense you, how you're feeling, if you were angry or sad or in danger, everything. I guess what I'm trying to get at is that my feelings as they are now might not be entirely my own. They could be a projection of your feelings onto me."

The girl stood completely still. She felt as though she was on a roller-coaster about to go down and was stuck at the very top, unable to descend. A chill passed through her while she did her best to deal with what was going through her mind at that moment.

"Anne." Link stepped forward, taking her hand in his. "I want them to be true, I really do, but I also don't want to lead you astray. When I get back, when this is all over with, we will figure this out together."

Before Annetta could say anything further, they were interrupted by the sound of shuffling feet. Soon after, Darius stood at the far side of the room.

Link withdrew his hand and turned to regard the elf. "I guess everything is set, then?"

"Good to go on my end," Darius told him. "You just get in there and get comfy."

"Not too comfy, I expect," Link flashed him a grin.

"You know what I mean, chuckles," the young mage replied. "Now get moving. We're wasting daylight."

"Looks like we'll make a Puc out of you yet," the Gaian snorted.

Annetta could not help but stifle a laugh, hearing the exchange between the two. Link then turned to regard her once more and closing in, embraced her in a tight hug before letting go.

"I'll see you soon," he said to her. "I promise."

"You don't have much of a choice," she reminded him as he walked off and began boarding the ship. "You're under oath, remember?"

Link's face beamed into one last smile as he disappeared into the ship. The staircase of the vessel then melted away with no trace of an entrance left. Seeing this, Annetta made her way over to Darius's side. This was where their paths would part, she needed to remain behind and prepare for the battle on Gaia when the time came. The young mage then created the opening, just as he had but a year before, when they had gone to storm Valdhar. Before she knew it, the boy with the crescent moon scar on his face was gone just as quickly as he had arrived.

Chapter 22

Later that evening, Annetta found herself sitting on the deck in the backyard of her house. A sombre mood filled her as she gazed into the night sky, the faint glimmer of stars peeking through on the celestial blanket of clouds. A lot had happened in the last few days, and the girl had no time to process any of it by herself. Now, in the quiet of the evening, it was all catching up. Her best friend was gone off to fight in another world because he believed his choice to be right, her mentor of two years had also abandoned her in the quest she was currently undertaking to rescue her great uncle, and the boy she thought had liked her back had told her his feelings were confused right before taking off on a spaceship to his home planet.

"Just another day in the life," she muttered to herself.

As she continued to look skyward, she realized again how much she missed the way things were before Venetor had come into their lives. She missed the long nights of sparring in the Lab with her friends while Puc instructing them. She missed the journeys to visit the races of the Four Forces and participate in events while there. She missed meeting up with Link in the lake biosphere, alone, just the two of them. As she reminisced about these, she also realized that things would never be the same again. The thought pained her.

The sound of the door gliding open could be heard, followed by two pairs of feet. Annetta did not even flinch, knowing whom they belonged to. Out of the corner of her eye, she watched as her mother and father took a seat to either side of her, both dressed in their boots and winter jackets to help fight off the cold.

"It's been a long time since we've caught you out here." Aurora smiled, settling herself on the step beside her daughter. "Alone, that is."

"We were beginning to wonder if you'd holed up in one of those rooms in the Lab," Arieus added as an afterthought.

Annetta felt the corners of her mouth form into a slight smile, as for a split second she forgot all of the burdens she carried. The feeling did not last long, however, and she found herself grounded once more in the present. "Hey, Mom, Dad. I've been around, just...busy."

"I take it Puc is not back, then?" Arieus inquired, only to be answered with a short bob of the head. "I see... what of Venetor and the others?"

A lump formed in Annetta's throat when the question was posed. She wanted to tell her parents so badly about everything that had transpired. She wanted to tell them about the Fire Elves attacking Aldamoor, Puc becoming First Mage, Jason, Sarina and Matthias leaving to go with Puc to fight the Fire Elves, Link leaving for Gaia and about Venetor being taken. These events, along with everything else weighed heavily inside of her, but she knew better than to say anything to them. Having them worry was the last thing she needed to add to the ever-growing list of problems that seemed to be piling up in her life.

"They're fine," she said in an absentminded and weary tone. "Everything is fine."

Aurora frowned, hearing how her daughter answered the question. "What's wrong, Anne? Is something going on that we should know about down there?"

The girl growled, feeling herself be smothered into a corner with concern. "Everything is fine, Mom. Trust me."

"Sweetie, you're going to have to do better than that to convince me," the woman snorted. "You're not very good at hiding your emotions."

Grumbling, Annetta attempted to give as honest of an answer as she could. "There's just been a lot of changes going on in the Lab. Puc's been sworn in to become First Mage, Venetor has Jason and I learning to tap into our feral forms, which by the way is so weird, and, well... I just kind of miss how things were before all of this. I never wanted to be a Gaian, I never wanted Puc to leave and now Link has gone off to Gaia and-"

Annetta felt herself becoming angrier by the moment as her hands shook out of frustration while she spoke, gesturing with them to get her point across. Dropping them to her side, she exhaled gruffly. "I just don't want any more things to change, not for a while at least."

"Annie, this is normal," Arieus said. "This is just the way of life. Nothing stays the same forever. That would be like if you woke up each day and wore a black shirt no matter what."

"But I would be totally fine with that," Annetta replied.

"After a while though, wouldn't you want to wear maybe a red or a blue one?" Arieus asked her, which made Annetta stop and think about it as he continued. "Change is necessary, even if we do not always agree with where it leads us at a given time. It gives us room to grow and experience different things. It's what allows us to realize our full potential as people, to become adults, warriors or teachers, whatever we need to be that can only be marked with time and change. I know right now it may seem like a lot of things at once, like the world is closing in on you from all angles, but this won't always be the case."

"I guess so," muttered Annetta. "Still doesn't change the fact that it sucks now and I miss things the way they were before."

"Maybe you just need the proper distraction to not think so much about it," Aurora suggested. "Helping Xander understand the Lab may be a way of doing that. He'll need someone to help him with his abilities. Your father and I are probably not the best people. He's in that stage of not wanting to listen to us."

Annetta wrapped her jacket closer around herself, feeling the cold begin to creep past it and frowned. "Yeah…that might help…maybe."

"He has no one else to help him get through his own changes," Arieus pointed out. "When you first came down, you had Puc and Brakkus who led you through things. With Puc gone…well… even if he were still there then I think there would be no one better than you."

"I don't even know what his ability really is, aside from what Titus told us," Annetta retorted, "So I don't really know how I would help him to begin with."

"It's simple, Anne," Aurora stated. "You just need to be his sister."

Annetta shook her head as she looked at the two of them. "That I can do."

They then sat outside this way for a little while longer, continuing to look up into the sky. While Aurora and Arieus simply enjoyed it for what it was, Annetta's mind wandered. Her thoughts turned to a distant world she knew very little of, yet it was such a large part of her. Inhaling, she discarded her doubts for the evening and focused what lay ahead.

⁂

The next day after his classes were complete, Xander came home from school. Stamping his heavy black boots outside, he took them off to leave by the door and proceeded to take off his grey winter jacket. Warmth began to creep into his nose and cheeks as he blew into his hands, rubbing them together. He had not taken his gloves with him in the morning, feeling them an unnecessary accessory he had to carry around and put on each time he went outside. Pockets served him just fine for this purpose, or so he deemed. Lost in his own world as he mentally prepared himself for the next game he would be playing once he got to his room, he scarcely noticed the figure watching him from above on the stairs.

"Hey, Xander," a voice greeted him.

Startled and feeling like a deer in headlights, the boy looked all around him, not seeing a single living soul. Looking up, however, he saw Annetta sitting on the stairs, her hands folded as she rested her elbows on her knees. She was sporting her usual jeans and black t-shirt combination with her worn turquoise sneakers, her jean jacket lying across her lap.

"Hey Anne," he managed to choke out of himself as he glanced up at her. There was a delayed silence between them before Xander spoke up again. "So… what's up? Why aren't you down in Q-16?"

Annetta stood up from where she sat, throwing the jacket over her shoulder casually, the elevation of the stairs making her seem a giant as she descended to meet with her brother at eye level. "I was waiting for you to come home."

Xander regarded his sister with curiosity, his train of thought being halted as the door behind him opened and in came Liam. Jumping back to make room for his friend, he was even more surprised.

"Hi, Anne," the second boy beamed to her, "I came straight after school like you asked. Can I just use the phone to tell my mom where I am before we go?"

"Sure thing." Annetta gave a short bob of the head.

"Go where?" Xander queried as his friend took off his winter gear and went to the living room to make the phone call.

"Down to Q-16, of course." She smirked. "Though I don't want you calling it that. From now on you refer to it as the Lab in conversation. Got it?"

Xander's face quickly went from questioning and shocked to ecstatic. He had been certain that since the last time he had gone down that she had not wanted him back there, due to whatever had happened and the apparent battle that had been lurking on the horizon. It had even crossed his mind that perhaps Annetta had not wanted him down there just because he was her younger sibling. They had gotten into spats over simpler things before. Despite getting along, they were not immune to jealousy.

"Yeah." He nodded.

Liam came back in the room, a somewhat disgruntled look on his face.

"I take it your mum wasn't too pleased with you going down again, was she?" Annetta mused, seeing the boy.

"Yeah, but she said do what you gotta do," he replied and then grinned. "And I wanna learn how to use these powers!"

Annetta chuckled, hearing his enthusiasm and crossed her arms as her face became more serious. "You will, but you will have to listen to everything you are both told when you are being trained, no matter how silly you think it may be. Understood?"

"Yeah, sure, how bad can it be?" Liam shrugged his shoulders in a matter-of-fact manner.

"Oh, you guys haven't got a clue. Put your shoes on and follow me."

ഇരുൻ

Their descent to the Lab having been made, Annetta led the two boys to the training room. The journey was silent, accompanied by nothing more than the buzzing of the halogen lights overhead and the sound of their feet along a metallic floor. Passing by one of the hangars which were filled with tarp-covered objects, the girl heard the distinct sounds of a drill at work. Diverting their course, she turned to take a peek into the room.

Inside, Skyris stood upon what looked like a raised platform. Her thick dark hair was tied back and her face was obscured by a welding mask as she fought with the side of a large vessel which appeared to be similar in shape to that of a space shuttle but with a military-green paint job.

Annetta watched quietly for a little while before making her presence known, mesmerized by the precision and nimbleness of what the Gaian female was doing. There was a grace about the way she moved that Annetta envied and admired. Each movement served a purpose, like a well-oiled machine. It was hard for Annetta to conceive it was the same person her and Venetor had picked up from the bar just over a month ago. Her doubts were confirmed, however, when the Gaian stopped what she was doing, lifted up her mask, put the drill down and reached for a large jug of orange juice to take a swig. The girl was certain at times the juice was not the only contents found inside the container.

"Hey, aunt Skyris!" she greeted her.

The Gaian turned around to regard the trio and flashed a grin. "Hey, Anne, Titus is waiting with Darius in the training arena for you already like you asked."

"Good to know," Annetta nodded and then glanced at the craft. "How are repairs going?"

"They're going okay," Skyris chuckled, "But won't be going if I stand around talking if you get my meaning."

"I hear ya. I'll see you later, aunt Skyris." The girl waved and continued on her way, with Xander and Liam in tow.

"That's our aunt?" Xander raised an eyebrow in surprise. He remembered hearing the name when they had come down the first time but had known nothing more past that.

"Yeah, and she grows on you," Annetta assured him. "She's just a bit stressed with repairing the ships for our trip to Gaia."

"Gaia? Sounds like a planet from a video game," Liam quipped.

"It's a planet alright," Annetta said. "It's the planet our parents are from, apparently."

"You mean we're-" Liam stopped mid-sentence and pointed at himself before looking over at Xander, who had an equally stunned look on his face, "...aliens?"

"Ouch, when you put it that way, it almost sounds offensive," the girl laughed. "Yeah, I guess we are, but the proper term is Gaian. The man you met last time, his name is Venetor. He's Skyris's brother and the prince of Gaia. He's been taken hostage by another Gaian named Razmus, who occupied the planet."

"Oh," Liam managed to get out of himself. "Is that why Jason hasn't come home in a while?"

"Jason is actually on another mission in Aldamoor," Annetta explained. "He's helping our mentor Puc deal with a threat of Fire Elves. I'll be going to Gaia with Skyris and the others to get Venetor back... when we get the ships ready, that is."

Reaching their destination, Annetta paused before the Calanite diamond walls and peered inside to see Darius and Titus both sitting on one of the benches off to the side. Darius was dressed in mage robes and staring at his feet, absentmindedly, trying to pass the time. Beside him, Titus polished one of his pistols, wearing what looked to be a white linen shirt with a tweed vest and dark brown pants that were tucked into high black boots. Taking notice of Annetta watching them, the two stood up.

"Ah, fresh meat," Darius cackled in an exaggerated tone as he rubbed his hands together, hoping to get a frightened reaction from the two younger boys.

Xander and Liam, however, were not to be moved, which came as a disappointment to the young mage.

"Right," Annetta breathed, "So, how do you guys want to do this?"

"I will take Xander with me," Titus declared. "The both of you will be of no use to us."

"Well, that was blunt," Annetta chortled. "Anything else, oh wise prince?"

"Yes," Titus retaliated. "Don't call me that."

Without saying another word, Titus moved towards the other side of the area, where wooden targets had been set up. Xander followed, though he was not sure what to expect from the Gaian.

"He's having a rough time with his father being gone," Darius concluded. "I tried to speak with him earlier, same thing. He's only doing this because he knows he can't do anything else to help Venetor directly right now."

Annetta watched from a distance as Xander and Titus stopped, having reached their destination. Titus began speaking to the boy, most likely explaining his abilities to him. The scene was very reminiscent of her own days of training under Puc with Jason. Snapping out of her thoughts, she regarded Liam, who was now waiting for their instruction.

"Okay," the girl sighed, running a hand through her hair and turned to Darius. "So...uh...where do we begin?"

Not responding directly to her, Darius placed a hand into his robes and produced two smooth stones from it. He then placed them on the ground side by side in front of Liam. "The beginning seems as good a place as any. Now, I want you to take the stone on the right and place it on top of the other one."

ೞೞ

On the other side, Xander did his best to follow along as Titus explained how his ability functioned to him.

"An Aerokinetic elemental," the Gaian began, "Is a person who can manipulate various natural resources he comes into contact with that deal with anything airborne, such as static electricity. Elementals can also amplify what they come into contact with, which means a simple spark for you can become an electric current. We will not know for sure if you are just Aerokinetic or if you have a mastery of other elements as well until you go through some exercises and have a better grasp on controlling your abilities. Is that clear?"

"Yeah, I guess so." The boy nodded, not very convinced still of what was being said to him. Part of him felt like everything he was being told was simply being made up on the spot by Titus. He didn't want to believe a word of it, but he knew he could not run from any of it, given the state of things. Titus passed a pistol to the boy, causing him to snap out of his thoughts.

"The first thing you need to do is to be able to focus your energy into the weapon you wish to use," Titus continued to lecture. "Different elementals use different weapons. I find for Aerokinetics such as myself, ranged weapons work best, especially those with projectiles like guns. The friction caused by the mechanism allows for a very quick and convenient reaction to be channelled and amplified into energy."

Drawing the second gun, Titus aimed at one of the targets. The moment the click of the trigger was heard, a blast of an overwhelming yellowish-white beam sprang forth from the gun, slicing through one of the targets and tearing it to shreds. Twirling the weapon on his finger with ease and sliding it back into the holster, he then turned to Xander. "Your turn."

The boy looked unconvincingly at the weapon in his hand, but pointed it at one of the other targets.

"Okay, now what?" he asked.

"Shoot."

Xander narrowed his eyes at the lack of instructions and pulled the trigger. Nothing happened. The boy, confused by what he had done wrong, tried to look down the barrel of the gun only to have Titus swat his hand away before he finished turning the gun.

"Rule number one; never look down the barrel of a gun with your finger on the trigger still." Titus exhaled roughly. "Did you focus your energy into it while you aimed?"

"You didn't say anything about that," Xander protested and pointing the gun once more, he concentrated. Hearing the repeated click of the trigger mechanism, Xander was pushed back by the force erupting from the weapon, the gun nearly flying from his hand. Shaking off the shock, the boy looked up to see his target destroyed. "Whoa!"

"The technique seems simple," Titus said. "However, aim, focus and learning to hold your stance is a whole other thing, but we will get to those as time goes on."

Before the Gaian could say anything further, Annetta teleported just a few feet beside them, snatching something with her hand as she did so.

"Sorry, rogue stone," she remarked, showing the small smooth rock in her hand before she teleported back to the other side of the room.

Xander stood wide-eyed at having seen what his sister had just done, causing Titus to speak further. "I take it you had no prior knowledge of what Annetta could do?"

"Not exactly." The boy shook his head. "I mean, I knew something was up, just...nothing like this."

"I see," Titus acknowledged, looking over in the direction of the other three. "It must be strange, then. I suppose growing up on Gaia, very little surprises me anymore."

"Anne said that planet is being occupied by a guy named Razmus and she's going to be going there with you to free Venetor," Xander summarized what his sister had told him. "He's your dad, isn't he?"

"Yeah." Titus nodded as he walked over to one of the remaining targets and began to drag it further back.

"Oh." Xander fell silent as he tried to think of something else to say, not wanting to be quiet for too long.

Titus sensed the boy's unease about the stillness and proceeded to remedy. "I don't know what you have and haven't been told, or what I can tell you, but things are pretty bad on Gaia. Razmus has taken control of the whole planet with his army of Hurtz."

"Yeah, I kind of gathered that much. How do you guys plan on taking it back with just like... the four of you?" Xander questioned.

"Six, with myself and General Atala included, if ye want to speak technically, lad," a thick gruff voice commented, causing Xander to turn around and stare. "Though we'll have an army if it makes much difference."

At the door stood Gladius, observing the ins and outs of what was occurring in the room.

"Gladius," Titus greeted them with a nod. "Is everything alright?"

"Making sure you didn't break the lad's bones is all." The Hurtz smirked. "Saw him nearly go through a wall from that first blast he did."

"I'll make sure it doesn't happen," Titus stated curtly.

"That ya best do," the Hurtz agreed. "Carry on!"

The hulking creature then moved to the other side where Darius, Annetta and Liam were working to check in on them. Xander still stood mesmerized by the sight of the being.

Titus caught him ogling Gladius and commented. "I take it you've never seen a Hurtz, either?"

"Nope, never." Xander shook his head. "First time."

"Seems to be that sort of day for you."

₧ℂ′

After training had concluded with Xander and Liam, Annetta lingered within the arena. Titus and Darius had taken on the task of bringing the boys back to the entrance, leaving her with some down time. Taking a deep breath, Annetta could still smell the charred wood from the targets Xander and Titus had been using, mixed with the metallic scents of the Lab she'd grown used to. Looking over to the side where the benches were, she noticed the rack with training weapons on it. It had been a while since she had gotten a good sparring session in, but there was no one left to spar with. Her hand went under the collar of her shirt as she pulled up a replica of Severbane on a thin black leather cord. With the battle against Mislantus having concluded, her father had told her what needed to be said in order to place the sword into a dormant state so she could have it with her at all times.

"Excieo," the girl commanded and watched as the pendant shifted into the blade with its scabbard and belt attached to it.

Fastening the belt around her waist, Annetta drew the sword, eyeing her reflection in the steel. There on the blade were etched the words 'Severed be he whom forgets', her family motto and words she did her best to always remember. There was something about the weapon she could not truly describe to others. It was a sense of completion, the holding of something which had in the almost two years of possessing it become an extension of her. At times, it felt like the sword was alive in her hands. Puc had dismissed the notion as nothing more than a fanciful flight of her imagination, for there was no magic in the sword. She still liked to think otherwise. Getting into her battle stance as she had been taught, the girl's muscles coiled in her body, her grip tightening on the leather bound hilt. Narrowing her eyes she leapt to strike at an invisible foe.

In her mind swirled images of Mislantus's soldiers, their faces taunting her as they swung weapons her way. Dodging and evading them all, Annetta hacked through the masses, not stopping for a single second. Twirling and pivoting as she used her blade to block incoming attacks, she lost herself in the moment and taking one hand off the blade, she flung the weapons rack across the room with her abilities, the clatter of metal on the floor bringing the girl back to reality. She grinned sheepishly, scratching the back of her neck at the sight.

"I'm thinking it works best with two," Gladius's voice rang from the far side of the room.

Annetta turned around to regard the Hurtz warrior standing by the door just as he had a few hours ago when the others had all been present. He seemed lost without Venetor.

"I'd be lying if I said I didn't like sparring with a partner better," she replied. "Just... no partners left."

Gladius strode forward and removed the massive double-edged sword from its scabbard on his back. The gesture mildly reminded the girl of Brakkus. "I think I can help ya out there, lass."

Flexing her back to remove the tension, Annetta went into her fighter stance. A familiar feeling creeping into her bones as she did so. "Bring it."

A wide grin spreading across his face, revealing a perfect set of razor-like teeth, Gladius attacked the girl without warning, his blade coming down full force.

"Whoa!" Annetta felt her body shake from the impact. "Aren't we going to use training blades?"

"What's the matter?" Gladius asked. "Ye seemed very confident a minute ago. Scared of a little scrape?"

While Annetta had trained using real weapons, Puc had always insisted on them using blunted sparring weapons while in the arena in case anyone got carried away. With the way things were on Gaia, Annetta was half-worried too. "How can I trust you?"

"Ah," Gladius retracted his blade. "Yer worried I might turn on ye? Fear not, lass, I simply want to see how ye handle yourself with yer weapon of choice. As much as people will try to fool ye into thinking a different sword of the same size is the same thing, it ain't. I saw ye swinging Severbane just seconds ago. I don't think ye'd get so into it with a dull blade. As for trusting me, if I do anything remotely suspicious, I think ye can take care of yourself. I don't see what reason ye may have to think otherwise, having trained with me brother and all."

Satisfied with the answer she had received, Annetta inclined her head and shifted back into her stance. In an instant, she was gone, having teleported behind the Hurtz. Whirling around, Gladius's sword collided with Annetta's causing sparks to fly.

"Fighting dirty are we?" he remarked.

"Puc always said not to hold back," she stated, and using her body weight, she bounced back from him.

"Glad to know my brother didn't encourage such things in sparring," Gladius smirked and ran at the girl once more, his sword close to his side as he did so.

Their weapons collided once more, the metallic sound of knife-edges accompanying each hit the two gave one another. Were Annetta not using her psychic abilities to level the playing field where strength mattered, she was certain the Hurtz would have had her within two moves. She remembered Brakkus being strong, but then she remembered he had always held back when the two of them had engaged in combat training. Gladius was not inclined to do so, she felt.

The assault continued wordlessly for some time, the occasional grunt from either party being the only indication of communication between them. Finally, Gladius pulled away, watching the girl with his great amber eye.

"My brother taught ye well," he said through laboured breaths. "Ye know the Hurtz battle style well."

"It was one of the first I ever fought against," Annetta replied, sheathing Severbane as she caught her own breath. "Brakkus taught J.K. and I everything we knew... until he passed away."

There was an uncomfortable silence for a moment. Annetta had not spoken with Gladius about Brakkus since the Hurtz had arrived. In fact, it almost felt wrong to even have mentioned it now. She was not sure how Gladius had taken the news of hearing his brother was dead.

"Aye, but he died a warrior's death and that is what matters." Gladius beamed and put his own weapon away.

Annetta nodded. Her curiosity was then ignited. "I heard you and Brakkus were both gladiators in the arenas on Gaia... what was it like?"

Gladius gazed out into the distance past the girl as he lost himself in thought, attempting to come up with an answer for her, the earrings on his good ear jingling as they twitched. "There's two sides to that story I can tell ya. The first that it's horrible and I'd never wish the life for anyone. The second, however…well, that's different. All Hurtz know what they be getting into when they sign up and many enjoy it. There's not a single other thing that can compare to it. The roar of the crowd screaming yer name as ye finish off yer opponent, the adrenaline of knowing that yer life can be taken from ya at any given moment and the humbling feeling of accepting that yer time in the arena is only marked by blood ya spill because once yers is spilt, ye be nothing to the watchers. Being that close to death, well… yer more alive than most ever be."

"I can see why some would feel that," she replied, causing the Hurtz to nod his head at her comment. "I think though that fighting for a cause seems like a better idea."

"And what is it you fight for, little lass?"

Annetta looked down and patted the hilt of Severbane. "For those who cannot fight for themselves, because when I asked who was protecting the Earth, they told me no one."

The Hurtz glanced in the girl's direction. His elongated snout curled into a smile having heard the answer she gave and chuckled. "Aye, Orbeyus's granddaughter through and through ye be."

Chapter 23

A heavy curtain of rain fell from the heavens as the hooves of Puc, Jason, Sarina and Matthias's horses could be heard pounding into the downtrodden soil. Approaching Aldamoor's gates, slews of tents could still be seen outside the walls. Jason swore the numbers had doubled, despite parts of the Four Forces having been divided to go with Annetta to Gaia. Dismounting in the midst of the pavilions and tethering their mounts to a post, Jason, Sarina and Matthias followed Puc's lead as he entered the main tent they had used previously.

Grateful to be out of the downpour and in the sight of lit torches, they dropped their hoods and were astounded to find the tent bustling with life. Jason sensed that even Puc was a little surprised, but he had no idea why. Their eyes were particularly drawn to five figures which stood in the centre, looking over various maps that lay sprawled out on the table. Four, in particular, seemed to be huddled closest, two men and two women that were all dressed in robes similar to that of Puc, with varying shades of blue.

"Jason Kinsman, Sarina Freiuson and Matthias Teron," Puc addressed them, "Meet the other leaders of the Water Elf cities of Terralim: Archmage Arton of Aridil, Archmage Haldinar of Oldund, Archmage Ralora of Enthrilnin and Archmage Sera of Nyver."

A formal greeting involving bows of the head was exchanged between them all when their eyes fell on the fifth figure in the room. He was a man who appeared to be in his late forties, with a bald head, atop which rested a pair of darkened goggles and large eyes so dark they appeared to be made of ebony with a small ring of gold around the edges. While he was tall, he did not tower over the other elves in the room, but his presence was made up for with his barrel-chested physique, accompanied by a pair of thick arms. He was dressed in a wool shirt, thick leather breeches, massive black boots and a duster jacket on top of it all. His square-jawed face wore a grim expression and was covered in what looked like soot. This was further accentuated by bushy mutton chops that were connected by a thick moustache.

"And this," Puc said, gazing upon the man, "Is Einar Steelstone, ruler of Alfheim, the capital of the Dark Elves."

"Thanestorm." Einar took a bow after he was introduced. "I see the rumours are true of Kaian's demise."

"It is unfortunate, but yes, they are true," the mage replied. "To what do I owe a visit from the famed Steelstone himself?"

Without the further need of questioning, Einar reached into his duster jacket, and with a heavy thud slammed a dagger onto the table. Judging by the design, Jason had a hunch that it belonged to one of the Fire Elves.

"I found this at a burnt down outpost not far from the mines. Fire Elves running rampant at our borders, pillaging," Einar spat, confirming the suspicion. "While I'm no friend to you, Thanestorm, I am also no ally to the Fire Elves. I will not tolerate those fire pixies prancing around my lands like some unruly children without a curfew."

"No offence, but who is this guy, Puc?" Matthias queried, motioning with his hand in Einar's general direction. "And why should we care if the Fire Elves attacked his lands?"

"Matt," Sarina hissed, feeling somewhat embarrassed for her adoptive brother.

"You know it." Matthias turned to her and then back to the others. "I know it, and I can guarantee the rest of these Archmages here know it, too. I'm just stating the obvious."

Jason ran a hand through his hair and sighed. He was starting to get confused with all of these new introductions. The only one who seemed to know what was going on was Puc, who was taking everything with a gallant stride. The youth was seriously beginning to regret his idea of going off alone without Annetta. Despite having Sarina and Matthias with him, he was missing her boisterous attitude in the times of change. He then remembered that this was her doing, to begin with, and his anger at the situation resurfaced.

Puc seemed lost in his own thoughts upon hearing the exchange from those present, analyzing everything that was being said. There was no room for error in any of it, he knew this from the last encounter. To make things worse, he was no longer certain which of the elves he could trust. His eyes fell to Einar as he composed himself.

"How long since the attack on your lands, Steelstone?" he asked. "More importantly, who led them?"

"Two days now," the Dark Elf replied. "They appeared from nowhere, a great smoking mass on the horizon. There were hundreds of them. I've not seen so many since before the days that Gaian, Orbeyus, came to Terallim. They were led by a female. Tamora, she called herself."

"Isn't that how they-" Jason paused as he looked over at Sarina and then Puc. "Isn't that how they disappeared from the battlefield when we fought them? I mean, the timeline matches up too."

"It is," Puc acknowledged the youth. "Fire Elves have never openly attacked Dark Elves, though. Some of your folk even trade with them as you do with us. This has been no secret. How then do I know that you are not conspiring with them?

"I have no love for either of your kind," Einar replied gruffly. "My interest lies only in that of my people and the ore in the mountains, Thanestorm. Why else would I come here?"

Jason listened carefully to what Einar was saying. The second he heard what Puc said about Dark Elves trading with Fire Elves, however, he got a bit wary. How exactly was he supposed to trust someone who just conveniently showed up when they were getting ready to launch an attack? He knew, however, that he had to be open-minded. He didn't know all the facts like Puc seemed to.

"What exactly do you want?" he spoke after considering his words carefully.

Einar turned to the youth. "Why, to do battle, of course! What other reason would I have to bring a thousand fighters and fifty war machines with me?"

Before anything else could be said, Doriden entered the tent, followed by Amayeta and Prince Snapneck.

"We got here as fast as we could," Doriden said as a greeting. "Troops have been fully divided, and the rest are making way for the Eye to All Worlds to set up camp and prepare for the journey to Gaia."

Jason took the distraction of the new arrivals to turn to Sarina and Matthias. "I don't know about the Einar guy."

He was unable to say anything more, feeling a hand grip his shoulder. He glanced over to see it was Puc, who quickly shot him a 'now is not the time' look before turning back to the others.

Archmage Ralora, a female elf in her mid-thirties of slight build with thick black hair that was pinned up to prevent it from getting in her way, moved forward to speak. "Whatever course we choose, we must do so quickly. The Fire Elves will not wait if they have in fact amassed an army the size of which they boast. What is our next move?"

The room fell instantly silent. All chatter ceased, and all eyes fell in the direction of Jason, who felt as though a set of spotlights had just found him on a darkened stage. He then remembered his place in all of this, and putting on a façade of confidence, he cleared his throat.

"If you guys want my honest answer," he said, "I haven't got a clue. I mean, one minute they're in Aldamoor, the next in Alfheim. How are we supposed to know where they will show up next? Like, is there a pattern to these attacks? I guess that's what I'm asking before I can say anything else."

Speech among those present resumed and Jason let out a sigh, feeling the wind knocked out of him from the address. He had no idea how Annetta always did it and made it seem easy.

Matthias observed everything going on in the room, before privately moving closer to Jason. "If I can propose one thing, it's that we find their base of operations. This was Mislantus's way, and a proven one. One of the first things he always did on a campaign of any sort was to establish where the enemy was and hit them there, where it counted most."

"You mean like attack their home city?" Jason asked.

"It was father's way," Sarina confirmed.

"It may prove to be a bit problematic with the Fire Elves," Puc interrupted, having overheard them. "Fire Elves are nomadic. They are plunderers and scavengers."

"But they must have some places they favour when stopping in between raids," Matthias thought out loud.

Puc's pale blue eyes found their way to the maps that were scattered on the great wooden table and studied them absentmindedly, searching for an answer. Wracking his mind and having found what he needed, the First Mage of Aldamoor spoke up. "We will meet them in the ruins of Edran, the grounds they believe to be the birthplace of their kind. There we shall face them in battle."

As soon as Puc had finished speaking, some chattering began, the tone of which was uneasy. Among those concerned about the plan was Archmage Arton, a tall middle-aged Water Elf with messy salt and pepper coloured hair and a neatly kept beard. He spoke his mind shortly after. "What assurance do we have that they will be present in that location?"

"Because the Fire Elves always go to the ruins of Edran to celebrate any victories they have," Sarina stated. "One of the books I read concerning the history of the Fire Elves says that upon the end of each raid they return to Edran to renew their pacts with their gods in the fire river Teil."

"That's a thing?" Jason raised an eyebrow, surprised at Sarina's knowledge.

"You really should read more," the girl told him.

"Seems as good a place as any," Einar mused.

"Is they any way we can get scouts out there beforehand?" Jason inquired. "I mean, it will take us some time before we manage to get all of our troops there to do anything anyway."

"I can take some Sky Wolves with me and have a look," Doriden offered.

"Done," Puc declared. "You will take a score of Soarin with you and investigate. I will have Captain Maria and the crew of Tessa go with you to have some mages create cloud cover in order to avoid suspicion of your activities. Matthias, I would also have you go with them. Contact us if anything is amiss or seems like they are planning a trap."

"Now you're talking sense, mage." The assassin grinned.

"The rest of us, prepare the camp to leave," Puc concluded his orders and everyone began to disperse. "If all goes to plan, we will catch them by surprise and show them they are not the only ones who know how to set things ablaze."

Jason watched as everyone began to leave. Relaxing his stance, he felt the weight of having been in the meeting slide from his shoulders. While Puc had done most of the heavy lifting with command, Jason could still feel the piercing gaze of everyone in the room whenever they fell to him. Mostly, it was the feeling of still being judged for his age, particularly from the other Archmages, whom he had never met before. He understood their concern, and it was not the first time it had happened since he and Annetta had come to know of their heritage. Still, it annoyed him. Snapping out of his thoughts, the boy saw that the only ones left in the room were Puc, Sarina and himself.

"So…" He tried to think of what to say. "Who exactly is this Einar guy and why are we letting him tag along with his thousand soldiers and fifty war machines?"

"He is the leader of the Dark Elves, as I mentioned," Puc said, turning to face him. "I am not sure how much you remember of our history, but Dark Elves primarily keep to themselves. We trade with them, as their ore is some of the purest to be found in the known world, but they, in turn, have traded with Fire Elves in the past, the reason why no alliance has ever existed between either species. Dark Elves have remained neutral in all our dealings, never taking either side, only wishing to make a profit from our wars."

"Let me reiterate my thoughts on all of this, then." Jason cleared his throat. "Why do we trust him?"

"We do not," Puc confirmed.

"What?" Sarina and Jason both exclaimed.

"We do not trust him," Puc repeated with a straight face. "We need his war machines and the thousand soldiers he has to offer. Do not think me ignorant of the things which have already transpired."

"If you say so." Jason shrugged his shoulders. "How exactly do we plan to keep tabs on him?"

"The same way one would in any finely tuned game," the mage said. "Observation."

ഇന്ദ

Later on that evening, Sarina and Jason returned to the tent they had been assigned with Matthias. The assassin had long since gone to prepare for his journey onboard the Tessa with the rest of her crew, leaving them alone. The light of the torches and candles in the room were the only things providing any light for them as Jason lay stretched out on one cot and Sarina sat cross-legged on hers, with an oversized book in her lap that she flipped through periodically.

Staring up at the tent ceiling and trying to make sense of any patterns he could see in the stitching on the fabric, Jason found himself growing more anxious by the second. The stillness in the room was unnerving him. He looked over at Sarina, who seemed not the least bit fazed by any of the events around her. He could only wish for such ease of mind in the midst of everything that was going on. It was a trait he was growing more and more to admire about her.

"What you reading?" he asked, breaking the silence.

"The history of the Fire Elves and the Water Elves," she replied, placing a bookmark in the page she was on and closing the tome shut. "I figured the more we know, the more we can be of help."

"More like you will," he huffed, settling back on the cot and put his hands behind his head. "I'm starting to ask myself what I'm doing here."

"Representing and helping to lead the Four Forces," Sarina reminded him as she got up and walked over to sit beside him on his cot. "Last I checked, anyway."

"Load of good I did today," Jason grumbled, suppressing a yawn with his right hand. "Seems like you could do that job for me just fine."

"I got lucky," Sarina reminded him. "Reading is just what I do, you know that."

"I know, but still, it feels like I haven't done a single thing since I got here but follow Puc around and listen to everyone at that stupid meeting," he griped.

"J.K., how else are future leaders to be born?" she inquired. "My father, whenever he had some important battle council to attend to, would have me follow him around exactly like that and it was worse because I was treated as a mere shadow in the room. Ordering troops and participating in war councils, it's something that isn't learned over night. It takes years to learn. Be thankful you have someone like Puc and the others to learn from."

Jason exhaled roughly, taking in what Sarina had said to him. He was grateful that he had not been left alone in any decision making, that they had been made for him in this case. While he was comfortable making choices for himself on the battlefield, commanding others was still new to him. Sitting up on the cot, he glanced over at Sarina, who smiled upon seeing him face her.

"Yeah, I guess you're right," he said, "Still doesn't change the way I feel though."

"Didn't say it would." She smirked and then tossed the book into his lap. "And if you're so worried about not knowing enough then use your mind and do something."

"Yes, Lady Puc." The boy rolled his eyes, causing the girl to chuckle.

✂✃

The orange glow of a thousand torches played off of the stone walls of the fortress as Amarok stalked through its halls. Razmus had long since gone into a dreamless slumber, passed out in his chambers over the stacks of parchments that adorned every corner of his living quarters. It was not something the assassin was not used to seeing. Mislantus had been the same in his pursuits of the Eye to All Worlds and Orbeyus's heir. He remembered the ruler of Valdhar as he would stare across into space and down at the blue planet once it came into sight, the hunger in his eyes ever prevalent. It was an affliction that enslaved all men of power, it seemed. However, it would not touch the silver-masked assassin and he made sure of that.

His meditations on such matters were interrupted when he turned the corner and was confronted by a young Gaian of medium build with short straight sandy hair and a defined jawline, dressed in a dark red leather jerkin drawn over the rest of his black apparel. He was a member of one of the few noble Gaian houses which had bent the knee to Razmus when he had taken power.

"My lord Mezorian." The new arrival inclined his head in proper Gaian greeting to him.

"Quintus of house... Brant." Amarok made a quick save as he tried to remember the youth's full name. "To what do I owe the meeting at this late hour?"

Quintus reached into his breast pocket and produced a crumpled piece of parchment, which he unfolded as hastily as he could before handing it over to Amarok. With an eager vigour to his visage, he then spoke. "I procured the materials you wanted from the builders of the tower, and have had them transported to the exact location you spoke of."

"Good, and you were discreet in your actions?" the assassin queried as he continued to walk.

"Yes, lord Mezorian," Quintus acknowledged as he followed. "Although I should ask, why all the secrecy in this preparation and aren't many of these materials not meant for structural building but for flight?"

"Ah," Amarok paused, pivoted on his heel and found himself standing directly before Quintus, who had almost run into him. "If I told you, it would not be a surprise for Lord Razmus, would it?"

"No, I suppose not," the youth agreed, taking a step back to regain his personal space.

Amarok realized the discomfort coming from the youth and withdrew himself a step back also, taking in the lad. He had chosen him for the errand due to his connections, but also for his lack of queries about the things he was told to do. His opinion on the young Gaian was starting to change and with the task complete, he was now dispensable in Amarok's eyes. Still, it would be a shame to waste such a being when he could still serve a purpose, if not now than in the near future and so the assassin held back. Instead, he placed a heavy armour-clad arm on his shoulder as a form of reassurance.

"Worry yourself not with trivial malcontent," he said. "I plan on throwing a grand spectacle for the completion of the tower when the day comes, one which will be spoken of for ages. Your name will not be forgotten when I mention with whose help the feat was accomplished. Now, go back to your mother, Quintus, for she must be worried sick about you for being gone after curfew. You don't want her to lose you as she did your father, do you?"

Quintus stood rooted to his spot with a look of terror in his eyes for a few seconds as he observed the assassin's one good eye before giving an exaggerated shake of his head. Amarok smiled beneath the mask. "Good...good...now, off with you."

He watched as Quintus went down the corridor from where he had emerged, fading into the darkness and finally vanished. Once he was certain that the boy was gone, Amarok resumed his original path.

"Youth," he spoke softly under his breath as he stopped walking. "It does not matter the race, the species, the time nor the age, they all can be bent to one's will if you are eager enough to find the tactic for them."

He stood in the hall for some time, the amber light licking at his silhouette as he listened to the distant sound of feet thudding on stone. Soon after, he disappeared.

Chapter 24

Engulfed in brilliant white light and accompanied by the feeling of weightlessness, Annetta allowed for her eyes to adjust to her surroundings. As soon as the buzzing in her ears dissipated, it was replaced with the chirping of birds. Blinking a few times as she got her bearings, the girl found herself standing in a garden as she always did in her meditations. The scent of earth and vegetation filled her nose as her sneakers padded along the soft grassy floor.

By this point, Annetta knew Orbeyus would be waiting for her. She was stumped, however, to find someone else waiting with him.

"Brakkus?" the name escaped her lips, which formed into a smile as soon as she spoke.

While before her, Orbeyus sat upon a fallen log as he had in their previous encounter, beside him stood the formidable Hurtz warrior just as Annetta remembered him, right down to his armour and sword. His long rabbit-like ears twitched, causing the slew of silver earrings in them to jingle.

"Aye, lass." He grinned, exposing a full set of gleaming white teeth. "That be ma name, and don't ya wear it out."

Overjoyed, Annetta threw her arms around him, embracing Brakkus in a firm hug. Remembering herself, she backed away, feeling slightly awkward for doing so around her grandfather. Orbeyus simply responded with a chuckle.

"It's so good to see you," she said and then quickly added, "Both of you."

"You've been busy of late," Orbeyus stated. "I haven't seen you around much."

"Yeah," Annetta sighed. "It's complicated."

"Well, ye might as well tell us," Brakkus prattled. "Not like we're going anywhere."

"Where do I even begin?" the girl wondered. "Fire Elves attacked Aldamoor in a raid and Venetor was taken prisoner by Amarok who is working for some guy named Razmus that has taken over Gaia. Puc is now First Mage, and he's gone with Jason and part of the Four Forces after the Fire Elves and I'm preparing with the rest to go to Gaia..."

Orbeyus observed the girl as she continued to rant, throwing in bits and pieces of information. Brakkus also stood unmoving from the spot as he listened to her, his ears twitching from time to time as he took it all in.

Annetta exhaled deeply once she had finished. "The worst part in all of this is I have no idea whatsoever if I am doing the right thing. Should I have gone with Puc and Jason and taken all of the Four Forces together against the Fire Elves or split us up like I did?"

"The mage can handle himself," Brakkus commented. "If he'd have any reason to think it would be a bad idea to split ye all up, he would have said so. He ain't known for hiding such things."

"Sometimes splitting up an army is the only thing that can be done," Orbeyus added, "And you need to do what feels right. Risks are a part of fighting any battle. Both Gaia and the Elves need aid."

"And Gaia was there in the Great War, so doesn't that make them part of the Four Forces in a way?" Annetta tried to reason. "I mean, I know they aren't officially or it would be called the Five Forces, but Venetor did come to help, didn't he?"

"Aye, he did." Brakkus shook his head and then looked over at Orbeyus as if expecting the man to say something more.

The Severio lord reciprocated his gaze to the Hurtz before turning to his granddaughter once more. "He did, though our parting at the end was not one of mirth, Annetta. It is however not a story that is mine to tell and it would be best if you ask your aunt Skyris about it. This being said, the actions of one Gaian cannot be held over an entire nation. There are innocent people on Gaia that had nothing to do with any of it, who are simply trying to get by day after day."

The girl nodded, somewhat confused by what Orbeyus had said about Skyris. She would need to approach her when she had a chance. She feared, however, that would not be anytime soon. Huffing, she allowed her shoulders to drop. "I guess that gives me my answer."

"No one can give you the answer, Annetta," Orbeyus interjected again. "Only you can decide the course of your fate and the person you are to become because of the actions you take."

"Right," she muttered, looking down at her shoes, then back up at the two of them. "I'd better get going, or they'll start to wonder where I've gone, too."

"That ya best do, lassie," Brakkus told her, "Make sure them horses are taken care of, too."

"I will, and see ya." The girl waved and took off in the other direction from where she had come.

"Take care, Anne," Orbeyus said quietly and watched as she disappeared.

Some time passed after Annetta had vanished when the Lord of the Axe spoke again, remembering another part of the prophecy he had once read:

'And though threat will be slain
Time will only slow the shadows bane.

There will come a day when a world split in two,
Will cry out for the white lion to rise anew,
In a land where brothers did once fight,
Basking in the unfinished tower's might,

Upon the darkest day,
When evil will no more keep at bay,
Destiny will no longer wait.
A leader of worlds will reveal true fate.'

Brakkus turned to regard the elder Gaian. "I don't think ya should have kept it from her. She has a right to know of it."

"Perhaps," Orbeyus replied. "But she also has a right to decide on her own."

ഇൻ

The trotting of hoofs overpowered all sound as Annetta brought Firedancer to a halt at the stables. Dismounting, she took the reins and led the horse to its stall where she would groom and take off its saddle. Taking in the wooden architecture, the girl sometimes found it hard to believe they were underwater, and not on a farm somewhere out in the country. Venturing further in, she was met with a strange sight.

"Uh...don't you have magic to do that sort of thing?" Annetta raised an eyebrow upon seeing Darius, dressed in an old t-shirt and jeans mucking out one of the stalls.

Hearing her comment, the young mage paused and turned around. "Magic isn't exactly the deus ex machina for all of life's problems."

"Really? Puc made it seem so," she replied, bringing Firedancer around to his stall and began the unsaddling process.

"Well, I'm not Puc," Darius reminded her bluntly and continued on with his task.

"Which you have tried to prove at every turn," the girl said.

"Yeah, I guess so," he muttered quietly.

The two of them carried on working side by side for a little while before Annetta spoke up yet again. "Hey, Darius, can I ask you something?"

"That usually implies you're going to ask anyway, so shoot," the mage remarked as he finished with his task, setting the shovel back to where it usually lay, walking over to the stall Annetta was working in and leaning against one of the walls.

"Your werepanther transformation," she began. "Was that something you learned at the Academy or something you just always knew?"

"It's something I just learned naturally," he answered. "I'm not part Gaian or anything, if that is what you're trying to ask. There are many species that can shapeshift into animals. It's more common than you think."

The girl frowned. Having completed unsaddling Firedancer, she reached for his brush. "That wasn't what I wanted to ask. I was going to ask how you knew what the animal you change into was."

"This about your feral form?" he queried.

Annetta nodded, her eyes going to her feet for a split second before she continued what she was doing. Upon deeming Firedancer clean, she finished and lowered her arm before she began talking again. "I still seem to be shifting between forms and I don't know why. I keep meditating and there's no change."

"If I can honestly state my piece," Darius said, "I think you're afraid to decide and deep down you already know what it is you want to be. You're just torn."

"Torn?" Annetta scoffed. "How am I torn?"

"I can't answer that," he said, "But I can say this, and it's something that was said to me many years ago by someone you may know: Sometimes it's not a matter of deciding but becoming what we are needed to be. As to how I knew about my form, it was gut instinct.

I didn't have much say in the matter. One day I just turned and that was that."

Taking some time to mull the words over in her head, Annetta wasn't sure what else to say. Before either of them could converse further, Dexter floated into the room casually, his single bright red eye observing the two youth. Annetta felt a chill go down her spine seeing the A.I., her mind wandering to science fiction plots where robots went rogue on people.

"I have been requested by Skyris to come fetch both of you," it said in its calm voice, turning its floating body back towards the exit. "Please follow me."

"What if we don't?" Annetta looked at it challengingly.

The A.I. casually turned around again, his hovering form coming uncomfortably close to Annetta, the single glowing crimson eye inspecting every aspect of her face. It did so for quite some time, making the girl want to take a step back and away into her comfort zone. In fact, Annetta felt her hands begin to curl defensively, ready to attack the thing if it displayed any hints of hostility.

Dexter, however, showed no further interest and floating back a little, said, "I cannot let you do that, Annetta."

Hearing the faintly familiar words, the girl froze, as did the mage.

Confused at the reactions but showing no change of his own, Dexter continued. "I do not understand the sudden jump of adrenaline in your systems. I simply meant that Skyris would not be pleased if you did not come. It concerns the state of the ships which are available to use for the mission to Gaia. Please follow me."

A wave of relief passing through both Annetta and Darius, the two complied and followed.

"How will I know when I'm ready to change?" Annetta asked, still focused on the previous conversation as she looked over at the young mage.

"You just will." Darius cracked a mischievous grin and disappeared behind the door.

80CR

Her eyes squinting as she stared at the translucent screen wall, Skyris attempted to decipher the engine blueprint that was being displayed to her three dimensionally beside the large metal war barge that she was currently working on in one of the hangar decks. Spread out on the floor all around her were parts and tools of every assortment and size imaginable. To her left, coming from a small squat black box, was a life-sized projection of the engine, while a screen to her right contained the blueprint. Pushing her loosely-tied hair back, Skyris rested her grimy hands on her temples and applied pressure, attempting to rid herself of the concentration headache that was beginning to set in.

The Gaian's efforts were thwarted when the chatter of Darius and Annetta began to echo in the background, causing Skyris to drop her hand from her face. Veering around, she regarded the duo as they were escorted in by Dexter.

"Hey, aunt Skyris," Annetta greeted her. "Dexter said you wanted to see us."

Before Skyris could answer, Atala, Titus and Gladius all appeared as well.

"Ya called?" Gladius questioned.

Skyris exhaled roughly, running a hand down the back of her neck as she attempted to find the right words to explain what she had to say. She hated being put on the spot like this, but there was no other way to go about it.

"We won't have enough ships for the troops," she confirmed. "I've been taking apart and putting together parts from different vessels to get the ones that could work in useable form, but the truth is that there is no way we'll have enough to get everyone onboard at once, and if the first trip to Gaia doesn't get detected by Federation scout ships, we certainly would on a consecutive run."

Everyone fell silent in the room. Annetta crossed her arms as she buried herself in thought. She had forgotten about what Venetor had told her about the Greys. She then remembered and thought out loud. "What about Link?"

"A single ship of that size could get through without any problems," Atala stated, "But Skyris is right, an entire fleet will set off an alarm."

"Then I guess our answer is quite obvious," Darius interrupted. "We'll need to create a portal."

"Wait, what?" Annetta turned to him.

"I was not going to suggest that," Skyris said squeamishly. "Although it's a means to an end, portal creation requires a lot of spell work. Worse, it can lead to unwanted attention from elsewhere, if you get my meaning."

"It's a means to an end as you said," Darius replied. "Also, last I checked, the entire planet is in danger. I think those unwanted attention parties can turn a blind eye. They have to other things."

Annetta looked around, not fully understanding who Darius was now referring to with Skyris. The older Gaian did not miss a beat, however, seeing Annetta's confused expression and explained. "Portal creation is highly regulated by the Intergalactic Federation since most portals are unstable if not created properly."

Skyris then turned her attention back to Darius. "Which is why I must ask, how would you even go about casting a portal in the first place that would fit the entire army through it without collapsing on itself?"

Darius muttered something under his breath and a small blue and white rectangle materialized in his left hand, which he then held out to Skyris. "Before the Pessumire was destroyed, the plans for the cannon were taken and stored on that key drive. No magic necessary."

Skyris accepted the drive with an almost childlike greed and plugged it into the box which was giving off the three-dimensional projection of the engine. Blueprints of Valdhar, followed by close ups of the cannon itself, along with hundreds of notes flashed before the eyes of those gathered. No one aside from Skyris was able to catch much of what was being shown, however, causing the Gaian's eyes to light up.

"Oh," she managed to say, covering her mouth with her hand as she did so, "Aren't you a beautiful little beast."

"Well, this could certainly change things," Titus mused, looking at the intricate blueprints. "Think you can build something like this, aunt Skyris?"

Engrossed by the possibility of this new project, Skyris completely forgot there were other people in the room. Her mind was already racing, assembling and creating a list of what had to be done. She had not seen anything as complex and elegant in a long time. Realizing again where and with whom she was, she turned around to face them.

"It may take a week," she estimated. "Perhaps a bit longer, depending on how quickly Dexter and I can fabricate the parts."

"A week? That's it? That cannon took them years to build." Darius's eyes widened upon hearing the proclamation.

"Yep, and none of them were top graduates from Pangaia's Engineering University with a PhD in Spacetime and Portal Travel Dynamics," the Gaian bragged.

"A week, then." Annetta nodded. "No pressure there, aunt Skyris, I'll go make sure the leaders of the Four Forces are notified."

As those gathered began to split up to go their separate ways, Skyris found herself taking a long glance at Darius. She admired his quick thinking. It was a shame he did not possess any of the knowledge she did for she could certainly use another hand with this project. Setting this thought aside and the other static within her head, she grabbed the discarded jug of orange juice, opened it and took a swig, feeling the citric bite hit her mouth. Her eyes then focused back to the blueprints and she prepared herself mentally to work.

"One week," she muttered as she pursed her lips. "No pressure there at all, Skyris. No pressure at all."

ಶಂಡಾ

The jump through the Speedway, as it was called, was the most difficult part of the journey to get to Gaia from Earth. While Link knew about the portal-based form of space travel, he had never attempted it himself. In order to reach many habitable planets, faster than light travel was required, however, it was not possible on the given plain of existence. This was why the engines within most modern space ships from what Link knew were able to 'ghost' into another dimension temporarily through the use of a specific type of generator. This method, however, used a tremendous amount of fuel and was good only for shorter distances. Ever since the Intergalactic Federation had perfected opening a portal leading to the dimension without the risk of causing the universe they found themselves in from imploding, it had been harvested, holes having been poked all throughout space, creating a highway system with exit points to various solar systems. This allowed for ghosting to only be used for short spurts and the ships to then naturally use the portal to slide through wherever they needed to. The portals were also conveniently unapproachable by less-advanced civilizations since they came in the form of black holes, which ships with a lack of proper technology had no hope of passing through, keeping them at bay. This was all he remembered from his lessons.

Coming out of the exit the coordinates on his ship had been calculated to, Link watched as the blinding light of the Speedway disappeared, replaced with the dazzling of a thousand distant stars on a pitch black horizon. Once out, he pressed a few buttons to enter coordinates closer to the planet and flicking a switch he shifted into ghost mode. The windows around him turned foggy as everything seemed to whiz by and then came to a standstill. Taking a moment to scan the screens and make sure everything was in working order, he then paused as he looked through the front windows. There, a tiny speck in the distance, he could make out the small green glowing gem, Gaia. Switching gears again, he checked for any signs of nearby ships, but found nothing. He wondered if this had anything to do with the Intergalactic Federation's lack of involvement in the conflict on his home planet. Perhaps the Greys had ordered all foreign ships to keep away from Gaia. It was not the first time exterior powers had done so to his home planet and yet Gaia had endured, having come back stronger and more resilient than before with each blow. Theirs was, after all, a warrior race.

Stalling no longer, Link put the ship into full speed and towards his destination. The vessel soon found itself orbiting the medium-sized emerald planet, its immense concentrations of vegetation and bodies of water visible from on high. The Gaian youth double checked his maps and bearings, until he set the ship to make its descent, the roaring sounds of the engine being picked up the second he touched the atmosphere.

Before he knew it, it was over and the craft had landed in the midst of a grassy meadow, despite having endured some turbulence. Turning everything off as he had been taught, he collected his things and opened the door. Descending the steps and setting foot on the ground among the waist-high stalks of deep green grass, Link allowed them to run past his fingers, feeling each blade brush along them, welcoming him home. His lungs inhaled the scents around him and for a moment he felt himself choke, not for lack of air but for holding back a sob in thinking he would never see Gaia again.

While he had frequented the forest biosphere in Q-16, it would never compare to his homeworld, and he had chosen the area he had landed in for a reason. Looking out in the distance, he took in the surrounding land until he had oriented himself, then headed straight. Undergrowth crunching beneath his shoes, he soon came upon a desolated and weathered cabin, the wood of the structure overgrown with moss and heavily decomposing. It did not matter to Link.

Reaching for the door handle and turning it, he watched as the rotting wood broke apart beneath his grip. Once the dust had settled, he stood wordlessly, before dropping the metallic object and proceeding inside.

"Well, that wasn't awkward," Link spoke quietly as he brushed his hands off on his pants, then strode inside.

The interior was not the largest, nor was it the smallest. It consisted of just the right amount of living space to have accommodated a family of three. The main room, now littered with sprouting vegetation from among the floor cracks, had contained a large hearth surrounded by furniture. Towards the end, a kitchen could be seen, the remnants of rusted pans dangling from a fixture attached to a ceiling. Link remembered the way they'd ring when meals had been prepared and the sound of logs crackling over a fire. Memories flooded back to him in waves. His father had been a woods guide, never having enjoyed life in the capital due to his obvious lineage. The two of them had kept mostly to themselves, Link's mother having died when he was just a child. Walking past his and his father's old rooms, he came full circle, selected a moss-covered armchair and flopped down in it, taking in the scent around him. He closed his eyes, focusing on the pristine silence.

He sat this way for some time, allowing for his mind to wander back into the past until the distinct sound of breaking branches could be heard outside. Eyes snapping open, Link focused his hearing on what was going on. His heightened senses immediately picked up the low rumbling voices of at least three Hurtz, two female and one male. Cursing himself for having been careless in his nostalgia, the youth rose from the seat and contemplated his next move. His sword hand reaching over for his blade, he realized shortly after that it would be no match for three fully grown Hurtz, but he knew what might. Taking off his sword belt, Link began to quietly strip off his armour and began placing it in the bag he'd taken with him for his gear.

The voices outside were now clearer, louder than before. The Gaian youth focused his energy, having been left in nothing more than a pair of pants. He raised his head and gave out an inhuman howl.

ෂාঞ

Outside, under the forest shade, the three Hurtz scouts froze in their tracks upon hearing the noise. Whatever wildlife there had been in the area had fled, leaving them as the only living creatures. They could see the remnants of the cabin before them now, the door torn open. Rotus, the male with loosely feline features and a crimson mane, turned back to his two female companions, Bertha and Mica, in question. Neither having a response for him, he turned back around and exposed his teeth, gripping the spear he carried with him tighter in both hands as he marched forward.

Everything then became a blur as a monstrous beast with the antlers of a stag and the body of a giant wolf crashed through the foliage. Rotus barely had time to brace himself when he was thrown into the air. Letting out a war cry, the Hurtz threw his spear at it, burying the shaft deep in the thing's shoulder. Rotus's efforts were in vain, however, when soon after the claws of his opponent slashed open his jugular, ending his life.

Mica and Bertha proved no worse in the assault, each female Hurtz drawing a cleaver-like blade from their belt and charging blindly towards Link. Pulling the spear free from his shoulder, the Gaian youth did his best to use the weapon to block the oncoming onslaught of fiercely pumping arms, throwing hit after hit on it. Gritting his teeth, focusing on the battle and ignoring the pain that now burned through his arm, Link waited for an opening. His efforts were rewarded when Bertha's blade lodged itself into the shaft of his weapon. Pulling the spear away as quickly as he could, he rammed the barbed end into the gut of an unsuspecting Mica, which then fell to the floor.

A meaty arm then wrapped itself around Link's neck, causing his legs to buckle slightly beneath him as he fought for control of oxygen flow. The struggle was short lived when a small projectile zipped past his head and struck the Hurtz, causing her to slide off and go limp. Looking up, Link saw not a living soul in sight. He didn't like it.

The muscles in his back bunching up, he prepared to flee when the soft treading of paws could be made out on the ground close by. Out of the overgrowth of bushes shot a haze of black and tan. Curling back defensively, Link allowed his eyes to adjust to his opponent. Before him stood a creature he was all too familiar with. Canine in shape, covered in shaggy black fur that melted into a mix of tan and white on its belly and arms, the beast stood at well over eight feet tall. Its huge ears were flopped over, unable to carry their weight like that of a German Shepherd pup, and from its elongated snout protruded two large fangs which hung down a little past the thing's lower jaw. Its massive paws with sword-like claws were alert, and the short bobbed tail swished back and forth in an aggressive manner while the creature's great amber eyes were locked upon him, tan markings where its eyebrows should have been further accentuating the anger on its face. Link had seen sabre-toothed dogs used by officers in the capital, but he had never actually seen one in the wild.

His defenses having been down for a split second, he then realized he was being watched from all directions. Whipping his head from side to side, Link took note of the two dozen men and women, which were concealed in various parts of the forest with a whole assortment of bows, spears, slingshots and anything else that could be used for ranged combat. Analyzing his situation, he could see no way around them. Worst yet, he had forgotten about his wound, which was still bleeding.

"I could really use Anne here now," he muttered to himself.

"Lincerious?" a voice asked.

Something in his memory triggered, Link's ears flattened against his skull. Turning around to face the sabre-toothed dog, he was greeted with another surprise. There, upon the beast sat a Gaian in her mid-twenties, tough of disposition, with a thick platinum braid which went past her chest. She was dressed in camouflage leather armour and wielded what looked like a spear, the head of which was a short sword tied crudely to the shaft. From beyond her gritty paint-covered face, a pair of emerald eyes glared back at him in question.

Relaxing, the transformed Gaian youth stood upon his hind legs, looking back at his captor. "It's good to see you too, Layla."

Chapter 25

Another day having ended, Venetor waited until the Hurtz overseers had finished their rounds for the night, leaving only the guards outside of the camp. Using the two moons in the sky as his guide to tell the time, he set out to the same spot he had designated at the first meeting. It was an area outside the main location with tents, close to the latrines where the Hurtz guards were less likely to come looking for anyone due to their sensitive sense of smell. It was an observation the Gaian prince had made when witnessing a few of the guards arguing with overseers about who would go to make sure no one was loitering there on a few previous occasions.

Walking clear past the last set of tents, Venetor took note of the few silhouettes he already saw standing there waiting, one of them belonging to Marianus, another to Janus. Coming closer to them, he could make out more silhouettes in the background, their outlines dimly illuminated by moonlight. Taking a central position among them, he had a good look around, counting the ranks of those assembled.

"What spoils have we today?" he asked in a hushed tone so as to not alert the guards.

No one so much as even flinched upon hearing the words initially, until Janus stepped forward and produced the broken edge of a pickaxe from under his shirt. He then handed it to Venetor.

"I had to lie and said it was lost in the mines," he explained. "I was taken off the evening rations for carelessness."

Venetor glanced down at the sharpened metal object in his hand while tapping the flat side of it against his palm, his face drawn in deep contemplation.

"You've done well, Janus," Venetor replied. "Your sacrifice will not be in vain. I promise you. Now, if we find a piece of wood, this can be fashioned into a spear."

Hearing what was said encouraged more to come forward, each individual dropping various parts of tools or sharpened stones at Venetor's feet. By the end, there was a heaping pile of rocks, metal and wood. Inspecting some of the pieces at the top, the Gaian prince nodded in satisfaction.

"Good," he smiled, "We will bury these with the others we have collected the last few days. Tomorrow we will meet to begin combining these into weapons worthy of an uprising."

"And how will we know when the time is right to strike, m'lord?" Marianus questioned him.

"The same way one prepares for any good skirmish," Venetor replied. "Observation and provocation of various scenarios, just like how we figured out the guards would be the least likely to come here. It's not a glamorous rendezvous spot, but it does the trick. Next, we must figure out when the changing of the guards occurs during the night. We may then have a chance of sneaking out of here to get to the tower and free some of the soldiers, so they can join us in the fight. The bigger our numbers, the better. Most of the soldiers have had feral form training of some kind. It will level our playing ground against the Hurtz. Now, I suggest you all get some sleep if you can once these are buried beside the latrines. Tomorrow, be here at the same time."

Venetor made out the bobbing of silhouetted heads as those gathered set to work, burying their collected spoils. Joining them, he began digging a hole with one of the broken shovels someone had acquired.

"Perhaps the tales were right," Marianus spoke, bringing up an armload of scraps.

"What tales are these, professor?" Venetor queried, depositing a shovel of dirt while keeping vigilant for any signs of guards.

"The stories they told us as children of course," The Gaian mused, "The legend of the white lion that would swoop into Gaia to save her when all hope was lost."

"A wives' tale," Venetor scoffed. "I'm no white lion. I'm just a Gaian doing his duty to his people."

"Perhaps," Marianus replied as he dropped what he carried into the shallow opening in the earth. "Then again, who are we as mortals to decide if we be legends or not? Razmus erred, for his declaration is false. He is not the white lion of prophecy. Such a decision is not ours to make. That is a gift the Unknown did not bestow upon us."

"No, but he gave us free will," Venetor rebutted. "And as you said, it is not our place to decide such things. What I can decide is how the fate of my people will play out. I will not stand by idly and watch us all die. That is not our way, never has been. If the Gaia we once knew is to end, then it ends in battle."

Retrieving a second pile to place into the hole, Marianus continued to observe Venetor as he worked on covering up their hiding spot. He knew no matter how much the Gaian prince disputed and rejected the idea of being the white lion of myth, there were many who had already made the decision for him when he had rallied them to rebel.

∞CR

Slush spattered from the sky early the next morning as Annetta made her way to her usual stop to catch the bus. It seemed odd, not having Link, Jason or Sarina there with her. It had been a strange few days, without her friends and to be surrounded by people who could care less about her existence. It was as though someone had taken away her shield in battle and she was exposed to the elements, in this case, teenage scorn. Not that she would ever show that this fazed her. Still, she could not help feeling the hollowness inside of her as she continued to trudge through the actions of each day until she went back down to Q-16. Even there, the isolation was still present.

"Hey! Wait up!" a familiar voice rang from behind her as the bus pulled up.

Annetta turned around to see Darius bolting towards her to catch up, a backpack slung over his shoulders, swaying as he ran. He wore a black winter jacket and blue jeans, which were tucked into high combat boots, no longer in the dress of a mage which she was used to seeing him in now. The girl raised an eyebrow, confused.

"Hey," she managed to say as she flashed her bus pass and stepped into the vehicle. "What are you doing here?"

"What's it look like?" he said through laboured breath. "Heading to school with you. Someone has to keep an eye on you with J.K., Sarina and Link out of commission. Why not me?"

"You don't have to." She frowned, finding a pole to grab onto as the bus doors closed and it began to move again, "Besides, what's your cover story this time?"

"Transferred back, that's all," he explained. "Other school I was in simply wasn't cutting it."

Annetta smirked, hearing his answer, and looked out the window at the mounds of slushy snow at the sides of the road. "Remind me why I have to keep going to school again?"

"So you can get good grades and then go to university," Darius snickered, then spoke in a more serious tone. "You remember what Puc said, about being able to get better intel by leading normal lives here on Earth?"

"Yeah, but still," the girl grumbled. "J.K. and Sarina are missing so much school now it's not even going to be funny, and we have finals

293

coming up soon. Also apparently we have to apply for college and university soon, and they're not here for that."

"I'm sure Puc and or Skyris will be able to come up with some way of getting them where they want to be," Darius reassured her.

"So much for leading normal lives," Annetta mused.

"As normal as can be given our situation," Darius corrected his previous statement.

Annetta rolled her eyes as she continued to gaze outside at the lazy grey cloud-covered sky and skeletal leafless trees that adorned the public side of the streets, behind which were slews of different buildings varying from townhouses to plazas with little shops. Coming to their stop, the two of them, along with other students that took the same route got out and began spreading out to get to their respective homeroom classes.

"I'm gonna go get my papers in order with the head office. I'll see you in later," Darius said, and took off without another word.

Alone and left again to her own devices, Annetta made her way inside and down the corridors towards her locker. Not having anyone to speak with, she had time to put everything away instead of rushing to get to class with a bag that was almost bursting at the seams from the number of books and binders she had to carry. Entering in her combination and hearing the ceremonial click, she opened the lock and began the process of storing all of the things she would not need until after lunch, including her jacket. Chances were if it did not stop raining then she was better off in the cafeteria than outside and even if it did stop raining, she would have time to retrieve it.

"I said quit it!" a prepubescent male voice shouted further down the hallway from her.

Alert and intrigued by the commotion, Annetta continued to listen as she organized her bag, unsure of what to make of the sudden outburst from the student.

"Stop being such a crybaby and let me see it," a slightly deeper voice demanded.

Shutting the door of her locker and putting her bag back on, Annetta looked out of the corner of her eye to see a somewhat heavier boy with messy black hair reaching out for a piece of paper that a taller boy dressed in a red and black striped sweater was dangling above him. Surrounding them were two other boys and a girl. Looking around to see no one else in sight, Annetta cursed under her breath. She wasn't about to walk away without trying to intervene. She couldn't. Turning in the direction of the group, she began to walk over. One plus side of her burlier and more athletic appearance compared to before was that it had its advantage in intimidating younger students.

"Give him the paper," she commanded once she was within hearing distance.

"Huh? What do you want?" the boy in the striped sweater grunted.

"Give him the paper, or I can have you in the V.P.'s office so fast you won't have time to even blink," Annetta threatened in a polite tone, folding her hands behind her back as she glared at the group. "So, what's it going to be?"

The boy turned back to the others in his group, who either shrugged their shoulders or muttered something half audible under their breath. Curling up his fists and turning towards her, the bully had little time to think of anything to reply when the indoor bell rang, signalling for everyone to get to class. Seeing the halls around them begin to flood with students, he dropped the paper and turned on his heel, followed by the rest of his group.

Bending down, Annetta picked up the paper and unfolded it to reveal an intricate pencil drawing of a samurai facing off against a fire-breathing dragon. Had she not known better, she would have thought it had been printed off the computer and drawn by a professional artist.

"That's very good," she said, giving it back to the shorter boy. "You drew that?"

"Yeah, it's sort of a hobby of mine," he replied shyly. "You're that Severio girl that used to get into fights with Lee aren't you?"

"Is that my rep?" Annetta chuckled. "Yeah, that's me. What's your name?"

"I'm Greg Carter." The boy extended a hand and shook Annetta's briskly. "Thanks for getting my drawing back, but I have to get to art class. I'm sure I'll see you later, though."

"Yeah man, take it easy," the girl nodded in reply and watched as he faded into the sea of students.

Seeing him vanish fully, Annetta turned on her heel and began to make her way to her own class. Walking past the guidance office, she paused briefly as her eyes wandered to the corkboard where she noticed a new poster had been placed. Most of the time they were black and white print outs with announcements, sometimes fitted on neon paper of varied colour to draw the eye, not that they ever did for her. This one, however, had fully coloured photographs on them of young men and women in uniforms.

"Hey Anne, there you are!" Darius shouted as he fought his way over to see her distracted by the pinup. "What's up? Thinking of becoming a cop?"

Pulling down a copy of the poster, Annetta looked at it more closely, "You know, that might not be such a dumb idea. I mean... I would be helping people and have access to anything happening in the city."

"Don't tell me you are actually considering this," Darius exclaimed. "You as a lady in blue?"

Feeling herself go red in the face, Annetta bit her lower lip and rolling up the poster, smacked Darius on the back of the head with it lightly. "Can it! Let's get to class before I get another earful of lectures for being late."

"Ten four! Roger, that constable Anne." Darius saluted her as he dodged another whack from the poster, causing both of them to laugh the rest of the way to class.

Chapter 26

The lands surrounding Edran were unlike the ones around Aldamoor. Where Aldamoor had lush seas of grass, Edran was barren, desert like. The odd tall stalks of grass could be seen clumped together with a sparse bush here and there, but aside from that, there was nothing. Among all of this were ruins of what had once been dozens of various structures. Their origins were long forgotten through the passage of time, save for the traces of brown half destroyed brick walls and towers that littered the area. This was where the Fire Elves returned to pay homage after every raid. Despite their nomadic nature, something always drew them back there. It was a sacred ground, one where warriors could replenish their strength until the next fight.

This was why they never knew what hit them. At first, it seemed like nothing at all, a thick mist rolling in on the horizon. Then, out of the clouds came the war zeppelins with Puc, Jason, Sarina, Matthias, and the rest of the fighting host. While it was obvious the Fire Elves had not been aware of the battle ahead, it did not take long for them to organize themselves enough to fight back.

The sound of ringing steel and splintering wood could be heard all around as Jason and Sarina stood back to back in the carnage, each engaged with their own opponents among the tall crumbling stone buildings of the ancient Fire Elf stronghold. Helbringer danced in Jason's hands as he blocked each onslaught of attacks from his foe, a particularly large female Fire Elf wielding what looked like a pole axe with a chain attached to it. The weapon seemed impractical to the boy, but somehow it was managing to hold its own against him. Behind him, Sarina locked blades with a jumpy male sporting short braided platinum blonde hair who wielded two short swords. His gleaming red eyes did not leave her for a single second as he came at her, each time with a more vicious attack. Gritting her teeth and parrying the blows with equal ferocity, the girl soon found herself being pushed back, despite her best efforts to remain in a stable position. Feeling her heel touch the back of Jason's, she was forced to acknowledge her situation in the fight.

Jason glanced back briefly to Sarina's predicament, and summoning his abilities, he sent the Fire Elf flying through the air to the other side of the battlefield.

"Hey! I had him!" Sarina protested as another attacker approached, this time a female with the side of her head shaved off, carrying a battle axe. She quickly set to work and began beating her back across the battlefield.

"Didn't look like it five seconds ago." Jason rolled his eyes at her and then refocused back on his adversary, which had almost taken Helbringer from his hands with the chain.

"Oh! And how would you know?" she scoffed, landing a fatal hit that ended her duel.

Distracted, Jason felt the chain of the weapon wrap completely around Helbringer. Pulling with all his might to avoid it being taken from his hands, he growled, glaring at the female he was fighting, only to see a flash of metal cut her neck, causing her body to go limp. Turning around, Jason saw Matthias standing but a few steps behind him, his gauntlets and arms smeared crimson. Both Jason and Sarina looked at him with perplexed expressions.

"A thank you would suffice," Matthias huffed.

The conversation was short-lived when five more Fire Elves appeared on the horizon with grim demeanours. The trio quickly turned their attention to them, raising their weapons on the defensive.

"ALFHEIM!" Einar's booming voice echoed all around as the Dark Elf catapulted himself into the midst of the enemy out of nowhere, his battle hammer coming down in pure malice, causing those few who it evaded to run from whence they came. The two Fire Elves closest to the middle had not been so lucky.

Jason swallowed anxiously, seeing their fate. "Well then, that takes care of that."

His attention from the scene was then taken when a Soarin crash landed on the ground beside them, a large bolt protruding from its wing. Taking note of the creature's eye patch, they knew who it was immediately.

"Doriden!" Jason ran over to help the Soarin up with Matthias and Sarina covering their back. "What happened?"

"Fire Elves weren't lying about the siege weapons." The Soarin gritted his teeth as he pulled the projectile loose. "We spotted two within the towers of the ruins, ballistae from the looks of it, or some variation. We couldn't get any closer to them, and lost three Soarin in the process."

"Damn," Jason muttered.

"What now?" Matthias asked. "Should we warn the zeppelins?"

"Scouts will have done that. I ordered them to keep at bay," Doriden informed the group as two other Soarin made the descent beside him and inspected the wound in his wing.

"Doesn't solve the problem," Jason thought out loud. It was times like this, he hated to admit, that he missed Annetta's quick thinking. He was still angry with her about forcing them to split up, but he knew anger would not help him here, so he did his best to formulate a plan on the go. "Matt, Sarina, you guys come with me, we can try to get as close to the tower as possible. Maybe we can level the siege weapons with psychic fire with Matt. Sarina, you cover us. Doriden, you get back behind the lines and have that looked at."

"Don't have to tell me twice, dude." Doriden grinned wolfishly and with the help of his comrades, was led away from the battlefield.

Einar then ran towards them again, now with a score of Dark Elf warriors behind him. "Might I be of assistance?"

"Cover us with Sarina and hope the Fire Elves don't spot us." Jason gripped Helbringer with both hands and turning his attention to the ruins behind them that loomed over the horizon, charged with the others.

୨୦୯୨

Further away, Tempest sang in Puc's grip as the First Mage of Aldamoor fought with Tamora once more. It had not taken him long to single her out amidst the chaos and he had a score to settle, if not for his honour's sake, then for that of the injury done to Iliam. Their fighting had led them all the way up one of the disintegrating tower-like structures which lay scattered around Edran. Neither of them wished to be disturbed this time around.

Breaking free from their latest encounter and ascending to the top of the structure where the roof was no more, Tamora turned around and faced Puc, the dreadlocks in her hair smeared in ash and dirt as she observed him with a vicious smile, twirling a sabre in either hand.

Sure of his target, Puc created and aimed a blast of green energy from his staff. Seeing the oncoming onslaught, Tamora quickly dodged, only to come face to face with the mage, their blades colliding once more.

"Your reign ends here Tamora." He gritted his teeth. "I will not let you continue raiding this land as you wish. Too long have the mages of

Aldamoor had your veil of deception drawn over their eyes, and I will see it undone."

"And what do you think will change now, Thanestorm?" she sneered. "You cannot destroy our whole race, we are as multiple as tongues of flame in a hearth. If I fall, another shall take my place, brighter and more brilliant than I. You know this. You have always known. You only came here with a vendetta of vengeance for Oberon and Titania!"

Puc did not reply and continued to parry the various attacks thrown at him, further egging on Tamora to speak, her amused crimson eyes flashing with each stroke of the blade.

"Poor little orphaned Puc, the son of the mighty Oberon left without parents due to a Fire Elf raid," she chuckled. "You were not the first and you shall not be the last, Thanestorm! That is the way it has always been."

Ignoring her banter, Puc continued his onslaught. The words of his opponent meant nothing to him, wind without substance. His perseverance was rewarded when the sabre in Tamora's left hand flew from her grip.

The Fire Elf did not miss a beat, and in place of her sabre, a ball of white light formed in her palm, which she threw at her opponent. Puc blocked it just in the nick of time with his staff. Tamora vanished from before him, and he quickly whirled around in time to block the attack that had been meant for his head with her other blade.

Swords locking at the hilt, the two elves struggled for dominance. Twisting his arm at just the right angle, Puc unlocked them, sending Tamora's remaining sword from her hands, his mind already calculating further moves. He then heard the ringing of steel, and dodged the other sabre flying through the air due to a spell that had been placed on it. Tamora was not ready to give up just yet, however, and grabbing hold of Tempest with her bare hand, she sent a shock of orange flames along the hilt. Dropping the blade before the embers could get to him, Puc rammed the end of his staff into her gut, causing the Fire Elf to lose balance. Recalling Tempest to his hands, Puc aimed both blade and staff at his opponent.

"I may not have been the first," he said through laboured breath, "and perhaps not the last, but I will make sure that in the future there will be no more. I will finish what my father started. I charge thee,

Tamora, and condemn thee as my prisoner. Call off your rabble and perhaps we may yet negotiate."

Tamora gave a shrill laugh as her mane of hair fell in her face. "Ever the peacekeeper, Thanestorm. You'll get no such pleasure from me."

"So be it," Puc said through gritted teeth and sheathing his sword, he raised his staff.

ଛଠଔ

Jason, Sarina, Matthias and Einar rushed past the Fire Elf ranks, every so often being caught in a skirmish as enemy soldiers assailed them. Their end goal, however, was drawing ever closer as they could see the ballistae dispersed among the collapsing buildings just beyond.

"Just a little farther!" Matthias called as he scanned the horizon, another wave of enemy fighters appearing seconds later.

Tired, angry and frustrated, Jason raised Helbringer repeatedly in a defensive manner as him and his friends were swarmed yet again. Before any further conflict could begin, the sound of a baritone war horn could he heard all around them. Confused, both sides glanced around, not sure what to expect.

"What in the Unknown's bane was that?" Einar questioned, holding his war hammer closer, his dark eyes darting back and forth.

The Fire Elves which had then come to attack them began to flee, further sending those present to question what was going on. The mystery reached its conclusion when something came bursting through one of the ruined towers, a thing the likes of which those present had never seen. With the debris flying everywhere at first, they could not tell if it was living or machine. It was not until the mechanical pumping of the many legs of the thing could be made out that they knew it to be artificial.

"I guess they weren't kidding about a siege weapon after all," Matthias managed to say, grabbing hold of Jason, Sarina and Einar. He teleported out of the way just in time to see one of the spindly legs come down on the spot where they had been standing.

Getting a better look at it once he had gotten his bearings, Jason felt his blood run cold. It seemed like a beast come out of a nightmare, resembling that of an enormous dragon made entirely out of metal with six mechanical legs, its jaws partially open to reveal a blazing inferno that raged inside of it beyond the gears. Mesh wings flapped, as steam and flames escaped from various holes in the thing, black bulbous eyes surveying everything around. Jason was not sure how it was holding together with the amount of heat it was producing. By all rights in his mind, it should have melted.

"What is that thing?" Jason cringed, looking away from its crimson eyes.

"That is a Clador, a destroyer," Einar said, clenching his jaw tightly, "Pure machine with no pilot. No collateral, all carnage and I am ashamed to say invented by my people on the behest of the Fire Elves."

"Great, now we got Dark Elf technology to worry about," Jason grumbled.

"How do we stop it?" Sarina asked, glancing sideways at Einar.

"Bunch of whelps like you stop it? It is called a destroyer for a reason," the Dark Elf scoffed.

Not interested in hearing anything more from Einar after that comment, Matthias decided to take matters into his own hands. Turning his attention back to the weapon, he did a quick scan of the thing.

His feelings being mutual, Jason took a step forward. "Any ideas?"

Glancing over at a pile of scattered bricks from the levelled structure, Matthias thought hard on his next course of action. "Just one. How's your aim?"

"Same old, why?"

"One teleports while the other stuffs it full of stone. We'll see how it likes that diet," the assassin indicated, and without further instruction, he teleported from where he stood.

"Watch our backs I guess," Jason told Sarina and Einar before following.

Matthias reappeared some distance away on a heap of stone that could have at one point been a tower. Analyzing his target, he focused as loose rocks began to rise around him. Jason teleported to a similar-looking landmark right across from him and began the same process. He had a good idea of what the assassin had in mind and he only hoped it would be enough.

'We alternate. Never from the same spot. Is that clear?' Matthias's voice rang inside Jason's head, to which the youth nodded, going into his fighter stance.

"Hey, pea-brain! Over here!" Jason shouted, waving his arms as he did and catapulted one of the smaller rocks to get the Clador's attention.

The creaking of gears paused for but a split second, then the thing's whole body seemed to turn on a crank, the legs only slightly adjusting to the new angle it now faced, smoke frothing from its open mouth. Jason felt the hairs on the back of his neck rise, but stood his ground.

Not wasting a second, Matthias hurled the first rock, the impact nearly throwing the machine off balance. Jason did not miss a beat and quickly did the same. The Clador did not seem fazed in the least bit by the second attack, and let out a stream of flame from its jaws that would have obliterated both Jason and Matthias, had they not teleported away.

'I don't think it appreciated that much,' Jason intoned sarcastically. *'Now what?'*

'Faster,' Matthias replied. Raising even more stone with his mind, he began to pellet them at the Clador in a constant stream.

Jason did not question what was being done, and attacked. It was not until a few minutes later that he understood what Matthias's plan had been. The Clador, weighed down by the burden of a mouth full of stone and unable to let out anymore flame due to the blockage, buckled on its legs and crashed into the ground, soon after igniting into flame.

'Good work, but we aren't done yet,' Jason told him and teleported away yet again to rejoin Sarina and Einar.

Arriving, Jason saw both Einar and Sarina had their hands full with more Fire Elves, and prepared to jump into the fray again. Aid came soon after, as a pack of Minotaur charged in, their hulking forms in full plate mail alone enough to put fear into the hearts of the enemy.

"Keep moving, Kinsman! We have this!" the familiar voice of Hideburn boomed among the chaos.

"Right, on it!" Jason acknowledged. Turning to his companions, he saw Matthias had not come back to join them. Knowing he could not afford to wait, the trio with the remaining Dark Elves Einar had brought moved forward.

Zigzagging through a few more of the broken down structures, it did not take them much longer to get to where the ballistae were stationed. It was a wall of towers that despite time had endured, remaining mostly intact. Two ballistae were left standing from the looks of it, the others having been overrun by mages as far as Jason could tell from the displays of flashing colourful light which emanated from the distance like lightning across the sky.

"What now?" Sarina asked, noting the concentration on Jason's face as he scanned the horizon.

"We take them out like we planned," he restated, then turned to Einar. "How long can you hold them off? I have an idea."

"After seeing you take out that Clador like that, as long as you need, Kinsman," the Dark Elf told him. Turning to his comrades, he lifted his war hammer into the air, charging for the enemies at the base of the closest keep.

Jason wasted no time after. Grabbing hold of Sarina's hand, he teleported to the top, bypassing all the chaos below. He was faced with two shocked Fire Elves that stood around the ballista. Drawing their sheathed weapons, they ran at him and the girl. Brandishing their weapons and readying themselves, Sarina and Jason braced for impact.

The clash of steel hitting steel occurred yet again as they soon found themselves engaging with the enemy once more. Jason and Sarina's arms pumped fiercely as they traded both defensive and offensive maneuvers with their opponents. Seeing an opening, Jason focused and sent his foe flying into a wall, cracking his skull on the stone. Free of the fight, he then turned his attention to the ballistae, which now stood unoccupied.

He began to turn the first siege weapon with his mind so it faced its twin, but his efforts were thwarted when a sharp pain erupted from his side. At first, he'd thought nothing of it, but looking down the realization came to him that a throwing axe now lay buried in his shoulder. Pulling the blade free thanks to an adrenaline rush powering his motions, Jason turned to face his attacker, a bald, brutish Fire Elf. A feral growl erupting from his lungs, Jason threw the weapon back and using his abilities, made the impact so grave that the axe buried itself deep in the elf's chest and caused him to fall over. Holding onto his shoulder as a massive wet spot began to form, Jason loaded a bolt into the ballista with his abilities. Before he could fire, however, he was drained of energy, and worse, it seemed another two Fire Elves had fought their way to the top.

"Just my luck." Jason gritted his teeth as he steadied himself and gripped Helbringer anew.

Seeing what had occurred, Sarina regrouped with him after having dealt with her latest foe, and readied her sword for another attack. Their worries were short-lived, however, when both invaders dropped to the floor without any indication of having been injured. The boy and girl looked on in confusion, until Matthias became visible from the dark behind them.

"You're all clear." He smirked, retracting his claws. "Let's end this and go home."

Nodding, Jason turned to his initial target and with Matthias's help, sent the bolt flying.

ഐ

The sun shone brightly through the green foliage, causing sunspots to form beneath Link's eyelids as he woke up. Blinking a few times to remove them, he got up and looked around at his surroundings. He had almost forgotten where he had been, lying on the small cot in a large tent that was filled with at least five more like it. Getting up and stretching, he began to get dressed, and upon being ready, wasted no time in going outside.

Peeking through the flap of the tent, Link was surrounded by an enormous campground. Multiple fires roared and were alive, the smells of meals being prepared wafted through the air, mixed in with the smells of sabertoothed dogs, horses, metal and Gaians.

His initial encounter with Layla had landed him a one-way ticket to the camp of refugees that were still loyal to Venetor, refugees who had escaped the capital after it had been overrun by Razmus and his army of Hurtz. Those who were able carried out guerilla warfare, while the rest stayed in camp. For the most part, those that remained consisted of children too young to carry a weapon and the elderly, for both men and women fought to regain their homeland, in the name of their rightful king. Link had learned much more had been captured and forced to work on the continued construction of the tower, and so their numbers were not great enough to do any true damage to Razmus's ranks, for the Hurtz were a force to be reckoned with.

His first day had been spent mostly in recovery from his injury as well as his transformation, and so Link had very little time to speak with Layla to learn more about the situation. Since then, it had been impossible to get a hold of her, as she was constantly out on raiding parties. Everything he had learned was from sitting around fires and speaking with those who had time to spare. He was determined, however, to get an audience with his old commanding officer and to be of some real use to the resistance, his thoughts being that it was also the best way also to gain information for Annetta and his friends back in Q-16.

"Oi, Lincerious!" A robust middle-aged woman with dishevelled blonde greying hair called out to him from one of the fires. "Ye looking for Layla again?"

"I'm going to find her eventually, Nadja!" he yelled back as he kept walking, throwing his hands into the air for emphasis. "There's only so many times she can evade me."

"Well, if you can't find her, be a good lad and bring some more wood over," Nadja told him, to which the youth nodded and smiled before turning back to his task.

Somewhere in the distance as he walked, the resonance of wind and string instruments could be made out as bored bards practiced their craft for the evening fires, offering comfort and an escape to those gathered. The sounds carried Link back to times spent with Annetta and the others in the company of different races on their visits. The memories brought a smile to his face, and the realization of how much he missed the friends he had made over the past two years of being on Earth, particularly Annetta.

Coming to the outskirts of the camp, Link took note of a few figures in the distance that seemed to be practicing with swords and a sabertooth dog that lay lazily in the grass close by. Watching them for a little while before making up his mind, he set off in their direction at a steady pace.

Layla rigorously shouted instructions to those that stood before her, drilling her subordinates just as she once had in the militia camps. She wore the same armour she'd had on the day Link had run into her, loose strands of her hair matted against her face and neck as she swung the spear vigorously, while war cries erupted from her throat with each blow. Her alert eyes catching sight of Link standing off to the side, she dismissed those before her and watched as they dispersed before turning her attention to him.

"I see you've decided to rejoin the land of the living," she greeted him.

Link felt his words catch in his throat as he tried to answer her. She still had the same hold over him as she did before and it showed all over him. Making a quick recovery, he coughed into his hand before addressing her. "My transformations still take a fair bit out of me. It's something I have been unable to rid myself of."

"Practice is the only thing which could lessen it," Layla stated, steadying herself on her spear as she caught her breath. "There's no other way around it."

"You know I won't do that," he answered flatly.

"Ah, and that is why you are the weakest link," she replied, reminding Link where his nickname had originated.

Link had no response to her teasing. In fact, part of him simply did not care, and so he glanced at her blankly as though she had said nothing at all.

Seeing her words not affecting him, she changed the subject. "So, tell me, because you have some nerve showing up here after all this time, just what happened to you? And why shouldn't I have you executed as being one of Razmus's spies."

Not knowing how to answer, Link reached into one of the pouches at his sword belt and held out his Q-16 card key. "Because I have spent the last two years with the heir of Orbeyus on Earth, and she is gathering a force to come here and take back Gaia."

Layla scoffed, seeing the piece of metal he held out in his hand and turned around to attend to her sabertooth dog. "Somehow I feel the heir of Orbeyus couldn't care less about what is happening here. Didn't Orbeyus abandon Gaia because he found us too corrupt, too proud in our nature?"

"I don't know the details, but Annetta wants to help," Link began.

"Bah! She has no idea what's going on here,"

"That's why she sent me," Link interrupted her. "She needs to know the state of things in order to plan for coming here. It's why I'm here, Layla. She knew that I could blend in easily and get the information she needs."

The young female Gaian warrior listened to what Link said while reaching into the saddle bag of the sabertooth dog. Finding a strip of dried meat, she fed the creature, who then lay down to have its belly rubbed. Obliging, Layla stroked the thick black and tan fur and analyzed what had been said. Link had forgotten how silly the creatures looked when they weren't on the war path, with dispositions similar to those of their smaller Earth cousins. Layla smiled, seeing the beast stretch, its tongue hanging out of its mouth happy for the attention it was getting.

"I saw it all, the day of the fall," she remarked. "The houses wreathed in flame, the civilians running around in panic and screaming as our Hurtz brothers turned on them. I witnessed the ascent of the Lord of the Unfinished Tower. I've also been there through the events in the days after, the struggles our people faced as everything they ever knew changed and a proud nation was forced under the heel of the very thing it had protected others from for years with no help on the horizon. I want to believe in what you say, Lincerious, but the truth of it is that we have been alone here for a very long time. Who's to say this Annetta won't change her mind and leave us as well?"

Link smiled and shook his head. "Because you don't know her like I do."

Layla caught the optimism emanating from Link. It was a trait she did not remember in him in their days when he was training under her. She also knew he would not have come back knowing the consequences of abandoning his training as lightly as he seemed to have. The death penalty for abandonment was not something Gaians dismissed with an ease of hand. She turned her head slightly back to face him and then back to the sabertooth dog that regarded her with a great lolling tongue and satisfied grin. Its all-observant amber eyes regarding her with full attention.

"I suppose there is little else we can do in the matter," she replied with a sigh, "But to see what this heir of Orbeyus is truly worth. I will need to fill you in if that is the case. Gaia is not what it once was."

Chapter 27

The shine of Gaia's twin moons peered from among the cloudy sky as Venetor and the others rallied in their meeting spot. It had been several days since their initial depositing of the various objects to the ground. Since then, they had managed to fashion them into crude weapons. Though they were not the swords, axes and lances used by trained soldiers, Venetor had assured each one of them that they would work just the same, or so he secretly hoped. The movement and change of the guards had also been studied furiously, no detail having escaped the Gaian prince and the rest of the enslaved.

Arriving first to the scene of the gathering, Venetor began the process of uncovering the buried objects. Laying them down on the tarnished grass beside him, he examined each one, noting the intricate imperfections of each, which lent an eerie beauty to them. Selecting a broken blade that had been fashioned to a stick hilt, he placed it in his belt and began uncovering another pile. His concentration was broken by the sound of feet padding on soil. Turning around and adjusting his vision, he saw the first of his fellow Gaians in the distance.

"Select what you will have," he indicated to the unearthed weapons. "We've much work to do this night."

ഇൻൻ

Armed and waiting for the appropriate time, they spilt forth from the compound, attacking the unsuspecting guards that had just come on duty. Leaving a trail of desolation in their path, Venetor and the others pressed forward like a torrential rain, their goal being the camp at the base of the tower where the Gaian soldiers were being kept.

High above, Janus, in the form of a white falcon could be made out, gliding on the wind and acting as a lookout. So far there had not been much opposition. Between camps at night, there was hardly a soul, and the few Hurtz that were encountered were caught unawares, an easy prey for the Gaians who followed Venetor with a fanatic fervour.

The host stopped, seeing the gates which led to the tower. Venetor remembered well seeing it in his youth, thick grass covering the fields all around, forgotten. It was not so now and turning around, he regarded those who stood behind him.

"My people, those who stand with me," he began addressing them. "This is not an easy task which lies before us and it would be a lie to say that we are all to make it out alive. What I can promise you is that there will be a better tomorrow, even if it simply means we place fear into the hearts of those that oppose us and that they know we are all lions. Gaians! Do you stand with me?"

There was no pause as the hands of all of those gathered went up into the air and a ground-shattering roar erupted from the crowd. Unsheathing his weapon, Venetor faced the direction of the camp and took off running.

The Hurtz soldiers, half-awake in the midst of the chaos, fell prey before the wrath of Venetor and his band. Taking on any of those who presented themselves, they spread like wildfire, making their way towards their destination. In the process of continuing their charge, they also switched out their crude weapons for those the Hurtz carried.

Having obtained two short swords, Venetor charged forward, allowing his feral form's instincts to take hold, the beast inside gorging on the adrenaline and smells of battle as he fought on. Fighting and felling his latest victim, he used the back of his hand to wipe the grit of battle from his forehead. His moment of peace was short lived when pain erupted from his shoulder. Snapping his head sideways, he took in the sight of blood oozing from an open wound that had been inflicted upon him by a particularly gruesome looking Hurtz, its face that of a boar sporting a thick mane of tawny hair with a braid running down the side while the rest flew freely.

A throaty growl escaping him, Venetor leapt at his enemy, slashing away with his twin blades. The Hurtz was not shy on returning blows, the double-edged axe pumping furiously in its hands as it attempted to undermine the Gaian prince. Taking the Hurtz unawares by throwing one of the swords at him, he curled up his free first and slammed it into the side of the creature's face with all the force his body could muster, causing his opponent to fall over. Pointing his second sword at him, Venetor was about to land the final blow when cold steel pressed against his throat.

"I would not do this if I were you," the voice of Razmus warned him from behind.

Venetor dropped his weapon and slowly turned around to regard the Lord of the Unfinished Tower standing before him, his pearl white plate mail gleaming a wicked pale silver under the moonlight. Beyond him, the Gaian prince took note that his followers had been rallied, and hundreds of Hurtz surrounded them. Even Amarok stood in their midst. This had not been a chance meeting.

"Did you actually think that you and your lot could best me?" Razmus spat. "Do you take me for a fool?"

"I take you for a man out of his time who has lost his mind," Venetor spoke plainly.

"You will soon know the truth." Razmus smiled slyly and then turned his head back. "Now, where is Marianus?"

At that moment, Amarok approached carrying a Gaian and tossing him at Razmus's feet revealed him to be the man he had asked for.

"Dead in the heat of battle." The assassin proclaimed.

"Him!" Venetor shouted in anger as he glared at the body lying at Razmus's feet, "I don't believe you."

Razmus regarded Amarok for a split moment as if not believing what the assassin had said before speaking again.

"A pity, I was to release his daughter in exchange for the information he provided. Perhaps even elevate him to the status of a noble." Razmus sighed and withdrew his blade from Venetor's neck before turning back to the Hurtz. "Take him away to the dungeons. The rest you strip of their weapons, send back to camp, double the guard and lower the rations for the rest of the week. They will be singing a different tune after that. I should have known better than to allow him among them."

Two of the closest Hurtz grabbed hold of Venetor under each arm and began to drag him away as he continued to struggle.

"This isn't over! As long as a single Gaian lives!" he shouted, only to be silenced by an elbow rammed into his gut by one of his captives.

"Of this we shall see." Razmus smirked.

Razmus watched as Venetor was carried away. His eyes then turned to the body of Marianus still lying on the floor. He was partially upset at the loss of such an asset. Marianus had proven useful in the short time that he had worked for Razmus, his only goal being the freedom of his daughter. Even when tested with the possibility of overthrowing him, Marianus had come in the dead of night to warn the king of the impending rebellion. It was a pity to see such loyalty wasted even if it was originally founded on threats. Turning on his heel, he began to walk away.

"My lord, what of the body?" Amarok asked as he followed him.

"Add it to the mortar for all I care," Razmus stated. "No sense in wasting blood and bone."

ℛℭ

Pulling the trigger, the weapon fired and a ray of white energy seared through the target, leaving a trail of smoke. Xander lowered the colt to see his mark had been made, a hole visible on the left side of the dummy, where the heart would have been.

"Impressive," Titus observed as he walked over and examined it. "You seemed to be a natural shot."

"Games," Xander shrugged.

"I beg to differ," Titus said as he faced him. "Quite different mechanics in both."

"I don't see what's so different," the boy replied bluntly. "You shoot in a game and you shoot here."

Holding his tongue, Titus simply smiled. He knew better than to lecture him, or rather, he had been on the receiving end too many times from his own father. He found the best course of action was for him to one day find out on his own.

On the other side of the arena, Annetta and Darius watched as Liam concentrated on the small stone before him floating flimsily in the air before landing on top of another stone. Breathing out once the task was done, he turned to look at the two of them.

"Okay, now what?" he asked.

"Again," the girl replied, using her own abilities to place the stone back at its original spot, causing the boy to groan.

"Oh, you've got to be kidding me!" he growled. "When do I get to do something cool like Xander?"

"Trust me when I say this, when you are ready," Annetta told him. "Now, again."

Liam muttered something nasty under his breath about wishing Jason was there, which Annetta did her best to ignore and watched as he started over.

"Way to bring down the whip, Anne," Darius whispered to her, causing the girl to punch him lightly in the shoulder.

"Can it." She gritted her teeth and then breathed out heavily. "I'm never going to look at Puc's lessons the same way again. We were horrible to him."

"No worse than any student at the Academy," the young mage chuckled.

"Still," Annetta sighed as she watched Liam repeat the rock's journey, only to have it fall but a few feet from its mark. "Why don't we call it a night for now with that. There's no point in you trying if you're getting angry about it. How about some sword fighting instead?"

"Why can't I use a gun like Xander?" he questioned her.

"Because." Annetta paused and flung her hand as though she was swatting a fly away, only to hear Xander yell in the background and the clattering of metal on the floor some distance away. "A gun is harder to psychic-proof than a close-range weapon, any other questions?"

Seeing what had been done, Liam shook his head. "Nope, I got nothing. Sword fighting sounds just fine."

"Good." Annetta nodded and observed as the boy went in the direction of the weapons rack.

Once Liam was out of hearing distance, Darius began to snicker. The sensation of flattening ears taking over, Annetta turned around to face him.

Seeing he had her attention, he spoke, "Taken from the pages of Puc Thanestorm himself."

ഇരു

Having walked Xander and Liam back to the exit, Annetta paused before the great doors leading to the front entrance of the base. It seemed like only yesterday that she had come down the first time with Jason. It also occurred to her how much reminiscing she had been doing the last little while, like she had aged horribly and skipped her young adult years. Wrinkling her nose at the upsetting realization, she threw open the doors with her abilities and strode back inside.

Allowing her subconscious to choose the course, Annetta wandered the halls of the Lab aimlessly, losing herself in her thoughts. The impending attack that was closing in was becoming more of a burden of late, mostly the worry of whether she was doing the right thing. Remembering her encounter with Orbeyus, she swatted the feeling aside and hearing voices ahead, she went in their direction.

In one of the vast meeting rooms, Atala and Gladius sat around a steel table, each holding a large metal stein as they spoke. Before them were sprawled maps of what Annetta could only assume were Gaia, with stone map markers that were placed into clusters on top of it.

"There is no way in all the realms of hell Razmus is gonna fall for it," Gladius protested. "Not a chance."

"Hurtz, I have been at this a very long time," Atala retorted in her usual bold tone. "I like to think I did not get my position just because the king wished to have a female general for equality's sake."

"Aye, and I can say the same for being a Hurtz who is the personal guard of the future king," Gladius grunted.

"Load of a good job you're doing now, aren't you?" Atala smirked, taking a swig of her stein before slamming it back down.

Doing his best not to be annoyed by the comment, the Hurtz exhaled roughly, running a hand through his shaggy mane. Folding his hands under his chin, he pondered the pieces for a long while with his good eye. His functional ear twitching, Gladius turned to the door to see Annetta standing in its midst. "Evening, lass. Yer up late for a school night."

"I have trouble sleeping with everything going on," Annetta confessed. "I was taking a walk to clear my head when I heard voices. What's all of this here?"

"Battle plans for how to take Pangaia, the capital city," Atala replied. "The Hurtz seems to think we are still outnumbered and outmaneuvered no matter how we post what troops we will have to our disposal, to which my reply is that we will not be."

"It's not the troops I be worried about," Gladius stated, glancing at the girl. "It be the fortifications. Most of Pangaia was rebuilt to withstand a full-on psychic attack after its dealings with Mordred the Conqueror."

"I thought we were going to go after this tower of Razmus's," Annetta said, walking over and taking a closer look at the maps.

"Yes, but a distraction must be laid," Atala informed her. "If we have all of our forces go for the second tower, then Razmus will simply bring the fight to us with all of his hosts in tow. But if we bring an army to Pangaia, which is the capital, he will have no choice but to defend it from us, giving the second force a chance to take down the tower, and if all goes to plan, leaving Razmus without an army."

"I see." Annetta nodded her head as she took it all in, then asked, "How many troops will he have, though? We still haven't heard from Link. We're planning this completely blind."

"Sometimes, lass, there be no choice," Gladius explained. "The lad should have contacted us by now to let us know he at least made it to the planet. We've heard nothing. Not to assume the worst, but…"

Gladius did not need to finish the sentence for Annetta to know what it could mean. Her heart sank into her stomach as she was faced with the potential realization of it. She could not believe it, though, she would not, not until there was proof, and empty speculation was never fact.

"I'll see if I can reach him," Annetta spoke finally, having given herself a chance to cool down. "If not by C.T.S., then by telepathy."

She did not say anything else, nor wait for a reply. Everything in her ears felt muffled after she had uttered the sentence to Gladius and Atala. Walking out of the room, Annetta walked some distance away from where the duo had been sitting. Certain she was far enough, the girl slid down against one of the icy metal walls before flipping open her C.T.S. and stared at it for a good long while. Could Link have simply forgotten to contact them, or was there something more sinister to the silence of the young Gaian warrior? Taking a deep breath, Annetta typed Link's number on the watch and waited.

Chapter 28

The clattering of horse hoofs and soldiers giving out orders was all that could be heard as Jason and Sarina rode back into Aldamoor. A roar of cheers greeted them soon after as they entered the main gate, citizens of every age marvelling at their return. Puc rode closely by them, a weary look present in his eyes from the events which had taken place. He did well to mask this from those who did not know him, and kept a steady pace astride his mount.

"Long live the Storm of Aldamoor!" many cried in unison among the crowd.

"You know, if I didn't know any better, I'd say they like you," Jason teased the mage.

Puc smirked, hearing the assessment. "Only the idea of me, I fear. Should they know me as you do, Kinsman, they would be singing a different song now."

The First Mage of Aldamoor then raised his staff, silencing those chanting. Clearing his throat, he began to address them. "Citizens of Aldamoor, my people. The threat of the Fire Elves has been eradicated, and it shall be many years till we ever see their like again on our borders, if they even dare."

The masses cheered once more as Puc hushed them repeatedly. "This is not to say that we should let our guard down, for the one thing I have learned in all my years is that the enemy never sleeps. Time and time again the Fire Elves have proved this, and negligence is not a mistake I am willing to allow. Too many have suffered at the hands of these...savages."

As if on cue, the cart which drew an imprisoned Tamora pulled up beside Puc, Jason and Sarina. The Fire Elf leader surveyed them like a jungle cat would her prey from beyond the bars, anger seething from her every pore.

Jason flinched, seeing the female Fire Elf handled in this way. He was alright with her being taken prisoner, but being shown off to a crowd this way just rubbed him the wrong way. He looked over at Sarina to confirm he was not the only one who thought this though she showed it much less than he did. The only one who seemed to have no issue with any of it was Puc.

"This is all only temporary," she warned them, through gritted teeth.

"As you say," Puc replied in an indifferent tone and then turned to the female elf that resided in the driver's seat. "Place her under arrest. I shall see to her later."

"Yes, First Mage," the female coach driver replied. Flicking the reins, she veered the horses, pulling the cart in the direction of the prison.

As it drove past Jason, Sarina and Puc, Tamora's eyes gleamed back at them from behind bars, a silent prayer of revenge forming upon her lips.

Jason turned back to Sarina, feeling a weight fall from his shoulders as the imprisoned Fire Elf faded into the crowd. It seemed the campaign was coming to an end, but he was also aware of what might be waiting for them when they return to the Lab. A faded anger resurged in him as he watched injured soldiers begin pouring into town, reunited with their loved ones. Many, he also knew, never would be, and some deaths could have been prevented if Annetta had chosen to stay together. Realizing he had not contacted her in all the time he had been away, Jason flipped open his C.T.S. and began punching in her code, albeit reluctantly.

"J.K., what are you doing?" Sarina inquired, seeing the abrupt change of body language in him.

"I never contacted Annetta while we were here," he explained. "We have no idea what we're going to be coming back to."

Looking back at the soldiers again, his brow furrowed in anger. "This is all her fault..."

"You need to let this go," Sarina told him. "What good is holding this grudge?"

Unable to hold it all in anymore, Jason snapped. "She abandoned her friends for what? Some would-be relative who showed up just because he needed an army? Then he gets conveniently kidnapped and she blindly decided she needs to go after him. I don't care if it's a whole planet that's in danger. Anne should have known better."

Hearing what he had to say, Sarina waited a good long moment before addressing him again. "Did you even stop to consider that maybe her outlook on family is different than yours?"

Jason paused for a moment as he contemplated what the girl said. "Well, I..."

"Anne grew up with a set of loving parents," Sarina continued, "Something from what I gather, neither of our pasts have had. For her, family is on the same level as friends, maybe even higher. Did you ever think of that?"

A light bulb seemed to go off in Jason's head upon hearing this, but was dimmed the moment he looked back at the city, his fist curling at the site.

"J.K., we would have lost soldiers and had them injured either way." Sarina tried to calm him. "That's what happens in wars."

"We would, but it would have been a lot less," he stated, his eyes lingering on the burnt city.

Turning back to his previous task and having completed the sequence on his watch, he waited to hear something, but nothing came of it. Frowning, Jason took off the small device and began to shake it, wondering if exposure to the elements had gotten the better of the watch. It was not the first time he had destroyed one in such a way.

"I can't get through to her," Jason told Sarina. "It must have been broken during the fighting."

"I'm sure she's fine," the girl reassured him.

"Screw it, if she needs anything, she'll call." Jason nudged his horse harder as he caught up to Puc, who had ridden further into the city towards the tower that was steadily being rebuilt. In fact, Jason noticed now that much of the inner city had been repaired since they had departed to go after the Fire Elves, which only meant that magic had been used as a means to accomplish the feat, and that Iliam had returned to the city as he had told them he would the last time they spoke with him.

"Puc, have you heard anything from Annetta?" the boy asked, more out of duty than concern.

"No, I have not," the mage replied. "Is something troubling you?"

Before further words could be exchanged, a dark shape materialized before them. Lowering the cowl of his navy blue cloak, Matthias revealed himself.

"I have good and bad news," he said. "The good news being Tamora was indeed in charge of the Fire Elves. The bad news is the ones that got away are involved in skirmishes across the countryside, burning everything to the ground in the name of their so called beloved leader. I just passed by two villages with the Soarin scouts, and it's not looking pretty out there."

"What? Seriously?" Jason groaned.

"Unknown's bane, I feared this would happen if we did not round them up thoroughly." Puc cursed at himself.

"We can't leave them to do as they please," Sarina added. "Skirmishes may seem like nothing at all, but over time they can escalate. I heard it happen on a few of the planets my father took over."

"We have little choice in the manner," the mage stated and then turned back to Matthias. "How many of these parties are out there? Have we a count?"

"I don't yet know for certain," Matthias replied. "Could be one, could be a dozen, could even be something entirely different."

"Mobilize every scouting troop we have," Puc instructed him. "These are details we need to know."

Nodding, Matthias vanished as quickly as he had appeared. Puc then looked over at Jason and Sarina. "Acquire fresh mounts and gather those still able to fight. Our work is not done yet."

Urging his horse forward, Puc stormed past them, a blur on the cobblestone streets of Aldamoor, as he raced out of the city, only having been there for mere moments.

"Never a dull second here," Jason exhaled, causing Sarina to nod in agreement and follow his lead as they prepared to leave once more.

ରଉ

A blazing red sun set over the horizon as cooking fires roared for miles around, the refugee camp coming alive with evening festivities. It was a way in which the people of Gaia were able to forget about their troubles for a time, exchanging songs and stories of long ago under a starry sky.

Link stood at a distance, watching as elders entertained the young with tall tales and musicians played their songs. Part of him feared their detection from Hurtz scouts, but Layla had assured him that the appropriate precautions were in place should such a thing occur, mainly of a magical nature.

Exhaling and inhaling the fumes of the flames deeply, the Gaian youth looked across one of the pits to see Layla surrounded by a score of children, her spear resting beside her as her hands flew in all directions in an animated manner while she spoke. Link could not help but smile, seeing her so at ease for once. Never in all his time of knowing her had he seen her in such a state. It was heartwarming. His gaze lingered on the scene for a little longer, until he felt something vibrating on his wrist. Looking down, he took note that it was his C.T.S. and flipped it open.

"105 here," he said, hoping he had remembered his code correctly and bit his lower lip, unsure of the results.

"01 here," Annetta's came through the device. **"Oh man, it's good to hear your voice."**

There was a pause in the communication. Noting how loud it was around them, Link moved away from the fires in order to be better able to hear her.

The noise still coming through, Annetta's voice came on again. **"You at a party or something?"**

"No, nothing like that," he laughed in response. "It's complicated."

"Try me," she rebutted.

"Refugee camp," he replied. Having found a log, he seated himself on it, the glow of distant fires illuminating his hand and the watch.

"Ah, I see," her voice seemed laced with worry now. **"It's bad over there then, isn't it?"**

Link sighed, running his free hand through his hair. "I'm not going to sugar coat it, Anne. People who are loyal to Venetor that escaped Pangaia and surrounding towns have fled into the wilds in order to avoid Hurtz scouting parties. Everyone who is captured is sent to work on the tower. Razmus is draining the planet of its resources to create the tallest structure possible and spares no one."

"Have you heard anything from Venetor?" she asked.

"No, nothing since I got here," he spoke into the C.T.S. "I haven't exactly been on the grid since I came here, though. All of my knowledge of what's going on so far comes from what I've been hearing in the camp."

"Damn," the girl growled. **"I was hoping we would know something more about this Razmus guy and what to expect when we head over and well...mostly..."**

There was another long pause and Link could distinctly hear another deep exhale happen through the speaker. **"I just wanted to hear your voice."**

Link felt his heart sink in his chest when he heard the last part, not sure how to reply after their last encounter.

"When I get back to Earth, we can talk about it." The words tumbled out of him automatically. "I may have said some things that didn't exactly express how I felt at the time, but right now we have bigger things to worry about."

"Yeah, I agree." Annetta's voice answered. **"Skyris is building a machine like the Pessumire on Valdhar to get us through without the use of ships. Turns out we don't have enough that will function here and building new ones would take years. I haven't heard anything from Puc, Jason, Sarina or Matt yet, so I have no clue what's going on over in Aldamoor."**

"They've probably got their hands full," Link reassured her. "A portal-creating cannon? What can't this woman do?"

"Spend a week sober, I think," the girl commented.

"I missed you, Anne," Link said with a smile.

"Good," she replied, **"That's how it ought to be."**

"I'll pass the details on of the plan to those running the place," he said. "Is that alright?"

"Yeah, that's fine," Annetta's voice responded. **"If you can, see if you can get scouts to where this city is, find out the situation there and see if you can find out about Venetor, too."**

"I'll do what I can." Link nodded and noted that Layla had gotten up from the fire and was walking in his direction. "I've gotta go, Anne. I'll call when I can. 105 out."

Annetta's goodbye came through just before Layla was in hearing range. Link closed the watch and turned to face her. "Good news, reinforcements will be on their way soon. Princess Skyris is in the process of building a portal-creating cannon to get them through."

"May the Unknown bless her." Layla smiled. "Princess Skyris is quite the engineer."

"There's something else," Link added. "Prince Venetor has been captured."

"What?" Layla's eyes widened in shock. "Where is he?"

"Here on Gaia," he stated. "That was part of the reason I left to come here. I don't know where exactly, though. I don't know where Razmus keeps his prisoners."

Layla's brows knotted as she thought on the subject for a little, the gears of strategy turning in her head.

"He'll be keeping him in the palace," she answered. "Razmus took up residence there once he took hold of the capital. All of my sources point to it."

"Can we get in?" he asked.

A mischievous smile spread across Layla's face as the reflection of the fires beyond caused a twinkle to form in her deep green eyes. "I don't know, can we?"

A week having come and gone had not even occurred to Skyris as she slept in a seated position in her office chair, her mane of hair sprawled out on the desk where she rested her head. In fact, time had all but stopped for the female Gaian when she had made a promise to deliver the replica of the Pessumire cannon to the others as an alternative for reaching Gaia. At first, it had been frustration and fury that had driven her to accomplish the deed, but as the days rolled on, the fury turned to stress and to Skyris this seemed a more efficient fuel than even the bottle of juice she had on hand. Finally, after a gruelling conclusion and set of tests, she considered it as working. The conclusion having been made, she promptly reached the end of her rope and deemed her workstation a most suitable resting place.

She had seen to minimizing the size without impacting the power, and so the current prototype was a little over twelve feet in size, versus its predecessor, which had been over thirty and took up an entire room aboard Valdhar. The design had stayed virtually the same, a large circular arc of metal which held together the cannon itself, a sleek cylindrical device, the firing end being larger in order to allow more force to travel through it.

After some hours, Dexter floated by and stopped a few feet from the sleeping Gaian. He kept a hovering vigil for some hours more before setting off an alarm that would have put any car to shame.

Jumping from her slumber in such a way that the chair rolled from under her, Skyris struggled to grab hold of the desk. She instead landed with her rear on the floor, her hair going off in all directions as adrenaline pumped her awake.

"What!?" she shrieked, coming to.

"A healthy sleeping period for a grown Gaian female consisting of eight hours has passed," Dexter concluded. "I set my alarm to wake you when the appropriate period of time had ended so that you may get the most out of your day."

"Well, did your calculations include all the days where I didn't sleep?" she grumbled, getting off the floor and stretching her sore form. "Unknown's bane... I could have slept so much longer."

"You know I cannot let you do that, Skyris," Dexter intoned.

"Yeah, yeah, healthy sleeping habits and all that," she huffed and waved a hand at it. "Remind me to wipe that from your programming."

There was a pause as Dexter observed her with his bulbous red eye before speaking again. "I also cannot let you do that, for you programmed me to prevent you from doing so in case you were in such a state of anger as you are now. Your adrenaline levels are raised quite high. Perhaps a sedative would be best right now to help you relax?"

Skyris pulled out a hip flask from her coat pocket and waved it in front of the A.I. "Don't mind if I do."

Tasting the bite of the liquid, Skyris quickly reached for the jug of juice under her desk and opening it, washed the previous pallet from her mouth. Coming to her senses from her initial shock, she observed her creation that lay before her. Walking closer to it, Skyris inspected the screen that was attached to the side, which allowed for calibration. Turning on the machine with a wave of her hand, she double checked once more to make sure everything was in place before turning back to Dexter, who still floated some distance behind her.

"I think it's time we test this." She let a sly smirk cross her face, satisfied with her work. "Patch me through for a mass communication on the C.T.S. for the numbers corresponding to Annetta, Titus, Darius, Atala and Gladius. I've got to let them know we're in business."

ഔരു

Annetta and Darius made their way down to the Lab at a hastened pace, having been told by Skyris to meet her along with the others at Severio Castle. Striding through the monotonous corridors of the Lab as quickly as their legs could take them, and then readying their horses, the duo crossed the portal separating the Eye to All Worlds from Q-16 in no time. Coming down the ridge which led down from the cliff, they took note of the group of figures gathered some distance away and hastened the pace of their mounts as much as travelling the steep path allowed.

Below were Skyris, Atala, Gladius and Titus, along with the leaders of the Four Forces, Lord Ironhorn, Natane, Entellion and Iliam, who stood in place of Puc. The group had gathered around a large metal structure.

"You made it!" Skyris beamed at them from the crowd.

"Yeah, we're here," Annetta replied as she and Darius dismounted. Looking up, she took in the sight of the cannon. "Uh... is that?"

"A replica of the Pessumire cannon from Valdhar? You're correct," Skyris confirmed, a wide smile forming on her lips as she crossed her arms. "Delivered in a week's time as promised and with improvements to calibration and size reduction for easier transportation."

"How did you exactly manage to get this thing here, anyway?" Darius inquired, studying the thing as he walked around it.

"Ye forget yer surrounded by technology when yer down in the Lab," Gladius said, his good ear twitching reflexively when he spoke.

The girl formed an 'o' with her mouth, her own thoughts on the matter having been answered. In truth, she did continuously forget, mostly because no one, it seemed, aside from Skyris knew how any of it worked. Annetta made a mental note to ask her aunt more about the gadgets within the Lab when this was all over, and turned her attention back to the Gaian female.

For a moment, it seemed like the jovial disposition of Skyris had been replaced with firm concentration as she set to work on calibrating the machine to create a portal for Gaia. Annetta and the others watched while she punched in coordinates and other variables on the screen with her finger. Satisfied, the Gaian then took a step back as a small tray emerged from the side. Reaching into the pocket of her bomber jacket, she withdrew a knife and slit the palm of her hand in a single swift motion. Cringing, Annetta looked at her questioningly.

Noting the discomfort of the girl, Skyris answered, "A part of Gaia is needed to locate the exact coordinates for the portal. Since we've not twigs nor stone nor earth, the blood of a native will do."

Placing her hand over the tray, Skyris allowed some of the blood to drip into it before withdrawing it. Taking a cloth out of another pocket, she wrapped the wound and watched as the tray closed, the calibrating beginning with a low humming sound coming from the mechanisms inside.

"Best take a step or two back," Atala warned Annetta and Darius. "It's going to get loud."

Having said her piece to the youth, the military leader crept up beside Skyris and whispered into her ear. "Is this wise to do, m'lady? We both know the dangers of creating portals."

Skyris turned to the side and regarded Atala. "What choice have we been left with in these dire times? Pray only the Unknown forgives us."

The humming of the machine intensified into a droning sound and reaching its peak, signalled with a blast of golden light from the cannon.

The wind rising around them at an incredible rate, Annetta braced her feet for impact as she shielded her eyes from the oncoming storm. Despite this, she felt herself being pulled towards the blast, and teleported a few feet back just to be safe. The light continued to intensify until it blinded those gathered. When the wind, light and sound died down, they opened their eyes to behold the portal that now stood before them. It was similar to the one which led to the Yasur Plains on Salaorin, the homeworld of the Ogaien, a mirror looking in on a world of immense trees sleeping in the night with two moons shining down upon it all in silver light. The portal shape itself was not formed to a frame like the ones contained in the Eye to All Worlds but instead resembled an open wound or a tear. Around the edges of the tear where the portal was made were a rim of golden flames. What surprised Annetta most was the size however, for it was large enough to fit thirty people across.

"Well, that is convenient," Lord Ironhorn said. "How accurate do we know what is being shown on the other side is?"

As if on command, Titus pulled out one of his guns, took aim and fired into the portal, his projectile going through the mirror image and hitting a tree on the other side. Lowering his weapon, he placed it back in its holster.

"If that is any indication," he stated, "I would say very."

"Well, that wasn't reckless," Gladius snorted. "What if yer father had been on the other side and ye just killed him?"

The thought drained the colour from Titus as soon as it had been uttered by Gladius, causing Atala to step forward. "A portal would not form in such a highly-populated area."

"It wouldn't even if that were a possibility," Skyris interjected. "I used map coordinates to plan the location of the portal, close enough to Pangaia, but far enough not to alarm anyone. I will say this, though, I would not risk waiting around for anyone to discover its existence."

"Agreed. We should mobilize our troops if we are to have any advantage," Entellion added. "What do we know of the enemy forces that will await us?"

"Link said there is a refugee camp with resistance fighters," Annetta spoke up, recalling her conversation with him. "It may be beneficial to see if we can combine our efforts with theirs."

"Do we know their location?" Atala asked in a stern tone.

"I…no, I didn't ask." The girl hung her head, somewhat defeated.

Dissatisfied, Atala huffed as she crossed her arms, burying herself in thoughts of strategy. Seeing this, Darius lent his voice. "We have to gather the troops either way. Perhaps Link will get back to us before then and we can somehow join up. Who knows, they could be close to where we will enter."

"It is true. We waste time here," Natane said and mounted up on her Aiethon. "I go to prepare the battlements. May Tiamet watch over you in the meantime."

With that, the Ogaien leader was gone, and soon after the others followed, leaving Annetta, Darius, Skyris, Atala, Gladius and Titus on their own. The girl turned around and regarded her ragtag team of fighters, not quite sure what to make of it all. Here she was, preparing for another battle, this one of her own choosing with companions, yet she had never felt more alone. A homesickness for the faces of her close friends she had made over the few years spent in the Lab washed over her again, only to be replaced with the need for action.

Folding her arms across her chest and straightening her posture, she remembered a line that one of those friends had said to her before. "Well, ladies and gentlemen… to arms."

Chapter 29

Night had fallen yet again on Gaia. Or was it day? Venetor was not quite certain anymore as he came in and out of consciousness, chained standing up to a wall at the far end of a vast chamber with no windows of any kind. Only two torches were lit on the opposite side of the room from him, Razmus preferring to resort to more primitive forms of energy that he was familiar with. He had quite literally sent Gaia back into a dark age.

He was alone in the room, for the Lord of the Unfinished Tower had made sure there was only one way in and out, and that way was guarded by a squadron of Hurtz. Closing his eyes and wincing at the pain of the open wounds that now covered his back from the whipping he had received, Venetor reflected on the moments which had led to his imprisonment. His recollections most vividly focused themselves on Razmus's eyes as they watched him the entire time. The amount of venom and loathing in the Gaian baffled even the grudge-holding prince. He knew full well the story of the two brothers, building their towers, vying for the throne, yet he could not understand it. He did his best to picture himself and Orbeyus as Razmus and Magnus, and still nothing. He had had his differences with him over the years, and even despised him for leaving Gaia when he did, but he still loved him. His memory then faded to one particular day he had spent with his brother so many years ago...

஁ଔ

An ocean wind assaulted Venetor as he stood on the shores of Pangaia, looking out into the vast body of water before him. The tide went in and out from under his feet, causing his toes to be buried in the grey sands of the shore. Overhead, oceanhawks squawked and crowed as they took turns diving into the water for their meal, creating an acrobatic show on the horizon.

"Don't go out too far, brother!" a boy's voice called from behind.

Venetor turned around on the stony shore to see Orbeyus sitting some distance away on a large flat rock. He was not yet the adult that would one day lead the Four Forces, but a wayward dreamer who was destined to become king of Gaia. His clear blue eyes beamed at Venetor, and were intensified by the indigo of the water. The sea wind whipped through his black hair, further accentuating the colour of his eyes, making him more spectre than flesh and blood. He wore simple woollen clothing of light colouring that would let the air through with ease, and around his neck, the pendant which proclaimed him as the heir to the Gaian throne.

"I can swim well enough," Venetor boasted as he wrinkled his nose at him.

"I never said you couldn't." Orbeyus chuckled as he slid off the rock and walked towards him. "But the tide is strong today, and the current swift."

"Whatever," the younger brother huffed as the wind blew his shaggy hair in all directions, causing it to tickle his neck and him to swat at it out of frustration. "I hate the wind."

"Why? The wind has a great purpose and more power than many give it credit for," Orbeyus stated, closing his eyes as he inhaled the ocean air deeply.

"Doesn't mean I have to like it," Venetor grumbled.

Orbeyus smiled at his sibling and then looked back out into the ocean, burying himself in deep thought. "Have you ever thought about what is out there, Venetor?"

"I don't have to think. I know because of all the maps we have to read in our lessons," the younger boy stated matter-of-factly.

"I don't mean on Gaia," Orbeyus smiled. "I mean beyond it."

"Same thing, maps of planets," Venetor answered with a bored tone.

Orbeyus sighed at the stiffness of his brother. "I need to tell you something, Venetor, and you have to promise not to tell anything to father until after I am gone. I'm going to be leaving Gaia to find the Eye to All Worlds."

"What? Why? You can't!" Venetor protested. "You have to stay here to be king. That's what you are supposed to do."

Orbeyus turned away from his brother as he collected his thoughts. "Venetor, if I stay, there won't be a Gaia to be king of one day. You weren't in that council meeting I was at today but…things are getting pretty bad. Mordred Freiuson stormed out, stating that he and his family are meant to rule all of the known worlds by divine right. Right now, these are but empty words, but I fear Mordred means to do much more. Venetor, if I don't get to the Eye to all Worlds and secure it with an army to protect it from him, then who knows what will happen."

"But who is going to be king here?" the boy answered, sadness starting to sink in as he realized there was no changing his brother's mind.

Orbeyus knelt down before him and slipping off the pendant he wore, put it around Venetor's neck. "I know of no one better."

Venetor clutched at the silver pendant bearing the rampant lion of Gaia on it. After examining it, he looked back up at Orbeyus. "But I don't think I can."

"I know you can," Orbeyus assured him. "This is the way it has to be, Venetor. One day you will understand, but know that I will always be your brother."

∞∞

What transpired in the days after, Venetor remembered without flaw. Orbeyus, along with Brakkus, his Hurtz guard, had taken off in secret, throwing their father into a rage unlike any Venetor had ever witnessed before. Abandoning his eldest, all attention was given to Venetor and his education on one day becoming king. It would not be until years later that the two boys would meet again as men.

"You would do well not to dwell on dreams, son of Balthazar." The voice of Amarok pierced his mind like a fine-edged sword.

Venetor lifted his weary head from its dangling position and opened his eyes to regard the man standing before him, the glare of his mask obscuring his vision somewhat.

"Then what would you have me do instead, Mezorian?" Venetor sneered.

Amarok observed the prisoner for a little while before he strode over and came up to Venetor's ear, close enough for the Gaian to feel the assassin's breath on his skin. "Pray for a quick death, for this is just the beginning of all that is to come."

"What in the Unknown's bane are you talking about?"

Amarok smirked beneath the mask, pleased with the peaked curiosity. "If only you truly knew the extent of what the Lord of the Unfinished Tower has planned, or the things which are currently brewing beneath the surface. This world and all others will burn, for they are a means to an end."

Hearing the words caused a surge of strength to course through Venetor making the Gaian straighten his posture as he looked at his visitor.

"Whatever you claim is to be will not come to pass," he spat defiantly "For every villain like you, a hero will rise. There can be no good without evil to stabilize it, nor any evil without good to defy it. That is the way it has always been."

Amarok gave a hearty laugh, hearing the words before turning on his heel towards the door. "Of that, Prince Venetor, we shall see."

Venetor continued to eye Amarok in a defiant glare. He knew the assassin was trying to wear him out mentally with what he said and he would not give him the satisfaction of thinking he had succeeded. Saying no more, Amarok exited the room, leaving the prince once again to the silence of his prison.

ഇറ

The sentence having been passed from Layla's lips, Link found himself thrust into the midst of events in camp. A plot was being drawn up for rescuing Venetor from Razmus's imprisonment, and no amount of power was being spared for the feat.

"The plan is simple," Layla explained to him beforehand. "A select few shall go in dressed as Apostles of the Unknown, and I in the guise of a noble. The cowls of the Apostle's hoods are always up, and no one dares them to be removed when in public, for they are seen as representatives of the Unknown and Razmus pays no heed to their doings. Where there are any persons of noble birth or religious order, however, there are always Hurtz. This is, for once, where your feral form will come in handy."

Hearing the words come from her mouth, Link stood dumbfounded, the orange glow of the fire illuminating their features and those of the few hundred people that were gathered.

"You want me to change into it?" he said, hesitation in his voice.

"Unconventional as it may be," Layla raised her voice slightly to silence those in the crowd that were already frowning at the idea, "It is our best way of getting in without raising any suspicion. Your altered feral form, as detesting as we may all find it, is the key to our success if we are to make it out with Venetor alive."

Link sighed, looking down at his boots, giving himself time to mull over the newly-acquired information. Had he been asked to do so a year ago, his decision would have been different, but his time on Earth in the company of Annetta and her friends had changed all of that. Shifting his weight from one leg to the other, he looked back up at her. "Alright, fine. I'll do it."

When this was said, those gathered set to work. It had been established that Hurtz armour would be needed for Link to wear as well as robes for Layla and five other fighters who would go in with her as a backup, not including the thirty warriors that would be lying in shadows spread out throughout the city as an escape route.

At first, having changed into his form, Link earned a few stares and even a few people who turned away. A scolding from Layla, however, turned everyone back on track. Soon, two blacksmiths were fitting him with Hurtz-styled chain mail and weapons that had been retrieved in raids. When they had finished, he looked just like one of them, except for the large antlers that still stood out from under his helmet which had been fashioned to make them seem as an extension of it.

"As long as you keep it on, they won't be able to tell," Layla said with a satisfied smirk on her face as she examined him.

"What now?" he asked and watched the team assemble.

"Now," Layla paused for dramatic effect, knowing of the band forming behind her. "We have a mission to get on with."

80C8

Slipping out of consciousness once more, Venetor's head drooped to his chest, only to have him awaken again with stiffness in his neck. What he would not do for a bed, or even just to lie down on the ground. Knowing it would do him no good to dwell on such things, he did his best to stretch. It was a difficult task in and of itself as his wrists were chafed to the point of bleeding. Perhaps if he chafed them some more, they would fall off and he could sleep on the floor. He then reminded himself of his title and purged such thoughts from his head. Closing his eyes, he did his best to remove himself from his current suffering by means of sleep.

His slumber was interrupted by the sound of raised voices outside of his door. Not caring enough to listen, he tuned it out, even omitting the sound of the doors ahead of him opening and closing. He was almost asleep when a pair of slender hands touched one of his forearms, causing him to jerk awake at the gesture.

"My lord," a female voice addressed him.

Snapping out of his sleep deprived delusion, Venetor saw a young woman with blonde hair dressed in a crimson gown with a burgundy cloak. She was surrounded by five others in long light grey robes that were piped in sapphire threading, the Apostles of the Unknown. Still, he did not know the face of the woman before him, and it bothered him.

"Who are-" the prince stopped as he looked further back. There, in the shadows, loomed another monstrous form, watching the door.

"Layla Ortal at your service, my lord." The woman bowed graciously, as did the others that were hooded. Even the beast in the back seemed to kneel as much as it could before him.

"I don't understand." Venetor furrowed his eyebrows. "How did you get past the guards?"

"You'd be surprised what a few rags and a would-be Hurtz could do." Layla grinned and reaching down into her dress, produced a lock pick kit.

Exchanging no further words with the Gaian prince she began to work on the locks. While she did this, Venetor's gaze zeroed in on the creature by the door. He knew it from somewhere, and yet, he could not pinpoint where. It was not until he caught sight of the golden crescent on the side of his face that he realized who it was.

"Lincerious?" he asked, surprised. "Never in my wildest dreams did I think to find you here."

"Then you thought wrong," the gruff voice of the creature replied. "Annetta sent me here while she prepares the Four Forces to come to your aid."

"Annetta is what?" Venetor inquired, only to wince upon his first wrist being released from its bond. "What exactly is she planning to do?"

"What else? Storm Pangaia," Link answered.

Words formed on Venetor's lips, but no sound came from them. He did not know what to think of the girl's strategy, nor what he had done to earn her loyalty. He had been anything but hospitable towards her or her companions.

"Why?" he finally intoned as the second bond came free. Weakened from his imprisonment, Venetor fell forward, bracing himself on his bloodied hands before hitting the ground.

"This is her way," the creature spoke. "She will fight because nobody else will. That is who Annetta Severio, heir of Orbeyus is."

"We need to hurry." Layla cut the encounter short as she helped Venetor up. "Can you walk?"

"Well, I believe they didn't break my legs," the Gaian prince stated as he staggered a little, regaining his footing.

One of the hooded figures came forward, producing a robe from inside his own and tossed it toward him. "Put this on and be quick about it."

Venetor did as he was bidden and threw the hood up over his face. They then proceeded out of the room, followed by Link at the end of the procession of monks that surrounded Layla.

"Say nothing," Layla whispered to him and then turned to the others. "If anyone approaches and asks what is going on, you are taking me to be sacrificed by the tower to ensure good continued construction."

"Razmus has revived Gaian sacrifice?" Ventor questioned in outrage.

Layla raised a hand to silence him. "Among his other decrees."

The journey out of the corridors leading to where Venetor had been kept went mostly without interaction. It was a common enough sight to see the Apostles taking a Gaian noble to be sacrificed. Venetor could still not believe such a thing had been brought back into practice.

Ascending the final steps to the main entrance, the group was met with two Hurtz guards at the door, whom quickly barred it with their spears in a threatening tone.

"Halt!" the one on the left barked. "The time for curfew is in place, where are you all taking this little thing?"

"She is to be sacrificed to the Unknown to ensure good continued construction," one of the hooded figures repeated what he had been told to say.

The Hurtz shot an angered glance at the one that had spoken. "Did I ask you? You filthy Gaian smut, I was asking your escort here with his...very strange headgear..."

The creature stepped forward and away from his post, leaving his comrade to guard the door. Wrinkling his face, which resembled that of a bear with hog tusks, he bore his eyes into Link. "I ain't ever seen you around here before."

"I guard only the Apostles, on Razmus's orders," Link stated bluntly.

"Oh really," the Hurtz snorted. "Because I have a brother who happens to guard the Apostles and he was just here this morning to do the very same thing you are doing right now."

There was an uneasy stillness in the group as they realized they were caught.

The Hurtz grinned, seeing his jackpot, "So, I suggest you take off that flimsy little helmet of yours and you all turn yourselves in, or I can't guarantee that what awaits you in the dungeons will be pretty."

Link continued to lock eyes with the Hurtz for a few minutes longer, before inhaling a deep breath and exhaling in defeat. He looked over at Layla, who gave him a small, curt nod before looking over at the guard.

"I suppose you are right," Link sighed as his hand reached up to his helmet. Then, with lightning reflexes, he head-butted the guard, driving his antlers into him with full force.

Before the other guard could respond, those in the robes were upon him and silenced him with a flash of their daggers, carefully lowering the body to the floor in order to prevent further commotion.

Link continued his struggle with the first guard, who refused to give up and was beginning to push back the antlers from him, a feral snarl beginning to erupt from him. As quickly as it began, it ended in a gurgling death cry as the creature slumped backwards, revealing Layla with a bloodied knife.

"Now we really need to get moving," she stated, looking around to see no guards anywhere else. "Shut the gates immediately behind us, walk steadily but at a hastened pace. We don't want further encounters."

Venetor watched from under the cowl of his hood as the others organized themselves, cleaning the blood from their instruments. "Not the rescue I envisioned."

Layla smirked upon hearing the comment. "Be thankful you got a rescue at all."

Chapter 30

They came upon them like wildfire. While the Fire Elves had expected to meet resistance, they were not prepared for the assault that was being led by Puc, Jason, Sarina and Matthias. A chaos fell among them as blades clashed and arrows flew from either end. It had turned out that several raiding parties were loose, and upon hearing that one was attacked, the others came to its aid like ants scrambling to the sweetness of sugar.

As the fighting raged on, Sarina and Jason found themselves separated from their companions. Any potential calls for reinforcements were drowned out by the sounds of sparring and of the torrential rain that the Water Elf mages had conjured to quell the fires that ate away at the surrounding buildings with a ferocious appetite.

Jason swung his mace at his newest opponent, a brawny-looking bare-chested man wielding a trident with three blades for prongs. His latest attempt being thwarted by the pole of the weapon, he teleported back a step, just in time to avoid impalement on the weapon's fearsome edge. Remembering his lessons with Venetor, he feinted an attack before teleporting behind, then swung again. Finally, he ended him with a fatal blow. Jason did not have much time to contemplate his achievement, however, when a thunderous, blunted impact threw him across the field. Colliding with the body of a fallen Minotaur warrior, Jason cringed as he tried to become aware of his surroundings. Anxiety took hold of him when he realized that he had dropped Helbringer during the events, which was further enrooted when an abnormally large Fire Elf wielding a club stood over him, grinning maliciously.

"Just my luck," Jason growled as he looked around for a solution to his problem of being unarmed. Seeing an axe buried in the corpse of a Fire Elf some distance away, he began to call the weapon with his mind to his hand. The grin from his opponent then disappeared. Dropping the club, the elf fell to his knees before collapsing on his side to reveal Sarina standing in his place, holding Jason's weapon.

"You forgot this," she said, tossing it to him.

Catching Helbringer, Jason felt himself go red in the face and quickly stood up, looking at the girl. "Uh...thanks."

"Anytime," she replied, then added, "Just so we are clear who needs protecting."

Jason growled, recalling their fight. "It was a one-time thing, and I said I was sorry."

Their bickering was cut off by the sound of hooves approaching. A second later, Amayeta materialized from the chaos atop her Aiethon. A glow emanated around her and the beast, preventing the rain from touching her, similar to the aura that Jason and his friends had on them when they had first gone to visit the Yasur Plains.

"The enemy loses heart!" she announced and was soon flanked by two other Ogaien. "We can make quick work of them, but only if we hurry and keep morale high."

"And how exactly are we gonna do that?" Jason raised an eyebrow.

"Simple." The Ogaien warrior's green eyes flickered. "We flood the foe in Tiamet's fury and let them know the son of Arcanthur is among them, or perhaps I should say, Jason Kinsman."

"If you say that will work," the youth replied, and turned to Sarina. "What do you think?"

"I say we make them quake!" the girl shouted and lifted her sword. "For the Four Forces!"

Turning their gazes, they faced the enemy and charged.

⊗⊘⊗

That night, the camp fires roared in a display of orange and yellow hues for miles around. The battle had been won with little casualties on the side of the Four Forces. There were no large festivities, though, aside from the usual campsite entertainment in case of a nighttime skirmish. Puc had suggested it to Jason, who complied with the wisdom of the mage. There would be time enough for celebrating when the fighting was over. Jason was also not particularly in the mood to celebrate as he sat huddled beside one of the fires, out of his armour and back in his runners, jeans and sweatshirt. He would not be in the mood until he was back with the rest of his friends in Q-16, with Annetta, Darius and Link. He was beginning to realize how useless his spat with the girl had been, even if he did not see eye-to-eye with her when it came to issues of family. This was all due to his recent conversation with Sarina.

Across the fire, Jason saw Puc staring into the flames, a drawn and fatigued expression adorning the thin face of the elf. During the day, the First Mage of Aldamoor seemed so full of life, barking orders to his troops, fighting, meeting with leaders. He seemed impervious to exhaustion and yet, when Jason looked over at him, he saw just that.

"You should get some sleep." Jason broke the silence.

Puc glanced over at the boy. "Was it but not over a year ago that I was the one giving you such advice, Kinsman? I believe I know when my body is in need of rest and when it is not."

"Sorry, you just seem tired," Jason snapped back.

The mage sighed, realizing the comment had not been malicious in any way. "Perhaps I am slightly weary from all of this campaigning, but it is a weariness of the mind and not of the body that plagues me."

"Really? Because it looks like the opposite on this end," Jason replied.

Adjusting his grip on his staff, Puc gathered his thoughts. "I am torn about whether or not we are doing the right thing here, Jason, continuing to chase a broken people."

"They attacked you guys if I'm not correct," the youth reminded him. "Though if I can be honest, you caging up Tamora like that in the public square did seem borderline dictator."

"They did," Puc agreed with him on the first part and then added. "Tamora needed to be humiliated, just in the way she humiliated the Water Folk. It was harsh but necessary. Anyways, at this point, we are the ones chasing them, I feel. That last battle, it was as though they had lost the heart for it. We have finished their morale."

Jason looked at the mage in confusion, not quite understanding what he was trying to communicate. The entire time, Puc had stated the importance of removing the Fire Elves from being a force of power.

"We are going back, Jason." The mage summarized his thoughts. "Tamora must be put to trial. They have done much damage, but genocide was never a part of this crusade. I will not stand for it, and it is not the will of the Unknown. No one has that right. I have done my duty as First Mage of Aldamoor and have driven the threat of Fire Elves back."

There was a brief pause before he spoke again. "I feel I have not however done my duty as the Advisor to the heir of Orbeyus and the son of Arcanthur."

"You did, and don't even start this I have failed crap," Jason growled. "You aren't allowed to play that card anymore. Things happened, things beyond our control and we just have to suck it up and go with it. That's what you taught us with Anne."

Hearing the comment, Puc said nothing else to Jason and instead resorted to studying the youth's face to the point that Jason felt himself go red in the ears.

"What?" Jason growled finally, unable to stand it.

"I was just trying to discern," the mage spoke, "When it was that you grew up."

Taken aback, Jason tried to say something in return, only to see the whirl of Puc's cloak as the mage spun on his heel in the direction of the tents, his voice carrying past the sound of the flames. "Good night, Kinsman."

Puc then made his way back to his tent. Barely having time to light the candles in his room, he was greeted by a visitor in a hooded cloak. Lowering the cowl, he revealed himself to be Matthias.

"You asked to see me?" he glanced at the mage.

"Yes, I have need to speak to you about some things, and have a favour to ask."

ഇൽയ

The escape had not been easy. The second the guards were found dead at the front gates, the blasting of a great horn could be heard all throughout the sleeping city. While Layla, Link, Venetor and the others were already a fair distance away, they had still managed to run into a squad of guards, a portion of whom were Gaian, not Hurtz.

"Some of the noble houses swore allegiance to Razmus. It was how he was able to take control of the whole planet," Layla explained to Link, noticing his confusion.

"Cowards and traitors," Venetor spat upon hearing this.

"Survivalists," Layla corrected him.

Their band was soon joined by the others that had been posted all throughout their escape route. Not long after they had done so, Link took note of what looked to be smoke on the horizon behind them. He knew better than to think it was friendly, and tapped Layla on the shoulder to get her attention.

"We've got company again, I think," he pointed out.

Annoyed, but focused none the less, Layla pulled out a pair of scouting binoculars from her belt and scanned the skyline.

"It's a whole platoon." She lowered them and confirmed her suspicion to the others. "We will be outnumbered and overpowered. Our best option will be to hide."

"I say we take them head on!" growled Venetor in protest. He'd had just about enough of skulking about in the shadows, and his warrior blood boiled within him for a fight.

"With all due respect, my prince." Layla turned to him. "We are neither properly armed nor do we have the numbers to defeat a platoon of Hurtz, even if some of those there will be Gaian. There is also not a psychic among us except for you, and well…"

Layla tapped on the collar which was still fitted around Venetor's neck. "Until this comes off, you are as disadvantaged as the rest of us."

His rage surfacing, Venetor curled his hand into a fist and struck at the nearest tree, the trunk burst into splinters. Layla, Link and the others watched in astonishment.

"The collar does not work on feral form abilities," he stated.

Those gathered began to mutter to one another in amazement, not having known about it. Aware they were wasting time, Layla interjected. "Even still, not everyone is fortunate enough to be a lion. Now, I suggest we leave before it is too late."

"Fine," huffed Venetor. "I still say we would have stood a chance."

They spoke no more on the matter and were off, disappearing among the trees which hugged the whole of the suburbs of the city in a great dense forest. Running through the thick greenery, they could soon hear the sounds of soldiers following behind, shouting commands.

"They will catch us soon if we do not stand our ground!" Venetor shouted as he ran. "We've no choice but to stand and fight!"

Cursing under her breath, Layla did her best to focus on a plan. Everything in her mind, was a blur as adrenaline clouded her thoughts. Something then caught her attention out of the corner of her eye. Stopping dead in her tracks, she looked over to see a grotto in the side of a hill. She looked behind, not yet able to see those pursuing her, and a desperate tactic formed in her head.

"There." She pointed to it and began to run in the direction of the cave.

"You can't be serious." The Gaian prince glanced at her.

"Oh, very much so," she said and turned to the others. "I need five of the fastest to keep going. You hear them coming in too close, you know what to do. The rest of us, we hide until they pass."

Their orders given, they split up. The grotto was not far from them, and it was much larger on the inside than it looked, giving them the advantage. Their eyes adjusting to the dark, they ventured further down the rocky path inside the cave, the roots of trees hanging overhead like thick vines.

Link, still in his cursed feral form, was able to see far better than most of those there, and what he was able to discern brought a feeling of unease to him as he examined the walls. On the few that were not covered in moss or lichen, he was able to make out scribbling and images.

"I've got a bad feeling about this," he grunted.

"You woulds too if yous homes be invadsin," a shrieking, shrill voice said from out of nowhere.

Everyone present sprang on edge, whipping out any manner of weapons they had on them. Using his abilities, Venetor adjusted his eyes to the murkiness of the cave. Upon doing so, he wished otherwise, for what he saw was not a pretty sight. The creature which had spoken stood about forty feet from their group. Atop its head was a tuft of shaggy brown hair which seemed to disappear beneath the many folds of the creature's head, which consisted of wrinkles coming from the giant Cheshire cat grin, or folds of fat. It hobbled about the cave with its scrawny arms tucked into both sides and a large, round belly protruding outwards, through the rags it wore. In Venetor's opinion, it was repulsive.

"What in the name of the Unknown?" the prince's mouth dropped.

"Now, nows, yous no usem Unknowns namesum in vanes. Only Fefj getsum to does that, we is homeboys after alls." The creature grinned.

A dragging sound could then be heard from the other end of the cave, as though someone were hauling an immense load they could not carry.

"Oje back, master!" a croaking voice called out a little too loud for the groups liking.

Fefj, losing interest in his guests, turned around to the new arrival, a creature of olive green complexion standing about two feet tall with an abnormally large nose and long pointed ears to match. It wore what appeared to be woollen rags wrapped around its body, and some on its head like a makeshift cap. A thin, fur-tipped tail trailed behind it as its huge yellow eyes regarded those gathered with a shifty disposition. Behind it, it carried a burlap sack almost as large as Fefj.

"You founds what I asked for?" The troll's grin widened.

"I think Oje has, master," the smaller creature assured him, and turning around, he opened the sack and crawled into it to rummage through its contents.

"You were dead," Link stated in disbelief, glaring at Fefj. "Puc turned you to stone."

"You know this thing?" Layla said off to the side to Link.

"We met him on Morwick in a cave," the youth replied to her.

"And the little one?" she inquired.

"No clue, but it looks like a goblin," he concluded.

"Fefj no turns to stoneses. Fefj livem high life in luxurious caves in…" the troll gathered attention to himself, then paused to belch, chuckled and continued, "Wherever diss backwater places be."

Taking a torch that one of the fighters had on them, Layla struck it with flint, igniting it. Everyone drew back a pace in revulsion upon seeing what they were dealing with.

"Cants takes the handsome face, me sees," Fefj chortled. "All troll ladies dies to be Fefj mate, mustum bees my pearlescents smiles."

The goblin then came back out of the sack, still oblivious for the most part to the visitors. Link, Layla, Venetor and the other fighters gaped in astonishment at what the creature carried in either hand, socks of varied colours, along with pens. Seeing these, Fefj's already naturally smiling face drew itself into an even bigger grin as the scrawny arms reached out for its prize.

"Yes! Single sockses and penses for writing the masterworks!" the troll squealed.

"Oje still not understands why master write on single socks and not papers." The goblin observed his superior revel in the sack full of socks and pens of varying shape and size.

Snapping out of his fervour, Fefj looked over at the goblin. "Why, to bring joys to all who reads it, makem it hards to reads, brings more joy."

"If master says so, it must be so." Oje nodded, having emptied out the entire bag. "Oje will fetch more for master now in other worlds."

"Goes! Goes! Thises only lastses for one chapters of epic troll saga of Fefj." The troll waved away his servant, who disappeared with the sack into the darkness of the cave. "Maybe one paragraph if I stretches it."

"We've no time for this," Layla hissed. "There is a platoon out there waiting to annihilate us if they find out where we are hiding. Now we all need to be quiet."

The creature flinched upon seeing that Layla was a Gaian female, but when he was sure she was not coming near him, he straightened his posture and looked to the group again.

"Quiet, you says?" The troll was intrigued. "So I singsum mating calls, brings pantaloons right heres."

"No, that is the reverse of what we need," Venetor protested.

"Don't argue with it," Link told him. "It will deliberately do the opposite to irritate you."

"Fefj knows best mating calls," the thing kept going. "Soooo louds, can be heards on other side of planet. Like sos."

The troll began to clear its throat in an overly exaggerated manner, coughing and huffing as everyone in the cave began to panic, not knowing what the thing would do next. Then, just as it was about to open its mouth, the creature went stiff. Its great grinning jaw going slack and eyes rolling to the back of its skull, the troll fell forward like a cut down tree and landed with a thud on the floor, face first. Standing behind it, was Layla with a large rock lifted over her head in both hands.

"Well, what? It wasn't like any of you were going to do anything," she intoned as she dropped the stone on the ground beside him. "Bind it, gag it and whatever you do, do not let it speak, and go find that goblin and silence it as well."

"Yes, Layla," one of the warriors acknowledged her as another went to go look for the goblin and with the help of two others. The first moved in towards the troll, only to realize, "I do believe it is dead."

Not the least bit fazed, she turned back to them. "Bind it and gag it nonetheless, then move it further in. I don't plan to stay here any longer than I have to. We move out at nightfall. They will be less able to track us in the dark."

"No sign of the goblin," the second soldier came back. "There was a small opening towards the end of the cave, it must have left that way."

"Stay there and make sure to apprehend it if it comes back," she commanded.

The soldiers set to work once their orders were given. Venetor observed all of this as it occurred, his gaze most focused on Layla as she worked the crowd of fighters, hearing what each had to say and giving out further orders.

"Where were you stationed before all of this?" the Gaian prince asked her.

Layla turned her attention to him. "I was a militia camp leader, my lord. Not one of any note, either."

"A pity, such wasted talent." He shook his head. "Had I been aware of you, I would have had you promoted quickly, until you reached a rank of some meaning within the Gaian army."

Layla snorted at the thought before replying. "And who would then be leading your rescue if I had been? The Unknown has strange reasons for things playing out as they do."

"Indeed he does," Venetor agreed. "When this is all over, however, I will keep my promise. When I ascend the throne, you will be at my side."

"You make it sound like a marriage proposal when you say that, my lord," she chuckled.

"I am a widower, am I not?" Venetor laughed. "To be clear with my intentions, however, I mean as a war councillor. I will need good minds like yours when we take back the Gaian throne."

The young Gaian female continued to look at him. She had heard stories of Venetor in her camp, knew of him only in passing as the heir to the Gaian throne and here he was, offering her a promotion, a better life. It was more than she could have ever asked for, but one question remained, would they survive the night? Turning her thoughts from wishful thinking, she looked to where the entrance to the cave was.

"Let's get you out of here alive and worry about military advancements later, my lord."

Chapter 31

Running was how the visions always started. Annetta's legs pumped faster and faster, her feet striking the solid earth beneath the sea of grass as she went. Even the scenery had not changed from her visitations, but then she realized what had. It was only her feet upon the ground, and on them were her sneakers instead of unidentified animal paws that padded against the earth. She then also realized that she was running not towards but from something, the adrenaline rush to her gut confirmed it. Conscious of her actions, she stopped and tried to summon Severbane from its dormant state on its necklace.

Before she could react, an unseen force knocked the girl to the ground some distance away. Shaking off the shock, she looked up in astonishment. There, but a few feet away stood a shaggy brown wolf that was about the size of a small horse, its yellow eyes observing her like two great moons, a pink tongue lolling in its open mouth. Feeling the leather-wrapped hilt of Severbane beneath her fingers, Annetta gripped it tightly and withdrawing it from its scabbard, used the sword to prop herself up into a seated position as she analyzed the beast before her. The wolf returned her stare and in the period of time that the two of them watched each other, she was able to gather that the creature meant her no harm. In fact, she felt comfortable around it, at home, as though she had known it her whole life, and the more she stared into the golden orbs that were the wolf's eyes, the more she realized that there was something uncanny about them.

As soon as her lips began to form into words of question, however, a thunderous roar could be heard all around, blotting out all other sound. Annetta rose and spun around with her sword in front to be confronted by a second creature. There, on the other side of her was a lion, also about the size of the wolf, its mane and fur the colour of light gold, contrasting its amber eyes. Its tail swished back and forth in a challenging and authoritative manner as it measured Annetta with its gaze. Again, the feeling of home came over the girl as she looked at it. Turning back to the wolf, however, the same feeling arose in her again, and then looking back at the lion, it was followed by confusion.

"Annetta," a familiar voice spoke from behind.

The girl fully turned around to find Link standing beside the wolf. He was dressed just as she remembered him when he left for Gaia, in his armour. A thousand things rushed through Annetta's head as soon as she saw him, and no sooner had her legs began to move in his direction, another voice came from behind again.

"You cannot trust the boy," it spoke in a commanding tone.

Annetta pivoted again, this time seeing Venetor standing beside the lion, his arms crossed across his chest as he usually did when in a casual stance.

"What are you on about?" she demanded of him.

"He left you to go to Gaia, remember?" the Gaian prince replied.

"I left to find Venetor, to get a way in just how I was commanded." Link reminded her.

Annetta glanced back and forth, turning sideways so that she could see both of them at the same time. A twisted feeling formed in her gut as she tried to make heads and tails of what was going on.

"Don't listen to him, Annetta," Venetor scoffed. "He's already forgotten the last encounter you both had."

The girl looked over at the boy with a forlorn face. Link returned her gaze, his eyes reflecting the same feelings the girl was going through at that moment. He took a step forward, his arms outstretched towards her.

"Anne, please," he whispered.

The girl lowered the sword as he came to her, and she too began to move towards him. Just as they were but a few feet from each other, Link stopped, unable to move. Confused, Annetta watched as he began to bang on what looked like an invisible wall that was dividing the two of them. Horrified, Annetta began to rap against the wall with her fist, trying to find some weakness in it, but all in vain.

"You may be bonded to him, but he already told you how he feels about you." Venetor continued to feed her uncertainty. "Is that who you really want to be with?"

Annetta turned back again to him and saw that beside Venetor now stood both Orbeyus and her father. The hairs on the back of her neck stood on end as behind them also materialized other figures, some of which Annetta recognized from paintings and sculptures in Severio Castle. An anger overcame her quickly as she realized that she was not having a vision, and what this all was, what it was meant to represent.

"I will never succumb to some stupid fate!" she snapped and turning back to Link, continued to pound furiously on the barrier between them.

"This is not a matter of fate, Annetta." Orbeyus was the one addressing her this time. "It is about understanding where you come from and who you are."

ഇൽൽ

Just as Annetta was about to reply with a venom-filled comment, everything around her went dark. Tossing and turning, the girl woke up to find herself in her room, her sheets soaked with sweat, her heart pounding in her ribcage and her muscles still tense from the temper she had submitted to in her nightmare. Peeling back the layers she was under that were no longer comfortable, she walked over to her window and opened it, letting in the cool suburban air.

Sliding down on the floor, she flipped open her C.T.S. watch and stared at the number panel for a few minutes. Just who exactly did she think she could bother in the middle of the night? Hesitating and finding herself embarrassed, she closed the watch, burying her chin in her arms as they hugged her legs. As soon as she had done so, her eyes began to droop once more. She then found her way back to bed, reminding herself it was all just a dream.

ഇൽൽ

They entered the camp by midday. Layla led the way, followed by her warriors as well as Link, who had now reverted back from his feral form and Venetor. The Gaian prince knew full well the state of his people by now, and yet seeing the shabby camp, he could not help but feel a renewed anger brew inside of him. From what he could tell, many had not had access to a proper bath, food nor a good night's sleep, things that once had been taken for granted on Gaia, things that were expected to be the norm. Those who recognized him through his own filth and unkempt appearance bowed as he passed by. The sight disgusted Venetor. He had no right to such a thing, for all the good he had done them. Gaia had fallen under his watch, even if his father had been king.

Once they had ventured far enough into the camp, the warriors began to disperse to tend to the wounded and to get some rest. No one ever knew when they would next be needed, and time for recovery was a rare commodity. Those left standing from the original party were Layla, Link and Venetor.

"Lord Venetor," Layla addressed him, "If you would please follow me."

Venetor complied with the request and trailed after the young Gaian female, with Link still accompanying them. It would be a lie to say that the younger Gaian's presence did not disturb Venetor, given the trespasses of the Heallaws family. Still, he did his best to ignore such facts, as he had his feral form when he had been rescued. Link had no reason to show his loyalty to Venetor after how he had been treated, yet he did, showing no blame to the prince for his family curse. It baffled him.

Soon after, they entered a medium-sized tent with a few cots in it, as well as a large table that had been cobbled together from various pieces of wood. In fact, the more Venetor observed the room, the more he realized how many things in it had been repurposed to serve as military quarters.

"My lord, now that we have you back, I feel we must turn our attention to other things," Layla began after a few more men and women had joined the three of them in the tent. "Pangaia must be freed from Razmus at all costs."

"This task is far easier said than done," one of the other women in the tent stated with a huff. "We are outnumbered, and the Hurtz are far stronger than any Gaian here."

"Not true," Venetor interrupted. "What many of you do not know is that the collars placed on everyone captured will not restrain your feral form abilities, only psychic. The hold Razmus has on the Hurtz can also be taken from him should one of the towers be destroyed He is using a stereophonic signal which has been designed specifically for the Hurtz to hear to control them.

Chatter erupted from those few who were in the tent as they began to question the prince all at once. Seeing the chaos, Layla slammed her hand down on the table so hard that one of the planks came loose.

"Apologies, but that needed to be done," she huffed, and seeing their attention on her, continued. "How do you know this?"

"Because we concluded it while on Earth," Link said as all eyes fell on him. "When Gladius, who had lost an ear, was not affected. Look, all of this began when Razmus was freed from the tower. It would make sense that there was something inside it that was affecting the Hurtz and that the other tower is somehow involved in it."

"The other tower is being guarded," Venetor added. "This much I know from reports I had received long before the fall of the capital. Hurtz were being drawn to it like mayflies. At first, no one could make sense of it, but once the facts were connected, it all did. One of the towers must be destroyed. Once this is accomplished, Razmus's hold on the Hurtz will be no more."

"What of the Hurtz we must fight in order to do this?" Link asked as his mind wandered to thoughts of Brakkus. "They are not killers, not out of their own free will. Sure, Hurtz love to fight, but so do many of us, and many resent the story of Razmus and their origin."

Venetor stood silently over the table. He stared absentmindedly at the hand-drawn maps of Pangaia and the surrounding areas. It was a concept he had not stopped to think about until that very moment. The Hurtz were not the enemy, and yet if they went down their current path, thousands would die. The aches of his recent imprisonment seemed to flare up with the extra burden added to his shoulders. A plan, however, began to formulate in his head.

"It may not have to come to that," the prince spoke once more and looked over at Link, "Do you still have access to your ship that you came here in?"

"I do." the youth nodded. "We hid it close to my father's house… or rather, what's left of it."

"Good, we will need the engine and fuel cells," Venetor spoke as he revealed his plan. "If we do this right, there will be a minimal amount of bloodshed."

"And what exactly is that?" Layla inquired.

"We're going to make a bomb."

"I'm sorry, you're what?" Link's eyes went wide.

"Standard military procedure," Venetor explained. "We sneak a few people in, set off the explosive, and minimize the casualties, plain and simple. The Hurtz will be out of Razmus's control, and we take back Pangaia."

There was a bout of silence around the table as those present weighed the option. It certainly sounded more appealing than full-out war.

"What of the noble houses that aligned themselves with Razmus?" One of the men that had come into the tent spoke. "Tower or no tower, they will fight."

"They may lose heart when they see what they are faced with," Venetor commented. "Still, it would be best for us to free those who are in the camps, the soldiers in particular. Our numbers here from what

I see are not ideal for open warfare and I assume none of your fighters are psychics either judging from the rescue efforts…"

"Annetta will have the Four Forces ready," Link assured him. "She's not one to pull out of something like this when her mind is set."

"We can only hope," Venetor grunted in reply. "For now, we need those parts, and a few brave ones to carry out the deed."

"I will go," Layla spoke without hesitation the moment Venetor finished his sentence.

"Layla, no!" the woman that had spoken earlier boomed. "We need you here to guide us."

"You do not need me." She shook her head and pointed to Venetor. "You've the future king of Gaia for that now, and I can't allow anyone else to go through with this."

"Then I'm going with you," Link announced.

Not a word was said from anyone when he made his decision. Link was aware that it had nothing to do with him not having been in the camp for long or of him not being a warrior of renown. It was something he had almost forgotten in the span of time that he had returned, but it had come back to haunt him nonetheless. He looked up to see the various glares which shot his way like hot knives. Touching his scar and tracing it in such a way that to the others it would appear he was brushing hair out of his face, he was made aware yet again of his place in Gaian society.

Venetor was among those who stared and breaking eye contact, he readied himself to leave the tent. "Do what must be done."

೮೦೧೪

As soon as the bell for their first period change rang, Annetta quickly left the classroom, Darius following closely behind her. Going to the office, she handed in her note that said she would be away for a week due to a death in the family, the funeral for which she would need to fly over to British Columbia to attend. The work was, of course, a forgery created by Darius himself, who had insisted that Annetta get time off school to be able to organize the attack on Pangaia more efficiently.

Finally, at the end of the day, after having received the pile of homework she would miss once her teachers had been told, the duo marched to the bus stop and waited.

"Still no word from Jason this whole time?" Darius asked, to which Annetta shook her head as she fidgeted with the bus pass in her hands. "You tried reaching him or Matt with your abilities?"

"I don't think you can reach across worlds like that," she replied, keeping her voice low due to the other students around them.

The bus pulling up at its usual time, they boarded, grabbing seats close to the back in order to continue talking.

"I know you guys fought before he left, but it's not like him to go on without saying anything," Darius commented. "I'd try reaching Matt, Puc or Sarina if that was the case. His childish skulking isn't helping any of this."

"Wouldn't they have reached out by now if something was up?" Annetta mused. "I mean, honestly, it doesn't take much. Just a quick call."

"Yeah, it's like when someone doesn't call their parents on time," he said. "They could be elbow-deep in Fire Elves. You saw what happened."

Annetta growled in frustration, raking her fingers through her wind-tangled hair. Her palm slapping her thigh as it came down, she glanced at the C.T.S. on her wrist. Perhaps Darius was right and she should try reaching the others instead. Still, it seemed odd that no one had managed to slip a single message through, Jason most of all. It was unlike him. She knew he had been angry with her when he left, but they had had spats before and recovered. That was, after all, the way of solid friendships. No disagreement was ever permanent.

She did not have much more time to contemplate this as the bus turned the corner where their stop was, and they made their way over to the door. As soon as they had exited, Annetta made sure they were alone and flipped open the C.T.S. watch. Typing in the code, she waited for a response of any sort as a ball of tension formed in her gut.

"05 here," Puc's voice rang across from the device.

Relief filled Annetta as her shoulders slumped under the weight of her bag. "01 here. I just wanted a status report, I guess."

There was a long pause before the voice of the mage could be heard again. **"Tamora has been captured. We prepare for trial."**

"That means you'll be back soon, right?" Annetta asked hopefully.

There was another pause. Annetta felt the tension resurface inside of her.

"I do not know when we shall return, 01," Puc concluded.

"What about J.K., Sarina and Matt?" she inquired. "J.K. hasn't answered anytime I've tried to call him on the C.T.S. Is he alright?"

"Everyone is fine, 01. There is no need for panic of any sort," the mage assured her. **"Now I must be going. The first phase of the trial is about to begin. 05 out."**

The communication was cut off and Annetta flipped the screen of her watch down in anger. On the brighter side, she knew Jason was alright. It also meant she would give him an earful when he came back.

"I guess that solves that," Darius chuckled, seeing the riled expression on Annetta's face.

"Yeah, no kidding," the girl grumbled as they continued to head to her house.

Still some distance away, Annetta flipped open the watch again and typed in another sequence.

"105 here." Link could then be heard from the other end.

"01 here. Status report," she addressed him in a commanding tone.

"We've freed Venetor," he told her. **"Layla, myself and a few of the others did it, but things are still looking bad. Razmus has an army of Hurtz under his command."**

"We knew that part already, what else?" she questioned.

"Venetor plans to send Layla and myself to blow up the tower using an explosive made from the ship I took to get here. It should remove the hold on the Hurtz that the waves are having."

Now it was Annetta's turn to pause during her C.T.S. communications. Something inside of her wanted to protest about the whole thing, but instead, something entirely different came out.

"Who's Layla?" she asked.

"My old commanding officer," Link said nonchalantly. **"She's the one that rallied the camp and ran the mission to get Venetor back. I've gotta say, she's really something else. I don't remember her being this daring back in the Gaian militia."**

"I see," Annetta did her best to maintain a steady tone. "Well, if you guys think it will work, then go for it. Who am I to say anything?"

"Uh...one of the leaders of the Four Forces?" the Gaian youth reminded her with a chuckle.

"Point taken," she replied as she and Darius reached the front steps of the house.

"There's one other thing, Anne," Link continued. **"Venetor wants to try going about this whole thing with minimal casualties,**

especially the Hurtz, because they're not in command of what they do. Among their ranks will also be Gaians that have bent their knee to Razmus, and those are the ones we really need to be on the lookout for."

Annetta sighed as she heard this. It had been something she had not stopped to think of in the whirlwind of preparations. Brakkus's grinning face came to the forefront of her mind for a split second, as well as that of Gladius. She tried to picture herself having to fight either of them on the battlefield, knowing they were not in control of what they were doing. A sinking feeling etched itself into her mind as she contemplated what to do.

"There could be a way around this," Darius interrupted. "We could create a tranquillizer of sorts."

"For the entire army?" she inquired.

"In potion form, yes," the young mage continued. "All it requires is contact to the skin, and the victim will fall into a slumber. We would only need it long enough for the tower to be taken down, after all. If you give everyone a blunted weapon, which every army is sure to have in their barracks for training, this could work. We would also give out an antidote to those with the weapons, rendering them immune to it."

The more Annetta heard, the more she liked this idea. She then turned back to the C.T.S. "Sound like a plan to you?"

"Best I've heard," Link replied. **"I should be off now. We have to go retrieve the ship to salvage. 105 out."**

Annetta closed the watch and then looked at Darius. "I guess we have our hands full."

"I'll worry about the potion," he informed her. "We'll get the other leaders together today and let them know what we just came up with, and tell them to mobilize the troops."

As the door opened and they crossed the threshold of the house, Annetta noticed no one was home. She shrugged it off, thinking her parents may have decided to go shopping or had other plans. Putting her bag away in her room, she took the card key out from the pocket of her jean jacket and slid it down behind the mirror. The teleporting pad appearing as it always did, Annetta and then Darius made their way down.

The sensation of waves crashing around her left her limbs, and the girl got up. She then waited until her friend materialized beside her.

Extending a hand to help him up, she opened the enormous twin doors with her abilities.

Annetta did not expect the sight she was to witness next on the other side. There, standing before her was both of her parents, her brother, Liam and Jason's mother, Talia. Annetta felt her entire body seize up like a deer in headlights.

"Uh... hey guys." She blinked a few times, trying to snap out of the confusion. "What are you all doing here?"

"Well, when we received a phone call from your school," Aurora spoke with her arms crossed, "with condolences about an Uncle Greg from British Columbia having passed away and how you were going to be gone a week, we knew something was up. So, talk, young lady. What is going on?"

Annetta looked over at Darius, who wore a blank expression on his face, unsure of what to say to her. The girl sighed, looking down at her worn sneakers and then back up at the faces of those present.

"You may want to sit down. It's kind of a long story."

Chapter 32

Jason felt his eyes drooping as he sat dressed from head to toe in his armour in the Mage Council chamber. Once everyone had gathered, they had been seated and Tamora had been brought in to stand trial before Puc, as well as a host of other mages. At first, Jason had done his best to pay attention to everything being said, alert and ready to enter the fray at any given moment. The longer the trial went on, however, the less enthusiastic he became, until he found himself being nudged by Sarina or Matthias in order to stay awake. Grumbling, he shifted himself in the seat he occupied while he tried to focus in on what one of the Archmages was saying to Puc and the gathered assembly.

"We shouldn't be here," Matthias whispered to him after a few minutes. "This whole thing is a farce."

"Oh, and what's your bright idea?" Sarina turned to him with a frown.

"Take the other half of the Four Forces and ride to meet up with Annetta," he stated. "Sitting here and waiting around isn't doing anyone any good."

"We need to be mindful of their procedures," Sarina explained. "Mutual respect. It's what the Four Forces are built on to begin with."

Jason sat in the midst of this while trying to listen to the proceedings. On the one hand, he completely agreed with Sarina. They had to respect the way that the Water Elves handled things, it was only fair. On the other hand, Matthias was right as well. The longer they sat around, the less likely it would be that Annetta would wait with whatever plan she had cooked up to free Venetor. In fact, for all he knew, it was already too late. If only his C.T.S. still worked.

"I'll talk to Puc the second I have a chance," Jason assured Matthias and then turned to Sarina. "How long do these things last, anyway?"

"Days, weeks," the girl mused on the subject as she tried to come up with a more accurate answer. "I've read even months."

Matthias gritted his teeth hearing what she said. "Annetta won't have that kind of time. If there's one thing I know, she's not one to wait around."

"I know that better than anyone," Jason growled. "So what would you have me do?"

"Let me go to her," the assassin spoke his mind. "I can take a portion of the army with me, join with her or go ahead and scout out what is happening. It's your choice, but as I see it now, I serve no purpose here but a glorified bodyguard."

One of the mages sitting close by shushed the trio, shooting them an angry glare with his feral blue eyes. They remained silent in response for a few seconds before Jason spoke again in a hushed tone. "As soon as this is done, we go to Puc. No more excuses about First Mage business. I want you to go ahead, Matt. Let me know what's going on with Anne. I can't reach her on the C.T.S. and it's starting to bother me."

"You mean in all this time you haven't communicated with her?" Matthias glared at him with a perplexed look. "Why didn't you say anything to anyone? That's kind of important, don't you think?"

"I…" Jason bit his tongue as the mage who had hushed them earlier turned around yet again with a nasty look, causing him to lower his voice even more. "At first I didn't want to talk to her. She really ticked me off when she decided to go after Venetor and split up the Four Forces. Then we were always on the march and fighting, so it was kind of the last thing on my mind."

Seeing the mage getting ready to rise to tell them off, Matthias rose first to leave, before turning one final time around to Jason. "Next time you have a communications breakdown of this kind, warn us."

"Where are you going?" Sarina inquired.

"To solve it."

∞∞

After having explained in great length and detail all of the happenings since Venetor's arrival to her parents and Talia, Annetta and Darius, along with the others in Q-16 had set off to work quickly in assembling what was available of the Four Forces. Before they knew it, tents were being raised yet again around the Eye to All Worlds as soldiers from all four races trickled in from their respective portals.

Annetta walked past clusters of soldiers and tents as she made her way around to the main tent where the meeting was to take place. Her reddish-brown hair tied in a braid, she was dressed fully in her armour with her overly large jean jacket overtop for luck. Severbane at her hip and her shield strapped to her back, the girl felt right at home among the scores of strange creatures. She remembered it had not been so long ago that it had been the opposite. Now it felt more like home to her than being a high school student on the brink of graduating and having to choose a career. It felt as though this was reality, and the life she always returned to was the make-believe one, a mask she had to put on to try and fit in. The depression of the thought sinking in for a split second, Annetta sighed and shook it off, then continued down her given path.

She was distracted, however, when the form of a certain Ogaien caught the corner of her eye. Turning her head fully, Annetta saw Natane speaking with three other Ogaien whom she recognized as Mothers Nita, Ahota and Enola. The Great Mother seemed to be giving instructions on where the Ogaien troops would be stationed in order to complement the other military units. Annetta waited off to the side until she was sure that Natane had finished, watching the other three depart in different directions.

Seeing an opening, Annetta approached her. "Great Mother Natane."

"Young Annetta Severio." The Ogaien's green eyes twinkled in recognition. "I will be at the tent shortly. There were some things I needed to discuss with the other Mothers, should we need to leave more urgently than expected."

"That's actually not why I'm here," the girl admitted. "I was wondering if I could speak to you in private…"

The Ogaien studied the girl curiously, not sure what she was driving at.

"It's about a dream I had," Annetta finished her thought.

"A dream?" Natane inquired.

"Yeah." The girl shuffled her feet as she centred her thoughts. "I thought with your experience with Visiums, you would be the person to approach with this. You see, Venetor had Jason and I meditating on our feral forms before he was captured. I continued studying on my own, but I haven't been able to figure out what my feral form is and last night…"

Annetta recounted her dream to Natane in great detail. The Ogaien woman listened intently to everything being said and only nodded the odd time to show she was paying attention, letting the girl finish without any interruption. She remained silent for some time after, before speaking.

"What is certain is this," the Ogaien concluded, "Your subconscious is torn and continues to tear itself apart as you are trying

356

to find your place in the world. This is not uncommon for one your age."

"But why am I feeling torn?" the girl asked. "Shouldn't what I want and who I'm supposed to be obvious?"

"No Annetta, it shouldn't," she replied, "Because very often those two things are very different, but eventually we are forced to choose, for we cannot continue to stay on the edge. In the dream, you said on one side there was a lion and members of the Severio clan, while on the other was a great wolf and Lincerious. It is a metaphor for choosing between the burden of the legacy your family carries or having a new start as a lone wolf, much like Lincerious."

The girl nodded, hearing what was said. It had been as she suspected, for the most part at least. Even worse was the realization that she could not choose, or at least it felt that way. No matter how much she tried to fight it, she was a Severio, and that part she could not throw away. She was also her own person, not someone who would bow down to fate, no matter how much someone claimed it had to be so because it was written.

"Thank you, Great Mother," she spoke, noting the tent they were to gather in further up ahead, "And we should probably get going, they'll be waiting for us."

🙤🙧

The light of the television screen flickering as the scenery on it changed, Xander and Liam's fingers moved across the video game controllers with athletic ease, controlling the army men onscreen in the first-person shooter. Having come down to the Lab with their parents and heard the story Annetta had recounted, the two of them did their best to tune out the earlier events. Finally, unable to bear the silence any longer, Xander allowed his character to be shot onscreen, watching the death replay from the game.

"Man, we almost had them," Liam growled in anger. "What gives?"

Xander tossed the controller down on his bed and huffed. "It's not fair."

"Uh... yeah, no kidding, you just cost us a seventy-plus kill streak," Liam fumed.

"That's not what I meant," Xander eyed his friend with contempt.

Snapping out of his gamer rage, the second boy then understood what Xander was going on about and put down his own controller.

Turning around, he saw the frustration building up behind Xander's blue eyes. His own feelings were not much different on the matter, but he knew full well the anger of his mother when he did not obey her, and so was not one to press an issue. Hell had no fury like a parent scorned.

"Look," Liam sighed, "You heard our parents. We can't go with Annetta or them to Gaia. It's too dangerous and we aren't trained."

Further infuriated with his friend's train of thought, Xander's scowl increased tenfold as he stood up. Walking away from his bed, he looked out the window. Everything he had ever known had changed so quickly in the span of just a few months. The powers, what his sister had been up to for the past two years, who his parents were, everything he had ever known was upside down, and now, when it seemed his family was to be involved with something yet again, he was going to be left behind, simply for the fact that he was, according to them, too young.

Liam was not blind to the annoyance of his friend. Perhaps it was because Jason had shown him his powers sooner, or perhaps it was the fact that his own brother was already away elsewhere and the ties he felt to his mother were not nearly as strong as Xander's were to his parents, but he did not feel as upset about everything going on. Whatever the reason was on a subconscious level, he did not know, but he knew Xander was taking it differently than he.

"I don't care what they said," Xander spoke, ending the staring contest with the window. "I'm going with them."

"Uh... and how exactly are you going to do that?" the second boy inquired as he slid off the bed they had been sitting on.

"I don't know, all I know is that I have to." Xander wracked his head as he tried to come up with an answer. "We need a key to get down there to begin with, but we..."

Before Xander could complete his sentence, Liam pulled out a metallic card key from his pocket and showed it to his friend. "Titus didn't show you those rooms with the hand scanner that get filled with whatever you want after you scan one, did he?"

The grin on the boy's face spread as he looked at the thin metal plate with renewed hope, a plan hatching in his head. "He did. How'd you get that?"

"Swiped it off the desk from inside the room I made when Anne and Darius took my inside one and they weren't looking." Liam smirked. "Not hard when they're fighting like two lovebirds."

"Ew, don't make me picture that." Xander scrunched up his nose. He was fairly certain Annetta and Darius were not together, and the fact that he had known Darius for so long made it even stranger.

"Too late now, I guess." Liam snickered as he headed for the door. "Come on, let's grab our shoes and get down there. We won't have much time."

ഇൻരെ

The meeting having come to an end, Annetta and the leaders of the Four Forces dispersed quickly from the tent. There was much to prepare and little time in which to do it, for Skyris had already begun calibrations to shoot the cannon. All that remained was some form of contact with Link on Gaia, and the plan could be set into motion. From there on, everything would happen in the blink of an eye.

Darius, dressed now in full war mage armour, spotted Annetta leaving and followed closely behind, using his long strides to catch up her.

"The potion is being distributed to all fighters," he informed her. "Have you told the leaders about the blunted weapons?"

"First thing I did," she assured him. "I made it very clear that they're to try and minimize the amount of Hurtz that are harmed during all of this. What really happens, though, we won't have much control over, and that's the sad part of it all."

"Yeah, that's true." Darius nodded its head. "For what it's worth, you've done a remarkable job here. Puc would be proud. I know I am. You've become an amazing young woman."

Annetta felt the base of her neck heat up underneath her chain mail upon hearing the compliment. She stood quietly afterwards, not sure how to respond to any of it. Darius had been her friend for years, even before she had known about Q-16. Through all of this, the two of them had also been brought closer together.

Sensing the awkward aura, Darius did not miss a beat. "Uh... I didn't mean anything by it. You know there's like a seven year difference between us. It would be so wrong on so many different levels..."

The girl could not help but chuckle, seeing the helpless stream of words flow forth from Darius's mouth as he tried to defend himself.

"That makes two of us," she chuckled. "Now come on, old man, we have an army to organize."

"Old man?" he raised an eyebrow. "I wonder what that makes Puc in your eyes."

"Antique or ancient, take your pick," Annetta chortled as the two of them continued on their way.

Making their way to where the horses were being prepared, Annetta found and mounted Firedancer. Accepting the reins from the elf that had been attending to him, she then checked to make sure everything was in place. Finally, she turned back to see the war banner of the Four Forces attached to the saddle. There was little wind to carry it, leaving it for the most part lying slack against the pole.

Darius, having found his own mount, joined with Annetta, and the two of them soon after ran into Gladius, Atala and Titus. The Hurtz wore his magnificent plate armour once more, while Atala sported her Gaian armour, as did Titus.

"Has the boy said anything yet?" Atala inquired.

"No, he hasn't sent any transmissions," Annetta told her.

"Aunt Skyris should be ready with the portal soon," Titus added. "Perhaps it would be wisest to contact him rather than wait."

"Aye, I wouldn't put my faith in waiting," Gladius agreed. "For all ye know, they could already be deep in the fray."

Though the girl liked to think differently of Link, she knew that trying to convince the trio would be impossible. Knowing her next move, she flipped open the watch and began to type in the number.

∞⟩⟨∞

The entire makeshift settlement on Gaia was in an uproar. All those able to fight scrambled as they attempted to arm and prepare themselves for the oncoming charge. Just as they had established at the meeting, the troops mobilized to take control of the prisoner camps. Once they held control of the imprisoned Gaians, they hoped their numbers would be enough to engage in head-on battle.

Link sat dressed in his armour on one of the logs by the fire pit, sharpening the edge of his sword with a whetstone. His mission would not carry him with the main forces, a fact that he did not resent after the last display from those in the command tent. Ignoring everything around him, he focused on the edges of the blade, losing himself in the sound of the stone on steel.

From a distance, Layla watched as he worked. She had not been proud of what had gone on. In fact, she was not proud of many things she had done to Link over the years when she had been his superior back in the militia. It was all just a circumstance of his birth, after all. Snapping out of her thoughts, she moved closer and settled on one of the logs further away, watching him sharpen the sword furiously.

"I remember that blade," she said finally, catching his attention. "It was your grandfather's, wasn't it?"

"It was," he replied with a grunt as he continued with his task.

"I remember how proud of it you always were," she reminisced. "How annoyed you were when I first made you train with blunted weapons. It drove you crazy not to use it."

Thinking back to his time in the militia, Link remembered the many times he was humiliated by her, further rubbing salt into his already open wounds from earlier in the day. He stopped his task and turned to look in her direction. "Is there a point to this conversation? I really don't see it."

Before she could reply with anything, the C.T.S. on Link's wrist began to go off. Sliding the sword back into its scabbard and dropping the stone into a pouch on his belt, he flipped open the device. "105 here."

Annetta's voice came through the device. **"01 here. What's your status in the camp? Final preparations are being made on our end. The cannon is nearly calibrated. We'll be ready to move out within the hour."**

"Understood," he replied. "We mobilize here as well. Venetor insists on freeing the prisoner camps before we join you. Will you be able to hold?"

"I believe so." There was an uncertainty in her voice.

Before Link could reply, Layla was at his shoulder, hovering over him. "01, we need confirmation if you will be able to hold. Yes or no."

There was a silence on the line before Annetta spoke again with a hint of annoyance to her tone. **"We will hold."**

"Good." Layla nodded. "Then I shall pass along your readiness to Prince Venetor. We will meet you on the field before Pangaia, I suspect."

"So be it. 01 out." The communication ended, and Link closed the watch.

"Your fearless leader of the Four Forces I take it?" Layla smirked.

361

"Yeah, that was Annetta Severio," he replied.

"Granddaughter of Orbeyus himself," she mused. "Well, we will see what she's worth. I'll go tell Venetor about them being ready. Meet me by the eastern entrance to the camp. It should be the quickest way to the tower. Make sure to load the device onto Rolf's saddle."

"Rolf?" Link asked.

"My sabertooth dog. Or have you not been paying attention?" She chuckled before disappearing into the bustle of the camp.

৪০೦৪

Preparations having been completed, Annetta, Darius, Gladius, Atala, Titus, Talia and Annetta's parents stood at the front of the army. There was an unsettling breeze which passed them by as they waited for Skyris to complete the last of the calibrations once they had been given coordinates from Annetta's communication with Link.

Annetta, more than anyone else, was beginning to feel the unease of waiting. There was an ominous feeling that resonated in her gut as she looked on ahead into the sea of grass before them, knowing how many now stood behind her. For what reason, really, did the rest of the Four Forces stand behind her now, other than a selfish quest to gain back her uncle and to help him restore Gaia? Those behind her did not owe her any favours, yet they followed her willingly to this. She lowered her head in thought, feeling the weight of her chain mail as it caused her shoulders to droop down.

"Mom, Dad, am I doing the right thing?" she asked.

"I think it is a little late for that, Anne," Aurora said.

"Even if we did tell you what we thought was right, you would still do your own thing," her father added.

Not receiving the reinforcement she had hoped for, the girl exhaled as she adjusted her saddle. Flicking the reins of Firedancer, she moved slightly forward and drew Severbane from its scabbard, causing those gathered to beat their weapons together in response.

"Warriors of the Four Forces," her voice rang loud and clear as she shouted. "You have no reason to follow me down this path, no motivation in truth to go and bare brute strength in the liberation of Gaia. Gaia is not our home, nor in truth our brother in arms. But this is not important on this day, for what we do here is beyond our bond as a single and united force. It is showing what we truly stand for, and that is freedom from tyranny."

A roar erupted in response, to which Annetta silenced them with a raised hand and continued. "Remember what you stand for when you are out there today, for today you do not fight for the oath you swore to be part of the Four Forces. You fight for the oath we all swore to ourselves when we dared to say no to those who would take control of our lives and what the Four Forces stand for!"

Another round of cheering erupted. The skies overhead darkened as Skyris let loose the blast from the cannon ahead of them. The portal opened with the sounds of crackling thunder. A final breath was taken, then the crossing began.

Chapter 33

The wax dripped off the pale candles lighting the large table littered with multitudes of parchment. In the sharp contrast of their blaze, Razmus's silhouette appeared a statue as he scanned the architectural drawings, searching for any way which would aid the completion of his work. His goal seemed so close at hand, and yet so far. His every thought when possible was always turned towards the tower, watching it climb ever higher into the Gaian sky. He knew, however, it would never be enough, perfection was not a thing by mortal hands attained, and yet he had survived over twelve thousand years. Was he still mortal, or something much more? His coming had been foretold. The white lion would lead Gaia out of darkness. That darkness had been evident as soon as he had been freed by Amarok. Lord and ladies running rampant without direction, abusing power at every corner and a king who allowed it to be so. Razmus would not stand for it. The darkness needed to be ended and he would be the one to make it so.

His thoughts were interrupted when a sharp wind wailed through the room, causing many of the candles to go out. Rising, the Lord of the Unfinished Tower turned in the direction of the open window opposite to him and walked towards it. Dusk had begun to settle on the horizon, bringing about an ambient twilight. Surveying a kingdom that was slowly calming into slumber, his gaze was drawn into the skyline as his vision adjusted to the dark. Squinting, he focused more, allowing his feral form abilities to take over. There, in the distance he finally saw it, dark clouds swirling ominously on the heavens. It was no natural cloud formation, this much he was certain.

"Amarok," he called. Instantly, the masked figure materialized out of the shadows. "Rouse the lords and ladies of the council. Tell them we prepare for battle and to gather the Hurtz. I think a certain black cub has come to bare its fangs in the face of Gaia."

හ෩ඝ

Trudging through the foliage of the vast forested area around him, Venetor made sure to look back every few seconds to take a count of those fighters that had come with him. The darker it got, the more paranoid the Prince of Gaia became, visualizing a hostile attack behind every rock and tree. A certain kind of alertness had taken root in his heart of late and try as he might, it had no intention of dying any time soon.

Then there came a fierce gust of wind that blew past, causing him to freeze in his tracks. Looking sideways, he could see clouds begin to darken and he knew full well what it meant.

"Is that?" one of the closer by fighters asked hopefully.

"Either that or the host of the Unknown itself has stopped by for a visit," he replied. "Keep moving! While Razmus's gaze is fixed elsewhere!"

No further comments were exchanged and the warriors leapt through the undergrowth with eager ambitions. Venetor remained behind a moment, revelling in the swirling of the black mass. Relief had begun to spread through him upon seeing it but on a deeper level, a thing he had not thought he would feel for any but his own son begun to emerge.

As he continued to gaze up, the feeling formed into words. "Hang in there, young one. I'm on the way."

&)(&

The sound of the charge overtook everything around her, shaking the very foundations of her soul as Annetta urged Firedancer on through the portal, roaring a battle cry so to not lose courage. Each portal had its own way of affecting the senses, and this one did not differ. At first, Annetta experienced weightlessness, which then turned into a sharp ocean breeze, followed by a dampness that proceeded to chill her down to her bones. Not that she had much time to notice with her mind set on other things.

Crossing the final part of the barrier, Annetta found herself looking ahead at what appeared to be a sea of forests. The trees were the biggest she had ever seen and seemed to eclipse any sign of grass around them. Peeking out from among the dense foliage, she could see in the distance roofs and multitudes of skyscrapers.

"There she be. Pangaia." Gladius confirmed her suspicion. "And that be the tower."

At first, Annetta could not see it, and then she was not sure how she had missed it. The thing Gladius had called a tower seemed to rise up from among the greenery like a massive black mountain. It was the smoothness and the perfection of it that finally gave it away as not being part of the landscape. The structure was so immense, the girl was certain that at some points during the day it blocked out the sun. Taking it in fully, she felt a sense of insignificance as she stood confronted with the unfinished tower. Yet among it all she managed to mouth one question as Firedancer came to a standstill. "Why?"

"What do ya mean by that lass?" the Hurtz asked.

"Why keep building it?" she asked as a proper question.

The Hurtz's mouth curled into a smile, his good ear twitching as he heard what she said and replied. "Lass, would I be a scholar I could answer, but I have and always will be a soldier. 'Tis not my place to ask such things, but to fight when called upon."

Atala pulled up soon beside them. "What are you both standing around here for? Forward!"

She was gone before Annetta could reply, and Darius soon bounded up on his mount beside her and Gladius.

"Uh... she does know it's still quite a way from the city, right?" the young elf asked. "Her horse will drop dead before she gets there."

"Never stopped Atala from trying," Gladius chuckled and urging his steed into a trot, he continued onward after the Gaian general.

Annetta looked over at Darius, who simply gave a small nod before taking off himself. Sighing, the girl looked up once more at the tower before she too joined the others in the continued march.

಄ఠ಄

Armed in his gleaming pale armour, war-like crown and flowing crimson cape, Razmus stalked through the halls, a grim expression adorning his face and a hand clasping the hilt of his longsword at his hip.

"Sire, the vanguard is ready to move out," a young messenger informed him. "Our cavalry and heavier units have not yet fully accumulated. Are there any messages you'd like me to deliver to Lady Brant?"

Razmus stopped in his tracks, causing the youth to almost collide into him, his only saving grace being a crack which made the boy trip far earlier and land on his face before him. The Lord of the Unfinished Tower looked down wordlessly, and reaching with a clawed gauntlet, he pulled the messenger up.

"Tell her to be prepared to do the right thing," he said. "To bleed and die for her king."

He then dropped the youth where he had fallen and continued walking. "And fix that crack!"

Reaching the outer gate, Razmus mounted his black sabertooth dog. Urging it forward, he moved to where the vanguard and the rest of his forces were amassing beyond the main gate. Looking up, he took note of the archers and the few psychics he had which were setting up their defences on the walls. Everything seemed to be in place.

Reaching the front ranks after checking in with his officers and having made sure everything was in place, the soldiers and Hurtz gathered froze upon seeing him before them. Razmus took note of the fear and respect they had for him, feeling it warm his insides like a good spirit. He did not show it in the slightest, though, his face remaining a mask of stone.

"I could say many words to you here and now," he began. "But the truth is that very little would have any sort of impact on your performance. Those usurpers out there mean to take your home from you and what do we do to those who would try to take our homeland? Our kingdom?"

The clanging of weaponry and war chants erupted from those gathered in an answer. Razmus smiled to himself. "Oh what a predicament you have played yourself into, little black lion cub. This battle is as good as won."

Turning back to his soldiers, he unsheathed the blade at his side and raised it into the air. "Onwards we fly!"

ഇരുൽ

They poured in like fire on an oil-slicked trail. Venetor and his fighters had little resistance at first from the Hurtz overseers as they plunged into the camps, taking out the minimal opposition with ease. It was not until the enemy began to mobilize that it became trickier. It was too late for them, however, for Venetor had pushed through enough to begin freeing those in the camps, who were quick to join in the fray, wielding anything that could serve as a potential weapon, from shovels and pick axes to large stones and pieces of wood.

Spreading out further and further, Venetor soon found he was cut off from much of his forces and facing an abundance of enemies, not that this bothered the Gaian prince in the least. Fists clenched before him in a boxer's style, Venetor's keen blue eyes were fixed on the two Hurtz foes he faced. Brandishing their weapons in a taunting fashion, they launched themselves at him.

Responding coolly, Venetor clasped the blade of the first opponent in the flats of his hands and applying pressure at the right angle, broke it off the hilt before throwing the torn-off metal at the other fiend to confuse him. Jabbing the first in the jugular, he spun around just in time to draw the short sword at his belt and block the oncoming axe which would have otherwise met with his face. Smirking triumphantly, he made use of the enemy's full weight in the attack and flung him over his shoulder. Sticking his boot onto the neck of the Hurtz he faced, he came to realize who it was that he was up against, Sentius, the overseer that had been in charge of his camp.

"So, we meet again." He grinned maliciously.

Sentius made no reply and snarling, did his best to fight past Venetor's foot. Applying more pressure to his leg, the Gaian prince glared down at the beast at his heel.

"I never did like your kind," Sentius snapped. "The coming of Lord Razmus was the most magnificent thing to befall my people. To finally rise above ya stinking Gaians and show ya the true glory of the Hurtz. I would enslave and torture ya runts all over again if I could, Lord Razmus or not in the picture."

It then occurred to Venetor that perhaps not all of the Hurtz needed the spell of the tower to be controlled by Razmus. Hearing Sentius just now had proven that to him.

"You..." Venetor uttered in a low growl. "If you think that torture and death are what will put the Hurtz above Gaians, then you are sorely mistaken. It's true. There's been no great love between our races for hundreds of years, but we are striving to be better, to work towards a better future. You can call us all manner of things, but there are three things all Gaians will never lack in their hearts no matter how much anyone will beat us down: Justice, honour and pride!"

Sentius continued to glare at Venetor and then replied. "Yer father talked a lot of talk too before I gutted him. Mostly though, he begged for mercy like a half-breed mutt."

To be called a half-breed in Gaian culture was the greatest of insults. Venetor's eyes darkened upon hearing what the Hurtz had claimed about his father. Calling the fallen axe to him, Venetor gripped it with both hands firmly and raising it over his head, brought it down before him with all the strength his body would allow. He did so multiple times in the seconds that passed driven by sorrow and rage. It made those foes that came near the scene question his sanity and to evade him, seeking another target. It was not until the friendly hand of a fellow Gaian fell onto his shoulder that Venetor retracted the axe, heaving heavily from the actions of his deed.

"My lord, are you alright?" the youth asked.

Recognizing the voice, Venetor turned to see Janus standing before him. There was confusion and horror written on the younger Gaian's face that made Venetor feel flooded with momentary guilt for his previous actions. He knew, however, he had been just in his doings.

"I'm fine," he replied coolly, burying what he had learned for the moment. There would be time to grieve later. "The true king of Gaia, Balthazar Severio has been avenged."

"The outer camp has been fully liberated. Shall we press forward, Prince Venetor?" Janus inquired.

Feeling the blood that had splattered from his earlier actions trickle down his face, he nodded in response, gripping firm the axe in his hand. Joined with a score of others, he charged forwards into the fray anew.

೮ೞ೦೪

It did not take long for them to reach the outskirts of the city, or at least, it did not take them long to reach the first wave of fighters. Chaos ensued when the tides of warriors collided, Hurtz, Gaians and the Four Forces alike. Everything turned to a blur and the perfectly-coordinated plan of using only the blunted weapons on the Hurtz failed almost instantly. There were simply too many enemies crashing in around them to take note of who was what and half the time the blows intended to tranquillize the Hurtz proved to be fatal.

Amongst the carnage, Annetta had lost track of Firedancer when she had teleported from the saddle upon coming into contact with the foe. She only hoped that the horse had gotten away and would not suffer the same fate that Bossman had when she'd fought against Mislantus's army. Delivering the war banner to the trusted care of one of the mounted elves, the girl focused her energies on the enemy around her.

With Severbane locked firmly in one hand and a blunted short sword in the other, she found herself surrounded by two Gaians and a Hurtz. Her eyes shifting from fighter to fighter, she watched as the Gaians came at her first, their swords raised high. Lifting Severbane in the absence of a shield, she blocked the attack, only to find the Hurtz charging at her from the corner of her eye. Seeing no other option, she teleported out of the way, watching the trio collide into each other.

She had only a split second to recover when another Hurtz charged for her. Pivoting on her heel, she met the attack head on, parrying the oncoming storm of assaults. The enemy Hurtz did not seem to slow in kind, raising a twin-bladed battle axe in large arching swings, each more devastating than the next. Had it not been for her training, Annetta was sure she would have been cleaved in two by now. Finally, seeing an opening, she dove for it, only to see the error of it all. The life leaving the eyes of the Hurtz fighter, Annetta watched helplessly as it slid off of Severbane onto the ground.

It was not the first time she had seen a sentient being fall on the end of her sword, but knowing that they had not been in control of their actions made it worse to think about. The mistake almost cost Annetta her own life as a searing pain cut across her left arm, causing her to drop the blunted sword. Spinning around, the girl found herself facing a Gaian female in full armour with a scimitar raised skyward. The foe's attack was cut short as the light left her eyes and she fell before Annetta. Standing behind wiping the blood from her blades was Skyris.

"Glad I found you when I did," her aunt said, "You'd have been a head shorter if I hadn't and I'm not about to explain to Arieus what happened."

Free of the potential threat, for the time being, Annetta took a good look around at her surroundings, watching the scenes of struggle around her. She then took note of the dead.

"We failed," she uttered.

"What do you mean we failed?"

Taking one of the blood clotting potions, Annetta downed it before continuing. "We failed to keep the Hurtz alive. Everything has gone to hell."

Hearing the words of the girl, Skyris also took in the scenery and getting a better meaning for what Annetta had said, she glanced back at her. "All's hell that ends well, think of the many that will live because the few die."

Brandishing her swords, Skyris then turned her attention back to the fighting and was off yet again, as quickly as she had appeared. Annetta continued to stand as Skyris's words sank in. She watched at a distance as the Gaian female she had come to know as the tech-savvy, heavily-drinking distant relative that never seemed to be short of quirks changed before her eyes into a mistress of war, taking on the enemy without showing any outward signs of remorse. Annetta could only hope one day she would be able to do so, to shut off the pain and do what had to be done. If she made it, that was. Seconds later, Darius appeared beside her.

"What was that about?" he asked.

"A reason to keep going, I suppose." The girl looked over at him and shrugged.

Still confused, Darius simply nodded and then saw her wound. "Your arm… are you?"

"I'm fine, I took a potion," she assured him, gripping Severbane tighter with her good hand. "Now let's get moving before we get any more unexpected attacks."

Giving a quick nod with nothing else to add, Darius trailed after Annetta as they rejoined the fight.

෨෬

Across the battlefield, another group of seasoned fighters held their own. Amongst their ranks were Arieus, Aurora and Talia. Standing back to back, their weapons raised, the trio had long abandoned their blunted weapons, seeing the flaw in the noble plan. Wielding their blades, they watched as another wave of enemy fighters spotted them and charged their way.

Aurora was the first to engage, striking outwardly with her two axes at the nearest opponent, a Gaian soldier in full armour wielding two great swords. He was a mountain of a man, at least twice the size of Aurora. This did not stop her in the least. Light of foot and catching his every move, Aurora whirled about him like a marionette would about her puppeteer while slashing away with her weapons.

Beside her, Talia created wicked blasts of psychic fire, throwing them at any larger packs of fighters that dared to look their way. Any who were still brave enough to come close to her, she challenged with the edge of her scimitar in a series of quick slashing attacks.

On the other side, Arieus found himself confronted by a Hurtz with the visage of a boar that had pointed canine ears. Were it not for his psychic abilities, he would have long ago succumbed to the mighty blows that were generated from the cleaver-like blade of his foe. Allowing added strength to flow into his blade, he parried, patiently awaiting an opening he was sure would soon present itself. It was not to be, however, for the duel was interrupted when the creature went slack and fell before him, an arrow protruding from its back. Distracted, the Gaian did not notice Entellion as he swooped down right after from the sky.

"I thought you could use a bow," the Soarin mused, "And a pair of eyes from above."

Becoming conscious of Entellion speaking to him, Arieus turned to the Sky Wolf. "Have you seen Annetta?"

"I saw the banner of the Four Forces," he acknowledged, "But it wasn't carried by her."

"She must have left it in a flag bearer's care," Aurora concluded, coming closer after having dispatched her foe.

"That's rather optimistic of you to say." Arieus turned to look at his wife. "That's our daughter out there."

"I still worry," Aurora corrected him, "But, as you said, she is our daughter."

Arieus muttered and grumbled under his breath. Try as he might, he still saw the little girl he was reading to at night, huddled up beside him under the blankets, waiting for whatever adventure they were reading to reach its end. His train of thought was derailed when Entellion howled and fell forward, a spear having gone through his wing. Prying it free, Arieus turned to see another three Hurtz charging towards them with raised weapons.

"I'll get him out of here," Talia said, examining the wound. "I'll be back as soon as I can."

It only took seconds for Talia to teleport out and back in after she had gotten Entellion to safety with some of the medics that had lingered closer to the portal. The trio gathered around where the fallen Soarin had been seconds before, readying their own weapons for impact. Clashing with the foe anew, utter chaos ensued as blades whirled in all directions, sparks flying from the colliding steel.

Arieus gritted his teeth with renewed ferocity as he struck at his enemy, dealing out hits. For a moment, it seemed as though his strength and momentum were infinite. Then it fell. His grip failing on the weapon, Arieus watched as it slipped from his hands. Teleporting just before the tip of the blade came at him, he reappeared above his foe, and summoning his blade he drove it into the neck of the Hurtz. A death cry erupting from it as Arieus leapt off as the creature fell to the ground. There was no time to celebrate, however, as another enemy warrior came at him, a Gaian female with a poleaxe.

An instant later, the Gaian's body crawled with sparks, seized up and fell to the floor. Standing behind her had been two rather short fighters, dressed in armour from head to toe, one of them pointing a colt where the Gaian now lay. It only took Arieus a minute to put the two together.

"Liam Kinsman!" Talia shrieked as she glared at the second newcomer, who seemed to shrink down even lower. "What on Earth are you doing here?"

"Making sure you guys aren't killed," Xander retorted in a muffled voice through his helmet, which he took off and threw to the ground. "What? No thank you?"

"Man, we are so busted," whimpered Liam under his helm. He was too terrified to take it off, in fear of what his mother would do.

"Busted doesn't even cut it close for you two," Aurora glared at her son, who finally understood how much trouble they were in, "Can I say power cut off and grounded till you are both of age?"

"I have a better strategy," smirked Talia, "Take away their batteries for everything."

"I quite like that idea," Aurora grinned.

The two boys gave extended groans upon hearing this but had little time to react anymore on the subject. Another wave of warriors was heading their way and there was not a moment to lose.

"Stay close to us," Arieus warned them as he gripped his sword with both hands, "And maybe if you behave, I'll see to it your mothers don't go through with that promise."

Chapter 34

Silently, the paws of the sabertooth dog padded through the dense foliage while Link and Layla remained flat on its back to avoid detection. They had seen the display of ominous clouds earlier and knew that Annetta had arrived, meaning their window to strike had begun. The world was naturally darkening and stars had begun to dot the heavens, adding further advantage to the stealth of their mission.

Link raised his head slightly and peering from the mass of bushy fur, saw the lights of the tower up ahead. The Tower of Magnus had been the tallest structure in all of Pangaia for twelve thousand years. Now, in the shadow of its brother, it seemed a meaningless skyscraper, forgotten in the toiling over the completion of Razmus's work. He remembered reading somewhere in a history book that the tower had once been the residence of Gaian kings and queens in the past. After sustaining damage in an attack of psychic fire, it had been abandoned in favour of a newer palace, Castrumleo, crafted by the monarch at the time and was left to its own devices, a monument from another age.

Layla halted the dog with a light pat on the side and then turned to Link. "From here we have to go on foot. Rolf won't be able to scale the walls and we'll have a better chance of remaining undetected."

"Like I have anything to argue with that," the youth stated and slid off the mount.

Layla jumped off and proceeded to retrieve the bomb from one of the saddle bags. Pausing, she turned to look at Link, who stood at a distance. "For what it's worth, I never thought any less of you for being what you are back then."

Doing his best to ignore what was said, Link turned away and crossed his arms, pretending to scout the area in case they were ambushed. "It doesn't matter what you thought. All of that is in the past."

The young Gaian continued to observe him for a few seconds longer after her proclamation. Seeing as it had rendered no results, she dwelt no more on it, checking the makeshift device. It was no longer than her forearm, consisting of two metal cylindrical containers that had once been fuel cells. Between these rested a power core, a small black box, along with some other parts that she was unable to identify and were all crudely strapped together by some belts that Venetor had managed to procure. From the ends of the various parts, wires sprung, wrapping the device, making it whole. How it was to work, Layla had no idea, except that Venetor had claimed it would.

Feeling the sensations of eyes watching him leave, Link looked over his shoulder, "Everything alright with it?"

"It seems to be all intact," she confirmed. Placing it in a sack, she slung it over her shoulder. She then turned to Rolf, who sat on his haunches. "You know the whistle and you know what to do until I return."

Wordlessly, the large beast rose from its resting position. Taking one good look at Layla and a short glare at Link, he trotted off into the forest and disappeared among the vegetation.

"I take it that it's not the first time he's had to hide like that," Link mused.

"Nor will it be the last," Layla confirmed. "At least before this is all over."

Exchanging no more words, the two of them made their way towards the outer wall which guarded the city. While the purpose of the wall seemed primitive, Gaia had, for the most part, decided to leave as much plant life intact as it could, and everything that was outside of the massive city border remained wild and untouched.

Coming to the foot of the structure, the both of them took note of the vast amount of thick purple vines that crawled up the side of the walls. Some of the tendrils were wide enough for a Gaian to sit in with comfort. While such a notion would appear appealing to a would be woods enthusiast, Link knew at once what they were.

"Cerebral Lianas," he growled as he wrinkled his nose.

"You know of them then?" Layla inquired.

"Hard to forget when you were playing in the woods, come across one, try to climb it and wake up in your bed with your father scolding you, saying you could have died."

Reaching into her pocket, Layla pulled out two vials and handed one to Link, who looked at it with a bit of confusion. "It's an extract. It should mask us from the Lianas's ability to drain energy from anyone who comes into contact with them."

Accepting the vial, Link analyzed it skeptically while sloshing the liquid around inside. "And how do we know this is going to work, exactly?"

"Brewed and created by one of the greatest thieves in all of Pangaia is how," she informed him and uncorking the vial, she downed the liquid, grimacing. "Don't let it hit your tongue and when you are on the vines, don't spit or get your sweat on it. Once they sense your bodily fluids, it won't work anymore."

Nodding, Link opened his brew. Catching a whiff of the rancid smell, he pulled it away from himself, coughing. Hearing a chuckle escape Layla's lips, he quickly regained his composure and wasted no time in downing the contents, even if he regretted it right after. His stomach churned as the liquid slid down like an eel into his gut, but he did his best to keep a straight face.

Before Link could say anything else, a pair of thick leather gloves landed in his hands as well.

"We'll need these to prevent sweat from touching the vines." She explained as she put on a pair. "It's a long way up."

Securing her pack and not saying anything further, Layla grabbed hold of the closest tendril and began the process of hoisting herself upwards.

Sighing deeply, Link proceeded to move towards the wall. Seeing Layla climb with none of the energy draining-side effects of the plant taking hold of her gave him the courage he needed to grab hold of the first vine. He then began the climb. This did not, however, stop his apprehension to the task, and before long he was starting to second-guess it. What if the antidote failed part way? If the draining of his energy by the mighty crawling vines did not kill him, then surely the fall would, and as far as Link was concerned, he had no intention of dying. Adrenaline pumping to his brain, he began to climb faster, hoping to reach the top as soon as possible. But it was not to be, and soon, he found his left foot stuck within the hollow of one of the larger vines. Cursing himself under his breath, he began to try and wriggle free.

"What are you doing?" Layla hissed, hearing the struggle from below.

"I'm caught, I can't get out," he answered her through gritted teeth.

"Unknown's bane, Heallaws." She rolled her eyes and moved downwards. "Whatever you do, don't get your sweat on it."

But it was too late for that and soon, Link's forehead was already beginning to show moisture as he struggled. Seeing this, Layla quickly tore a piece off of her tunic and threw it down at Link from above. It landed on the top of his head.

Twisting and freeing his foot seconds later, the dampened rag fell from his face downwards. The cloth then hit one of the lower vines, and the thing they had feared began as the creepers began to stir from their sleep.

"Damn it, Heallaws!" Layla cursed. "Move!"

She did not have to tell him twice as Link redoubled his efforts, the vines beneath his feet beginning to awaken, coming to life with the scent of a potential meal. Hands and feet tearing upwards as fast as his coordination would allow him, Link found himself nearing the top of the wall. It was not to be so easy, however, and not long after one of the sentient tendrils wrapped itself around his foot. Hissing, Link began to feel its effects, but was not about to lose his head. Unsheathing his sword, he glanced down at the purple serpentine vine. His aim clear, he swung the blade, cutting clear through it. The whole plant seemed to recoil from the blow and shook violently in the aftermath. Scrambling, he reached the top and with a final lunge, was on the wall.

"Please tell me there will be another way down," he spat in between laboured breaths.

Seeing his anxiety, a grin cracked on Layla's composed face. "That depends on if we disarm the tower. Come on!"

Finding a set of stairs, they began their descent into the city.

ഇരുഈ

In the midst of the chaotic mass of fighting troops, a battle axe came crashing down onto its latest opponent. Releasing a guttural war cry, Lord Ironhorn retracted his weapon and continued forward, flanked by two other Minotaur. Ending another enemy that had come into his path, Ironhorn's gaze fell to a tattered crimson cape. Locking eyes with the Gaian in white armour, the Minotaur king made it known that he was to be his next target, pointing his dagger, Fearseeker, in his direction. The Gaian simply grinned at the mock invitation and turned to face him, taunting Ironhorn with a clawed gauntlet.

Nostrils flaring at the challenge, Lord Ironhorn raised his weapon anew and threw himself at the foe, charging madly, while his companions occupied themselves with oncoming Hurtz warriors. Colliding, Ironhorn's axe locked with that of his opponent's longsword. Sparks flew as each of them dealt out blow after blow, not faltering in their speed nor stamina.

Impressed, Ironhorn withdrew but for a split moment. "And whom is it that I have the pleasure of fighting and killing this day? Speak, and perhaps I shall have your likeness adorn one of the many halls in my castle."

"Fight yes, but kill…that is not likely," the Gaian chuckled. "I am Lord Razmus Severio, king of Gaia, the white lion and once known as the Lord of the Unfinished Tower."

Lord Ironhorn's brow knotted as he heard the name. "So…you are the one who is the cause of all of this? Well then, it shall indeed be an honour to finish you."

Raising his axe over his head, Ironhorn struck once more, hitting Razmus's blade, the sound of ringing steel reverberating through his hands, all the way up his arms. Sidestepping, Razmus broke free of their second encounter and proceeded with his own offensive set of attacks. Parrying, Ironhorn roared and locking the sword with his axe, used his immense strength to throw Razmus into the air as though he were but a mere rag doll.

Somewhere at a distance, Annetta peered over her shoulder to see the scene unfold as Lord Ironhorn battled with the Gaian in white armour. Free of her slew of attackers, she made her way hastily towards the scene, hoping to be of some aid.

It was all in vain, however. Reaching the last stretch between herself and the fight, Annetta watched helplessly as Razmus recovered from his projection into the air, teleported and reappearing on Ironhorn's back. After some struggle, and avoiding multiple near death throttles from Lord Ironhorn, he slid his sword into the Minotaur's jugular. The move killed him instantly.

"No!" Annetta screamed, to the point of feeling her throat go raw.

The hulking body of the Minotaur king fell to the ground with a metallic thud. Razmus's gaze then shot in the direction of the scream, his eyes fixed on Annetta. The hunger of battle renewed itself upon his visage as he chose his target, her.

"So," he mused as he wiped his sword on Ironhorn's tabard before proceeding further, "This is the fabled heir of Orbeyus Severio, the little black lion cub of Earth."

Anger pulsing through her like scalding hot water, Annetta shifted into a fighter stance, observing the Gaian. He was a psychic, this much she knew now, and it meant he was that much more dangerous to her. She would have to be one step ahead of him at every turn, just as Venetor had taught her.

Razmus sensed the girl's wariness and smiled with a flash of white teeth. "Come now, Annetta, I just wish to talk. We are family, after all."

"What kind of family member kills the friends of other members, creep?" She sneered.

"I could also ask what kind of family member brings an army to another member's doorstep, but you don't see me doing that, now do you?" Razmus retorted as he sheathed his weapon and extended a hand to her. "I'm going to give you this one chance to surrender, go home and go about whatever business you have on Earth. Whether you take it or not is your choice."

Annetta glared at the hand before her, clad in white armour, the clawed fingertips on it stained in blood. Her nose wrinkled in disgust knowing to whom it belonged.

Eyeing the Lord of the Unfinished Tower she replied, "No way."

Teleporting from where she stood, the girl reappeared to the left and swung Severbane with all the might she could muster.

Razmus did not miss a beat and brought his sword out to meet her own, the sounds of metal clashing on metal thrumming through the steel. Not the least bit intimidated by the girl's display of prowess, Razmus used the distraction of their duelling to bring his right hand down and strike at her with his claws.

Barely having time to move, Annetta sidestepped just in time to have the claws tear through the chain mail on her arm as though it were nothing more than cloth. Gyldrig was not a soft metal by any means. The girl could scarcely imagine what manner of material the Lord of the Unfinished Tower's armour was made of if it had managed to do that much damage with so little effort. Calling the shield off of her back to her arm, she slammed the flat of it into Razmus's face, temporarily throwing him off balance.

Grimacing, the Severio lord held his face, taking note of the blood on the palm of his hand and then looked up at the youth.

"We would have called that fighting dirty back in my day," he spat.

Annetta smiled wickedly. "Times change, old man."

With that, they clashed anew.

සⓒ෬

The clattering of horse hoofs could be heard echoing all around as Matthias urged his mount onward, through the cobblestone courtyard of Severio Castle. A look of desperation decorated the face of the assassin as he searched for anyone he might know among the Water

Elves, Soarin, Ogaien and Minotaur that had remained behind. His prayers were soon answered when he noticed Entellion in the medical tent with two elven medics surrounding him.

"We may need to amputate the wing," the first of them said with a concerned look as he examined the puncture wound the Alpha had obtained on the battlefield.

"Where are Annetta and the rest of the Four Forces?" Matthias demanded as he got out of the saddle and strode towards them.

Though he was in pain, his fur matted with blood and sweat, Entellion lifted his head from the sickbed to regard the newest arrival. "They have gone to fight. The battle rages on Gaia."

Matthias's eyes widened at the revelation. He'd come too late.

"How long have they been gone?" he questioned as the medics ignored him and continued to move about the Soarin, trying to figure out the best course of action.

"An hour maybe more," Entellion managed to gasp in pain as one of the two elves poked at his wound, trying to see if there was any nerve damage. "Everything happened so fast."

"Then there may still be time," the assassin confirmed for himself and turned on his heel to leave.

"Where are you going?" Entellion asked weakly.

"To get aid," Matthias replied. Getting on his mount anew he pressed his heels into the flank of the horse and was off again.

Chapter 35

Elsewhere on the battlefield, the arching flashes of scythes crisscrossing could be seen as they went for their nearest target. The sweat on Atala's brow created a slick and glowing feeling to her skin as she fought. Sheer will guided her actions, and soon the general of the Gaian forces had managed to fight her way to the main gates of the city along with other members of the Four Forces, which now had dispersed all around. Landing a roundhouse kick to the chest of her latest victim after her blades had found him, she sent the Gaian warrior soaring some distance before he collapsed. She had little time to contemplate the fact that the unknown soldier had once been under her command, for a new challenger was waiting, a Gaian female who Atala knew all too well.

Staring her down, she spoke. "Lady Andromeda Brant. I find it strange that you of all noble Gaian houses would align yourself with Razmus."

Lady Brant was a slight Gaian who appeared, in human terms, to be in her late thirties. She sported a tanned complexion that was further marred by the blood of her enemies and the grit of battle. She wore traditional Gaian military armour, her auburn hair worn to match in a single long braid, done up into a bun to prevent it from getting in the way while fighting. Beyond all of this, a pair of green eyes glared at Atala without any hint of mercy.

"I do what must be done for the sake of the Brant name," she stated in an icy voice as she raised the bastard sword she carried and moved towards Atala.

Their blades meeting in a singular clash, Atala put her full weight on her weapons as she pressed forward to gain an advantage.

"What of house Pelleio?" Atala questioned with venom in her words.

Hearing her maiden name, a name which she remembered her sister fully slighting in their youth, Lady Brant found inner strength and pushed as well. "That name, as well as my sister, are dead to me now."

"Is that how you really felt about me, Eda?" another voice spoke from close by.

Withdrawing her weapon, Lady Brant turned around to its source, the look of malice dissipating from the creases in her face.

"Sister." She mouthed the word as she gazed at Aurora. "What in the name of the Unknown are you doing here?"

"Rescuing Gaia from you, apparently," Aurora stated, her voice still cold as she raised her weapon, though half-heartedly.

Seeing what was about to occur, Lady Brant looked around to see that no one was watching and dropped her weapon before going on her knees, placing her hands behind her head. Surprised by what had occurred, Atala and Aurora came closer. Not soon after, Arieus and Talia joined the trio, followed closely by Xander and Liam in tow.

"Things are bad on Gaia," Lady Brant confessed. "If Razmus is truly the white lion of prophecy, then all he brings is the end. I'd sooner peg him for Korangar than any saviour of this world. The Hurtz are all under his command and have the run of everything. He's placed some nobles in charge of other cities and continents but they are just figureheads with no say."

"It won't be this way for long," Atala assured her once she was certain Lady Brant would not revolt. "As we speak, there are those inside who are breaking Razmus's hold on the Hurtz, the question is how many of the Gaian houses that have aligned themselves with Razmus will continue to fight once the Hurtz are freed."

Lady Brant thought for a moment before speaking. "A few will continue to fight, but not many. No, many of us have been blackmailed, had spouses or children killed or sent to work on building the tower. I only fight because if I do not, Razmus threatened to kill my son, just as he did my husband when he first opposed to bending the knee to him."

"Will you be able to call your warriors to turn sides when the time comes?" Talia questioned.

"Yes, they will heed my call," Lady Brant confirmed.

"We've only one choice then," Aurora concluded. "We fight until that tower goes down."

"And I with you, sister," Lady Brant stated. "But first I must find Quintus before doing so...if I may."

Aurora turned to Atala, who still wore a puzzled look, not fully trusting Lady Brant's sudden change of heart. Still, she was Aurora's sister and so the Gaian general complied, taking a step back from their prisoner. "As you'll have it. But note that when the tower collapses, I will be watching."

₧₧

Jason's head began to droop yet again as the prosecution of Tamora continued. It seemed the Fire Elf had an endless list of crimes she had to answer for. He wondered how much longer it would all take before he got to change out of his armour into something that did not obstruct his blood flow after a few hours of being in one position. Feeling an elbow go into his side for another countless time, Jason stirred to look over at Sarina, who regarded him accusingly. Shrugging, he rubbed the sleep from his eyes and looked down at the pale-haired elf in chains once more as one of the Archmages continued to speak.

Further delegations were interrupted, however, as the doors slammed open with the force of a hundred soldiers. In came striding Matthias, his hair wild from the wind and his demeanour filled with the sense of unfaltering determination.

Confused by the manner of entry, many of those gathered began to speak among themselves. Out of all of them, Puc seemed the most composed and rose from his seat.

"Annetta and the rest of the Four Forces have left," the assassin announced as he walked further inside. "They are on Gaia, right this moment."

"And what of it?" Alaric spoke as he rose from his seat. "We were aware of young Annetta's campaign, but there are delicate matters which require our attention here. Tamora must answer for her crimes. This cannot wait."

Matthias felt his blood boil upon hearing the illogical response. "And what of your troops sent to Gaia? What of the people you are so willing to sacrifice?"

"They have plenty of soldiers," another mage from on high spoke. "Everything will be fine."

"How long have they been gone?" Puc asked. "Was anyone able to tell you?"

"What does it matter?" the mage who had spoken before scoffed.

Puc looked over his shoulder at the source of the voice with his steel gaze. "It matters to your First Mage."

Puc turned to regard Matthias fully, having silenced his opposition. "How long?"

"A few hours at most, from what I gather," he confirmed.

Hearing what was going on, Jason sprang to life from his bench. "Are they winning? Do we know?"

Matthias looked over at him. "Entellion had fallen, and he was in the medical tent when I came."

"If my father is in danger then I must go," Doriden, who was present at the trial, spoke. "He is the Alpha."

"And what of your oath to the Four Forces?" Puc questioned him.

"I have an oath to my Alpha before all others," Doriden glared at him, "And those that are fighting on Gaia are also part of the Four Forces, last I checked."

Jason felt tension spread through the air in the room like smoke, and remarks of resentment and panic began to trickle through among those present. The only ones who seemed to show none of the symptoms were Puc and Matthias.

"We need to go to Gaia, and we both know it," Matthias finally stated as he continued to stare down the First Mage.

"That is not as simple as you think it to be," Puc replied, glancing back at the Archmages that studied him from their seats.

Unable to hold his tongue any longer, Matthias let loose his final ammunition. "I think it is, in fact I think it's so simple that it's been hiding under everyone's noses. Tell me, what exactly did you do to Venetor? Did you best him in a competition? Actually, forget I said that. Did you fall in love with his sister?"

There was a silence in the room. After some time, Tamora, who was still chained in the midst of the room began to laugh a long and hysterical laughter. It became so intense that two of the guards were forced to remove her back to her holding cell in the prison. Puc returned his gaze to Matthias with some semblance of anger in his eyes.

"A speculation and nothing more." he spat.

Matthias crossed his arms, unflinching and looking back at the mage. "You forget that I was once an assassin. It was part of my job to spy on people."

Jason continued to listen to the scene as it unfolded between Matthias and Puc. His mind eventually zoned out as his thoughts went to Annetta and the others. He was having an eerie sense of déjà vu. Was it not over a year ago that he had also found himself in an altercation between Matthias and Puc due to Brakkus's death? The fight with Annetta had left a sort of damage on him in the aftermath, even if he did not speak of it. It had also made him question just how far he was willing to go for a friendship. Was he willing to let her die? The argument from the assassin and the mage reaching its pinnacle snapped him back into reality. Standing up from his seat, the youth vanished and reappeared with his mace drawn in front of Matthias. He then slammed the weapon down into the ground with full force, producing an echo in the room.

"That's enough!" he shouted, further getting everyone's attention. "I don't really care what Puc did in the past to Venetor, and I'll be honest that I don't particularly care for Venetor's company after seeing his training methods. The fact still remains that Annetta is out there, as are my other friends, and I can bet that at least one of you here other than myself and Doriden have people you care about there too. The Four Forces were meant to be one power with one goal, to protect people, and right now people are out there possibly dying because the other half of the Four Forces isn't doing its job."

Stillness fell over the room, allowing for Jason's words to resonate long after he had spoken. No one said anything back. It was Puc who finally spoke, having let the words sink in.

"I am in agreement with Jason and Matthias," he said. "We have ensured the safety of Aldamoor and secured the Fire Elf threat. The trials can wait, those we are sworn to cannot. Ready all troops. We ride for the gate of Pangaia."

After having declared this, he turned to leave, causing some in the room to go into an uproar, while the majority hurried to prepare.

Having exited the room, Puc was then met with Jason and Sarina, who hurried towards him.

"Puc, I'm sorry for what I did but I-" the boy began to apologize in a speedy manner.

"There is no need for any of that," the First Mage assured him.

"But didn't he just break so many different regulations?" Sarina questioned.

"As far as I am concerned, I am glad he did for once." There was a hint of a smile across Puc's face. "Honestly, you did not both believe I wished to wait till all was said and done to go aid Annetta, did you? Also, who do you think made sure Matthias had a mount to leave and check on the situation? I thought you knew me better than that."

"Honestly, sometimes it feels like we don't know you at all," Jason said. "I mean... what is your issue with Venetor? Did you and Skyris actually..."

"A story best saved for another time," Puc replied flatly.

Just then, Matthias came around the corner to join them.

"Troops are beginning to take position. It shouldn't be long," he informed them.

"You gave them the order I wrote ahead of time then?" Puc asked.

"Like we discussed," he nodded.

"Wait, wait, wait!" Jason stopped. "You were both in on this the whole time? That argument in there..."

"Was staged." Puc finished the sentence. "You did not actually think those other mages would have allowed us to leave the trials for later if there was not a dire need, did you? I forget your youth at times, Kinsman. Here is a lesson for you to carry forth for the rest of your life. In politics, nothing can ever be straightforward."

Chapter 36

Toiling among the carnage as spells of varied caliber shot from his battle staff, Darius fought alongside a slew of fellow mages. Many he did not recognize, but there were a few faces which he was able to pick out as either having been in the Academy around his time there or as fellow students. Working together as a unit, they found themselves facing a score of Gaian soldiers, loyal to Razmus. Keeping their distance and readying their staves, they fired off spells, alternating between ranks to ensure a steady stream of assaults.

In the midst of all of this, Darius's eye was drawn beyond the battle as he noticed a familiar figure on the horizon. He had to squint for a moment to be sure, but after seeing the great shield being raised to save its owner from an attack, he was certain that it was Annetta up ahead. It didn't look good, however, as the figure in white armour with a crimson cape slashed away in a continued string of offensive moves, alternating between his longsword and his clawed gauntlet.

"I've gotta get over there." He patted the closest mage to him on the shoulder, who gave a gruff nod in response.

His mages robes whirling behind him as he removed himself from the group, Darius made his way towards Annetta and her opponent. Coming within range, he positioned himself behind the debris of one of the fallen airships. Aiming his staff, he prepared to fire. An orange blaze erupted from the tip of his staff and shot in the direction of the white armoured figure.

Without so much as glancing, the Gaian's hand shot out sideways and backhanded the blast so it landed some distance away from him and Annetta, causing the ground to rupture. Debris flew everywhere and before Darius had a chance to orient himself, he was thrown into the air and carried forward to where the fighting duo was by an unseen force.

"And what have we here?" said the Gaian, who Darius assumed to be Razmus.

Given an opening, Annetta slumped back on the ground, her breathing short and raspy. It was clear the girl would be going nowhere. Razmus smirked at the sight and continued to study Darius. "Black of hair but no blue eyes, yet you fight like a Water Elf mage...curious."

Struggling, Darius tried to break free of his invisible bonds. His thoughts turned inwards as he realized his psychic-blocking amulet must have gotten loose during the battle and fallen out somewhere on the field. There was no other explanation for him being unable to move. Cursing himself for not securing it better, he stared into the face of the ancient Severio lord.

"Not much to say for yourself, either," Razmus mused, "Generally people in your predicament would threaten to gain vengeance or something to that extent. I suppose if you've nothing to say, I can just kill you instead."

Seeing no other way out, fear began to course through Darius as he realized he would die. It was not meant to be, however, as the malevolent smile disappeared from Razmus's face and the hold he had on Darius weakened, dropping him instantly. A yelp of agony escaping him, Razmus turned and glared at his attacker. A battle-weary Annetta stood just behind him, propping herself up on Severbane with her shield hand, a ball of blue and purple flame sprouting from her free hand.

"Why don't you pick on someone your own size?" she sneered through laboured breaths.

Wrath coursing through him, the Lord of the Unfinished Tower forgot his earlier victim in the face of the newest slight done to him. Tearing off his burned cloak, he tossed it to the ground in disgust.

"Insolent brat, this will be the end of the line of Magnus and ALL of his descendants," he snarled in full fury. Dropping his longsword, his arms began to circulate with blue sparks. "Starting with you, black cub."

Raising his right hand, a ball of blue and purple flame began to form and a snarling guttural noise built in his throat.

Annetta braced herself for the oncoming attack. She was too tired to teleport, having used much of her energy fighting Razmus. The final attack using psychic fire had pushed her over the edge. Cursing herself internally, she had only two regrets. They were the way she had left things with Link and her fight with Jason which had led to splitting the Four Forces in two. All else she could leave behind, knowing what awaited her on the other side of death. Closing her eyes, she let out what she thought would be her final breath. Nothing happened. She then heard what sounded like the thud of a fist and a body crash to the ground. Opening her eyes, she saw Razmus lying on the ground before her. Beside her stood Venetor.

"I believe you misheard my niece," he stated, cracking his knuckles as he did so and stretching his arms, "because she clearly said for you to pick on someone your own size."

Razmus rose from where he had fallen, his eyes not leaving Venetor as he studied the shorter fighter closely. Touching his neatly trimmed beard, he noticed the blood that had trickled down the corner of his lips and spat out some more. A grin formed on his mouth soon after.

"And I suppose you're the one to do so?" Razmus chuckled. "You clearly didn't make the height requirement for the job."

"You know the old saying," Venetor smirked, "The taller the mountain, the greater the ruins when it is toppled."

"You don't even know the origin of those words do you lad?" Razmus cackled. "The mountain refers to the height of a legacy, not a person. Had you known this, you would know that the only mountain falling this night shall be Magnus's!"

Not wishing to continue with any more words, Venetor teleported, reappearing behind Razmus with his left fist extended backwards, ready to throw an earth-shattering punch. Razmus was no fool, and as soon as the hit was close to contact, he too disappeared, leaving Venetor with only seconds to anticipate his next move before he reappeared again, claws ready to tear through the Gaian prince.

Sidestepping out of the way, Venetor blocked the oncoming attack, using his psychic abilities to create a shield around his skin. Baffled, Razmus struck again and again, but in vain.

"How can I not hit you?" he hissed.

A hearty laugh escaped Venetor as the Gaian bloodlust rushed to his head. "I am not called the Ironfisted without reason. Twelve thousand years of advancement in the arts of psychic training plays a factor."

Calling forth his rage, Venetor focused inward. Since the day his psychic training had begun, Venetor had been taught one thing by his mentors, and it was to understand what it was he hated most in the world. It took years, but he soon learned what it was. It was not a personality trait or the prospect of having to do some deed he disliked. With Venetor, the answer had been far more obvious and yet complex, for the thing he hated most was watching the people of Gaia suffer. The pride he had for his people overtook all else. Controlling the psychic fire as it burst forth from both hands, he used his mind to shape them into clawed gauntlets around his hands, similar to that of Razmus's. Then, he struck.

While this encounter began, Darius made his way to Annetta, who was barely holding on as she was. Placing her free arm around his neck, he allowed her to lean on him as they watched the two Severio lords clash. He took notice of the many nicks and cuts which adorned the tattered chain mail she wore, as well as the large cut on her arm.

"Those don't look good," he whispered to her. "We need to get you out of here."

"What? We can't leave! What if Venetor needs help?" she protested.

Darius rolled his eyes and placed a finger on one of Annetta's deeper wounds, to which the girl squirmed and grimaced further. "What good will you do him in the state you are in, other than be a liability?"

Growling, Annetta watched in defeat as Razmus and Venetor continued to fight, hacking and slashing at one another with their clawed hands. Their fighting styles resembled that of two wild animals wanting to tear each other apart. Whatever the outcome was to be, neither side would show the other a shred of compassion. Mesmerized and unable to look away from the seemingly perfect dance of death, Annetta finally snapped out of it when Darius began to pull on her arm anew.

Exasperating in disappointment, she turned to face him. "Fine, let's go."

೫ଓଔ

Skyris thrust her sword towards the enemy, always remembering to keep her second one at close range and ready to parry. While she did enjoy the occasional bar brawl, which rarely ended in someone being dead, she had never enjoyed fighting as much as her brother. Still, she was taught from a young age to wield a variety of weapons. It was a Gaian custom. Gender did not prevent one from learning to fight and often throughout history, it was females who had proven to be the greater warriors.

Catching her opponent off guard, she disarmed the Hurtz before her, who wasted no time on confusion for lack of an arsenal and lunged at her with fangs and paw-like hands extended. Curling into a ball and rolling in between the legs of the giant, Skyris emerged on the other side and with a powerful blow, planted the hilt of her sword into the head of the Hurtz, knocking it unconscious.

Scanning her surroundings briefly, she made out Titus some distance away, wielding a sabre in one hand, his pistol firing off shots in the other. To the opposite side of her, Gladius swung his two-handed blade as he faced off against another fellow Hurtz. Distracted as she was, she did not notice the sound of armour clanging until it was too late. Pivoting on her heel, Skyris deflected the head of the oncoming pike from a male Gaian soldier only enough for it to pierce her thigh. A yelp of pain escaping her, Skyris did not waste a second longer, bringing down her sword with full force, breaking the wooden pole with an uneven cut. Anger pulsing through her, she hurled herself towards the stunned soldier.

Falling backwards, the fighter struggled to rise to his feet as Skyris's weapons came towards him. "Mercy! I beg thee, Lady Skyris!"

Hearing the pitiful plea, Skyris recoiled momentarily, thinking to humour the soldier. Looking down at her bloodied thigh, she sheathed one of her swords and removing the spear tip pointed it at him. "Is this what you call mercy?"

"I swear my lady, had I known it was you, I would have-"

"Oh! If it was me you wouldn't have, but were it some other poor wretch, you would not have thought about it for a second longer, would you? Is that it?" she snapped.

"I'm sorry, I really am." The soldier was on the verge of sobs.

Skyris felt disgust roiling up in her throat and spat on the ground, hoping to rid herself of some of it, but it was all in vain. Looking down, she took note of how fast the blood was escaping the wound. She would have to deal with it soon. Her duty called her elsewhere at that second, however, and her gaze fell back to the soldier.

"You think because I am a female that I will spare you?" Skyris stated coldly. "That because I am a female I must automatically show compassion? What are you? An Earthling? I am a warrior of Gaia, and I will not show mercy because someone will weep for it."

As she spoke, Skyris continued to circle the soldier, the broken tip from the pike tracing the shape of his slouched shoulders.

Feeling his fate was sealed, the soldier did the best he could to compose himself. So be it, he thought, and closed his eyes. He awaited the sound of the blade to pierce his neck, but was instead greeted by the sound of a metal thud as something hit the ground right beside him.

"I only show mercy when I feel like it," Skyris spoke into his ear. "Consider yourself lucky this time."

Opening his eyes and nodding, the Gaian scrambled to his feet and scurried away as quickly as he could. The adrenaline of the moment leaving her, Skyris felt the pain of her leg come to the forefront of her mind. She gripped the wound fiercely as she rummaged through the pouch on her belt for a potion.

"M'lady!" Gladius called as he rushed over to her side and immediately offered his arm for support. "Are ye hurt bad?"

"I've been worse," she managed to say as she downed the contents of the vial she found.

"Aunt Sky!" Titus called as he came over and saw the leg. "We need to get away from here. I don't think we can take the city. We underestimated the amount of backing Razmus would have."

"We will do no such thing!" Skyris snarled and tried to break free of Gladius's arm. "We came here to win, and that is what we are going to do."

"M'lady, look around ye and tell me what ye see," Gladius spoke.

Hearing his words, Skyris did take a good long look around at her surroundings. It was a wreck. Warriors from both sides lay on the battlefield and while many had fought, many had lost their lives and if they continued, many more still would. Gritting her teeth, Skyris did not want to admit defeat. How could she when her brother was Venetor the Ironfisted? She was not about to be known as Skyris the Fleeing for the rest of her days, and she was certain Annetta had no desire for a similar title either. Where was the girl, anyway? She had seen her briefly earlier, but that was it. She had to go find her, she was blood after all, and Annetta had risked everything to get Venetor back.

"We must find Annetta." She voiced her thoughts.

"Skyris, we must leave," Gladius repeated himself. "We are losing this battle and we will lose much more if we don't go."

Before Skyris could speak any further she saw it, or rather she heard it before she saw it. The cry of thousands of voices filled the air from the woods. Out of them came the imprisoned Gaians, armed with all manner of weaponry, but most importantly of all, armed with their courage to take back their home. They were the prisoners from the camps that had been building the tower judging by the state of their clothing and the remnants of chains they wore. Someone must have freed them and Skyris only hoped that Venetor been involved. A smile spread across her face as she turned to her two skeptical companions.

"Come on! We're not finished yet!"

ಬಾಣ

Were it not for the cover of darkness and the disruption caused by the battle outside the gates, Link was certain they would have been detected by now. The descent down the wall, once they were on the other side, had taken no time at all. Locating one of the nearest keeps, they snuck past the guard on duty and went down the winding staircase. After that, it was a matter of staying close to the shadows of the various buildings which populated the great city, a task at which Layla excelled.

Before they knew it, they had reached the base of Magnus's Tower. The structure did not look like much in comparison to the behemoth that was Razmus's Tower, and even less so with part of it having been burnt. Regardless of this, on either side of the barred entrance, the banners of Gaia decorated it, a white rampant lion in a shield of crimson on a field of white and red that was cut vertically in half, symbolizing Gaia's warrior heritage. Link found no time to dwell on them as he was pulled inside by Layla clutching his arm once she had opened the door. Wincing, he went along willingly, his vision going dark once they were fully inside.

Rummaging through her pack, Layla produced two small stones. Clicking them together, they lit up as bright as any torch.

"Hold these," she said as she passed them along to Link.

"Light stones," he mused as he looked at them. "My father used to use these in the woods. Handier than any lighting device, even if some find them primitive. I never thought I would see someone use these again."

"Well, you thought wrong," Layla assured him as she moved forward.

Link looked around, shining the light to get a better idea of his surroundings. What once he imagined had been a grand entrance was now a desolated, dank room with overturned rotting wooden furniture and debris lying scattered. It had also been evident that some rebellious youth had once inhabited the room after its desertion and used it as a place to drink and take out their frustrations on the world they lived in. On one of the walls had words scrawled across it in red paint.

"Beware, for the white lion arises and his reign shall deal swift justice. Death to all usurpers and false believers." Layla read the words in disgust. "I still don't believe Razmus is the white lion of prophecy."

"A prophecy is just words," Link said. "If there's one thing I learned in Annetta's company, it's that there really is no such thing as fate. We all make our own choices."

"How exactly do you know that?" The young Gaian female eyed him curiously as she continued to walk further into the tower, trying to find a place to set the fuse.

"Because she's always said so," he replied, "and from what I've seen, it's proven to be right."

"No, what I mean is how do you know that her actions and her thoughts are not just part of the grand design of the Unknown and she only thinks she has free will, but ultimately her fate is already written?"

Pausing, Link thought hard on what Layla had said. Was it true that Annetta, himself and all of his friends already had a predetermined destiny they could not escape? The innocent thought slowly boiled into anger as he looked over at his companion to retort. It was not meant to be, however, as the sound of one of the structures being knocked over could be heard from a distance. His body coiling for a fight, Link handed the light stones to Layla and readied his sword.

"You get that fuse set," he whispered to her. "Go now."

Though he disliked it, Link did his best to tap into his feral senses as he had once been taught, his vision becoming a little clearer. He had to be careful, however, since one of the downfalls to his curse was that he had little control over his abilities and risked phasing fully into his feral form. Walking in the direction of the noise, Link found an overturned table and hid behind it, utilizing it as a wall. Peering from around the corner, he saw the forms of two soldiers, a Hurtz and a Gaian, armed with great barbed spears.

"Oi, we know you're in there!" the Gaian called out, "Come out willingly and we'll go easy on you."

"Ruddy kids," the Hurtz grunted. "Always breakin' in where they shouldn't be."

"Can you blame them? Pretty nifty place for a late night excursion," the Gaian retorted. "My concern is deserters, or worse."

The short canine ears of the Hurtz flattened as he thought about it. His nostrils flared, taking in the smells around him. Then, without warning, he overturned Link's table, revealing the youth. "And what have we here?"

Link drew his sword as he took a fighter stance. "I'm warning you, stay back!"

"Oh, or you'll do what, lad?" the Hurtz grinned, fully exposing his jagged yellow teeth. His eyes then narrowed when he caught sight of Link's scar. Hissing, he withdrew. "Unknown's bane! This one is cursed! We best not touch him!"

"That's right," Link prodded them. "I'm as unclean as they come."

The Gaian soldier was not fazed, and moving forward he pressed the tip of his spear into Link's chest. "And how's we to know there aren't more of you in here? Speak, half breed, or I will spill your guts where you stand."

"Go ahead and try." Link gritted his teeth and knocked the spear to the side, rolling out of the way as the Hurtz's weapon came crashing down onto the ground.

Recovering and pivoting on his heel in the nick of time, Link's sword met with the blade of the Gaian's spear. Throwing it back with full force, he was faced with the reality of being outnumbered. Still, he remembered facing worse odds beside Annetta. Remembering his training with Brakkus, he took in a deep breath, grabbed a chair as a shield and lunged at the Gaian. His attention during the fight needed to be divided, however, for the Hurtz warrior had no intention of waiting his turn.

Further away, Layla made the final preparations for setting the charge. Her ears had long ago picked up the commotion of the fight, intensifying the speed at which her hands worked. Sure that she had completed the task, she set the timer, reached under her shirt and produced an amulet of a spear. Touching the blade, the pendant sprung to life, transforming into the weapon in her grip. Turning from her work, she made her way into the fray.

Meanwhile, Link took hit after hit from both opponents, doing his best to buy Layla as much time as he could spare. Taking out the tower was their only shot. He was not prepared then to see an ally appear at his side and release him of one of his foes.

Layla jumped in to take on the Hurtz, her spear acting as both a defensive and offensive weapon, a spinning mass of silver swirls in her hands as she attacked and parried, never in the same order.

From the corner of his eye, Link watched in awe as she not only countered her foe but gained the upper hand. Losing control of his own fight briefly, he gave way and the blade of his enemy found a weakness in the joint of his shoulder, cutting him. The blade entering him was the signal for his full awareness returning. Link refocused his efforts twice over and soon, the Gaian soldier was no more.

"You need to get out of here!" Layla called not long after as she fought on.

Clutching his injured shoulder, Link looked over at her with a determined gaze. "I'm not leaving you here."

Hearing the overly sentimental and overused words come from his mouth, Layla could not help but smile a little. "You truly are the weakest link, Lincerious Heallaws. Get out and help them win this fight. Your task in this place is done."

Realizing what she meant by the task being done, Link felt a chill go down his spine. He then also realized how close they were to the exit now, seeing the moonlight coming through the open door. Had she planned this? Before he could even contemplate, however, a deafening noise, like thunder, crashed down around him and everything turned white.

Chapter 37

Venetor swung at Razmus, claws colliding in a display of sparks over and over. Jumping back, the two psychic warriors removed themselves from their fighter stances, but did not unlock eyes. By this point, each of them wore a collection of small cuts they had received from one another, but none were serious. They were evenly matched, and this only drove the urge within them for a challenging fight further.

"You are truly a Severio," Razmus spoke after a lengthy pause. "It is a shame that you are not of my line. I'd imagine had I any descendants, they would be just like you."

"You should have thought about that when you first awoke," Venetor responded. "Had you bent the knee to your rightful king, none of this would have happened. Twelve thousand years of punishment would have been enough in the eyes of anyone."

"Ah, but you see, I am the rightful king," Razmus replied. "I was the white lion of prophecy and I came to lead the people onto the correct path, the right path. I saved Gaia."

"You are destroying it," Venetor spat. "Gaia is not perfect, but she was thriving until you rose from your slumber."

"Lord and ladies that would squabble all over each other, Hurtz being mistreated and seen as less than citizens of Gaia, and a nation so proud it thought to travel the stars," Razmus retorted. "No, I think I did save it. It is you who are the blind one in this situation."

Before Razmus could speak further, an earth-shaking boom came from the direction of the city. The fighting all around seemed to stop as everyone's attention turned to where Magnus's tower had erupted with white smoke. Seconds later, the great structure fell as though it had been nothing more than a pile of children's building blocks.

Seeing this, Venetor glanced back at Razmus with a triumphant smile. "It is finished. Without the tower, you have no power over the Hurtz and therefore, no power here."

The reflection of the smoking mass of where the tower had been could clearly be seen in the blue orbs that were Razmus's eyes. There was a degree of shock on his face, seeing his brother's tower fall and the last remaining testament of anything from his time that had existed in the present turn to ash. Hearing the words that Venetor had spoken, however, the Lord of the Unfinished Tower was brought back into the present and sent into a fit of laughter.

"You flummoxed fool. Who would give you such an idea that their will is bound to something which could so easily be destroyed?" he guffawed.

Venetor felt the colour drain from his face as he heard the renewed sound of battle form around him again. The worst of what he felt, however, was not that. It was a feeling he had experienced just a year before all of these events. It had happened when he had been ordered by his father to leave, when he had raced to get to one of the last existing vessels left on Gaia to flee for help, and when he had left knowing his people would suffer. It was a feeling Venetor Severio had vowed to never experience again, defencelessness. Glowering at Razmus, he did his best to keep his internal turmoil to himself.

"How did you do it?" he asked coolly.

"That is a secret that will live and die with me quite literally," Razmus stated with no further explanation as he raised his claws. "Willing to try, Ironfisted?"

Calling forth his psychic fire yet again and bending it to his will around his hands, Venetor redoubled his focus. "Whatever it takes."

He then leapt towards his calling, engaging in the battle anew.

ജ‌ଓ

Blinking, Link felt a sharp pain in his left leg as he came to in addition to the wound he had sustained earlier in his shoulder. His world spun and there was a buzzing in his ears. As he tried to get up, he noticed that it was covered in stony debris. Sitting up, he did his best to begin to uncover it and try to see if it was broken. Applying pressure, he winced. Something was definitely not right. He then remembered the last thing that had happened, his flight from the tower with Layla and their encounter with Razmus's soldiers. Looking around, he saw no trace of their foes, but neither could he see Layla. Struggling to get up, he tried to reach for the hilt of his sword to prop himself up, only to realize it was not in its scabbard. Cursing, he crawled over to one of the closest large broken tower pieces. Grabbing hold, he lifted himself up higher to get a better look. Link then saw the body of the Hurtz warrior. Not far from the creature was his sword. Getting back down, he did his best to slink over. Once he grasped the sword hilt, he propped himself up on it and resumed his search.

It did not take long to locate Layla. She had landed in such a way that her hands stretched out from under the debris, like a sailor drowning at sea. Rushing over to get to her, Link knelt down as best as he could. With his scraped and bloodied hands, he then began to move the rest of the rocks which covered her. As he worked to free her, a shuddering gasp escaped Layla's lungs as she came to, prompting him to stop.

"Easy, it's just me," he hushed her. "I'll get you out, just stay still."

"I can't feel my legs," she managed to say in a raspy and torn voice. "I can't feel very much at all."

"I'll get you out and get you to one of the Water Elf medics. They can help you," he assured her.

Her face, a mixture of blood, dust and ash contorted as involuntary tears streaked down her face from the lack of feeling while she shook her head. "We'll never make it."

"Yes, we will." He corrected her and continued to work. "I'll get you out, you're going to be fine, you'll see."

"The weakest link as always," she chuckled, a choking cough taking its place soon after. "My time here is over. The embrace of the Unknown comes for me."

"No, you stay with me," he growled, working more furiously.

"I'm feeling somewhat cold, is death cold?" she asked faintly and then smiled. "You know, had things worked out, I could have seen myself falling in love with you, curse or no curse."

The words brought an extra sting to Link, and having finished removing the debris, he used the last of his remaining strength to drag Layla out of the hole she had been in. Holding her in his arms, he said, "We can still have that chance, you and I."

Coughing, the Gaian female shook her head. "No, no Lincerious, you were fated to another, to a Severio."

"I don't even know if my feelings for her are real," he said.

"Or maybe you're just scared that they are more real than anything else you've felt before-" Layla was cut off by a gurgling cough as she spat out some blood. Shivering again, she rested her head against him. "I think...I will just sleep here for a while...it's so cold..."

With that, Link felt her last breath escape her. He had failed yet again to protect a friend, failed to help. It was a feeling he had forgotten since Brakkus's death and now it was present again. A rage filled him as he shook her, trying to reawaken her to life.

"Stay with me!" he shouted.

He continued to yell for some time, hoping that she would open her eyes, hoping that she would wake. Deeper inside, he knew that

Layla was no longer there and what he held in his arms was a husk that would soon grow cold. His mind coming to terms with this, he looked down at her helplessly as a sob began to form in the back of his throat.

"Weep not for those who have gone from this life," a familiar voice spoke behind Link. "but for those who yet live, for they are the ones who endure the struggles."

Becoming conscious that he was no longer alone, Link laid Layla down and turned to the source of the voice. Some distance away stood two beings, a man and a woman both dressed in identical black suits, crisp white shirts and matching black ties. The woman, pale of complexion, wore her long crimson hair tied back in a clean ponytail while the man, of darker skin, had short pale blonde spiked hair. None of this really struck Link as strange, but what did were the eye colours matching their hair. There was something oddly familiar to them.

"You have done well, young Lincerious Heallaws," the woman spoke again as she strode forwards. "A testament to the loyalty of the Heallaws clan as it has been for years, even before what befell your family."

"Who are you and what do you want of me?" he asked, attempting to rise by propping himself up on his sword.

Without saying a word, the man in the suit came at Link. Reaching down, he placed a hand on his leg. Gritting his teeth, Link did his best not to make a sound from the pain, only to realize it had vanished along with his other wounds. Taking a step back, he then recognized who he was speaking to as an image of a phoenix and a thunderbird flashed before his eyes. Instantly, he knelt before them.

"Forgive me, Bwiskai and Fulgura," he said. "I did not know you in this form."

"Nor should you have." Fulgura smiled. "We felt this shape would stand out less in this world."

"As honoured as I am to see you again, I don't understand why you are here."

"Rise, mortal. We come to say this," Bwiskai began. "Your journey here may come to an end, and another journey can begin."

Link glanced at them both with a perplexed gaze as he got up. "I still don't know what you mean."

"What do you know of the Order of the White Knight?" Fulgura asked.

"The White Knights of the Unknown," Link replied. "My father told me stories of them growing up. I had always wanted to be one since I was a boy. They are an elite warrior class comprised only of fighters selected by the messengers of the Unknown. Trained by angels, they are fully devoted to their cause. They have no spouses or children, don't claim any sort of title and are also absolved of all past sins in the eyes of the Unknown."

"The Unknown has seen your courage and your loyalty," Bwiskai commented. "And so he wishes to offer you a place among their ranks."

Link was taken aback by the proclamation, his head still dazed from the explosion, the ringing present in his ears was only now slowly beginning to dissipate. "But I'm no one. I'm an outcast among my own people. I couldn't even save Layla from death. The White Knights are all great heroes that are renowned to all who know and believe. I couldn't even save-"

"None of the White Knights were heroes when first they accepted," Fulgura reminded him. "They were no different than you are now."

Link thought long and hard before speaking again. "What about my friends? What about Annetta and Jason and-"

"You will not be able to speak with them until your training is complete. The task must be finished with no outside interference," Bwiskai explained, "should you choose to accept."

"We cannot linger here long," Fulgura added. "Layla's soul has been collected and brought over to the other side. Our time here is fleeting."

Link bit his lip as he buried himself in thought once again. His life had always revolved around fighting. His dream, as with any soldier, was to be the best, to be the greatest, to be remembered, to train and master every possible fighting style, weapon and ability he could get his hands on. The White Knights of the Unknown had access to all of these. They were able to protect people, the one thing Link wanted to be able to do most of all, and yet at every turn, he had failed. His eyes lingered on where Layla lay as the last thought entered his mind.

"If I decide to leave, how long will I be in training?" he questioned.

"You will train within the Citadel of the Unknown," Bwiskai explained. "For those here, it shall be a span of but a few months, within the citadel, it shall be thirty-three years."

"Will I age?" Link panicked.

"Have no fear of becoming old, Lincerious Heallaws." Fulgura smiled. "Time will pass but you shall not age, only gain in knowledge and in strength. Such are the gifts the Unknown can bestow upon you, should you accept."

"My friends, I want them to know I'm alright," he said again after another pause as he weighed the consequences.

"No one can know," Fulgura intoned. "The training of a White Knight cannot be spoken of to just anyone."

Link paused at this. He did not want to leave Annetta, Jason and the others without saying anything. They would worry if he did, especially after everything that had just happened with the tower blowing up. But a part of him deeper inside felt that he would be of no use to them. He had failed Layla and the sting of that failure echoed in his ears along with the ringing he still heard. He was being given a once in a lifetime opportunity to become one of the greatest fighters in the world. It was a chance he had always dreamed of, to be able to protect those he cared about and to overcome the circumstances of his birth, to no longer be an outcast. While not great, the sting of having been back home and realizing he would not be accepted as he was made it obvious that something needed to be done, and he would not find the answers on Earth. As a White Knight, he could gain that acceptance and the skills he needed to prevent any more of his friends being taken from him. What were a few months of being absent from his friends compared to that?

"Okay then," Link sighed. "I've nothing else to lose."

"Just one thing," Bwiskai said as his eyes wandered to the sword Link held.

Glancing down at the blade, a sword that had been passed down to his father, Link looked back over at the two beings with a pleading expression in his eyes.

"No titles," Bwiskai stated. "Even those of belonging to one clan or another."

"You will have another," Fulgura assured him. "Now come and follow him."

Link's eyes gazed down at the sword. He could feel the weight of it as he held it in his hand, the texture of the grip beneath his fingers and the resistance to obey what was asked. Closing his eyes as he finalized his decision, however, he let the blade fall, hitting the ground with a thud that was louder in his ears than it seemed. Looking up to see everything illuminated in a blazing white before him, he felt the sensation of water washing over him and touched his face. He felt that the scar he had worn his whole life had vanished. He then felt a weightlessness, as though all of his cares were gone, that what he was doing was right. With no further reservations about where the future was to take him, he stepped towards the light.

Chapter 38

Her arm slung over his shoulder, Annetta continued to walk with Darius's assistance. They had left most of the battlefield behind and were now on its outskirts, where the edge of the forest began. Their attempts to escape were thwarted, however, when a pack of Gaian soldiers rushed in. Annetta drew Severbane from its scabbard and held the blade in an unstable two-handed grip before her. Waiting until her adversaries lunged forward, the girl summoned up the last reserves of her strength and unleashed an adrenaline charged counter-attack, a whirl of sword strokes that would have left many opponents dizzy. Ending the enemy fighter closest to her, she spun around, having felt the eyes of the other soldier on her, who after seeing what the girl had managed to do in her current state, was having second thoughts.

Annetta gritted her teeth and pressed forward towards him, her sword before her. Her attention was wrongfully placed, however, and a second later, she found herself flying through the air as a mighty Hurtz club swatted her aside.

"Annetta!" Darius called, still occupied by his own fight and unable to reach her.

Landing some distance away and only being spared broken bones due to her armour, Annetta cringed. She knew she would most likely be black and blue the next day, if she made it. Looking over to the right, she saw Severbane lying but a few inches from her and reached out to grab it, her fingers barely able to touch the pommel. Too exhausted to use her abilities, she stretched further, hoping to grasp it. She then heard the sound of approaching feet. Panic gripping her, she tried to tap into what was left of her psychic powers, only causing the hilt to rattle as it attempted to move towards her. Seeing the massive boots inching closer to her from the corner of her eye pushed further adrenaline into Annetta. Snatching up the sword in the final moment before the shadow engulfed her, she lifted the blade above bracing for impact. Closing her eyes, she waited.

She continued to wait for some time but nothing came, and soon a firm grip caught hold of her wrist. Annetta opened her eyes. There to greet her, was a pair of green eyes and ruffled brown hair she never thought she would see again.

"J.K.?" she asked, quizzically. "But how?"

"Well, you left a pretty big gaping portal back at the Eye to All Worlds. You were sort of easy to follow." He smiled and helped her up.

Still perplexed, Annetta glanced around to gain her bearings. Turning around completely, she saw Puc and Sarina standing some distance away, the second half of the Four Forces that they had taken with them to fight against the Fire Elves in tow.

"You came, all of you," she managed to say.

"Astounding as it may sound, you did not honestly think we would let you get yourself killed a second time, did you?" Puc retorted with his usual sarcastic candour.

Before Annetta could reply, Darius scrambled towards them, having freed himself of his nemesis. Seeing the new arrivals, he was just as taken aback as Annetta had been, if not more.

"Whoa, is it really you guys?" he asked.

"In the flesh, or so last we checked," the First Mage stated.

"As happy as I am to see you, we have our work cut out for us," Darius said, "It doesn't look like whatever had been planned with the tower worked and the Hurtz are still attacking."

"What? I thought that one was in the bag!" Jason exclaimed.

"You sure it maybe just doesn't take time to wear off? Like a poison or a spell?" Sarina asked.

"Unknown's bane, we must have missed something," Puc muttered to himself.

"The question is what," Darius replied. "Everything seemed to point to the tower having been the cause of it."

While Puc and the others continued to speak, Annetta had begun to slip into a fatigue-driven delirium. The world around her slowed down as she observed the happenings on the field around her. Further away, she could still see Venetor and Razmus engaged in their struggle, the light of their psychic fire prominent on the darkened field. Airships and Soarin alike sailed through the air, while on the ground, the hordes of Minotaur, Ogaien, Water Elves and freed Gaians all banded together, trying to overtake the enemy, but there was something missing. Annetta had felt it ever since she had arrived on Gaia, a pang in her heart where something should have been but wasn't. The more she had fought that day, the more she had felt it slip away, like trudging through concrete which continued to rise and thicken around her. The word she was looking for then came to her, and she realized what it was that gave her a sinking feeling in her gut.

"We may have greater numbers now," she muttered, "but we are losing this fight."

"What do you mean, Anne?" Jason asked.

"Exactly what I said," she continued. "We have greater numbers, but we are losing the fight. Everyone's morale is low."

"The separation of the army may have had something to do with that," Puc agreed. "As well as the fact that many do not wish to be fighting the Hurtz in the first place."

Annetta looked over to the field once more. She knew she had to do something, but she had no idea what she could do in the state she was in. Every part of her body ached and burned, and she was barely standing. She then remembered who else was out there now, possibly hurt or even worse, her family, those she loved and had wanted to protect.

"I have to go back," she said, and those around her knew she would not change her mind on the subject.

"Before you go off again." Sarina interrupted her and reaching into the pouch on her belt, produced a vial that she handed to Annetta. "You may want to take that."

Accepting the vial, Annetta looked skeptically at the blue liquid inside of it and recognized it at the same potion Puc had given her the day she had arrived in Q-16 for the first time. Remembering the vile taste of it, she scrunched up her nose as she popped the cork and downed it, only to be surprised there was no aftertaste at all. She looked over at Sarina questioningly.

"An improvement I made." She beamed.

"A great one." Annetta smiled, feeling her energy return, and glanced over at Puc. "You could use a few pointers."

"Watch your tongue, young Severio," he warned her.

An idea then came to Annetta. Flexing the fingers in her hands and seeing she was able to move again, she handed Severbane to Jason and dropped her shield. "I'm not going to need this for what I'm about to do. You'd best hang onto it for me."

"What? Are you crazy?" he protested. "No way are you going out there without a weapon!"

"I won't need one. Just trust me!" she called, already having started moving away. "Meet me at the tallest point on the field, over there by that ridge where the big hill is."

Having pointed to where she wanted them to go, she was off again, running as fast as her legs would carry her.

"What exactly do you think she has planned?" Darius inquired of Puc.

"Do I look like some omniscient being to you?" the First Mage retorted. "I know a great deal about many things, but what goes through Annetta Severio's head is certainly not one of them. I will say this. I do believe she is finally beginning to understand her place in the world."

"What do you mean understand her place in the world?" Jason motioned frantically to where Annetta had vanished. "Unless it's dead, then I don't get it. My best friend just went without a weapon into a fight!"

"Did you not see the look in her eyes?" Puc asked, only getting a blank stare from the trio with him. "It was a look of understanding who she was, what she has to do. It is the look a child gives when they decide to leave their childhood behind. I have only been privileged to see it once in my life before, and it was with Arieus and Arcanthur when they were boys. What Annetta plans to do I cannot say, but whatever it is, she is not going in there with fanciful notions. She goes to fight."

While this all went on, Sarina noticed something was out of place. Glancing around, she figured it out. "Has anyone seen Matt anywhere?"

ಬಂಡ

Having slipped away from the others the moment they had come through the portal had been the easy part. Teleporting past everything on the field of battle had not. It had been a reckless move on Matthias's part, but the assassin knew that beyond the great doors of the capital city waited the prize he had sought out for so long. He felt without a doubt that he would cross paths with Amarok Mezorian should he stride through the gates, and nothing else could convince him otherwise. He had a score to settle with his old master.

Downing an energy replenishing potion once he had gotten inside through teleporting past obstacles, he found himself standing at the base of the building he assumed to be the stronghold of Razmus. Dropping the vial and hearing the distinct shattering of glass, Matthias strode inside. He was greeted by two Hurtz guards that came charging at him from the main corridor once he had opened the door. Extending his claws, he made quick work of both of them. Nothing would stand in his way for vengeance.

He continued to trudge through the building, not at all meaning to conceal his position. He wanted Amarok to know who had come for him. Having finished his trek on the first floor, he ascended to the next one, and the next one, and the next one. Reaching the final level and having taken the last step down the lengthy stone hall, he waited. The wait felt so long that he had almost given up his crusade, thinking it foolish to delay any longer while his friends toiled below. His muscles beginning to twitch in response to his command to turn around, he froze as his ears picked up a subtle metallic echo through the hall.

The resonance continued to grow louder until Matthias was certain that the cavernous sound was coming from behind him. Pivoting on his heel, his suspicion was confirmed as before him stood Amarok, his broken silver mask glinting from the firelight of the torches around them.

"And how long, pray tell, did it take you to find me?" Amarok mused.

"Doesn't matter." Matthias gritted his teeth as he got into a fighter's stance, his gauntlet claws extending. "The point is that I did, and now we finish this."

"As you'll have it," the masked assassin replied, not moving from his spot, placing his arms behind his back.

Angered by the lack of passion for the fight, Matthias roared as he charged head first towards his opponent. As soon as he began to run, the silver studs on Amarok's armour all down the lengths of his arms begin to move to meet him, extending like pointed tentacles. Colliding halfway, Matthias attempted to cut through them as a house cat would through a forest of ribbons. In his case, however, the ribbons fought back, hoping to take him out in the process.

Amarok stood rooted to his spot, watching Matthias dispassionately. It was not an absence of wanting the battle that clouded the assassin's mind, though, but the thoughts of a more immediate task at hand. Other things were unravelling around them, things which Amarok needed to see through. The elder assassin's patience having reached its end, he teleported from sight.

Matthias fell slightly forward upon Amarok vanishing. Rage seething through him, he turned around to see the masked figure standing close to one of the large open windows, his weapons retracted in their dormant state.

"Coward!" Matthias spat. "Come back and face me like a psychic warrior!"

"Where did you ever get the notion that all of this was just about our little rivalry?" Amarok questioned him. "You have still much to learn, Matthias, and the first thing is that not all is as it seems in this world and that everyone, whether they like it or not, is just a game piece, only a shred of the whole fabric of reality. Above this, above all of it are the few gods who oversee it all, and unless you are in their ranks, you count for nought."

"What in all the hells are you talking about?" Matthias scoffed.

"This: You are a chess piece, and I a god," Amarok informed him, an icy malice trickling off of every word as he spoke. "And now, I go, for this was all just a means to an end."

Teleporting towards him and thrusting his claws forward to tear at his throat, Matthias found himself grasping at air when he reached his target. He stood beside the window, lost for a moment, looking up into the night sky, and then he saw it. There, hiding in the clouds, he was certain he was able to see a familiar shape. It was a great castle with large rectangular towers, giving the structure an almost industrial instead of medieval shape. Multiple tiny windows dotted the structure like a thousand stars as it became more prominent through the swirling mist-like clouds.

His mouth agape, he whispered, "Valdhar."

෯ඏ

Following Annetta to where she had told them to go, Jason, Darius, Sarina and Puc noted something from the corner of their eye as they rode. Looking up, they saw a vast form in the clouds.

"What on Earth?" Jason asked.

"Is that?" Darius raised an eyebrow.

Puc studied the slowly diminishing form in the clouds as it grew more distant, disappearing into space. The floating structure resembled a castle. Everything in his mind spoke against it being what his logic pointed at.

"Valdhar... but it cannot be." He whispered.

"We'll have to worry about it later." Sarina interrupted his stream of thought. "Annetta needs us now."

Hearing what she had said, the others nodded, continuing their course.

ଋଦ୍ଧ

The wind whizzing past her ears and the sound of small stones and twigs snapping beneath her was all Annetta could pick up as she continued down the path. Every so often, she would stumble over raised roots and uneven ground, but this did not deter her from her course of action. Branches brushed past her legs where trees bowed too low along the path, further obstructing her, but she did not care. The smell of dampened earth filled her nostrils, making it harder to breathe the further she ran, but still she continued. All she knew was that she had to keep going. The only thing that frightened her was that when the time came, she would not know what to do, and she hoped that if there was such a being as the Unknown or whatever their name was, that they would guide her. Her family needed her. They along with the countless others below, depended on her to make a difference. Tripping and falling forward, scraping her hands in the process, she growled under her breath, rose, and kept going.

Drawing closer to her destination, Annetta focused, channelling every bit of herself into her thoughts, particularly into the ones she had gathered about her feral form. It was true that she had never used it, but Venetor had said it was a matter of simply knowing, and that her Gaian biology would take care of the rest. She could only hope he had been right, and she could only hope that what she was doing was right as well.

Maintaining her course, Annetta had been certain that nothing was going to happen, that her crusade was to fail. As she was about to give up hope, however, she began to feel it. At first, it was a low reverberating tingling in her fingers and toes, the kind one got from their limbs having fallen asleep and then waking up. As she continued to run, focusing on the dreams and visions, it all intensified, until it became a burning sensation all over her body. Fighting against it, she forced herself towards the edge of the hill. Her knees buckling beneath her from the scorching along her body, she dropped to all fours and with all the speed she could muster, persisted in making the climb.

ଋଦ୍ଧ

The turmoil of battle continued. Blow upon blow collided, the Lord of the Unfinished Tower and the Ironfisted. There seemed to be no end. Their psychic fighting style had led them to flight, mixed with teleporting every so often as they tried to outmaneuver one another. Led away from the battlefield, they soon found themselves on the towering city walls.

Landing on the stone walkway, the two duelling warriors faced off one another, their eyes locked in a staring contest. Neither moved a muscle, silently regaining some of the energy spent on the strenuous form of brawling.

Not eager to wait any longer, Razmus was the first to attack, rushing at Venetor with a psychic energy-projected leap that made him appear to float through the air. Seeing the oncoming onslaught, Venetor braced himself, only to see Razmus disappear seconds before impact. His muscles coiling, ready to move away at a moment's notice, Venetor looked around, trying to predict where he would resurface. His looking away cost him the advantage, however, when Razmus reappeared in the same spot he had been. His fist colliding with Venetor's jaw, the Gaian prince was sent through the wall, the only thing saving him from his body being reduced to a heap of contorted flesh being the psychic shield he had held up around himself the entire time. He would still be incredibly bruised and possess more than a few fractures when all would be said and done, but he would not be broken. Not completely. Sailing through the air and impacting some distance away on the ground below, he groaned in agony as he did his best to rise.

Razmus floated over but mere seconds later, descending gently on a raised pile of rubble with his arms crossed over his chest. Seeing the state Venetor was in, a smile formed on his face.

"Give it up, spawn of Magnus," he told him. "It's over, I have won. I who am the rightful king."

Venetor raised his hand to his left arm, feeling how tender it had become from having absorbed the majority of the shock. He was vaguely aware of what was happening on the field as well, but part of him ignored it. He had no choice. He would not surrender, this was not his way. His pride would not let him, and when stripped of all his power, that was all he had left. Straightening his back, his chest out and his fists curled for further encounters, Venetor stood defiantly before Razmus.

"Last chance. I will not stop until you relinquish the crown and let my people go," he intoned.

"You take me for a fool?" Razmus spat as he came closer. "Never."

Gritting his teeth, Venetor mentally prepared himself for another round of attacks. The muscles on his back arched and braced for impact. He then heard it in the distance, the faint thunderous sound of troops marching. Isolating it, he turned back to gaze upon a hill that stood not far from them. At first, one could see nothing significant about it. Then over the ridge it came, basked in a platinum glow against the rising red sun. Venetor felt his guard drop as he gazed upon it, a lioness, its fur, the most pristine of whites. Behind her were a slew of warriors, Water Elves, Minotaur, Soarin and Ogaien. Gazing down below, the lioness surveyed everything with its keen blue eyes. Certain she had all in her domain under her attention, she let out a roar. Taking one last look at the battlefield, she took off in a single leap, bounding forward, followed by the slew of soldiers behind. Weapons drawn, they charged into the fray, led by the white lioness.

Many had turned to see what happened when she had roared, and many of the Gaians fighting for Razmus could not believe their eyes. Neither could those who fought for the Four Forces. Seeing the new incoming fighters, they cheered and pressed forward with renewed faith.

Seeing this shift in power and seeing many of his own Gaian soldiers lay down arms in reverence of what had just occurred, Razmus sneered and turned his attention back to Venetor.

"Is this your last desperate attempt to try and tips the scales of war? A cheap parlour trick?" he spat, pointing at the lioness, which was now deep in the fray.

Watching her go, Venetor could not help but crack a grin that turned into a deep rumbling laughter as he threw his head back. Composing himself, he looked back at the ancient lord. "Well, I did try to warn you, didn't I?"

Seething with rage, Razmus let out a howl and threw himself at Venetor, resuming their fight.

಼ೱಐ಼

Rushing through the field, Annetta felt as though her senses were on overdrive. Everything in her body seemed amplified upon her transformation, just as Venetor had described it to her. Though her course was set to find her family and make sure they were out of harm's way, she was still faced every so often with oncoming enemies, angry Hurtz and fanatic Gaian warriors who claimed they would take her pelt and present it to Razmus himself. In most cases, she was able to outmaneuver the fighters until she was able to attack. When she was not, Jason, Puc or Sarina were in close enough range to assist, having followed her as she had asked them to do earlier. It was like old times again. The one person that was missing was Link, and she hoped to catch a glimpse of him somewhere on the battlefield.

"Too bad we can't understand a thing going through your head now, Anne," Jason commented when they had come to a short stop.

Annetta let out a low pitched rumbling sound in response to the comment as she sniffed the air. Certain of her path again, she took off.

Watching her go, Jason and Sarina lingered behind for a little while, during which time, Puc had dispensed with a foe he had been sparring with and caught up to them.

"How do we deal with the Hurtz?" Jason asked, turning to the mage.

Puc scanned the field as he tried to formulate a plan of attack in his head. The forces they had brought with them had increased the chances of victory, but at what cost? The slaughter of thousands of Hurtz who had no control over their actions? The more he thought about it, the more he understood why Annetta had tried to undertake the plan she had at the beginning of the battle. At the same time, he knew its futility as he looked at the broken bodies scattered throughout the grounds, both ally and enemy.

He glanced sideways at Jason. "The same way you deal with any enemy, Kinsman. You fight."

"But they-" he began.

"They are the enemy." Puc cut him off. "Have you not figured it out by now? War is an ugly affair."

"There must be something else we can do," Sarina thought out loud. "A spell to put them to sleep perhaps?"

"We would risk hitting everyone around us, including ourselves." Puc shot the idea down.

"Oh... well there has to be something." The girl frowned.

"Aren't you supposed to be like, one of the greatest mages alive?" Jason questioned him.

"I may be many things, but I am not the Unknown himself," the First Mage replied.

Having quieted them both down, Jason and Sarina turned to each other to try and come up with something. Looking outwards, Puc's eyes lingered on Venetor and Razmus as they fought again in midair, slashing at each other's throats.

"Perhaps there is some form of hope," he spoke again after pausing, "and perhaps the fate of this battle does not rest on our shoulders at all."

He then realized why they had thought the Hurtz had been linked to the two towers and why they had been wrong. There was another factor they had not taken into account. Razmus himself. Seeing Annetta grow more distant on the horizon before them, Puc urged his horse forward yet again before he could share his thoughts and called to Sarina and Jason. "These things do not mean that we do not fight. Onwards!"

Chapter 39

Dodging the latest assault, Venetor countered with his elbow, pushing Razmus's arm away. Teleporting upon every hit, they soon found themselves in the air again. After another round of struggle, Razmus managed to feint a blow, and struck Venetor square in the gut.

His psychic shield being his only saving grace yet again, Venetor felt himself sailing through the air, and soon after collided with a rocky surface. He had no time to contemplate his surroundings or even to orient himself in the slightest, for just as he attempted to rise, Razmus's clawed gauntlets came at his throat. Grabbing his wrists, Venetor struggled to prevent the spiked ends from coming any closer to his neck. Soon after, the two of them found themselves grappling, fighting for dominance. Neither seemed to give way to the other. It was only brought to an end when Venetor managed to look up and teleport away to the bit of ground he could see.

Having freed himself, Venetor sat up and was able to feel every bruise and cut on his body. His psychic energy was fading, and he was not sure how much longer he could keep up with his adversary. He could see Razmus was not much better off, as the Lord of the Unfinished Tower turned to face him anew. Cuts marked his face and his once pearl armour was now tarnished with earth, soot and blood.

His breathing heavy from the labour of the fight, Razmus addressed him with his arms raised. "It ends here, spawn of Magnus, right where it should."

Confused, Venetor looked around and realized that they had both ended up on top of Razmus's tower. The floor beneath was completed, reinforced with dark wooden planks, while the walls that meant to climb even higher than they already did, stood in pieces like sentries that were to witness their bout.

Straightening his posture and curling his fists before him once more, Venetor closed his eyes as he focused, allowing the last remaining reserves of energy to flow through him, encircling his limbs in a protective aura. He had one last shot he felt, and after that it would be over, one way or another. Yet Venetor did not fear death. The name Severio would live on through his son and through the grandchildren of Orbeyus.

He then remembered the white lioness upon the hill, her presence and the charge. Razmus had been exposed as a fake, there was no denying to anyone what they had seen. The prophecy his people had waited on for so long had finally surfaced, during his own lifetime. It all had to count for something.

Resolution filling him, Venetor glared into the eyes of his enemy. "It does end. For you."

A ragged roar escaping his lungs, Venetor launched himself at his foe again in a series of strikes that would define the fate of his kingdom. He held nothing back, sending punches, kicks and the occasional slash from his psychic claws at Razmus. His fury, however, created a blind spot, which Razmus found with ease, tripping the prince and sending him on his back. Venetor struggled to rise, but soon after, found himself grappling with his foe, their hands entwined and thrashing for dominance.

"I don't think you heard me correctly," Razmus spat. "The line of Magnus Severio shall fall and Razmus Severio shall endure. Perhaps if you say long live the king, I may spare your life so that you may rot in a dungeon as an example, or better yet, in the base of this tower. Wouldn't that be fitting?"

Gritting his teeth as he fought to prevent Razmus's hands from reaching his neck, Venetor then replied, "Long may he reign."

Summoning everything he had left in him, Venetor used his energy to bring down the closest wall. The massive stones rushed towards Razmus as if they were leaves carried by the wind, and collided with the Lord of the Unfinished Tower. Looking over his shoulder to see the source of the commotion, Razmus was met with a block that smashed his head, ending his life. Everything that occurred after was a blur of rock and dust as Razmus's body crumpled and was sent over the edge. Still on his back, Venetor watched as he attempted to lift himself into a seated position.

With no strength in him, he soon dropped his hands. Closing his eyes, he muttered under his breath, "Long live the one true king."

He lay there for some time, unsure of how much of it had passed, when something gripped his forearm. Opening his eyes, he saw a familiar face looking down at him.

"Teron?" his brows knotted in confusion.

"Good to see you too Lord Venetor," Matthias answered as he pulled the Gaian prince to his feet, draping an arm over his shoulder for support.

"How did you?" Venetor asked in half cohesive thoughts.

"It's what I did before for a living," Matthias stated as he rummaged through a pouch he carried at his belt. "I'd find and kill people. I was watching you and Razmus for a while. If things had gotten worse, I would have stepped in."

"Yet you did not," the prince replied.

Wordlessly, Matthias handed a vial to Venetor. Seeing he was unable to even lift a hand towards it, Matthias opened it and poured it down his throat. "I remember Gaian pride being a sore spot for you."

Feeling some vitality return to him as the liquid washed down, Venetor looked over at the assassin, a sly smile spreading across his face. "At least you gathered that much."

ജ

Down below, Skyris and Atala found themselves back to back, facing off against a pair of Hurtz warriors. Many of the Gaian soldiers that had fought for Razmus upon seeing the appearance of the white lioness in the field had promptly changed allegiance. The Hurtz, however, were not so quick to have a change of heart over their bond to Razmus.

Her short swords flashing before her in a display of lights and metallic clashing, Skyris found her prowess seemed little more than child's play to her formidable opponent. Worse, she had begun to lose stamina from the lengthy fighting. There were only so many sword strokes she could deal out in a day, and Skyris Severio was beginning to reach her limit. Her weariness finally showed and Skyris found herself disarmed of one of her blades. Hanging on by a thread, she continued to block the attacks of the Hurtz, unable to land any defining blows of her own. Finally, her other sword knocked from her hand, she braced herself for the inevitable and closed her eyes.

"Lady Skyris!" Atala's voice boomed from behind.

The sound of her voice echoed through Skyris's ears for far longer than she thought it would. Afraid to open her eyes, she remained still, waiting for the Hurtz to cut her in half as she had seen happen to others on the field.

"Lady Skyris," a gruff voice spoke again.

Confused, Skyris opened her eyes to see the Hurtz she had been facing standing before her with an outstretched hand, the massive blade it was wielding stuck in the ground. Skeptically, she accepted the hand and was pulled up. Looking around, she saw that all the Hurtz on the field had dropped the weapons or were looking around, confused as to what had occurred.

In the midst of the field, the white lioness that had appeared strode through, behind her an entourage comprising of Puc, Darius, Jason, Sarina and a score of others including Aurora, Arieus, Talia, Liam and Xander. The creature looked as weary and tired as Skyris felt, a great pink tongue lolling in its mouth as it continued past those present. Coming to a rest, she stopped to take in everything around her. Many Gaians and Hurtz had gathered around, their eyes filled with wonder as they looked upon her.

Some distance away, Venetor and Matthias soon teleported in. Venetor looked as though he had taken an incredible beating. Seeing the white lioness before him, the Gaian prince moved towards her. Standing before the great beast, he knelt, and soon after, the many gathered joined.

"My people are forever in your debt," he said. Standing up, he turned to face those gathered. "Long live the White Lioness of Gaia!"

They replied in cheers. While many lay dead or injured on the field, they knew there would be no more on that day. The fighting had all but come to a halt as the last remaining rebels surrendered. Weapons dropping to the ground, the ringing of metal on metal came to an end. The battle was over.

Chapter 40

What transpired in the time after the battle was somewhat of a haze to Annetta. She remembered being told briefly that the Hurtz were actually controlled by Razmus himself and not the towers, his death having triggered their regaining of control. She also vaguely remembered seeing a massive structure flying overhead at some point that looked familiar, but she failed to believe it was what she thought it had been. Valhdar had been destroyed after all. It was little surprise to her that when she awoke, she found herself in a strange room and a bed she did not recognize. Bolting into a seated position, she found the bed she lay on was big enough to accommodate at least four of her. White and red sheets adorned it, and from the canopy above hung stark white cloth which draped down four mahogany posts. Getting a better look around, she saw the walls matched the paleness of the cloth, upon them hanging tapestries depicting ancient battles that seemed very similar in style to those found in Severio Castle. A large regally-carved closet stood on the far end of the room, and on the opposite wall, a shelf filled with books. Annetta was only finally thrown off from thinking she was in a medieval castle by noticing the mannequin beside her bed, which was dressed in traditional Gaian armour. Beside it, was what looked like one of the work benches with a touchscreen interface built into it from Q-16. Next to these lay Severbane in its scabbard, and her shield.

Getting up from her bed woozily, she found herself wearing a long white nightgown. She walked over to the armour, running her fingers down the finely-made black scale mail. It was cold to the touch. Her hand stopped at the cape. Thinking it had originally been red like the one Venetor had worn when he had first come to Earth, she noticed it was not, and lifting it up, she revealed a white lion embroidered into it upon the crimson.

Just then, the door crept open and Jason's head popped in. Seeing his friend awake, his straight face instantly turned into a smile.

"Oh good, you're awake!" He grinned, swinging the door fully open to reveal Sarina, Puc, Darius, Matthias, Annetta's parents, Xander, Liam and Talia, all waiting behind it.

Looking down at what she was wearing and seeing so many people present, Annetta's face flushed red. "Guys! I'm not dressed yet!"

A slew of 'Oh's' was exchanged, and the door shut once more. Annetta rolled her eyes before turning her attention back to the armour.

She scanned the area around her, but saw no trace of any of her regular clothing. More pressingly, she saw no trace of her jean jacket. Part of her was quite certain it had not survived the transformation process.

"I guess I'll get to buy a new one," she muttered to herself. Turning to the armour, she began to don it.

ℝℛ

In the hallway, Jason and the rest of the companions waited impatiently. So many questions swam through their heads after seeing what had transpired that it brought an air of tension around them. Hearing the door handle move, they turned back to it. Out came Annetta dressed in the armour that had been placed by her bed, with Severbane at her hip and her shield strapped to her back.

"Anne!" Jason cried out, unable to contain his enthusiasm as he tackled the girl with a bear hug.

Returning it, Annetta barely had time to recover as her family rushed in next, closing in around her in a protective circle. She could feel their concern radiating from them as they pressed in. Remembered who else was present, she pulled away slightly.

"I'm okay, I swear," she chuckled, somewhat embarrassed.

"Well, we had some doubts about when you keeled over like that," Matthias said.

"I did what now?" Annetta raised an eyebrow.

"All much less dramatic than he is making it seem," Puc assured her. "Though you did give us all a fair scare when you ran off that way."

"Oh," she managed to say. "Sorry, it's just… it seemed like a good plan at the time."

"Since when has running into a battlefield with no weapon, not telling anyone what you are thinking of doing ever been a good plan?" Sarina inquired.

Annetta sighed as she collected her thoughts. "Look, I'm sorry but when I realized it, it couldn't be helped. I just…I had to go."

"What are you talking about, Annetta?" Puc asked.

"My feral form," she replied. "Or rather, what it needed to be."

The mage nodded, "I see."

Annetta tried to remember the fragments of the end of the battle, organizing her mind. One thing stood out above all others. "Did I… did I actually see Valdhar?"

"I'm afraid so." Matthias confirmed. "It seems Amarok was using Gaia as a front to hide rebuilding it, but to what end I haven't got a clue. He always was an enigma with his plans."

"Do we know where he went?" she inquired.

"Not a clue, but he'll be easier to find if he travels in it, that's for sure." The assassin told her.

"And the Hurtz, what happened to them? I lost control towards the end and I... well it all went black."

"It would appear Razmus had the Hurtz tethered to himself and not the towers as we originally thought." Puc explained. "A form of magic similar to the one that bonded young Lincerious to you. In this case, the enchantment allowed for Razmus to bond his creation to himself so long as he lived. He probably had it cast when he created the first of them. The bond was then passed down through generations of Hurtz without them knowing it due to him being encased in the tower all these years."

Before the conversation could continue, they were interrupted by the sound of approaching feet. Looking over down the hall, a Hurtz dressed in full plate armour stalked towards them with a set of earrings jingling from its one ear. His fur neatly groomed and a new eye patch in place of his old one, Gladius paused some distance before them, placing his hands behind his back.

"The coronation is set to be in an hour," he announced. "Prince Venetor has asked that ye all move towards the main square where the event is to take place. Thanestorm, ye'll be needed for the crowning, and I am to take young Annetta with me now."

Annetta looked at the Hurtz skeptically, but moved forward nonetheless. Finally realizing who was missing, she paused and turned on her heel to look back again. "Where's Link?"

Hearing the question, everyone seemed to avert eye contact with her, fuelling a certain thought that could go with such actions. It was only further fuelled when finally, Puc came forward with a very familiar object in his hand.

"I am sorry, Annetta. He was in the tower when it collapsed. All the workers found was his sword."

A lump formed in Annetta's throat when she accepted the weapon from Puc. The heaviness of the metal seemed to triple in her hands, making it difficult to look upon the blade. It had not even been cleaned, and the blood of its final victim still adorned it. Trying her best to keep calm, Annetta reminded herself that she would see him again when she meditated, and this thought kept her tears at bay. She knew now was not the time to mourn her friend.

"Thank you for telling me," she managed to say as she handed the sword back to Puc, before turning around again and leaving with Gladius to their destination.

๑๛

Much of the debris had been cleared away for the ceremony. While still in a state of ruin, the sombre main square with its cracked marble-like floors served well and reminded all those gathered that what they were to witness was the rebirth of a nation. Standing on an elevated platform where a great tree, now broken, once grew were Annetta, Puc, Atala, Titus, Skyris and a score of other lord and ladies. Escorted by Gladius, Venetor passed through the crowd, dressed in full Gaian armour with a longsword at his hip. Stopping at the foot of the stairs, Gladius allowed Venetor to go up first and followed suit.

Reaching the top, Venetor knelt before the people, just as he remembered his father had done once, many years ago. There was a bittersweetness to it all as he looked out at the crowd of broken people. They had won, but at what cost?

Knowing his place, Puc moved towards Atala, who held a heavy silver coloured war-like crown wreathed in sharp spikes upon a crimson velvet cushion. A single red stone glistened in the centre of the regal headpiece with the light of the sun. Taking the crown into his hands, he moved towards Venetor. Extending his arms outwards with the crown, they hovered over the head of the future king of Gaia.

"Here kneels before you a Gaian who would wish to call himself your king," Puc spoke in a loud and clear voice. "As has always been the case with Gaia, a king is not chosen by blood, but by his acts, and should he be worthy, he takes the mantle from his sire, else another king be elected. Is this Gaian here, Venetor Severio son of Balthazar Severio, worthy to be your king?"

A series of nods, 'aye's' and 'yes's' could be heard from the crowd. It was clear that none opposed the succession. Puc then moved to his next order of business and placed the crown upon Venetor's head.

"By the power, granted to me from on high as First Mage of Aldamoor I crown in the light of the Unknown and give you your king!"

Those gathered below erupted in cheer as Venetor rose from his spot. Puc took a step back, and making eye contact with the new king, let him know their quarrelling would be downplayed for the time being.

Nodding back in respect, Venetor then turned to the masses and raised his hand to quiet them.

"My people," he began, "Gaians and Hurtz alike, we have both bled in the course of this terrible time, and it shall not be a time that will be easy to forget. It is sure to become a source of woe in future feuds, yet we can avert this, should we truly be devoted to a better tomorrow. That is why I pardon every Gaian who willingly fought for Razmus's side, and I ask that all Gaians pardon every Hurtz here for actions which were not in their control. In turn, I also vow in my time as king to erase the last of the prejudices that have been woven into the fabric of our history of two proud races, Gaian and Hurtz. We are both of this world, and neither is greater or smaller, nor does one race have more rights over the other."

He then drew the sword from its scabbard and turned to Gladius. "I put meaning to my words as of this moment. Gladius the Hurtz, kneel before your king."

Confused, Gladius did as he was told without second thoughts, having full trust in whatever Venetor had planned.

The Gaian king then placed his sword on the shoulder of the Hurtz. "Gladius the Hurtz, you have served me faithfully all of my life. You have given blood, sweat and tears in my service. You have laughed with me and you have counselled me when none other could. Now I tell thee to rise as a lord of Gaia and choose a surname for you and all of your descendants to come."

Those gathered were in shock as Gladius rose, for no Hurtz had ever in the history of Gaia carried a noble title.

"If it is allowed, my king," Gladius spoke, "Then I shall take on the surname of Arcusson after my father's name, for it is who I am, my lord."

"So it was spoken, so it shall be done." Venetor nodded.

He then turned his attention to Annetta, who stood off to the side with Skyris and Titus. Motioning for her to come forward, the girl approached with a somewhat hesitant walk.

Seeing her uncertainty, Venetor addressed her. "Of all the heroes born on this day, none have surprised me as much as that of you, Annetta. Please kneel."

Obeying, Annetta did as commanded, though somewhat painfully with the score of bruises she had acquired. She then felt the weight of the sword on her shoulder.

"Annetta Severio, from this day forth and for all of time, carry with you the title of the White Lioness of Gaia. Rise, and never forget where you come from."

಄಄

Not long after, the celebrations shifted to the castle. The empty stone walls were decorated with bright royal Gaian banners, upon them a proud white rampant lion, wearing a golden crown atop its head. The crown was an addition Venetor had insisted be added to symbolize the rebirth on Gaia. Seated on his throne, the new king was constantly being swarmed by thankful subjects and well-wishing nobles. Annetta and her companions were seated off to the side, united at last. It seemed like a long time since they had been able to enjoy each other's company, and yet Annetta could not help but feel a pang of guilt for trying to appreciate the moment when Link was no longer with them. She promised herself, however, she would visit him as soon as she had the opportunity in her meditations.

"Hey, who is that?" Jason whispered into her ear, which threw the girl off her train of thought.

Looking over, Annetta could scarcely believe her eyes at what she was seeing. Coming down the hall and towards the throne were three creatures she had only ever seen in movies. Hovering on what looked to be small pods were beings that may have only been about four feet high, with thin spindly limbs, dressed in dark suits with what looked like circuits running through them. What truly gave them away, however, were the large bulbous heads and enormous pitch-black almond eyes.

Jason could not avert his eyes from them. "Are those?"

"Kinsman," Puc hissed. "What have I taught you about staring?"

Their prattling in the corner ignored, the beings came to a halt before Venetor. The Gaian king locked eyes with them before speaking.

"Greetings," he said. "To what do I owe the presence of the Greys?"

The Greys looked at one another before turning to Venetor, and telepathically spoke. *"We come but merely to congratulate the new king of Gaia on his post and on the victory he has won this day."*

"A victory indeed." Venetor nodded. "One I could have won with greater ease had the Federation stepped in to aid."

The aliens looked over at one another without a single smidge of emotion on their faces before turning back to Venetor again. *"The Federation was not aware how great a threat Razmus Severio posed. We felt the Gaians were capable of handling his ilk. We come with a full apology for you, Lord Venetor, and assure you that the Federation will aid in the restoration of your space fleet due to its destruction."*

"At least there is that," Venetor huffed and put on a fake smile for the Greys He knew their sentiments were only for political show and they did not mean anything sincere by it. "Very well. You have my thanks and the gratitude of Gaia. I shall report to the Federation with the outcome of this affair when all is set into accord here."

"Happy tidings to you," the creatures spoke, and then their eyes turned to Annetta and her companions. *"And to the one they now call the White Lioness of Gaia."*

As quickly as they had entered, they left, allowing the celebration to resume.

Jason's gaze lingered as he watched them leave. "Okay, I don't care what you guys say. That'll be in my nightmares."

"The Greys?" Sarina questioned. "Well, I mean, they have always been a bit on the eccentric side..."

"Eccentric? How about terrifying!" Jason continued, "Imagine seeing those things when you wake up after a blackout, and being... probed."

"I'm pretty sure probing isn't an actual thing they do," Annetta added in. "It's probably just a thing people came up with on Earth."

"Sorry to be the bearer of bad news, but it's real," Matthias interrupted as he took a swig from his goblet. "That and crop circles too, although that was always more of a pastime for their teenagers, like graffiti, from what I gather."

"You mean that stuff means nothing?" Jason's eyes widened and his hands then went below the table. "I'll never sleep, not unless I want to have nightmares about-"

"Kinsman, may we please speak on a different subject other than the violation of your rear end?" Puc groaned, to which the rest of the table burst into laughter.

The conversations and merry making continued late into the evening. The topic, as per Puc's request, did not surface again.

The celebrations went late into the night and soon, many had dispersed to sleep and heal their wounds after the hard-fought battle. Standing upon a large open stone balcony, Venetor gazed down into the sleeping city, his people safe. He felt a sense of peace in knowing this.

He was soon joined by Skyris. His sister was dressed in traditional armour and a cerulean cape that was fastened to the side in the Gaian style, marking her as the sister of the king.

"Not out cold yet?" he chuckled lightly, seeing her.

"Oh, I'm just getting warmed up." She pointed back jokingly to an empty keg that was still present on one of the tables.

The king of Gaia gave a hearty laugh upon hearing the proclamation. "It's good to be with you again, sister."

"Which is what I have come to speak to you about." She said. "I've decided to return to Earth with the others. I feel like my work in Q-16 needs to be completed."

"This doesn't have anything to do with a certain elf, does it?" He asked.

"What bound Thanestorm and I before is no longer there, I'm afraid." Skyris sighed.

"I see."

There was a lingering silence after the exchange as the both of them gazed out into the horizon, lost in their own thoughts, reflecting on the battle, its outcome and those lost. Gaia would never be the same.

"I need you here, Skyris," he finally said. "Earth can wait."

"Damn it Venetor, with what?" she groaned. "If this is about marrying me off again, I refuse to take any part in it. I am a grown female Gaian, and not your chess piece."

"I meant in replenishing our ships, Skyris," he stated. "I am well aware of your feelings regarding marriage."

"Good. Then we are agreed," Skyris huffed. "I'm leaving for Earth whether you like it or not, I hope you know."

Venetor felt the will to argue with Skyris vanish as his shoulders slumped, feeling tiredness creep into his bones from the day's events. Despite his love for a good fight, he was too worn out to wish to start another.

26

"Very well, you have my permission to go," he finally said. "I would still like for you to be available to communicate with, should I need you."

Skyris smiled and bowed. "So it shall be done, my king."

Venetor rolled his eyes and watched her leave to go back inside.

"And brother, thank you."

⊰⊱

Early the next morning, Annetta, Jason, Sarina, Puc, Matthias and Darius set out into the fields beyond Pangaia. Having spoken with Venetor about the whereabouts of the Heallaws house, they soon came upon an overgrown cabin, just as the Gaian king had described it.

Setting to work, they created a burial mound before the broken down structure. Sarina adorned it with the wild flowers she had found in the fields, while Jason, Darius and Matthias laid stones around it. Finally, Annetta placed the sword upon it, a symbol of a final farewell to her friend.

"Here, though his body does not rest, lies Lincerious Heallaws," Puc uttered, "Warrior, companion, friend and son. He died in the service of Gaia and of the Four Forces. Tormented his whole life by a curse not his own, he rose above this. May the Unknown accept you into his light, now and always."

Raising his staff, Puc slammed it into the earth with full force. The mound lit up, and in its place, a crypt of marble with the likeness of Link sleeping upon it, holding his sword appeared.

"Rest easy, buddy," Jason sighed as he patted the slab.

All those gathered paid their respects to the fallen warrior, and after some time began to disperse, until there was only Puc and Annetta left standing.

"I still can't believe he's gone," she finally said. "I feel like... I would have felt it, with the bond and all."

"There was no trace of him at the site," Puc replied. "No one could have survived the blast if it was as great as those who found the sword said it was."

Annetta frowned as the tears she had held back finally rolled down her cheeks. "Perhaps that's just the dreamer in me wanting it to be otherwise."

"There is no wrong in this," he said. "We all deal with grief differently."

There was a silence among them for a few moments as Annetta regained her composure and wiped her eyes before speaking again.

"Yeah, I guess so."

The two of them held a silent vigil for a little while longer, until Puc spoke.

"Did you know about your feral form?" he asked. "About what it would be?"

"I only had hints," the girl responded. "I was confused for the longest time as to what it could be. I kept having dreams like I was being pulled in different directions. In all the chaos on the battlefield, I remembered what Darius said to me, that it's not a matter of choosing sometimes, but a matter of becoming what we needed to be. Gaia needed a white lion, so I became one."

Hearing the words, a faint smile formed on the lips of the elf as he looked down at the young girl. "Wise words. You are truly growing up to be the heir of Orbeyus I always thought you would be. He would be proud to see you now."

"I hope so." Annetta smiled faintly. "Which leads me to what I have to say next. I'm going to stay on Gaia for a little while. I'll finish my exams. I've even decided to go into Police Foundations in college. But for the summer, I think it would be a good idea if I stayed here, maybe help Venetor out a bit and learn a bit more. It would help me get away from what happened, too. Maybe I can even figure out where Amarok took Valdhar."

"If that is what you desire." Puc nodded.

"You know what I'd really want more than that?" Annetta glanced over at the mage, "To figure out where all those stray socks went."

"That, young Annetta, is a mystery many would wish solved."

A light smile forming on her face, the girl looked back into the horizon where beyond the behemoth trees lay the walls of a city that only now was beginning to wake.

Epilogue

Excerpt from the chronicles of the Eye to All Worlds:

For once, none of us truly knows what the future holds, and in this lies the beauty of life. It is the uncertainty of where things will go versus what is planned that makes the grand design the marvel which we witness as we journey along.

Annetta has left for the summer to stay with Venetor and oversee some of the restoration of Gaia. She wishes to learn more about her ancestors, as well as her abilities. The wisdom she has begun to possess baffles even myself, and I assure you, Orbeyus, that wherever you may be, she carries forth your torch with all your vigour.

Jason and Sarina prepare for their post-secondary education. They seem to be receiving letters of acceptance daily and continuously come to me for aid in a decision, to which I only say that it is up to them. How else can one truly take the next step in life if it is not by following one's heart?

Liam and Xander have now also come under my charge, though I have left much of their training to Darius, as my attention is needed in being First Mage of Aldamoor. To add to this, he seems to have a better understanding of how to deal with them, having known the two boys far longer than I.

The Four Forces have all returned to their lands, the wounds of the battle on Gaia not soon to be forgotten. The funeral of Lord Ironhorn was a sore affair, and I only hope that Lord Snapneck proves to be just as wise and fair a ruler. Doriden has also taken up the mantle of Alpha after his father suffered the loss of a wing.

Skyris has opted to stay on Earth and to work on some of her long-forgotten projects in Q-16, much to the protestations of her brother. I believe her exact words to him ran along the lines of, "I am a grown female Gaian, and not your chess piece."

Matthias continues his search in the stars for Amarok. His confession about his last encounter with the assassin has left me with much worry. If what he said is right, this war is far from over, and I am not certain that we are prepared to deal with much more at the current time.

Speculation, alas, never did anyone good, and has been the cause of more than one grey hair. To this, my friend Orbeyus could once attest.

To those who come across these words long after we are all but legend and legacy, remember that change is not a thing to be feared, but to be embraced. You will find that with courage, you have more impact on your destiny than you dared to dream.

-Puc Thanestorm, First Mage of Aldamoor;
Chronicler of Severio Castle through the lives of Orbeyus, Arieus and Annetta Severio, Defenders of the Eye to All Worlds

Acknowledgements

As I said in the acknowledgements found in Q-16 and the Eye to All Worlds, a writer is never alone. While I have my muses partially to thank for that, there is a lot more to it than pure inspiration. First off, to my family, who have given me a wonderful environment to soldier on and keep writing. Mom, Dad, I'm sorry for the mess at times, but they say that is a healthy sign of a creative mind. Thank you for the wonderful gift also that is my Polish heritage, I wouldn't have been aware of it were it not for your perseverance in sending me to Saturday school and on all my summer trips. To my brother, Adam, thank you for continuing to be a motivating pillar in my journey. You know how to crack down the whip. I also cannot forget my four legged friend Meesha, who lay on my bed as I wrote each night. Though you cannot read, you are one dedicated fan. My head editor Anthony Geremia, for continuing to put up with my late night texts about plot holes, grammar questions and for attending multiple conventions, during which, you have endured many a storm with me. You are the Sancho Panza to my Don Quixote as I continue to fight windmills in this writing quest. Chris Barfitt, thank you for being quite possibly the most patient person on the planet whenever I've needed time to plot, write, edit and when I've needed help while attending live events. Thank you for understanding the madness that is me. Sylvia Powers, for your help with editing, I am incredibly grateful for having an additional pair of eyes look over these pages. One is never enough. Krystina Kwiatkowski, thank you for helping to bring the flag on the front cover to life, and Anthony 'Letch' Letchford, thank you for helping with the crown on the back. To Bethan Riehle-Johns for helping inspire, based on true facts, the pen-thieving goblin Oje, of whom we still to this day are convinced that haunts the office of Groupa Ltd. To those I was with in the dealers room with at SFContario, Brandon Draga, Deanna Laver, Pat Flewwelling, Chad (I don't have your last name on Facebook, and felt really silly after thinking it was Simon due to your Facebook name being Simon Dalek, so I apologize for not listing it here), we will always have the Cantina, and thanks for all the fantastic memories of that and many other conventions I've attending with you there after the fact. Lastly, to MJ Moores and the other members of the W.C.Y.R. (Writers' Community of York Region) for their imparted knowledge on writing as I continue to spread my wings in this venture. If there are any I have missed in these acknowledgements, I apologize and know that whatever support, wisdom or smile that you gave was not a gesture I have forgotten. Until the next adventure, keep it awesome!

About the Author

A.A. Jankiewicz (known to most as Agnes) hails from the city of Pickering, Ontario. Her debut novel 'Q-16 and the Eye to All Worlds' was published as part of her thesis project at Durham College as part of the Contemporary Media Design Program. Prior to that, she graduated from York University with a BFA in Film Theory, Historiography and Criticism. When she's not busy plotting the next great adventure, writing, doodling, tinkering in the Adobe suite programs or mellowing out with her friends, she enjoys walks with her four-legged companion Meesha. When not at work she is working on the next instalment in the Q-16 series.